The Interloper Trilogy: Book One

Hope you enjoy the book Becki!

Icebreaker

by Steven William Hannah

Chapter One

In the dead of night, there comes a knock at the door of a frozen tin shack. Old Simon would have jumped in fear, had he been surprised - but he is expecting a visitor. He merely sparks the match that he has been holding in his frozen mittens, lights the candle by his bed, and carries its weak light with him to the door. Shivering in his oil-stained denims, he unhitches the rusted lock and eases the door open. Flurries of snow force their way in, curling around the door and buffeting his legs, bringing the frozen night air with them; the smell of salt and industry. Old Simon shivers, longing for a night when he has oil to burn for warmth.

The visitor looms in the doorway, tall and bedraggled. He wears a dark leather raincoat, hood up, and carries a heavy leather satchel. Old Simon starts to shiver a greeting, but is cut off by the stranger.

"You asked for a *doctor*?"

Old Simon hears the question, the real question, and nods in answer. This man is no normal doctor. He steps back in invitation. The stranger - the *doctor* - steps inside. The door clacks shut behind him as he sheds his cloak and hangs it on a wall hook. Without the soaked leather distorting his silhouette, he seems far less imposing.

He's tall but slight; his face is long and stubbled, but his eyes are dark and kind, and he wears the thick yellow fleece of a fisherman up to his neck. Early twenties in the face, late thirties around the eyes. Somebody who has seen much; Old Simon knows the look well. As if to dispel any doubt as to his intentions, the stranger offers his hand to the old man, smiling.

1

"Bear," he introduces himself. "I'm the *doctor.*"

"Simon," rasps the old man, nodding. The stranger has a firm and honest handshake, though he isn't what Simon had expected from the rumours. "I'd offer you a drink but -"

"No need," says Bear, raising his hands and taking in Simon's shack. Bear has a spark to his eyes that puts Simon at ease. Everything seems to interest him. "Can't drink on this job anyway," he gives Simon a knowing smile. "It's hard enough as it is."

Bear sets down his satchel and begins taking in the shack. Simon, the old fella, is lurking about in the background, lingering next to a cellar door, the type that inevitably leads to a concrete underground shelter. Every house in Forgehead has one, every single house.

The rest of the shack is what he expected. Old Simon is close to the docks, where the most unfortunate of Forgehead's workers have their dwellings. This far from the forges and workshops, the temperature is lowest. Ice is quick to form on the outside of the shacks, leading most people to sleep underground in their shelters. The shacks are for storage.

Simon seems eager to get started, and so Bear puts him at ease.

"Just gathering data," he says, looking over the shack. Everything might be important. This is not just work – this is research. Simon loses some internal battle with himself, and opens drawer, pulling a flask out. Simon watches him, awaiting judgement. Bear can smell the alcohol coming from it - but he does not judge.

The shack, thinks Bear. Uneven concrete covers the floor, and the roof is low enough that Bear can reach up and brush his hand against the rotting beams. It resembles the cramped tool sheds of Bear's youth, where he spent many long gaslit nights with his father, tinkering with old electronics from before the Cataclysm.

There's no light, save for the dim flicker of the candle in its glass tube; no windows, no moonlight by which to see. There isn't a surface that doesn't hold some box of scrap metal, or some bundle of fabric. Bear has seen this setup before: this is a tinkerer's place, someone who works with old machinery. He recognises ruined old direct-current motors and spools of copper wire. He immediately feels at home.

The shack has a grand total of two doors – little more than planks and corrugated metal sheets held together with nails. One door is the entrance that he stepped through. The other is where his work likely is.

Simon hovers near him like a fly, impatient, hovering from one foot to the other, taking sips from his flask. When he finally breaks the silence, his voice is trembling;

"So I don't know how much you've been told, but I just -"

Bear waves his polite ramblings away with a smile as he investigates the boxes of scrap up close, taking his time. "Don't worry, Simon. The message got through, and here I am." Bear pulls a large writing pad out of his satchel, rough recycled paper that rasps as he turns the pages. He tries his best to look professional.

"I have to ask you some questions first, Simon – if that's ok?"

"Oh. Of course."

"First – I assume that you asked for *my* help because the usual channels are... *unavailable* to you? You didn't want to tell the militia? The Forestry?"

Simon sits on the edge of a desk, his eyes tired in the candlelight. Bear would guess at Simon's age, but in Forgehead people start to look old at thirty.

"Aye," says Simon. "I mean, there aren't any doctors here that I can afford anyway." At the mention of cost, an uneasy silence falls over Simon. He gives Bear a questioning look.

"I don't charge for these services," says Bear, answering his unasked question.

"Oh thank Gaia," he breathes. "You're a better man than I."

"I can't charge for this work, man," shrugs Bear. "It's too important. Now – to get us back on track. You can't go to the usual channels? You haven't told anybody else?"

"I mean – I would tell our Council reps, but anybody who's Council will tell the Foresters, and if *they* find out what's happened to my boy -" Simon stops talking and holds a clenched fist against his mouth. Bear sees the stress that he is under. He understands what it feels like – those that are taken like this end up something worse than dead.

"No need to continue," he tells Simon. "Thank you."

Bear understands exactly what the Foresters would do too, if Simon were to mention his son's fate. He has seen it done. Simon's son is already a statistic, something to be burned – along with his house and anything he owned. Better safe than sorry, of course. Marks of this practice are everywhere – the streets of Forgehead are littered with sealed, burned buildings. Tombs by any other name.

Still completely necessary, thinks Bear. Better than to risk an outbreak.

"Now Simon," he pushes. "I need to ask you some questions about your son. Is that ok?"

Before Simon can answer, there's a sudden, sharp wailing from downstairs that makes the candle flicker. Both Bear and Simon freeze as the shadows dance against the wall, and the wind rattles the door against the frame. Every box of scraps begins to rustle, then settles. It dies off, and Simon looks at the door in tired resignation.

"That's my son," he whispers, and looks at the ground. "What do you want to know?"

Bear catches his breath and tries to play it down, but some things he suspects he will never get used to.

"Of course. I've heard that kind of thing before. Apologies for my reaction, I should really be used to that by now. Am I right in saying he's below us?"

"In the shelter, aye. He's there so the neighbours don't hear the things that he shouts."

"Of course," says Bear. "So. Before I talk to your son -"

"Can you help him?" Simon blurts out. as though he doesn't know the answer.

Bear holds his gaze in the darkness, staring into his milky old eyes. This is the point where he always considers lying. It would be so easy to give them a little hope, just enough to sustain them; but really, they should already be grieving. Bear doesn't answer, and in doing so, tells Simon what he already knows. The old man sighs and his shoulders sag inwards. He looks up from his hands after a pause.

"Have you *ever* gotten anybody back?" he asks Bear. "Is there a chance? Any at all?"

"No." There's a long silence whilst the wind howls. "But the data I'm collecting could point us to possible cures; prevention, treatment... To that end, Simon, again: I need to ask you some questions. Ok?"

Simon gives a weak nod and stumbles backwards onto a bed that Bear had assumed was a low shelf of some sort. It's covered in thin coats, clothes and straw. There's no fireplace, Bear realises, and shivers as the cold starts to seep through his fleece.

It dawns on him that Old Simon has been sleeping here, in order to keep his son and his condition hidden. He must be suffering. Bear makes a note to try and get him some kind of help after he is done here. Bear prepares a stubby engineer's pencil and rests the paper on his knees.

"Ok," says Bear. "How long ago was the exposure?"

"Eight days."

"Eight? Really?"

Simon nods. "Is that unusual?"

"Rare to find one that's made it past seven," Bear tries to brush over it. "Has your son ever worked with the Forestry?"

"No."

Bear makes a note. Unusual again. These are answers that he expected to hear. His heart begins to beat in his ears. "Has your son lived here all of his life?"

"Forgehead? Aye. Raised him myself."

Bear makes another note and tries not to hear the implied story that Simon is telling him. Mother died in childbirth, Bear reckons; still a common occurrence this far down the coast. Few doctors, next to no contraceptives, long nights; sad story.

"Has your son ever left Forgehead for any period of time? At all?"

"No."

Bear notes the fast answer – of course he hasn't left

Forgehead. To do so without the protection of the Forestry or – rare though it is – a Crawler, would be suicide.

"So," Bear puts the pencil down and starts looking for deception. He needs to know if Simon is lying, because if he isn't, then his son's case is exactly what Bear has been looking for all these years. "If your son has never left Forgehead, how did he come to be exposed?"

"Is this a trick question?" asks Simon, and Bear hears the indignation rising. "How the fuck should I know? He fell through the front door – I thought he was drunk – rubbing his eyes and, and, ah, hell -"

Simon's brief flare of indignant anger turns to grief again. His breathing is coming short – hysteria is setting in, and Bear leans forward to stop him from going down that road; anger won't answer any questions, and Bear has many. Simon is shaking when he puts a hand on his shoulder, trying to fight back tears.

"Stay with me, Simon, we're almost done. So, your son was afflicted somewhere in Forgehead?"

"He must have been."

"That's..." he stops. That's impossible. Absolutely impossible – and exactly what Bear was hoping he would say. "That's good information, Simon, I can use that. And he *told* you when you asked? That he had encountered the, uh -"

"Gaia?" Simon asks. "Stared into the Devil's eyes? Whichever name you call it by. Yes. He only managed a few words, but that's what he was saying."

Bear tries to remain polite, to not indulge superstition, but he cannot help but correct Simon. "Are you Gaian, by chance?"

"In name, I suppose. Hard to call it faith when we know she exists. I'm Gaian the same way I'm human."

He believes that the awoken mother earth is trying to kill us, thinks Bear – but not enough to drop out of society and start drawing runes on himself, covering everything in dream catchers, and eschewing personal hygiene. It would be fair to say that Bear has a low opinion of Gaians, little more than a cult in his eyes.

"I only know what we call it here in Forgehead," Simon shrugs and waves Bear away. "Christian or Gaian, doesn't matter. We both know what we're talking about, what does it matter?"

Bear stops scribbling and looks up from his notes. "It always strikes me that to call it anything other than an unnamed phenomenon is to give it a kind of mythical property. It implies that we cannot, and will not, ever understand it."

Simon laughs. "Do you understand it?"

Bear gives an awkward cough. "No."

"Then what difference does it make?"

"Fair," says Bear. "Back to the questions; your son confirmed that he'd seen Gaia's eyes?"

"He'd seen her, aye," whispers Simon after a pause. "I asked him what had happened to him and he just – he screamed like a man shot. You ever heard that noise, when someone gets hurt so bad that they know it's over? When it's just suffering left? It's like this weak groan. Acceptance."

Bear can't see much time left in the old man's eyes. "Yeah," says Bear. "Yeah, I know what that sounds like."

"He knew what he'd seen." Simon stares into the darkness, away from Bear. "We both knew it was over then. I -" Simon cuts himself off, before finding the strength to continue. "I couldn't do what he asked me to."

Bear knows that his son would have asked him to end it. By any means necessary. He knows because he was once asked to do the same thing, and did no better than Simon.

"Few of us can," says Bear. "Don't judge yourself for that."

"Doctor, if it comes to it, will *you* end his suffering?"

Bear forces himself to meet Simon's eyes. "That's not for me to do, Simon. I can't make that call."

"But you're a doctor?"

"Not of medicine," says Bear. Simon looks at the ground, defeated. "No life is mines to take. He's in the basement now?" Simon nods, and Bear feels reluctant to push Simon much further. Here, though, he has to. He cannot do this alone.

"Simon; are you familiar with the established stages of the, uh, *psychosis* associated with -" There's a blank look in Simon's eyes, and

Bear realises that the man probably can't even write, let alone familiarise himself with the stages of mental breakdown that accompany exposure sickness. "Sorry," says Bear, "let me walk that back a bit. Has he begun to draw or scratch symbols onto the walls?"

"Aye – spirals that go into lots of little spirals. I try not to look at them."

"Good man. Keep your eyes off of them," says Bear. "Has he tried to speak to you at all?"

"He has, aye. In rare wee moments, lucid moments. Sometimes he gets right up to the door, and he whispers under it while I'm asleep."

Bear feels his stomach curdle at the thought.

"Does he talk about people who are deceased?"

Simon nods. "He said his mother wanted to talk to me. Told me to come in close and listen. Told me to open the door."

"And?"

"And I didn't. Crazy talk, all of that. It didn't sound genuine. Sounded malicious. Didn't sound like him at all."

"Smart of you to resist," says Bear. "What about mimicry?"

"What's that, Doc?"

"Pretending to be other people? Trying to sound like other people to deceive you?"

"No," he says. "No, not that. I don't think so. His voice changes sometimes, but otherwise, no."

Bear continues, eager to hit the big questions now. "He didn't exhibit the usual dreams in the lead up to an incursion? My records don't show any phenomenological event eight days ago - nothing might have caused his exposure."

"No dreams," says Simon. "Not that he told me, no. And there wasn't an incursion, you're correct. It was just him that got it."

Bear feels something catch. This is it. This is the case that he has been waiting for.

"And *you* didn't experience any dreams?" asks Bear.

"No, no, I'd have told the Forestry immediately."

"Perfect, thank you Simon."

Bear hefts his bag and begins to rake through it, leaving Simon in silence. The old man breaks in with a nervous question.

"Do you believe me, Doctor?"

Bear stops and raises an eyebrow. "Why wouldn't I?"

"But I mean – this isn't how it happens, is it? Gaia ain't something you see down an alleyway after four pints, right? It doesn't just burst into our town like this, that's not how it works. She can't get past the walls. You're supposed to get the dreams, first too, aren't you? Gaia warns us. Then we all spend a few days with our eyes bound shut and our ears clamped over and the Forestry burn it back to hell with their weapons. It's always *all of us* dreaming – all of us at risk. There's always a warning. It ain't supposed to work like this – is it? Just to one of us? Have we –" Simon stops, and Bear sees the guilt in his face "Have I brought this on him somehow, doctor? Did I do something bad? Or -"

Bear shakes his head, and puts a hand on Simon's shoulder before he starts to lose it again. "No. No, Simon, you have not brought this upon anybody. But you are correct: this is not how the phenomenon usually presents itself. This isn't how it usually works – and that's why it's so important to study what has happened here. That's why I'm going to go and talk your son."

"Has this ever happened before?"

"Once," says Bear. "Just once that I know of. Now. I need your help to collect the necessary data from downstairs."

From the bag, Bear begins to build a pile of equipment: An electronic music player, small headphones, a wind-up LED flashlight, and a thick fabric blindfold. Next, Bear produces a plastic box the size of a walkie talkie, adorned with dials, valves, switches and antennae. Finally he finds and fastens on a thick leather glove covered in steel pipes and gas cylinders. He tests the pilot light on it, briefly lighting up the room.

"What *is* that?" asks Simon, standing up. "Your glove has got fire coming out of it."

"It's a leather blacksmith's glove with a pressurised aerosol mixture and a pilot light. It's got about six seconds of protective flames in it, to about ten feet of range." He sees the look on Simon's face, and backtracks. "Don't worry. I'm not going to burn your house down, this is just for my protection."

"But – why would you – I mean, do you think it's still down there? With him?"

"It could well be," says Bear. "The things he's drawn on the wall – if they are what I think they are – have been proven to cause similar, if minor, psychoses to those that your son is suffering from. We aren't entirely sure what they are or how they interact with the phenomenon yet, so we have to be careful There is vague evidence to suggest that they could cause a phenomenological incursion, so I just want to be safe." He smiles, and wiggles his fingers in the pyrotechnic glove. "Its like having the Forestry in your pocket for a few seconds. Enough for me to hold back an incursion and run, at least." Simon looks at him blankly, having understood nothing that he just said. Bear simplifies and repeats:

"Look. You believe he saw Gaia; now I think there's a bit of Gaia in him. This is for my protection," he shifts topics. "I still need your help." He puts the headphones in, and rests the blindfold above his eyes. "I need you to point me to the door, tell me how many steps there are, and then help me put this blindfold on."

"I - " Simon stops, obviously nervous. "You're not going to burn my son, or -?"

"Of course not, of course not," says Bear, and takes a shaky breath. "Unless he attacks me, and then I'll try to restrain him. But if he tries to remove my sensory equipment, Simon -"

"He wouldn't -"

"*He* wouldn't," says Bear. "I'm sure *he* wouldn't – but I don't know if it's *him* down there any more, Simon – you understand?"

"He's not ate anything since it happened," he says. "He won't be strong enough to attack you."

"Maybe so, but I try not to assume that my safety is a given when I do this."

Simon nods, and lifts a dream catcher from the wall, covered in Gaian symbols. He seems far smaller now than when Bear arrived.

"My son is dead, doctor," he says, and Bear hears the acceptance begin to set in. Bear gives a grim nod.

"Yes."

"My son is dead, and yet I can't bury him. I can't grieve. Instead I have to listen to him wailing and scratching at the walls."

Bear knows all too well the feeling of mentally burying somebody before they have died – but there is no time for him to sympathise. He has to concentrate, lest he make a fatal mistake.

"Simon?" he refocuses the conversation. "I need you to help me, now."

Simon sighs, and helps fasten the fabric blindfold over Bear's eyes to prevent visual exposure. Bear hefts the electronic box and switches his sensor to high-sensitivity. The pilot light flickers on his glove, and Bear pulls the blindfold over his head.

Everything falls dark for Bear. He hates this, but he has grown somewhat accustomed to it. Simon mutters a Gaian prayer, and Bear hears the door creak open, the locks and chains falling to the floor. Bear feels himself standing at the edge of a very different kind of darkness, and waits at the top of the stairs.

All is dark. The temperature drops. He can hear breathing in the distance, muffled and strained, like panting. Bear puts one hand on the damp wall and the other, gloved hand out in front of him.

Around his neck, the sensor starts to beep. The panting stops, and in its place, he hears whispering from below, someone giving a sermon to no audience. It barely sounds legible. Bear knows that by now, the boy has likely chewed through his own tongue and won't be able to form words. Probably for the best.

"Simon?" asks Bear.

"Doctor?"

"Before I block out my audio; how many steps?"

"Ten."

"How large is the room?"

"About eight by four."

"Metres?"

"Aye."

"What's your son's name?"

11

Silence.

"Simon, what's your son name?" he repeats, louder.

"Addie," he sighs. "Aiden by birth – always called him Addie."

Bear nods, and lifts the ear buds to his ears; but before he puts them in and presses the PLAY button, he tilts his head towards where he can hear Simon shaking.

"Simon, you've been great so far, so I need you to do this one last thing, ok?"

"Aye," he grunts.

"No matter what you hear," says Bear. "No matter what manner of screaming and wailing comes from down here, you *cannot* come down. Ok? It's unbelievably dangerous. You have to stay up here. Lock this door behind me. When I return, I'll let you know it's me by knocking seven times, ok? If it's your son at this door, Simon, then you don't open it. Worse still, if I ask to be let out without knocking, assume that I am dead. Anything except me knocking seven times, you are to go and get the Forestry, and you burn this place to the ground. Repeat it back, what do you do?"

"Go and get the Forestry," he weeps. "And burn this entire house to the ground."

"Good man. Now is no time for cowardice on either of our parts," says Bear, and begins to laugh as the adrenaline hits him. "We're on the cutting edge of science here, Simon. This is where great discoveries are made." He secures the earphones. "Besides," he says to himself, "I've done this before. I'll be fine."

Bear puts the headphones in, and hits PLAY on the music device. Beethoven's Symphony Number Five in C Minor (Op. 67), scrolls across the screen as it begins to play in his ears. It's loud enough to drown out the sound of the whispering in the dark. It'll stop him from suffering a potential audio exposure.

He feels the door close and lock behind him, and Bear steps down, blind and deafened, into the darkness.

Chapter 2

Afternoon the next day, and Bear is enjoying the sunlight despite the cold.

He sits on a creaking wooden chair on the veranda of a pub, sheltered from the constant snowfall. Along the street, Forgehead's workers scurry through the snowy wisps and whirls, clutching their belongings. Visibility is about thirty feet, and though his thick coat and gloves are barely enough to keep him warm, he refuses to retreat indoors to the pub's fireplace, which is already crowded.

At least it keeps his beer cold, he thinks, and takes another sip of it as he scans the street. He's watching for a particular silhouette, that of the friend he is supposed to meet. The findings and papers that he has brought with him are burning a hole in his pocket. This is the awkward moment, the space in between, where his findings and his life are most at risk.

If his research is to ever have any impact on the Coastal Union, on anybody's life, then it has to be seen by the right people – the same people who have made such research illegal: the Council of the Coastal Union, in the capital city of Union. He has never been, but he has heard stories of it's towering walls and pre-cataclysm architecture.

Bear feels himself fidgeting and takes another sip to calm his nerves. His head runs through numerous possible events: that his friend has gotten cold feet, maybe even betrayed him to the Council. He dwells too long on the thought that his friend has been caught and, under torture, given up his name – that at any moment he will feel the cold metal of a militia pistol against his neck. It wouldn't matter to the militia that his work is something that will help them.

He takes another drink and tries to relax. His friend wouldn't betray him, he reassures himself. They've known one another since they were boys.

Bear jumps in fright as the door opens to his side – but it is merely a half-drunken steel worker staggering outside to try and find his way home through the snow storm, to a no-doubt-cross wife. He doesn't even notice Bear.

He curses his brain, and its endless capacity for imagining disasters. He has lost a lot of sleep through his life over this unwanted talent. Too many nights spent staring at the ceiling imagining everything that could possibly go wrong, at any time, for any reason. That said, it has saved his life more than once. He wonders sometimes if the positives of his gift has ever balanced out the negatives.

A figure approaches through the snowfall, and climbs the stairs to the veranda with their chin tucked in their jacket. Bear relaxes as he sees the olive coloured greatcoat beneath the rain-cape, and the unmistakable outline of the Woodsman's hat, shaped like an old ship captain's with a brass, flaming acorn pinned to its front.

"Chief Woodsman," says Bear, and raises what remains of his pint.

Out of the snow, the Chief Woodsman of the Forestry shakes his rain cape and removes it, hanging it over a chair, and seems to unfold from his thick jacket.

"Bear," grins the Woodsman, his voice muffled through his thick red beard. He slaps Bear's shoulder, almost spilling his pint, and sits down. His entire face is the hue of burned skin, red and blemished, covered in pockmarks and scars. He looks twice as old as Bear – despite having been in the same class at school. He has a constant cheer to him, despite having one of Forgehead's most stressful jobs, positions, and lives. Bear has always wondered if that's just how he copes with it.

"Calum! You're a little late," says Bear. "Drink?"

"No, no, none for me," he waves him away. "On duty. Can't stay long. Good to see you, by the way."

"Likewise. Been a while."

"I've been busy, man, sorry," Calum exhales and seems to deflate a little. "Gaians and Christians at each other's throats. Arguing about how they think the world will end. Dumb reason for a riot, but what else is there to do around here?"

"You handling it ok?"

"Surviving," he shrugs, and Bear can see now in his eyes how tired he is. "Worst part is how many people they're convincing. Now everybody thinks the slightest bad dream is an omen and comes running to report it. Everyone is on edge, which means more fighting, more drinking, more... work for me." Calum takes off his gloves and wriggles his fingers, chirping up. "Speaking of bad omens... you have your research?"

"I do. I think you'll reach the same conclusions from the data that I did."

"Spoil me: what conclusions are those?"

"That what people experience during an exposure event is similar to a nightmare, at least in things I can measure like symbol and texture."

Calum gives him a long sideways look, as if waiting for something more. "So... a thing that we all consider to be a nightmarish experience is kinda, nightmarish? That's what you discovered?"

Bear laughs. "Missing the point a bit. Ok, science time, paying attention?"

"I'll try," he gets comfortable.

"Pre-cataclysm science thought that dreaming was how the brain files things away, makes space for us to think, right? Like clearing out space."

"Right."

"The longer you go without sleep, the more intense, more vivid, your dreams. I've read pre-cataclysm papers on it, it's well documented. Now, why is that?" Bear answers his own question before Calum can throw out something daft. "Because you're cramming more processing into less time. So during the rare times that an exposure case can make a lucid statement, you find the *same things* coming up all the time. Symbols, patterns, and so on. Like the brain trying to process far too much at once -"

"Like dreaming," says Calum, nodding along. "Ok. So that's your big discovery?"

"Big *theory*. If I'm right, it means that exposure madness might be linked to a kind of information overload, an overstimulation of the brain, maybe. Which raises questions and ideas about the nature of the phenomenon." He leans back, struggling to hide his excitement. "That's what the data suggests, but now I need to work on disproving it," he stops, yawning into his hand. "Sorry, up late working last night. That's the other thing that I want to speak to you about."

"You were working last night?" There's alarm in the Woodsman's voice.

"Aye, I got a referral right here in the worker's quarter" says Bear, faltering as he sees the look in the Woodsman's eyes. "Is everything ok?"

"Was it – was it fresh? Nobody reported any exposure incidents last night – and it was me that was manning the desk. That's unusual."

"Fresh? No. Eight day, though," he says quietly.

"Eight? Bloody hell, that's a while."

"I know – and worse still, I could find no linked event. Nothing happened eight days ago to cause this."

"Who was it?"

"Gaian lad, tinkerer's son called Aiden, father called Simon, old guy. Aiden was in the last stages. Drawing on the walls – self harming, hadn't eaten, no self care, non-vocal when I saw him, tongue chewed through... Had a few lucid moments and brought up his dead mother. No mimicry, apparently. Evidence of numerous suicide attempts, bites on his wrists, you know. The usual."

The Woodsman reaches across for Bear's pint and takes a sip of it despite Bear's frowning. "Where did he get exposed then? Was he one of mine? Forestry?"

"Walking home from the pub, apparently," says Bear, with the tone that says *doubt*. "Father said he wasn't Forestry. Hadn't left town. Ever."

Bear believes Simon, in his heart – but the scientist in his head tells him to doubt everything until it can be proven. Deserters from the Forestry are punished with death – it is likely that Simon's boy was, in fact, one of the Forestry, and that his exposure led to his dessertion, and that Simon was trying to hide that fact.

Still, thinks Bear. It didn't *feel* like Simon was hiding something.

The Woodsman waves Bear away. "Gaia doesn't look at any of us without warning us first. No dreams?"

"No dreams," he shakes his head. He resists the urge to correct Calum's terminology – he decided long ago to let people have their superstitions, whether Gaians, Christians, or anything in between.

"Well, I have to ask if you've considered he might be lying?" asks the Woodsman.

"Of course I have. And I don't think he is."

"So he isn't one of the Forestry, didn't leave town... but still got exposed. Very strange case. You know what I'm thinking, Bear?"

"I know, I know -"

"This sounds like your father all over again."

"I *know* – that's why I was so anxious to meet you today. Every other account in my research is a Forester, Cartographer or Scout who got too close to the phenomenon, suffered an equipment malfunction or whatever, and got exposed, whether via eyes or ears. I've spent two months setting up contacts and referrals, finding men and women who – and I can't blame them – don't want to go into the Council's post-exposure care program."

The Woodsman laughs – they both know what the post-exposure care program does. Both have stated before that they'd prefer a medically administered gunshot, if it came to it.

"It's been a hard couple of months," says Bear, "and it's good data, useful, whatever you think the phenomenon is. But Calum - " he pauses, checks that they're alone. "Calum, this guy was final stage. You can't fake that; he wasn't a Forester, wasn't a Scout or a Cartographer or any other guild. Somehow, the phenomenon managed to reach him. What if this is it? Same thing that happened to my dad? Maybe there's something *inside* Forgehead? Something related to the phenomenon, that can cause exposure? Could any of our sensors have failed? Why didn't anybody get any dreams?"

Calum the Woodsman hasn't moved. Bear sees the cogs turning in his head – he's a smart man; has had to be a smart man to survive in a profession with a fifty-nine percent annual casualty rate. Few men get old in his line of work.

He's a Forester: one of the poor – or brave, depending on who you ask – bastards who are sent to man the walls where the phenomenon is breaching. They are blinded and deafened with sensory headgear, and must trust someone's voice telling you where to aim and shoot your flame gun. That's if and when the radio works, and the radio gets more and more unreliable the closer you get to the phenomenon.

Bear prompts him again. "Calum? What if it's inside -"

"That's impossible," he says, but his tone has changed. Bear sees him weighing up possibilities. "Ok, what if it had a delayed effect? Maybe he's lying about the timescale, and we can point to an incursion that *could* have caused it."

"There's no recorded evidence of delayed exposure effects. Could be possible though." Bear takes out a sheet of paper and makes a note of this interesting theory – he'll have to work out how it could be disproven.

"Or," continues Calum, "could somebody else have infected him? Can exposure even be transmitted like that?"

Bear mulls it over. "I've considered that too. Those in late stage exposure sickness tend to make markings on things. Those markings have been shown to cause minor psychoses – but never a full blown exposure. He didn't just see some wiggly lines on a wall, Calum, this was the real thing."

"He *definitely* didn't get the dreams first?"

"No dreams."

There's a long and heavy silence. Both men know the weight of what's being said. They both have the same feeling; the feeling that you've left the door unlocked, that you didn't check under the bed before you got in.

"This isn't something I ask lightly, Bear," Calum lowers his voice and leans across the table. "But we've already mentioned your father. Random exposure in the middle of a secured town, right? You've always told me you thought it might have been deliberate, that your father sought out exposure on purpose. Think this might be the same deal?"

Bear looks away, irritated. Of course they have to consider the parallels to his father; a scientist, a wildly intelligent man, who taught him almost everything he knows. Till, when Bear was sixteen, his father stumbled in the door, unable to speak, in mental anguish. Exposed, in the very place that they were meant to always be safe. *Impossible. They have sensors, they have walls, the phenomenon can't get in.* He had never worked out why, and his father's moments of lucidity were neither long or common enough to get any answers.

All of his research had been about the phenomenon, it was an obsession. It has gradually eaten away at Bear, the horrible suspicion that his father may have left town to deliberately expose himself to it, to gather more data first-hand. That's the narrative that he has worked to for years. Could Aidan have done the same? He was a Gaian, maybe he wanted to meet her up close? Is the answer that simple?

"Bear?" Calum prompts him. "Bear, it's *very* similar to your father's case."

Bear snaps back to the conversation, waving it away. "I think my father might have chosen to do that to himself. This one? Nah, didn't seem deliberate to me. I was thinking that a Gaian lad might have wanted to meet his goddess?"

"That's not how it really works for them," shrugs Calum. "Trust me, I deal with Gaians every day. They don't want to be exposed."

Calum rests his hand on Bear's research notes, keeping them hidden as militia soldiers walk by. He lifts a hand to them, and they throw a loose salute. They owe him no allegiance, but he does command their respect. "Ok," he says when they are gone. "I think I want to see this for myself. Where is this lad, right now?"

"At his home, locked in a cellar."

"I want to talk to his father. We need to find out how this happened. If the rules have changed -"

"Let's not frighten ourselves," says Bear. "There's no reason to assume the rules have changed."

"You're so old school," laughs Calum. "The rules could change at any time. Our world hasn't followed rules since the Cataclysm – but here you are, still trying to put everything in boxes as if the rules still matter."

Bear ignores the well-meaning jibe, and points to where Calum 's arm is covering the research notes.

"Give this a look, will you? While I'm here and can answer questions."

Calum checks over his shoulder, then flips the folder open and skims over the title and abstract, reading under his breath.

It reads:

COMMONALITIES AMONG VICTIMS OF PHENOMENAL-EXPOSURE

Bear leans over and points to the well-drawn bar graph on the first page, which he had to draw by hand with what tools he could find or buy. The graph is nestled among thick paragraphs of compound words and semi-colons.

"This is the frequency of exposure cases by several easy variables. Age, height, so on. It gets more interesting as you go in, but I had to establish a foundation."

"This may take me some time to read," says Calum. "And I'd rather not wave it about out here. If any of the militia read it -"

"If any of the militia *can* read," laughs Bear. Calum smirks with him over the top of the papers. "If I may make a recommendation," Bear continues, "on pages six to nine are a collection of some of the more unnerving statements; what people saw when they looked at the phenomenon, what they heard, what they remember... Really difficult stuff to get from them, patchy as hell and barely coherent, but... that segment? Don't read it in the dark."

Calum looks up, curious. "Now I *know* I didn't just hear some superstition from the good, rational doctor."

"I'm a rationalist, Calum, not an idiot. I read it by candlelight and the wick ran down, room was pitch black for a few moments. I immediately got this awful feeling. Like I wasn't alone. Now we don't understand the phenomenon, sure, but I *know* that I don't understand it. This new case is weird enough to frighten me, and I'm not taking any chances. Neither should you."

Calum nods. "Ok. Is that our most likely option for our boy's exposure then? Some kind of exposure rune drawn by another person? Because if so, we need to find it and destroy it. We might need to retrade his steps."

"I don't know – there are many, many cases of migraines, minor psychoses, nightmares, and so on, all brought on by viewing runes drawn by exposed people. They can certainly cause discomfort, strange feelings, unease... there's *some* evidence tying them to incursion frequency, but honestly? Nothing concrete. I don't think someone could just have drawn it on a wall and, *boom*, exposure." Bear thinks for a minute, and jots down the possibility anyway. "If it turns out that they can, then we may have to consider more sinister explanations." Bear takes a long drink. "But back to the more mundane options..."

"Noted, and glad you brought this to my attention, Bear," says Calum, leaning back as he stuffs the report into his coat.

"Well I've got another favour to ask," says Bear.

"Go on."

"We can rule out him being Forestry – score off a theory."

"You said he wasn't lying."

"But we can be *certain,*" says Bear. "If we just check."

"Fine," says Calum. "You want me to run through my casualties and desserters?"

"That would help a lot."

Bear sinks his beer and clinks his empty glass against the wooden table, as though he's been checkmated and is knocking over his king.

Calum and Bear pull their coats on, wrapping up against the cold.

"Come with me," Calum motions with his head. "I've got half an hour left on my lunch, then it's back to work. Let's go and prove a theory." He rolls his eyes, and means to mock Bear, but the dig goes over Bear's head.

"You can't prove a theory," says Bear. "You can only *disprove* a theory."

"Well then let's do that instead."

Bear is anxious to see if Calum is right – but something in the way that Simon spoke last night, something about his manner, makes him think that he was telling the truth – and that frightens Bear to his core.

He can't help but think of his father, and he hates it. The sooner that he has an answer to this, the better.

Chapter 3

The streets of Forgehead are a mess of churned snow and dirt, like walking through thick soup. Bear's boots slosh in the mud as they pass churches – to both Christ and Gaia – and rambling street preachers talking to curious crowds. Militia soldiers have formed a line between the two opposing faiths. To one side, Gaians are singing, chanting, dressed in their strange robes. They have far more dirt on their skin than most, covered in body paint and sketchy tattoos, with dream catchers, beads and feathers woven into their hair and clothes. They're making their call to the end times, asking for Mother Gaia to take them first, to make them part of her again.

The Christians, on the other hand, are shouting at the militia for allowing this to go on without a single arrest.

"Idiots," says Calum. "Doomsday nutjobs are going to get shot if they keep trying to call Gaia down upon us. They're frightening the normal people. People keep asking us to crack down on them."

"If anybody could call it down," says Bear, "then we'd be in far more trouble than we are. How long have they been proclaiming the end times now?"

"As long as I can remember," says Calum, and his smile fades. "Much louder recently, though."

One of the Christians tests the line and everybody surges forward, screaming at the singing Gaians, ordering them to stop tempting the devil, begging them to think of their families, of their children. He is wearing the horizontal crucifix of the Last Testament Church, those who believe that the apocalypse has come and gone, that they are living in the times of darkness before their saviour returns to take them to heaven. The militia forms a slim line of black body armour and face masks, struggling to hold it back.

Bear tugs on Calum's sleeve, and stops to watch. As expected, one of the Christians breaks through. The Gaians stop singing, and a brawl immediately breaks out. The militia rally before they lose their position, firing a few shots into the air. There's scattered screaming, and the fighting disperses with some panic and scrambling. Regardless, the militia produce their steel rods and start cracking bones. As Bear leaves, he sees two young men, a Christian and a Gaian, trying to help one another up. One of them clutches a broken forearm from trying to block a steel rod.

Bear shakes his head, but pays it no more mind. As of late, the end-times chanting has gotten a little irritating for him. No evidence for it, he has told everybody who asks. Nothing to suggest that things are coming to an end. No great change. Till last night, of course.

Ahead of them lies their target, behind sandbags and barbed wire, machine gun nests and concrete walls. The Forestry Headquarters.

From the barbed wire hangs charms of every kind,, and though he detests the thought of charms and trinkets, he can appreciate the mural of the Coastal Union's cultures that it has created.

Calum motions to the guards and they scrape the huge metal gates back by hand, allowing them entry. Bear notes the various charms as he enters. Machine guns will be no use against the phenomenon if it ever came here – but maybe the charms will. Bear has his doubts. There are petrified wooden charms and flower wreaths from Gaia's followers, crucifixes both with and without Christ upon them, most of them horizontal as always; and then Bear sees a charm that makes him pause.

There's a sheaf of wood with writing burned onto it. He asks Calum to wait for a moment and raises his hands to show the Foresters that he means no ill will, and gingerly lifts the strange charm from the wire.

Somebody has burned various notable formulae onto the dry oak. Bear recognises them, of course. He sees the single line equation that explains general relativity, and below that, a series of brackets and notation that describes the calculation of gravitational force.

Bear considers why somebody would ever do such a thing.

Whilst not considered a religion by any means, rationalists are often derided by the churches of Christ and Gaia for their attempts to impose mathematics, logic, and the scientific method onto the phenomenon – which, to them, is so innately and obviously supernatural or divine.

Is this, Bear wonders, what this charm is for? That if the phenomenon were to try and pry its way into the Forestry HQ, it would come up against a reminder that - by the laws that govern the universe, the laws of physics - it cannot exist? He laughs at the idea, and hangs it back up before joining Calum on the walk to the main building.

"What was so interesting?" Calum asks him.

"Nothing," says Bear, still laughing. "Just superstition – everywhere I look."

Calum shrugs. "Superstition has saved us, a lot of the time. It might be all we have."

"We also have flamethowers and sensors that tell us where to aim them," says Bear, preferring to trust in tools over symbols. "That's a pretty big advantage, too, and it was men like my father that gave us them."

Men and women in drab olive uniforms jog past them, rolling cylinders of fuel, heading towards snow-tracked trucks and groups of dogs around sleds.

"Preparing for an operation?"

"Restocking after one, actually. We're low on just about everything after helping to defend Red Lake."

"Red Lake had an incursion?"

"Aye. Thirteen dead. Twenty two exposures."

"Well done," says Bear, for what is a miraculously low casualty count.

"Finger's crossed that we kept enough of our own stuff back, though."

Bear looks at him in alarm. "Should I be worried?"

"We've got enough fuel, fire and explosives for another fight, if it comes to it. Manpower we're a bit short on – but I'd rather have twenty veterans than a hundred more recruits. Men who know not to take their helmets off no matter how bad it gets; as opposed to prisoners with no experience who want to see what Gaia's eyes look like. Idiots."

Bear looks for fear in Calum's face, but finds none. "What if you run out of supplies?"

"We shouldn't," says Calum, shrugging. "Crawler's arriving today with a fresh load of stuff from White Anchor. Thank Gaia."

"The Crawler's coming today?" Bear suddenly feels a weight lifted.

"Should've arrived by now actually. Must have ran into new terrain or something – but they always make it through."

Bear, for a moment, feels like a child again. A lifetime ago, his father would put him on his shoulders to let him see over the crowds, crowds that would come solely to watch the Crawler's arrival. The ground would start rumbling first, and his father would show him the vibrations in a cup of water, explaining to him how vibrations travel faster through solids than air.

Then they'd hear the churning of its treads, each as tall as a man and a half. People would start shouting and pointing. The treads were so wide, his father had explained, to spread out the thing's immense weight and stop it breaking through ice sheets or sinking into deep snow.

The huge body of the crawler resembled, according to Bear's father, a submarine or a stubby self-contained boat. Bear wouldn't even see a picture of a submarine until he was much older. Apparently it had the same capacity for pressurisation – allowing it to go beneath the ocean if required.

But the Crawler went to much darker places than any ocean bed.

In those early years, Bear hadn't quite understood what the Crawlers meant to people. He didn't understand then that travel between the various settlements of the Coastal Union is nigh-impossible due to the constantly moving phenomenon, driving itself like prying fingers across the lands. Then there was the shifting landscape to consider. Whatever the phenomenon did, it changed and rearranged the world as it went. Maps were useless after it had been and gone – hence the Cartographer's Guild.

Only in a Crawler, with its heavily armoured body, vast array of heavy weaponry, and unstoppable momentum, could any human make it through the phenomenon unscathed and with their mind intact. It insulates the crew and passengers from the madness just outside the vessel, sealing them in pre-Cataclysm armour.

The Crawlers were, to Bear, mankind sticking its fingers up at the phenomenon that had plagued them in the century after the Cataclysm. Proof that they could still rise above any problem nature threw at them. Seeing one had always given him shivers.

Seeing a Crawler meant that trade and travel were about to happen. Goods from other settlements, luxuries that Forgehead could not grow or make for itself, would be sold to the town. People would disembark, people who had bought the expensive right to travel aboard the Crawler for a few days.

Bear had never been on one – couldn't afford it back then. He'd considered saving up for a trip to another settlement all his life, now that he could afford it – if only to see the interior of the Crawler's chassis, to understand how it was built, what it could take, what it was capable of. Work, however, always kept him rooted firmly in Forgehead.

The childish wonder recedes, and he realises he's been staring into space as he walks. Calum has led them into a low-roofed office building that looks like an old school building, with huge windows and rickety wooden doors, giving it the appearance of a flat-headed beast peering up from the grey sludge that coats the ground.

"Ok, my office," says Calum, and leads them down cold, grey corridors.

On the walls are pictures Bear takes for graffiti every time he sees them. They depict a man lifting a masked helm off his head, with a pained expression on his face.

Below that reads a slogan:

It's Not Worth It!

And below that:

It Only Takes One Mistake For Exposure To Take You

In the bottom left is the bronze, flaming acorn of the Forestry, their sigil. Bear has always thought it fitting, since they generally ended up burning forests to the ground when they burn back the enroaching phenomenon.

Calum unlocks the door to his office and leads Bear into what looks like a storage cupboard with a desk and some filing cabinets. The cabinets are scavenged – Bear can tell because they are all different styles.

"What was his name again?" asks Calum, pulling drawers out. "Aiden?"

"Aye, went by Addie. Father was a tinkerer."

"Surname?"

"Didn't ask – plausible deniability in case the militia asked me where I'd been."

"Seems redundant," laughs Calum. He opens a drawer and lifts out a folder, sifting through its contents. "Ok, let's see."

He looks through it, frowns, and gets another folder out. He sifts through that, clears his throat, and then looks at Bear.

"Theory disproven," he says. "He wasn't one of mine."

"I knew it," whispers Bear, nodding. "Unless your Foresters have kept an exposure from you?"

Calum instantly dismisses it. "They wouldn't. There's shouting and alarm bells all down the fire-line when an exposure happens. We get warnings on the master screens when somebody removes their sensory blockers anyway, or in the event of a breach. Impossible." He scans through his own records. "We did have a turn-away, recently. About two weeks ago, doesn't fit your time frame though does it?"

"A what?"

"You know, a turn-away. Turning Gaia away before she reaches us? We'll sometimes get early warnings from Scouts or Cartographer's, and send a squad out with some sensors, a remote command unit, and some flame guns. Y'know, just give her a nudge, remind her we don't want her company."

"Two weeks, you say?"

"Yep. No exposures reported."

"Doesn't fit. So then we're back to my initial theory," says

Bear. "Something which has the same effect as the phenomenon is inside Forgehead. Alternatively, the phenomenon *itself* is inside Forgehead – though there's no precedent for that."

Calum closes the filing cabinet as though he's closing a coffin lid, staring into the distance, thinking. Bear sees his doubt; feels much the same. This shouldn't be possible.

"We could go and visit the boy?" suggests Bear. "You can see for yourself."

"Visit a final stage exposure victim?" asks Calum, giving a joyless laugh. "And what, see if we can interpret his dribbling? Put his teeth back in?"

"I've got my sensor and my work gear in my bag. Maybe there's some information I missed, something that I overlooked. Maybe a second opinion would catch something new?"

Calum considers this, and Bear sees the fear starting to work on him. He knows neither of them will be able to rest until they know the answer:

How did an exposure occur within the walls?

"Bear, I'll be back in two minutes, wait here."

Bear nods, and sits in Calum's seat behind the desk as he leaves the room, closing the door behind him. Bear looks around at the cold, grey room, and uses his time alone to go over the details, over the facts, and see if he missed anything. Some people would get bored being left alone in such a dull room, but Bear is unfamiliar with the sensation of boredom. Solitude and quiet are just other places to work, for him; ideal conditions for his mind, if nothing else. And so he thinks.

The phenomenon can move – everybody knows that. That's why the Forestry exists, after all – to burn it back when it gets too close.

Walls don't stop it – he knows that. They slow it down, apparently, and give the Forestry a high vantage point to launch flames from. Walls didn't stop it wiping out Heap, though, the poor bastards.

He lifts the sensor out of his satchel and considers it: a wooden box with a range of sensors, radio detectors, diodes and rickety electronics held inside with tape. Home made. It uses two finely tuned lasers to alert him to distortions in space, based off old pre-Cataclysm papers on gravitational wave experimentation that his father had bought years ago. The papers had barely cost his father anything: the scavengers didn't know what the words even said, let alone meant. They *know* that the phenomenon disrupts space – it's the one real, clear lead that they have.

The little sensor had probably saved thousands of lives – it was the basis for the standardised detector that most Foresters and Scouts carry with them now. Larger ones are built into the ground and walls around all settlements – allowing Calum to command his Forestry from a secure location during an incursion, and tell them when to start firing.

Calum comes back in, and sees him toying with with his father's old sensor.

"Still using the old model, I see," he laughs, and sits on the edge of the desk. He's carrying something in his hands; it resembles an old diver's helm. "Shouldn't you upgrade it to a smaller model?"

"I like it as it is," says Bear, and stows it. "Simpler, less likely to fail, easier to fix."

Calum sits the helm on the table; a brass diving helmet with wires leading to haphazardly installed headphones cut into the side, with the glass face-panel spray painted black.

"Your old sensory blocker," says Bear, confused. "Why's that here?"

"Because I can't take a modern one out of the armoury without signing for it and being asked questions. Pass me that paper. What's the boy's address?"

"Uh, twelve. Mill Street."

Bear passes the paper to him, and Calum begins writing on it, in his blocky, capital lettered scrawl. Bear reads over his shoulder.

It's a will, of sorts. It says that should he not return within three hours, Twelve Mill Street is to be sealed and purged with fire. Below that, he writes that he suspects something is loose in Forgehead, and to start patrols.

"What if someone finds this before we return?"

"I'm leaving it sealed with my second in command, who will

keep track of the time. These are the orders I'd be giving out this evening anyway."

"What? You're starting patrols?"

"You're damn right I am. If something is loose, then we need to start emergency protocols immediately. I'm just giving it one last try in the hopes that it's some misunderstanding, and we find proof that you're wrong."

Bear nods, understanding. It makes sense and covers all the bases, from Calum's perspective at least.

"What are the emergency protocols?"

"Half-sense patrols; one Forester in sensory blockers, led by another without, taking turns. I'm going to need more kit, more fuel, more flamethrowers, more -" He trails off. "More soldiers."

"What?" asks Bear, growing nervous.

"I'm going to need to issue a conscription order. Bear, you know what that means."

"I'm not joining up, Calum," Bear laughs, though his voice is trembling. "I'm educated – I'm exempt."

"It's a lottery, you're a citizen; I can't promise your name won't come up."

"So take me out of the loop; offer me a job doing something in an office somewhere."

"While other people put their lives at risk?" asks Calum, as though insulted.

Bear leans forward, raising his voice. "I'm probably the only person in Forgehead who knows how to research and understand this, Calum – I'm not cannon fodder."

Calum goes silent. "Maybe I could find something. You're right. The Crawler is due in later today, I can't miss that – but if everybody goes to see it arrive, we can use that as a distraction to investigate this place."

"Good," says Bear. He's letting Calum strategise – that's his area of expertise. Bear is far better suited to the aftermath where the facts and figures have to be analysed. "Anything else? Can we get help from anywhere?"

"If we get the dreams - if we know that an attack is coming - then standard procedure is to put out a broadcast, emergency frequencies. Then the other settlements will send Forestry backup – or a nearby Crawler will come, if we're really lucky. I have to tell the radio tower to do it personally, though."

"But we don't *know* that an attack is coming. Just that an exposure occurred within the walls, without precedent. We don't know *what* we're dealing with – if anything."

"It's too much of a risk," says Calum. "We have to treat this like an attack is coming. If it's nothing, we're fine. All that happens is I get less popular than I already am."

"And if you're right?"

"Then we're ready for whatever Old Mother Gaia throws at us. We won't disappoint her."

Bear bites his knuckle – this is far from what he expected when he handed his research over to Calum. Which raises another question:

"What about my research?"

Calum pats his pocket, as if only just remembering that it's there. "Oh, of course, of course. Well this is more important than ever, now. We'll need to get it to my contact – they'll ensure that the Council see the research, and they can decide how we proceed."

"All done anonymously?"

"Obviously. Nobody's getting disappeared for this, Bear, don't worry."

Bear feels himself growing smaller as their peculiar situation starts to tighten around him like a noose. He's neck deep in potential crimes, risking execution or imprisonment and torture, and he's plastered his name all over everything. Calum sees the fear on his face, sees him go white. "Bear," he leans in, "I won't let anything happen to you – you've probably saved a lot of lives by bringing this to me."

"Ok," says Bear, breathing and calming himself. Calum's ability to embolden people paralysed by fear was part of what made him a good leader. "Ok. Time to go?"

"Time to go. Twelve Mill Street."

Bear hefts his satchel, and Calum grabs a rucksack from a cabinet in the corner and stashes his old diving helm in it.

They leave without a word, stern-faced to hide their anxiety.

.

Chapter 4

Twelve Mill Street is a quiet tomb on an empty, silent street. Far off, Bear can hear the muffled fanfare of crowds: people awaiting the arrival of the Crawler, the arrival of fresh food, family members, and letters that are cheaper to send than radio messages, if a lot slower.

Calum, his old diver's helm under one arm, knocks on the rickety wooden door as Bear did the previous night. There's no answer, and the two men give each other curious looks.

"Should we -?" begins Calum, motioning towards the door.

"Do it," says Bear.

Calum steps back and kicks the door right next to the handle, shattering the lock from the wood and throwing the door open.

The sun shines through a thousand motes of dust and dead skin. Nothing has changed since Bear visited. Simon is nowhere to be seen.

Calum briefly checks that nobody is watching, and enters the house. Bear sits the door in a position as close to 'shut' as he can manage, and Calum produces an LED lamp to illuminate the room, holding it high. Sterile electrical light shows them an empty camp bed, a mess of a house, a barely used cooking stove and a pile of wet firewood.

"This place is barely lived in," whispers Calum. "Poor bastard was just scraping by."

"I made a note to tell you about how this guy was living. He was gonna need help one way or another."

Bear looks through the boxes of screws and parts. "A lot of this is rusted," he says quietly. "I missed that the first time. Thought he was just a tinkerer. He probably hasn't done anything with this stuff in years. Do we definitely know that he works here?"

"What about this?" asks Calum, lifting the straw mattress of the camp bed. There's a Gaian dream catcher under the mattress. "Your boy got bad dreams, it seems."

"Don't all Gaians do that?" he asks.

"Not unless you want to ward off nightmares," says Calum.

"Well, I can forgive Old Simon some nightmares, given what he has been through," whispers Bear.

Crossing to the basement door, Bear pulls out his earphones, blindfold and music-player. As he prepares to lock his senses shut, Calum stops him with a hand on his arm.

"Let me go down," he whispers. "One of us should keep watch, no sensory blockers. In case the father returns. You've met him before, you can make something up."

Bear weighs it up; can't find fault with it. "Ok," he shrugs. "I'll keep watch. Just be careful."

"I've been in worse places than this, Bear," he says. "Right. How do you usually do this stuff? What do you look for?"

"Calum this is your job," laughs Bear.

"No, my job is burning this shit to the ground. I don't *investigate.*"

"Ok, well," Bear relents, "the walls are scratched up with post-exposure runes; the boy himself – if he's still alive – is really too weak to move, he's confined to a bed. There was a big cabinet in one corner, empty when I checked it – think it used to be used for meat. There's a lot of – y'know, no toilet, so..."

Calum understands. "Ok," he says. "I'll see if I can find anything that implicates him as Forestry or something else. A thorough search – I'll bring anything back up. Take me through your process."

"Ok, take this," says Bear, and pulls his phenomenological

sensor out of his satchel. "I've set it to short range sensitivity, and you can plug your earphones into *this* slot here – on this setting, it'll only beep if you point it towards a rune or something that might be an exposure risk. You use that to figure out what way is ok to look, then you can open your eyes, but mind your peripheral vision."

Calum taps the helmet. "That's what this thing is for. Keeps the field of view very narrow."

"Good, well, keep your ears guarded too, whether or not you think it's quiet. No telling what audio risk there might be down there."

"And the boy?"

"I couldn't get anything out of him," says Bear. "Even if I were to wait for a lucid moment, I couldn't risk opening my audio channels to hear what he was saying."

"Ok, I'll see if I find anything new. Good luck."

"Good luck."

Calum pats his shoulder, passes him the LED torch, and opens the door. There's silence from the basement – no wailing, no breathing. He puts the diving helm on and closes the front hatch, and presses a button in his coat pocket. Bear can hear the muffled heavy metal music echoing through the brass.

Calum descends, leaving Bear alone in the cold light. Bear shivers, and starts looking around the house. He checks all the usual places; under the bed, behind picture frames with drawings of Simon and his son in pencil, in the drawers of the makeshift kitchen.

Bear finds everything that Simon owns, and realises how little it is. As many pieces of cutlery as there are people under the roof, a floor of concrete and mud, and a roof of corrugated steel filled with rust holes. No home at all – no life, just an existence. It saddens him.

His train of thought is distracted by the sound of footsteps outside, and Bear curses under his breath and creeps to the basement door. He can hear Calum rummaging around down there, and little else.

The footsteps grow louder on the slush outside. He hears murmuring voices by the door. Bear needs to warn Calum, but he can't go into the basement with his eyes open. There's no time.

He takes a chance, and steps into the darkness of the stairwell as he switches the LED lamp off, closing the door behind him. There's no strange sounds – he's safe for now, no audio risk.

Bear screws his eyes tightly shut, and descends into the basement. Calum won't hear him coming – he'll have to use touch; meaning he can't block his ears with his fingers. He's going to have to risk it – but if he can't hear anything from here, he's *probably* ok.

It still makes his stomach turn. This is one of the most basic rules that his father taught him when dealing with the phenomenon; no sloppy work, no risks, always assume the worst and prepare accordingly.

He has no choice – it sounds like somebody else is entering the property. Militia, given the heavy footfalls of their boots and the metallic jangling of their equipment. That means they're in far more trouble than just an angry homeowner returning.

Calum does not have any control over the militia: they'll be arrested, investigated; maybe the research in Calum's jacket will be found and... Bear tries not to dwell on it. He tiptoes down the stairs. He'll have to rely on touch to communicate with Calum.

The Forestry long ago developed a basic touch language for communication between people undergoing sensory blocking, in the event that their radio was blocked, or there was an emergency or malfunction. Bear navigates by sound, listening for the tell-tale whispering and out-of-key singing that is present in every survivor report, the sounds that will tell him he's entering an area of phenomenological effect.

But there's only silence and shuffling.

Whatever was once here is gone now.

He heads towards the sound of Calum's movement, and acts quickly. He grabs his arm, and Calum jerks away and throws a wild punch, catching Bear on the cheek. Panic – and no wonder. Bear grimaces and tracks his hand down Calum's arm until he finds his hand, and squeezes it as hard as he can:

Friend.

Calum stops flailing, and Bear keeps both his hands clasped over his, so that they can communicate. Calum returns the *Friend* gesture.

Bear taps the ears of Calum's helm hard enough that he'll either feel or hear it.

Audio-safe.

Calum reaches into his pocket and turns the music off. The two men stand in silence, breathing heavily, unable to see one another.

"Bear?" whispers Calum.

"Sorry to frighten you -"

"I'll say," he laughs, still whispering. "Nearly had a heart attack, man. What's wrong?"

"Someone was coming. Might be in already -"

Bear is cut off by the creaking of the floorboards. Then, two distinct sets of footsteps.

"Shit," whispers Calum, "I kicked the door in, they'll know something's wrong."

Bear hears him push his jacket back and feel for his pistol. "Put that away," hisses Bear. "We don't know who it is, and you aren't shooting militia. Into the cabinet, in case they come down."

Bear feels his way along and they open the cabinet, climbing into it. The cold brass of Calum's helm presses against Bear's forehead. The two of them crouch there together in the dark, closing over the door with a *click*.

Just in time. The basement door opens, and two sets of footsteps descend the stairs. The two intruders start talking. Bear immediately labels them Rat, who has a nasal whine of a voice, and Pig, who continually snorts into the back of his throat as though he's unwell and has a low timbre to his tones.

"What a shame," says Pig, and sniffs. "He had real potential."

"Bright boy," says Rat. "Really thought he'd pull through."

They are talking, Bear realises, about Addie. His body must be there – meaning that his suffering is over, at the least.

"You know how rare it is," says Pig. "Look at the etchings, too. Barely enough cohesion to even register. I can't see shit in them. No elegance, no evidence of real understanding."

"Yeah, good point," says Rat. "This wasn't even close."

Bear wonders how they can even discuss the runes – can they *see?* Are they down here without sensory gear? Bear risks opening his eyes at a low squint, covering his eyes with his hands and separating his fingers just a little. Through the cracks in the cabinet door, he sees the yellow light of an old battery-powered torch. Pre-Cataclysm technology, horribly inefficient. The men cast in that light are looking around, eyes wide open. They do not seem to be affected.

"Messenger called it wrong again," sighs Pig. "That's a couple in a row now that haven't survived exposure." Bear feels Calum tense up at the mention of the word. "Think he'll be angry?"

"I hope not. I hate when he gets angry."

They hear the humming of a man deep in thought, and frustrated. "He was so certain about this one, too, wasn't he? Said he had nailed it. So why aren't these new ones surviving?"

"Gotta remember: he can only show these people the truth, my man. After that, it's up to them to endure it. Addie wasn't worthy – that simple. Shame – Messenger said he'd have been really useful. Engineer in training, I think. Let's get on with things, then."

Bear is already making mental notes on all he's heard. He can feel his heartbeat in his ears, feel his shallow breathing making his head light.

The footsteps retreat up the stairs, and as the basement door closes again, Bear lets out a tense breath. Neither he nor Calum says anything – Bear pushes the door open and they unfold themselves. Bear keeps his eyes shut.

Above them, the house door opens, and then closes. They're alone again.

Bear takes Calum by the arm and leads him up the stairs, eyes shut, into the dim light of the house, and switches on the LED lamp. They're safe here, for now. Calum wrenches the helm from his head and sits it on the bed as Bear wipes sweat from his brow. Both of them are breathing heavy, still tense and full of adrenaline.

"What the fuck?" asks Bear, barely keeping his voice down. He's pacing up and down. "Who was that? Who the *fuck* was that? They were looking at the runes Calum, they were looking right at them and it didn't bother them, what were – what the -" Bear swears and rummages in his pack, pulling out some paper and a pencil. He starts scribbling down words, trying to recall exactly what they heard.

Calum is holding his brass helm in his hands now, and staring into it with a bright, fresh fear in his eyes.

Bear looks up from his scribbling. "You going to say something, Calum? I mean, we just – that was -"

Calum looks up. "The boy was dead. Far as I can tell, he choked on his own vomit."

Bear stops, lets out a tense breath, and nods. "Least he isn't suffering now."

"Those men -" begins Calum.

"They were talking about deliberate exposure. They said something about *surviving* exposure."

"I know," says Calum, as though irritated at his own confusion. "There are rumours -"

"*Nobody* survives exposure," says Bear. "It's terminal."

"Is it?" asks Calum, and both men look at one another in nervous fear. "Are we absolutely sure about that? Are *you*? You hear some weird stories from Cartographers, man, folk who've been out in the field. People from out near Heap who'll tell you there are prophets who've survived it, who've been changed by it."

"Those are rumours and drunken stories. I've seen a *lot* of exposure cases Calum; I've never seen someone survive it." Bear scratches his chin. "I mean – I've never seen any data that indicates otherwise. Gaians *do* talk about their shamans enduring exposure but that's bullshit and everybody knows it – otherwise there'd be some great accounts of it by now."

"Those guys seemed fairly confident about it, didn't they?"

"What if -" Bear stops, and rubs his hair back as he does when stressed. "Ok. I need to think about this. This is a lot. I mean *if* it's possible to survive exposure then that could change everything. If I could *replicate* that..."

"We're out of our depth aren't we?"

Bear laughs. "I know I am. What the hell do we do? What's happening here?"

"I think," says Calum, "that we should single out what we *know*. That people might be deliberately causing exposures."

"Experimentation, perhaps?" suggests Bear, talking more to himself. He's thinking about his father again. "It's what I'd do if I *really* wanted to study exposure, if I needed the numbers for a data set..."

Calum shrugs again. "Maybe. Maybe. Perhaps looking for people who *can* survive it?"

"Like a natural selection type deal?" says Bear. "If they're doing something like that, at least we'd have an explanation – though I still don't know how one might cause a deliberate exposure without being near the phenomenon. How do you bring the phenomenon to someone within the walls? Unless, y'know, they drag some poor bastard outside during an incursion... I don't know. This doesn't make sense. Calum, I think we need help."

"I think you're right. And I think I know who to ask."

Bear looks up, as realisation dawns. Calum answers his hopeful look with a smile.

"Let's go and watch the Crawler coming in. They'll be able to help us."

Chapter 5

The Crawler's arrival always pulls the largest crowds that Bear ever sees in Forgehead – and these days, the crowd seems that much larger. People, he imagines, must need the reminder that there's a world out there beyond their walls.

Crowds of bedraggled workers wrapped in shawls and leather coats stand in Forgehead's main square. Children are already climbing up the old armoured bulldozer that is half sunk in concrete – a memorial to the Scavenger War twenty years ago – a war that ended when it reached Forgehead. The children climbing ignore their parental demands to come down – they want to see the Crawler.

Snow begins to fall, soft and faint in the dying evening light, casting a hush on the crowd. The silence is broken by the great gates grinding open. The Crawler is taller than the gates, taller than any house or building in Forgehead except the great chimneys. It turns the road into two roads, creating great trenches where its treads fall.

They can feel the engine through the ground as it approaches. When it goes past, the world seems to drown in the beat of its machinery, roaring like the waves. As it passes by the crowds, Bear can just make out movement from the cockpit at the front, the only window in.

Bear holds his breath as the trembling behemoth shudders and coughs, coming to a stop; the Crawler has turned and parked itself near the square, and is lowering its ramp, revealing the cargo bay.

People peer and tiptoe to see who is coming down the ramp, what goods and luxuries the Crawler has brought them.

Instead, Bear joins them in a collective, low gasp. Three people stand on the ramp, limping down it. One of them isn't standing, but hanging between the other two.

"Hang on," whispers Calum – they both sense something amiss. "There should be four of them."

There's an elderly man with his long grey hair pulled back in a pony tail, wearing a long duster jacket. Then a huge, broad man two heads taller than Bear, at least, with blood streaked across his torn t-shirt, and a woman. The woman is blonde, with a gold circlet around her braided hair, and she hangs by her arms between the two men. Blood is dripping from her mouth, her shoulder, and her abdomen, where poorly applied bandages hang. Her guts are almost hanging out from them – it's a miracle she can stand at all.

The old man stares at the crowd in disbelief as the trio stumble down towards them.

"Don't stand and stare," he barks. "Get us a medic, now!"

Calum surges forward through the crowd, donning his Forestry cap and shouting his credentials as he pushes forward. Bear can think of nothing useful to do – so he follows.

When the clamour has died down, Bear finds himself in the role of nurse. He's the closest thing they could find to a doctor – even if it's just academic, he at least has an understanding of anatomy and shock treatment, and that makes him an acceptable substitute. It is one of the many things that his father insisted he learn to do well.

They stand in the same tavern where Bear sat earlier, inside this time, with the candles pushed off the table and the injured woman lain atop it, unconscious now. She's half naked under a blanket, after Bear has cut her blood soaked vest off to treat her unimpeded. Having removed the poor bandaging of the Crawler crew, Bear has done his best to put her insides back where they belong and stitch her shut. Bloody bandages bind her three largest wounds, with a soaked cloth on her forehead to try and take some of the heat from her body. She wears a thin layer of sweat over her skin – deathly pale, feverish. Her breathing is shallow, fast. She's right at the precipice.

On the tavern seat beside her sits the large statue of a man, hands clasped in front of him. He hasn't spoken a word – but he watches everything that Bear does, never blinking. The tavern door is locked, and the room is empty by order of Calum's authority. Bear remembers it still: watching Calum kick the door open with his pistol in one hand and his golden acorn badge in the other, screaming orders as the injured woman was carried through the door.

They had called for a doctor over and over again. Nobody had come forward – and so Bear had taken a deep breath, and did his best. It might not be good enough.

Behind Bear, in the dim half-light as the fire dies down, Calum is in whispered conversation with the old pony-tailed man, who wears a knitted wool jumper and old pre-Cataclysm jeans, covered in oil and coal stains, with that huge leather duster jacket hanging off of his slim frame. He looks somewhere between sixty and a hundred, and Bear can't quite place it.

Bear looks at the silent giant beside him, and then back to the woman, fighting for her life.

"She's lost a lot of blood," says Bear, and watches the giant. He doesn't react, doesn't speak. "I don't suppose – you know – if the Crawler was bringing supplies, they might have brought plasma, or adrenaline, maybe, anything from Red Lake...?"

Bear trails off. The giant says nothing, just stares. Bear instead turns his attention to her wounds. Deep gashes, down to the bone, mark her shoulder. Her abdomen had been torn open so cleanly that he could see her intestines beneath, split from hip to rib. Then there's her mouth. Her cheek has been slashed open from lip to ear, so badly that Bear could see her jaw muscles at work when he tried to apply an antiseptic mixture.

He has stitched the gashes together as best he could, and sewn a mesh over her jaw. Now they have to wait and see if she pulls through. Bear still can't tell what the wounds were caused by – a bladed weapon of some sort, he imagines – but who would attack a Crawler crew? They were the lifeblood of the Coastal Union – there'd likely be a complete collapse if the Crawlers stopped their work.

"What's her name?" Bear asks the giant. He says nothing. "Ok, great, thanks a lot, huge help my man. Do you speak English?" The giant just stares. "Do you *speak?*"

Breaking the tension, Calum approaches with the old man in

tow. "Bear – this is Dusty, he's their captain."

Dusty leans forward and shakes Bear's hand. He feels warm, and he looks calm despite their situation.

"Bear," says Dusty with a voice like cigarette papers, shaking his hand firmly. "Thank you for everything – when Bee pulls through, it'll be thanks to you. We did what we could, but we aren't doctors."

"Ah, it's nothing," Bear manages. Something about the old man's blue eyes and faint smile make it impossible to be anything other than humble. "I'm no doctor, either, y'know -"

"Forgehead isn't known for its medical care," blurts Calum, as if in explanation. "We're far from Red Lake. Few to no doctors."

"I'm grateful nevertheless," says Dusty, and folds his arms as he looks at the woman. "Bee's a tough lass. She'll pull through."

It dawns on Bear that Dusty is reassuring himself, as much as he is reassuring them. Bear notes that whilst Dusty is uninjured, the giant of a man who remains unnamed has two smaller gashes across his chest, through his thin t-shirt. Bear had offered to look at them earlier, and been quietly, politely, pushed away.

Calum taps Bear on the arm. "Bear, I told Dusty about your research."

Bear feels his stomach drop. "I – what -"

"Relax, son," says Dusty, smiling. "I'm no fan of the Council's research ban. The Chief Woodsman here -" he nods at Calum, "- says that it's good work. Then there's your other issue, right? An exposure within your walls, isolated – very unusual."

Bear feels like he's being interviewed or examined suddenly – he can see it in Dusty's face; he knows more than he's letting on.

"Highly unusual," rasps Bear, still suspicious, looking to Calum for answers.

"Calum tells me that you overheard a conversation, too – about deliberate exposures?" Dusty sees Bear's face change to surprise, and he holds up his hands. "Don't worry yourself son, I do this for a living. This isn't news to me."

Bear nods, and he realises that he feels relief that Dusty knows everything. He feels a weight lift from himself. This isn't just their problem any more. He drops his defences, something that feels natural with Dusty already. Dusty clearly has a lot of experience here.

"That's what it sounded like," he says. "Do you know something about that?"

Dusty says nothing – but he looks down at the huge man who remains silent. "Glass," says Dusty, meeting the giant's eyes. "You can speak. Tell them about the Dreamers."

The giant – Glass – has a voice like gravel beneath tyres, and he doesn't blink once. He talks directly to Bear, as though he were the only person there

"There exists a cult of men and women. Across the Coastal Union. People who have survived exposure to Gaia. Looked dead at her. Emerged unbroken. Different. They believe that they are chosen by Gaia. Tested. They seek others out. People they believe to be capable of surviving the experience." He pauses for the first real time, as though for effect. "Then they expose them."

Bear meets his gaze, but sooner or later he has to blink – and when he does, Glass looks away, back to Bee.

Calum sighs. "They call themselves Dreamers – Dusty thinks that we've got some in Forgehead."

"You have," says Dusty, shrugging. "Though most of them are dead now."

Calum raises his eyebrows. "What makes you say that?"

"They ambushed our Crawler eight hours ago. Now most of them are dead."

Silence. Calum eventually speaks up. "Does that happen often?"

"No – otherwise they'd *all* be dead," he smiles. "They've never been so brazen as to attack us before – they must have been pretty confident. A Crawler is probably the most well equipped, well protected thing in the Coastal Union."

"Misplaced confidence, clearly," says Calum.

"Not entirely. They got us pretty good." Dusty nods at Bee's unconscious form. "Hit us hard."

"If I can ask," says Bear. "What did this to her?"

"Whatever happens inside an incursion, son. It wasn't gunfire anyway." Dusty pats Bear on the back. "Ask her when she wakes up."

Calum nods sadly. "I've seen Forestry casualties like this. Usually dismembered. She got off light."

Bear – everybody, to be honest – knows that death for the Forestry usually comes through exposure. Sometimes, though, when things have been particularly desperate, the bodies of Forestry conscripts show up in neat, thinly cut pieces. Bear has never been allowed to autopsy them – and no explanation has ever been offered. Gaia's wrath, they'd say. Demons that live within the Hell That Walks, tearing people apart. Bear wonders what he'd see if he looked at her wounds under a microscope. What was it, exactly, precisely, that did this?

"So is Forgehead in any danger of an incursion?" asks Calum, breaking Bear's train of thought.

"Could be. They ambushed us right in the midst of Gaia doing her thing," says Dusty. It unsettles Bear – he's talking about an incursion, about the phenomenon coming down over them. Such an event is enough to plunge Forgehead into a siege for days, but Dusty almost takes it in his stride. Dusty continues. "If the Dreamers were trying to stop a Crawler, then maybe they wanted Forgehead isolated – or without the munitions and fuel we've brought. Maybe they wanted us? Who knows. We didn't get to ask them."

Calum nods. "Munitions, of course. Wonderful – I'll have some men unload our stuff at once." He turns to Dusty, and Bear sees his professional veneer reappear. He becomes the Chief Woodsman again, and extends a hand – Dusty shakes it. "You've done Forgehead a great service by arriving when you did, Dusty. You've put to rest a lot of questions, and raised many more. Now I have to see to my duties; radio broadcast for help, start the patrols, handle logistics... Bear, continue to care for this woman, please."

"Aye-aye," sighs Bear, and Calum leaves. Outside, there's a crowd waiting. Bear hears Calum clear his throat, and address them – putting fears to rest, calming them. Urging them to return home, to return to work. He makes no mention that in twenty-four hours he'll be ordering Forestry conscription in preparation for a possible incursion.

"Your name is Bear, right?" asks Dusty, taking a seat at a nearby table, a few metres from the woman's unconscious form. Dusty rests a hand on her wrist, and for the first time he looks truly solemn. He could be her father, given their age difference.

"Yeah," answers Bear. "That's me."

"I reckon they left the taps on, Bear – you could pour yourself a pint. I won't tell a soul."

Bear considers it, but shakes his head. "Not while I'm caring for someone."

"You don't want a drink? I'll watch her."

"I'd *love* a drink – but until she wakes up and is stable, I'll hold off."

Dusty nods. "Good man." Bear feels like he's passed a test of some kind. "Calum told me that you're educated?"

"Aye – doctor of the sciences."

"A doctorate eh? In this day and age? Where'd you get your degree?"

"My father – he was the son of a university professor himself, pre-Cataclysm. Taught me all I know. Our family inherited a lot of pre-Cataclysm books from our ancestors. Apparently the sciences ran in all my family."

"That's good to see. The old knowledge is very valuable. We've lost much."

Bear notes what he says, about the world before it broke, and takes a look at old Dusty. He certainly looks like he's lived a long time, but how long? Old enough to have witnessed the Cataclysm himself? That would make him – Bear does the maths quickly in his head – at least ninety years old. Older, if he was able to remember the Cataclysm. It'll be a century, soon, since the world changed.

Dusty sees the curiosity in Bear's face. "You want to ask me how old I am," he laughs.

"I've been told I have an inquisitive nature," says Bear, laughing. "No need to answer."

"Makes you a good scientist, I imagine. Curiosity isn't exactly a survivable trait these days. Honest attempts at investigation are likely to leave you biting your fingers off while your brain melts."

Bear dislikes the topic, considering what happened to his father. "Yeah. Dad said a lot of science-minded folks died in the early years. Trying to figure out what was going on – losing their damn minds, before we figured out that you couldn't look at it, couldn't listen to it."

"Then they were trying to figure out why people were losing their minds," says Dusty, as though he's heard the story before. "And ending up with the same fate."

Bear sighs. "Aye."

"That what happened to *your* father?" asks Dusty. "Right?"

Bear looks at him as though he'd pulled a gun. "How do you know that?"

"I'm old, Bear. Forgehead does one thing: makes stuff. I knew the only scientist in Forgehead a while back – not well, not by name, but I knew he was doing good work. Heard he fell to the madness. I'm sorry. You must be the only scientist in Forgehead, now. Am I right?"

Bear shrugs, and collapses back into the seat. "Aye. And yeah, dad was an exposure case. Probably wanted to *see* what he had been researching. Maybe got sick of waiting for answers. Found him on the doorstep, gone mad. He wrote a bunch of stuff as he faded, in those few, lucid moments. One last piece of work. I've still got it, actually."

Bear has no idea why he tells Dusty these things. They've only just met, but Bear feels a magnetism to Dusty. He *wants* to trust him.

Dusty is staring at him, sombre now. "You've not read the notes he wrote on himself, though, right?"

"Of course I haven't," says Bear. "I imagine half of it is illegible insanity anyway."

"Has anybody else read it?"

Silence. Bear looks at the table. "No."

"What if there's something useful in those notes? Something that could ease the suffering of the world? Unlock some enigma, maybe? Don't you want to know?"

"No. I don't really *want* to know what he wrote," admits Bear. What he doesn't say, is that he is terrified that he might learn his father's motivation. Bear has to assume that it was deliberate – maybe spurred on by his scientific curiosity, frustration, desperation...

The real question, Bear would never admit, is this:

Why did he think it was ok to leave his son behind?

The unwritten truth in Bear's head is that this latest exposure case mirrors it so closely that he has began to doubt his own narrative; no longer is he sure that his father might have left him alone by choice. If he can prove that someone is deliberately exposing others, like those men talked about, then it might be that his father was a victim. He could patch that deep wound over, and move on somewhat. Put his father to rest, in his mind. Forgive him.

He has to prove it first, though, and that alarms him. His father always warned him about letting emotions cloud his objectivity when it came to research, to drawing conclusions. If he wants to find an answer, he will; that doesn't make it correct. He has to temper his assumptions, to look at the data thoroughly.

Dusty is watching him. Bear has obviously wrestled with what he is going to say.

"Yeah. I don't want to know what's written. It would be unscientific. Might cloud by objectivity."

Dusty leans on the table, talking in a low hush. He knows what Bear is really saying.

"That's fair, no reason to put yourself through that," says Dusty. Bear looks for condescension or smugness, and finds none. Dusty is totally genuine. "Did you know that people could survive exposure?"

"Not until today," sighs Bear. "Feel like I've had about fourteen rugs pulled out from under me."

"Get used to that feeling," says Dusty, totally serious. "There's more questions than answers to this stuff."

"How do they deliberately expose people?" asks Bear. "What's the method?"

"Wish I knew, son," he sighs. "Wish I knew. That said, we *have* found people tied to stakes out in the wilds. Might be that they just leave them in Gaia's path and wait for her to take a stroll nearby, expose the poor bastards. I've seen the stats. Less than one in a thousand survive, we reckon."

"Christ," whispers Bear. He shivers at the idea, that anybody would do that to another human; but he also dislikes it as an answer. It wouldn't explain Forgehead's internal exposures. How did they get something past the wall? It's not a solution.

It's dark outside when Bear stops worrying about the woman. Her pulse has regulated, she's breathing steadily, and she's warm but not feverish. Bear takes his first real look at her. Though her face has been torn almost in half, she has the look of a Valkyrie – blonde hair in a braid, golden circlet, strong jawed, pale as snow.

"What's her name?" asks Bear, and Dusty stirs from where he is resting his eyes, nearby.

"Beatrice," he says. "She goes by Bee."

"Bee," says Bear, and checks her pulse again. Stronger now. She's going to make it, provided that she is spared an infection. Bear fills a flask with water and prepares fresh bandages next to a bowl of boiled water from over the fire.

Dusty has been quiet for a while now – and Glass, the giant, remains staring at her as she sleeps. Bear works to keep the wounds clean as he replaces the bandages and checks the stitches. His eyes keep closing despite his attempts to keep them open. The sounds of Forgehead die down, till there's just the howling wind outside; the quiet slushing of footsteps; the crackle of the fire. He hasn't slept since before the night in Old Simon's house. Coming up on twenty four hours awake.

"Dusty?" Bear eventually asks.

Dusty jerks up suddenly, and Bear realises that he had been asleep after all – with his eyes open.

"Everything ok?" asks Dusty.

"Fine, aye, fine – listen, I'm falling asleep. I was going to ask you to keep watch, but -"

Glass raises a hand, and Dusty answers him. "Go on, Glass."

"I have no need for sleep," says the giant. "Not now. I will watch Bee."

"What a champ," says Dusty, and leans back into the chair. "Get some shuteye, Bear. Feel free to go home – Bee seems to be doing just fine."

"I said I'd care for her," says Bear, leaning back. "I'll sleep here just in case. I want to be here when she wakes."

"Good man," mumbles Dusty as he drifts off. "Good man."

Bear shuffles until he's comfortable.

What a day, he thinks to himself, and promptly drifts into the land of dreams.

Chapter 6

The tavern room is as it was when Bear closed his eyes.

Glass is sitting in the same position, Bee is lying prone on the table with her head tilted to the side and her limbs hanging loose. Dusty is slumped in his chair, fidgeting with one finger at the edge of his mouth as though he has something stuck in his teeth.

Bear stays silent. There's a strange air to the place – everything is still, and dim. Glass has his eyes open, and there's a gas lamp crackling gently behind them. They sit in a bubble of light whilst flurries of snow whisper by the windows, ghosts in the dark of the night.

The only other sound comes from Dusty, who's finger is squelching against his gum as though it's porous. It sounds infected. It worries Bear enough that he has to wake the giant, Glass, up. He overcomes his shyness and whispers:

"Glass?"

No reply. The silent giant stares ahead, so Bear leans forward.

"Glass?"

When there's no reply, he reaches out and tries to squeeze his forearm.

The forearm crumples like paper, and motes of dust puff out as Bear squeezes. He reels back in shock and stares at Glass, who is still unmoving. The huge man is now starting to slowly disintegrate, and Bear feels panic overcome him.

"Dusty? *Dusty,* look at Glass, what's -"

Dusty has worked several of his teeth free by now, and is wrenching at the skin of his gums, trying to peel it loose. He pays absolutely no mind to Bear.

Bear has no reference for this; no basis upon which to build a response. All he feels is fear, primal fear – the need to get *out* of here. Everything is wrong suddenly. The room seems so much larger than it was previously, the walls are so far away that they're blurring, fading into shadow.

Anything could be in that distant fog.

Things are moving in it.

He turns to flee, stopping only to see if he can carry Bee out of this mess.

But Bee is already airborne, drifting upwards towards the ceiling, still unconscious with the blanket draped across her. Something is pulling her up, something huge and unseen. Hundreds of strings lead up into the shadow, attached under her skin.

He hears Dusty mumbling through his hands, asking for help, having forced both of his hands through his dislocated, distended jaw. Glass slowly becomes a cloud of motes that choke the air.

The light flickers.

Someone is whispering something, nearby.

There's a figure under the table, crouched, dark, humanoid and staring. It's been there the whole time.

Bear runs for the door and throws it open, but there's nothing outside.

Just snow, and darkness. No light.

A shape in the darkness, on all fours like a dog, padding forward into the low circle of light. Bear can only really hear it, sliding, dragging itself, wheezing.

There's more whispering behind Bear. He hears the table scrape and the cracking of bone as something unfolds to fill the entire room. Black tendrils drift out of it, as though they are underwater.

He should run forward to escape, but *something* is coming towards the tavern.

It comes closer, and becomes clearer.

Bear sees a black wolf, with eyes too close together – and human. Human eyes, with human eye lashes, open wide in a very human kind of joyful anticipation.

And its mouth is full of human teeth. It smiles wider than seems possible, and Bear realises that the wolf-thing extends back into the darkness as far as he can see, on hundreds of legs and one long, elongated torso that is writhing with something thin and reedy growing inside it, tendrils emerging from that human mouth, black and razor thin.

Something grabs him

and Bear opens his eyes, gasping, as Dusty shakes him awake.

"Bear? Bear, wake up, you're -"

"Dreaming," whispers Bear, and takes a breath. "Nightmare."

Which means the horror might just be starting.

It's barely morning, still almost dark, and the lamp holds them in a small circle of normality like it did in his dream. Dusty and Glass are looking pensive, staring at him as though waiting for something. Dusty lowers his voice,

"Bear," asks Dusty. "Do you remember your dream?"

Bear nods. He's done this test before; testing for shared dreams, the most concrete omen that an incursion is about to occur.

Dusty looks at Glass, and gives a grave nod. "You know what I'm about to ask?"

"The basic symbols," says Bear, still shaky from his memory of the terror. "See if any match. See if we've just been warned that an incursion is coming."

"So describe it," says Dusty, sitting down. He turns to Glass as if to say something, and Glass seems to understand without words. Glass begins to pack their kit into one large rucksack that he shoulders, whilst Bear talks.

"It was this room – Glass dissolved into spores, you were tearing your own teeth out... Bee was floating skywards. I saw something under the table -"

"Saw what?"

"Something small, humanoid, crouched -"

Dusty grabs his forearm. "It unfolded? To fill the whole room?"

"Yeah. And there was a wolf. Except it was more like a centipede or something, and it had -"

"- human features," says Dusty, finishing his sentence. "Teeth like a person."

They both nod to one another.

"Shit," whispers Bear, and stands up. "Similar dreams. There's an incursion coming. We need to tell Calum – wake him, if he hasn't gotten up already, the Forestry need to know!"

"Well, you do that," says Dusty, brushing himself down and throwing on his long overcoat. "I need to get my crew back to our Crawler. We shouldn't be here when an incursion hits."

The door is suddenly thrown open by an exhausted man in a trench coat with the golden acorn of the Forestry on his lapel, and a pistol in his hand.

Calum.

He looks around at them all, steam coming from his snow-soaked clothes, silhouetted against the low morning twilight outside.

"Wolf?" he wheezes. "Human teeth? All long and -"

"Aye," says Bear. "Shared dream, Calum."

Calum screws his eyes shut and pinches the bridge of his nose. "Ok," he says, recovering himself. "I need to get an emergency broadcast out before the radios go down. Dusty, what are you going to do?"

"Leave," says Dusty, with the tone of an apology. "We have other stops to make."

Calum understands, and nods. "Ok. Well, at least you've armed us."

"I'd stay if I could, Chief Woodsman, but -"

Calum cuts him off. "The Crawlers hold the Union together.

No need to justify yourself, Dusty. Go and see to your Crawler. Is the girl ok?"

"She'll live," says Dusty. "You have my thanks."

Dusty turns to Glass and motions to the table, and Glass picks up Bee in his arms as though she were a child, the blanket draped over her warm body. Her bandages and dressings hold.

"Bear, you ok?"

"I'm fine," he shrugs.

"Good," says Calum. "Then get yourself home and prepare. Your sensory gear all working?"

"Of course," says Bear.

Calum pats his arm. "I'll see you on the other side. I have much to do."

Bear nods, and wishes his friend well. The Crawler crew shuffle out of the door with their unconscious crew mate, leaving Bear standing alone in the same room he just dreamt of. The burst of cold air from the open door jolts him out of his daydream.

He feels weariness settle in despite his sleep. Nightmares do not make for good rest.

Now, he likely won't sleep for three or four days, whilst the incursion rolls through. Four days of sensory deprivation, with his food and water and piss-bowl lined up where he can find them by touch, fearing at every single movement that if he reaches out, something will grab him and pull him into another place.

The meditative techniques taught to him as a child – taught to all children now – are only effective for so long before one starts to get lost in their own mind. Incursion or not, the evidence that Bear has seen indicates that sensory deprivation causes hallucinations and distorted perceptions. It might be a danger to lose track of what is and isn't in your own head. It was used as torture, pre-Cataclysm. Or so he has read. Now it's a matter of survival, lest the incursion expose everybody in Forgehead to the phenomenon.

It could be worse, he knows; he could be in the Forestry, following orders brokenly transmitted into his sealed helm, trying to burn back something that he can't perceive with just a flamethrower.

Bear hefts his satchel, somewhat lighter now that Calum has

his research papers, and walks out into the snowstorm.

"Bear?" comes a call from Dusty as they pass on the street. He turns back to see the old man and his warm smile. "Thanks for everything – and good luck."

"You too," he nods, and leaves, a little starstruck.

Bear walks the fastest way home as the sun rises, on easy concrete paths, though it takes him past the Gaians and Christians. They're out early, trying to get the best spots for preaching to the workers. There's no fighting now, and the militia seem to have left for elsewhere. There's blood on the snow still, where people still rest by fire barrels, tending to the injured from yesterday's riot. Some of them are wearing the clothes and decorations of each other's side. Something close to peace has fallen, just as they're about to be plunged back into the abyss. As Bear passes, he hears two young women discussing the coming apocalypse, about how they're both curious about what it will feel like.

It seems to have just been accepted into common knowledge. The phenomenon destroyed the South some time ago. It moved in and stayed, and everybody put on their sensory gear, but the all-clear never came. The same will happen to us one day, say the doomsday fetishists. Every time you put on your blockers, might be the last. The Gaian shamans are sure of it.

It angers Bear, who has been taught that you don't have to accept anything that is forced upon you. To him, it sounds like defeatism, like a quiet surrender to a long night. He will not indulge it, and it gives people something else to be afraid of, as if there isn't enough already.

He is halfway home in the grey gloom of the early morning when the siren sounds. It's a long wail that is only ever heard on well-planned test drills, and it keeps going past the ten second test, letting the entirety of Forgehead know that this is no drill.

It cycles through the three discordant tones like a butchered animals last squeal. The few people on the streets that Bear can see freeze and grab onto each other in terror, their faces like that of children as the siren shatters the air. The townsfolk turn and flee for their homes.

Most of them.

One or two of the Gaians are sitting on the street, smoking, looking up at the sky with a faint cheer on their face. They seem to be waiting. Either the Forestry will force them to take cover, or they'll face exposure when the phenomenon comes. Then they'll be quietly taken somewhere quiet, and shot. That's what they consider a mercy, in the Forestry. Otherwise, they'll be taken to post-exposure treatment, something that Bear declines to think about.

He keeps his eyes low on the ground as he makes it home, as he was always taught to by his father:

Don't look up.

We build walls to stop us from looking at it.

To stop it from looking at us.

We don't know if it appears in the sky or not.

We build walls to keep it out. We set fire to it, and we push it back, but it has been a long time since we've looked to the skies.

Bear is alone in his house. He kneels on battered old cushions, listening to himself breathe. The town of Forgehead goes silent as the sirens fade. No machines will run today, no forge will light, no anvils will be hammered, no steel shall be produced. Only the Crawler will move, and it will be driving away, leaving them behind.

There will be silence, and – if they are truly unlucky – fire.

Bear has lain out his sensory gear and music player, his weeks worth of dried rations and bottles of water, and the jug and bucket that he'll use as a toilet. He places his blindfold and earphones on the floor and hooks them up to his radio. He won't move from this spot until the radio squawks to life and gives him the all clear. God bless the radio tower, his father always said, but Jesus, do they scare the shit out of him every time. From absolute silence, to someone talking right in your ear. For most people, at least those not in the Forestry, the all clear is the best and worst thing to happen during an incursion.

Even in drills, that moment of sudden noise has always caused Bear to jump and cry out in terror. Nothing builds tension in a man like days of sensory deprivation, wondering if every breeze and shift in temperature means that something has *found you,* that the Forestry have failed in their defence, that you're going to be taken. If you're lucky you'll only be cut neatly into tiny pieces by whatever dwells within the phenomenon.

It could be worse. At least he's lucky enough to *have* a radio. For those in the poorer areas, they rely on the Forestry doing the all clear rounds, tapping the safety signal on the arms of the townsfolk. It's why nobody can lock their doors during an incursion, which just adds to the anxiety. Many times Bear has sworn he has heard his door creak open, and spent the rest of the incursion certain that something is in the room with him. No wonder people often remove their protective gear. Not knowing what's beside you for days on end; it gets to Bear every time.

Numerous Forestry recruits have had noses bloodied by accident when waking people from an incursion. In better days, he thinks, maybe Bear would have liked to study ways to ease people back from sensory deprivation without moments of abject terror – but there are more pressing concerns for now.

He lays another two objects out before him: his sensor, and his glove. Part of him has always wondered what he'd find if he could listen to his sensor and record the readings as the phenomenon passed nearby. He's never even had the nerve to just leave it switched on. He can't imagine waking up to find that it's brushed just past him.

His glove is more for comfort; he could keep it on, and if the phenomenon gets close then he has six seconds of purifying flame with which to fight for his life. More likely he'd incinerate some poor Forestry recruit trying to give him the all-clear, when the radios fail again.

Bear is deciding where and how to sit, what to lean against, how to position his kit around him, when there's a scuffling sound outside. He stops and looks up, waiting, tense. His unlocked door flies open and Bear scrambles for the glove, stopping when he sees who has arrived. Calum stands with his pistol in one hand and his old diving helm under his arm. Bear's relief dies as he sees that his friend has blood running from the inside of one sleeve.

"Bear," he wheezes, struggling for breath. He closes the door and leans against it, fumbling to lock it.

Bear stands and runs to catch him as he stumbles. "Calum,

what the fuck happened, are you -"

"Just a graze," he winces as he leans on Bear's counter top, struggling to breathe and talk. "Bear. *Bear -*" he grabs Bear by the shoulders, and Bear sees real fear in his friend's face.

"What?"

"Bear, the radio tower. Everybody inside was dead. There were two guys there. They dropped this when I opened fire, what can you tell me about it?"

Calum produces a hard drive with a bullet hole through it – it must have gotten hit in the crossfire. Bear takes it, turns it over, and shrugs.

"Pre-cataclysm hard drive, for a computer or a laptop, I guess. What the hell, man? What happened?"

"They killed the radio operators, then they were trying to hook this up to the broadcast gear. Can you find what was on it?"

Bear shakes his head sadly. "It's wrecked, man. You need serious pre-cataclysm tech to recover data when it's this bad. Maybe in Union they have something but -"

"Bear, they escaped," he says. "I don't think I hit them. They might be coming back for it." He throws his hands in the air, ranting. "We have no radio, Bear, the radio kit got caught in the crossfire. I couldn't hail Union. We can't call for help."

Bear feels his world drop out through his stomach. "Shit."

Calum wipes his brow and takes off his hat. Seeing how pale he looks, Bear's medical instinct kicks in. He gets his water jug and starts pouring, trying to get Calum to show him the bullet graze. Infection is still the biggest killer in Forgehead – he has to clean it, no matter how small a wound it is. Calum takes a gulp from the water jug as it is offered, and half-removes his jacket, showing Bear where his jumper has been zipped by gunfire. There's a dull brown patch where he's bleeding, but it has mostly stopped. He's talking fast – adrenaline.

"They got away when I stopped to check the radio operators. Soon as I tried to get back here, the wood to the side of my head fucking exploded, Bear. They were taking shots at me – must have known I'd want to catch them up. Couldn't see them – small calibre, barely any muzzle flash, no idea where they were shooting from. I took cover and fired back, but they kept me pinned. They know what they're doing. By the time I tried to sneak out the front and flank them, they'd moved again. I ran back here."

"Think it was those two we overheard?"

"Almost definitely. Gaia's tits, Bear, imagine if I hadn't made it back. There'd be no orders given, it'd just roll right in and we'd be all alone, with two psychopaths loose and everybody blind."

Bear realises that they might still be in danger, and pushes a brush up against the door to jam it shut. He motions for Calum to get down.

"You think they could have followed you?" he hisses.

"They might have, that's why I came here first. We need to get a message out, Bear. If the all clear never comes, what happens to everybody? They'd starve, or take their helms off and get exposed – or the phenomenon would get in and everyone would be pulled apart and... We'd lose the whole town. Gaia have mercy, it'd be the South all over again. Just like at Heap. Maybe that was their plan, Bear, just like you said. Deliberate exposure. What kind of maniacs would -"

"Calum, wait," he stops him – and not just because he's rambling.

There's movement outside the door.

Calum looks at the door, shaking from the adrenaline. In the momentary silence, the door thuds and scrapes forward an inch. The lock holds

He was followed.

Calum grabs Bear and throws them both to the floor as bullets punch through the wooden door and across the room, blowing chunks out of the walls. Bear clamps his hands over his ears and curls into a ball, as glasses and mugs explode above him.

There's no rattle of gunfire, only the muffled coughing of the suppressor on an automatic weapon. Calum points his revolver at the door and fires one, two, three loud shots, putting fist sized holes in what remains of the door.

There's a flash of movement in Bear's peripheral vision, a figure in the gloom by his kitchen window. He lunges for his glove, but he barely has it on his hand before the masked figure raises his submachinegun and opens fire, shattering the window.

Calum is already up on his knees, one hand on Bear's shoulder, and as the floor and wall around him burst into splinters, he fires twice.

Red mist bursts through the broken glass and the gunfire momentarily stops.

There were two of them, thinks Bear – one by the door, and the other at the window. If he was attacking a house, and saw his comrade go down, he'd know that the occupants were facing away from the door.

Bear realises that they are going to be coming in the front door. He rolls over onto his back and secures his glove, cranking the gas up to full. The pilot light flares and the gauntlet hisses -

- and as he'd anticipated, the lock snaps and the door bursts open.

Calum has the wrong angle, his gun pointed almost one-eighty degrees away from the assassin. He turns as though in slow motion as the second gunman breaches like a trained soldier, gun up.

Bear clenches his fist, and the gauntlet's valve opens wide.

A pressurised mixture of petrol and pre-cataclysm polystyrene erupts from the glove and hits the gunman like a flaming fist at chest height. It has enough force to knock his aim off, and he gets two shots off that go wide as he throws his arms up in defence. The ammunition in his gun pops and bursts. Bear can only watch, horrified, as the attacker tears at his own clothes and jacket as they erupt in flames. In seconds, he is consumed. He is silent, panicking, flailing as the fire spreads, falling back out of the door and onto the snow-soaked street, but nothing is extinguishing these flames. His face is consumed by the flames as they crawl across him.

He discards his clothes as Bear and Calum give chase, but the fire has burned through his coat and onto his skin, down into his bones, and his black charred skin reeks as it burns. Smoke pours off of him like an oil fire. His muscles are burning through. He stumbles on blackened shin-bones as he falls.

Bear hears himself apologising, though he doesn't know why – nor to who. Calum breathes, aims, and shoots the gunman once in the head, ending his pain. Blood sprays against the snow, and he abruptly stops collapses, as the fire devours his body.

Bear lets out a sigh, but Calum has yet to relax. He is scanning the street with his revolver, grabbing Bear and pulling him back inside his house. Bullet holes have riddled most of his room, and now it smells of burning flesh. Calum finishes reloading his gun, thumbing rounds into the revolving chamber. He snaps it back into place.

"Stay here," says Calum, and practically drops Bear to the ground. He leaves.

A minute later, Calum returns, and closes the door behind him. Bear is looking at his glove, and fiddling with the dials. His mind has briefly shut down; no matter how hard he tries to focus and think his head keeps spinning, too fast to keep up with.

He can still hear the first abrupt scream, as though the attacker is still doing it, but when he checks outside there is just a limp corpse, burning still, belching thick black smoke skywards. There's the occasional squeal and pop of fluid and fat.

Calum kneels in front of him.

"Bear, look at me," says Calum, clicking his fingers. Bear manages to focus on him. "You did good, ok? You saved us both. You did good. Just focus on your breathing and try not to -"

Bear doesn't feel it coming, but he can't stop shaking. Without warning he vomits onto the floor, and his mind slows a little. He realises how badly his chest hurts now. Every muscle in his body has gone tense without him noticing, until now. His heart is pounding, and he can't make it stop, it's getting faster, faster still, he can feel it struggling.

"My chest – I think I'm having a heart attack."

"It's just panic, you just need to breathe, ok? Look at me, copy my breathing, in for three, out for three, come on, do it with me -"

"I killed that guy."

"Breathe man," Calum shakes him, and Bear copies him, following the pattern of breathing until his heart doesn't hurt so much, and some measure of sense begins to return. Calum puts a hand on his shoulder. "Bear, listen – this whole thing is fucked, ok? But I need you to take a breath, and get back in the game. I'm gonna be all on my own here if you can't straighten your shit out, ok? You do it for me, right? Back in the room, come on. One-two-three."

Bear nods, and reaches for the water jug to wash his mouth out, spitting onto the floor.

"Ok," says Bear. "Ok, I'm here. I'm listening."

"I found nothing in their pockets, and I don't recognise them. They're using shitty scavenger auto-guns with home made suppressors; low calibre, sub-sonic ammo. Not the weapons we make in Forgehead. They aren't from here. This was planned. There might be more."

"Are they Dreamers then? Calum - are we going into an incursion with people in town trying to kill us?"

Bear hears the fear in his own voice, and hates himself for it. Just a day ago, he gladly walked into a basement and risked phenomenon-exposure for the sake of science. Now he just wants to take a break from it, to catch his breath. The phenomenon is dangerous, but this is something else. This is *malice*.

"*I'm* going to be dealing with an incursion," says Calum. "You, on the other hand, are leaving Forgehead."

"What?"

"The radio tower was a mess, Bear. No distress call made it out, there's no guarantee we can fix it in time. We're sitting ducks, isolated. When Gaia wanders our way, we'll be all alone. We're going to be under siege, and there might be Dreamers among us, and Union City won't be coming to help us. Which means that I need you to take your research and this hard drive they were trying to plug into the radio, and everything that's happened here, and go join the Crawler crew. Once you're far enough away from here, get them to broadcast to Union, ok? They have really powerful comms tech onboard that thing. Get a message to Union City, and tell the Council what's happening here."

"But -" Bear's brain shuts down. It's been a long, sleepless couple of days. He rubs his eyes, and tries to get a handle on what's going on. "But I don't -"

"Look," says Calum. "You said it yourself – you aren't canon fodder. I'm going to need every able body I can get behind a flame-gun, or monitoring sensors. A lot of people are probably going to die before this is over. But Bear, listen to me," he puts his gun down and grasps Bear by the shoulders, looks into his eyes. "Bear, *everybody* in Forgehead could die if you don't get that broadcast out. Tell Union we need help, ok?"

Bear nods. "Will you be ok? Is everything -"

"Gaia's arse, Bear, of course not," he laughs. "The biggest bitch of all time is about to come for us, of course there are going to be casualties. Me included, maybe. That's my job. But we'll pull through; provided that help comes in time. We need to know that someone is coming, right? We can't hold forever."

"Ok. Ok. Has the Crawler left yet?"

"Almost. You'll hear the engine warming up before they embark." Calum reaches into his coat and produces Bear's research papers. "Here. Make sure you have everything, then get yourself out of here. I'm counting on you."

Bear's brain finally catches up. Dreamers, sabotage, isolation, phenomenon incoming, fate of Forgehead at stake, broadcast to Union City for help.

"I've got it," he says, and turns to grab his things. "Ok. I'm good."

Calum watches him pack quickly: everything that was on the floor, including his food and his now-empty glove, plus a couple of spare napalm-aerosol cylinders.

He pauses, and crosses to a desk, pulling out a sheaf of papers in a beige folder.

"More research?"

"My father's notes," says Bear.

The writings that Bear dare not read, the nonsense that his father wrote whilst Bear did his best to care for him. He might not get another chance to read it; he stuffs it in his bag alongside everything else.

"Ready?" asks Calum.

"Yeah."

They walk outside, Calum's gun still in his hand, and survey the empty streets. The body is still burning, and Bear will not look at it. Not now.

Bear turns and shakes Calum's hand, then embraces his old friend.

"Stay safe," says Bear. "Don't die. I'll see you when this is over."

"Bring the Union City Forestry with you, and I might even be glad to see you," laughs Calum.

They nod their goodbyes, and walk their separate ways. Calum goes back towards Forgehead, to a long, quiet siege full of fire and fear; and Bear walks towards the distant shape of the Crawler.

Chapter 7

Bear finds the Crawler ramp open, leading into their huge vehicle's cargo hold. It has stables for livestock, huge shelves for crates of goods. Glass appears from the craft, unloading crates of ammunition and fuel, one in each hand, as Forestry soldiers ferry the deliveries away with haste and little talk. Glass sits them on sledges for the smaller men, who work two at a time to ferry the crates that Glass held one-handed.

Glass sees Bear, and says nothing, not as much as a nod, before he turns and steps back up the ramp, continuing his work.

"Glass?" shouts Bear after him, afraid to follow or take a step onto the ramp. The scuttling Forestry workers take no heed of him. He feels like a ghost.

Glass reappears with a crate on one shoulder, and a barrel under his other arm. He thuds down the ramp, hands the stuff over to the Forestry men, and then turns back up the ramp again. Bear watches, dumbfounded.

"Hey, Glass. *Glass?*" Bear turns to the workers. "Is this guy deaf or what?"

"Glass doesn't speak mate," says one of them, rolling a barrel as though building a snowman.

"I've *heard* him speak," laughs Bear. "He's not mute."

"Only speaks if old Dusty tells him to though," says the man, and turns to continue his work.

Bear watches as Glass reappears with a single crate, and one of the Forestry men asks,

"Last one?"

Glass gives the faintest nod that Bear has ever seen.

"Glass?" he asks, before the giant can leave. "Glass, I need to speak to Dusty, is he onboard?"

Glass looks at him, and then goes to walk away.

Bear is exhausted, coming down off adrenaline, and he is not used to being so blatantly ignored.

"Hey, don't just *walk away,* this is important -"

Bear reaches out and grabs his wrist. Glass stops and turns, looks down at Bear's hand on his wrist, and his face shifts into a frown. Their eyes meet. Bear can see it in his face: Glass is challenging him to let go, lest he take action.

It must be the adrenaline, but Bear isn't intimidated. He just killed a man. He tightens his grip and meets Glass's gaze. Glass jerks his wrist away, and makes a hand gesture that says:

Wait A Moment.

He walks back up the ramp, leaving Bear standing with his heavy satchel, shivering from more than the cold. He hears laughter, and looks around. Two of the Forestry men are shaking their heads.

"Good way to get killed, mate," says one of them, and they turn to carry their cargo away. Bear idly wonders if they'll survive the next couple of days.

Up the ramp, Glass has activated an intercom of some kind, and Bear hears Dusty's voice through a speaker, too faint to make out details over the wind. Glass looks down the ramp at him, and jerks his thumb over his shoulder, motioning for Bear to follow him.

He doesn't look happy about it.

Bear takes a breath and walks up the ramp of the Crawler for the first time in his life.

The air inside the Crawler is warm, and the hallways and

walkways resemble that of a submarine; metal pipes and hand rails line the claustrophobic corridors, and every movement causes creaks and groans from his surroundings. Bear follows Glass from the sparse cargo bay up near-vertical stairs and through a maze of corridors.

At every turn there are sounds of clanking and hissing, and though the corridors are tight, Glass moves through them like a racing snake, ducking and twisting as Bear bangs his head and shins on valves and pipes.

Glass brings them to a pressurised door with a wheel lock. Bear knows better now than to ask questions or to try and make small talk. Instead he watches Glass spin the handle. A hiss of air escapes and, before he pushes the door open, Glass turns and gives Bear a look of warning. His eyes say: *Behave.*

Glass opens the door. On the other side is the navigation deck and on the far end of it, the cockpit. Bear steps forward, and the reality finally settles for him: he is standing aboard the command centre of a Crawler. This is the kind of thing that he daydreamed about as a boy, always wondering what the view from the inside was like.

He takes it in. There are four heavy pilot seats, two on his left and two on his right, each nested behind four complex looking consoles covered in valves, meters and buttons. Bear feels like a child again – already he wants to know what every button does, what the readouts and sensors measure.

Beyond the four command modules, Bear sees the pilot seat. Seen from outside, the cockpit always looked to Bear like the 'head' of the Crawler, it's singular eye. It has a sharp bough like that of a boat, for cutting through the snow. The top of the cockpit is made of thick glass, divided into four wide windows, to allow for visual manoeuvring. Right at the glass, near a broad set of controls, is the huge captain's chair with a co-captain's chair just to the back and side of it. All of the chairs are on gyroscopes, Bear notes.

They must be at least thirty feet off the ground, thinks Bear, and with a sharp pang of fear he realises that he can almost see over the walls of Forgehead. Fear of the open sky, of the open snowfields, has always been taught to him. Out of instinct, he averts his eyes, lest he accidentally catch a fatal gaze at the phenomenon. There is no guarantee that it will be there, but he only needs to glimpse it once and he will share his father's fate.

Glass closes the door behind him, and Bear becomes aware that he is gawking. Dusty and Bee are sitting opposite each other in the captain and co-captain's chairs, seemingly mid-conversation when he entered. The way that they were sat reminds Bear of a therapist and their patient. Dusty smiles when he sees Bear.

"Our friend from the pub," he says, and leaps from his chair to shake Bear's hand. "Welcome aboard. I'm sure you remember Glass, but you probably haven't seen Bee up and about?"

He nods to Bee, who is watching him with a kind of impatience – he feels like he may have interupted something important to her.

"And of course," Dusty continues, "I'm Dusty, Captain of this vessel. This is Crawler Four, Callsign: Icebreaker. Glass told me you wanted a word, and I said: for our friend, no less than the navigation deck itself will suffice! I -" he stops, and sees that Bear is in distress.

He wants to meet Dusty's eye, but at his back is the open horizon, and Bear cannot force himself to look up. Bear is trying to look confident, but the adrenaline that has kept him going is now gone, and he realises that he is shaking.

Dusty seems to know exactly what is happening.

"Oh, hold on." He turns to Bee, and motions covering his eyes. Bee nods, spinning around in her chair, and with the press of a button on her console, the cockpit window is sealed by thick metallic plates that unfold and slide over it, plunging the cockpit into shadow.

Warm red emergency lights flicker on, followed by bright strips of glowing white light. The snow fields no longer terrorise Bear.

"Better?" asks Dusty.

"Better," says Bear, blinking the ache from his eyes. "Seems a little risky to just keep your viewports open at a time like this."

"There's no risk at the moment," says Bee, and from her voice is is obvious that she is still badly injured. It's the first time Bear has heard her speak. She has a gravelly voice, like the rest of them, and a constant scowl – perhaps, thinks Bear, because she was torn to bits less than a day ago and must be in agony when she's awake. Bear reluctantly finds himself intimidated, though that might just be his nerves talking. Her cheek is covered in bandages, though her other injuries are hidden by her snow-grey overalls.

"Sensors are quiet," she continues. "The moment they pick something up, they automatically close any audio or visual exposure points."

"Ah," says Bear. "Clever use of them. The range on them, though -"

"It's all calculated by our onboard computer," says Bee. "We trust her to keep us safe."

"Onboard computer?"

Dusty motions to an empty seat at a control deck. "Sit down, Bear, sit down. Relax. There's not enough time for all the questions. We're about to leave, so be quick; so what brings you here?"

"You didn't leave a scalpel in me or something did you?" asks Bee, though she's smirking. How she manages to smirk through the mesh holding her cheek and jaw together is beyond Bear. Aside from her hand hovering over her abdomen, she hides the pain well.

Bear takes a deep breath, aware that they're all watching him. He had never considered until now that they might reject him. This seemed easy in his imagination. He falls back on professionalism, and tries to be an adult.

"I need to secure passage out of Forgehead. By order of the Chief Woodsman."

It is Bee who answers. "We don't do evacuations -" she begins, but Dusty cuts her off with a raised hand.

"Why are you leaving?" he asks. "Won't the Chief Woodsman be issuing a conscription order in a few moments?"

Bear lets go of any pretence he had of being in control, and spills the entire thing to Dusty.

"He wanted me to leave because the radio tower is busted. Two men shot it up, killed the people inside. They were trying to use *this,*" he produces the hard drive, "probably to play something on the radio to everybody with a headset. No distress call to Union City has been made, none can be made. Then those same men made an attempt on the Chief Woodsman's life – and my own."

The atmosphere in the room turns to ice. Dusty turns and looks at Bee, then at Glass.

"Dreamers," he mutters, before turning back to Bear. "So the

Chief sent you to get the message out?"

"Once we're far enough away that the phenomenon stops interfering with radio? Yes, if at all possible, I'd like to use your broadcasting capabilities. Please."

Bee shrugs. "We can do it ourselves, no reason to take on another passenger. Your job is done, lad, go help Forgehead survive. Well send help."

Bear frowns at her. "I also have something to deliver to Union City."

"The hard drive?" she asks. "We'll take it, no worries."

"Not just that. Research and findings that need to be seen by the Council."

Dusty folds his arms. "Isn't that the same research that would get you hanged by the Council?"

"It is. I'll cross that bridge when I come to it, but they need to know about what's going on."

Bee laughs. "You think that your research is better than what the Council has found on its own?"

Bear is already souring on her. "I do, yes," he says. "You can read it, if you want."

"I'll pass," she snaps, and that is the end of it. Bear can see that he's touched a nerve. She avoids his eyes, and he wonders what it is about the research that she wants to avoid – and why she doesn't seem to like him?

The crew all exchange looks, and unspoken words. Bear sees the doubts on their faces, and sighs.

"Ok, look, I can pay, as a passenger, if you want. I'll buy passage. I can afford it. I think?"

Bee rolls her eyes. "It's not about paying, lad. Dreamers came for you for a reason. They tried to kill you -"

Dusty silences her with a look. "Bee, I'll thank you to remember who captains this vessel. This is my decision."

She leans back in her chair, pursing her lips, wincing at her wounds. "Sir."

Dusty turns to Bear. "You're asking us for a lift to Union City,

Bear, correct?"

"Yes, but honestly, that can wait – the main thing is to get this broadcast out. Calum – sorry, the Chief Woodsman – asked me to do it, because he trusts me. The lives of thousands who live in Forgehead are in jeopardy. I mean, is this really such a big issue? I'll stay in the cargo bay, I don't need a room or anything."

Dusty shakes his head. "Bee is voicing her concern because the last time we encountered Dreamers, they gave us a fairly good beating. You saw her wounds. It didn't go very well for us. If you're a target for them, then we're making ourselves a target too."

"It sounds like you're already a target," says Bear. "Plus, not many people even know that I'm here – Calum, and maybe some workers from the Forestry. The men who tried to kill us are dead."

Bee chirps up again, eyes lighting up. "Don't tell me *you* killed them?"

"Well -" Bear stops himself.

He hears the screaming. Smells the charred flesh. Feels his heart beat fast and cold. It feels like it did when he first felt it. Like he is having a heart attack. He feels it coming on, and worse: in front of the crew. Bear begs with his head, with his heart, to slow down. He tries to breathe like his father taught him. He tries to meditate like he does during an exposure event. He imagines the music drowning out everything else.

"Well," he manages after a pause, fighting for control of himself. "One of them, yes."

Bee nods her approval, turns to Dusty. "If he kills Dreamers then maybe he's got some use. I mean... We *are* down a man -"

"I patched *you* up as well," Bear tells her. "Look, I'm not useless. If you want me to pitch in, I will."

"We aren't looking for another crewmember," says Dusty. "Yet. But if you want to help out, that'd certainly be useful."

"I'm a fast learner," says Bear. "Just tell me what you need me to do."

Bear sees Dusty weighing up his choices, looking at Bee and Glass for answers. Bear can see him arriving at his decision.

"We could use someone that can stitch a wound," he sighs,

talking to his crew. "We owe him one. That's my decision. Strap yourself into that seat, Bear, watch and listen; and don't touch *anything*."

Bear sighs with relief, and leans back in the seat. In doing so, he becomes aware that somebody else has already made a solid indent in it that must have taken years. He feels like he's standing on an unmarked grave. Bear tenses up, trying not to look too comfortable out of respect. He takes the time to relax, to get his heartbeat under control with the usual breathing techniques.

When he is sure that he isn't going to die of nerves in front of these people, he fastens an X-shaped harness over himself. The array of buttons lies before him, triggering some ancient desire to press everything, and see what it does. He resists, for now.

The others take their seats, with Dusty in the pilot's seat at the front and Bee just behind him. Glass sits across from Bear at the back, leaving an empty pair of chairs in front of them both. The crew strap in, and Dusty starts messing with dials. Bear can hear distant parts of the Crawler cough and splutter to life like some sleeping giant.

Bear watches in wonder. He has never seen so much technology in one place.

"Glass," says Dusty, without turning from the controls. "You can speak. Is the cargo bay clear?"

"Yessir," he growls.

"Bee, armaments and sensors?"

She pores across dials and readouts. "Weapons and sensors both nominal."

"Navigation and assignments?"

"Online," she says, pulling a cork clipboard out from her chair. "Our next route takes us to White Anchor, where we exchange a portion of Forgehead's steel and tools for fish. We'll need to prep the freezers. ETA two days, God willing."

She pulls the sideways crucifix from her overalls and kisses it, touching it to her forehead, and Bear makes a mental note of her faith, wondering if that's the reason for her being so short with him.

"Any high peaks along the way?" asks Dusty. "Anything for good broadcast range?"

"Yeah," she says, murmuring to herself as she tracks her finger along an LCD screen, upon which is a map of the Coastal Union territories, with red dotted lines marked in for possible routes. She then pulls out a paper map and compares the two, noting several differences. "Latest Cartographer's release shows two new peaks, seems we've lost one as well. Relatively high range anyway, we can find out by eye if we need to."

"Good," says Dusty. "Let's wake up May."

Bear looks around in confusion, wondering who or what May is. The speakers crackle with feedback before resolving themselves, and a voice comes through, yawning as though up from a long sleep.

"*Morning, sweethearts,*" comes the tired but charming voice. Bear already imagines her to look like some pre-cataclysm model in his head, pale featured with red lipstick. He can't place her accent. Definitely old-world, like the accents on old Scavs from the South.

"Morning, May," chimes Bee and Dusty together. Glass says nothing.

The voice comes over again. "*Glass? You not going to say good morning?*"

Glass folds his arms, remaining silent until Dusty turns and nods to him.

"Good morning, May," he eventually grumbles.

"*That's all I ask,*" comes to sweet reply from May. "*Now either someone is deceiving me or there's a new acquaintance to be made.*"

Bear darts his head around, looking for a camera. How does she know?

"Go ahead, Bear," says Bee. "Say hello to May."

"Uh, hello May. I'm Bear." For some reason, he looks at the ceiling when he says it.

"*Morning darling,*" she coos. "*Staying with us long?*"

"Uh, a couple of days I guess. As long as you'll have me?"

"*Not a problem, I'll just recalculate our estimated fuel usage for you. You're about what, eighty-five, ninety kilograms? Got some heavy stuff with you?*"

"Eh, probably? I guess?"

"*Got it, thanks handsome.*"

Bee is laughing as one might at a friend making fun of someone, and Bear realises that he's blushing. The crew is looking at him expectantly.

"She sounds nice?" he offers.

"Good luck getting her to have a drink with you," says Bee. "I don't think you're her type."

Bear sees the smiles on every face - except Glass, of course.

"I'm being made fun of, right?" he catches on. "What is it? Is that a recording of an old actress or something?"

Dusty shrugs. "That's what we used to call an English accent, from far south – pre cataclysm. I always said she sounded like that actress, who was she, the one with the mouth, she was in that show with the spies -"

Bee rolls her eyes. "Nobody is going to remember your ancient actresses name, Dusty," she says, turning to Bear. "She's a computer. That's basically the Icebreaker you're talking to. She is the Crawler."

Bear looks around, confused. "Like, a text-to-speech program?"

She sighs. "Like, a pre-cataclysm artificial intelligence, who helps us run the ship."

"You've got an AI in here? Seriously?"

Dusty nods. "Every Crawler has a fair amount of automated tech, but May is unique. Ask her yourself, she hears everything we say. Unless we ask her not to. Go ahead."

Bear looks up at the ceiling, unsure of where to field his question. "May?"

The speakers crackle. "*Hey, little bear.*"

Bee laugh, and Bear smiles through a curious frown. "Um. May, what are you?"

No hesitation. "*I am a self-learning general intelligence, originally designed to assist in the running and cyber-warfare suite of a T-2050 Kraken Class Dreadnought, before the global societal and environmental collapse that you call the Cataclysm.*"

Bear laughs out loud. "Really?"

"Really, darling," she says, and he can hear her smile.

"And what is a Kraken Class Dreadnought? A ship?"

"A pre-Cataclysm batttleship and drone carrier."

"And running the Icebreaker isn't so different to running a battleship?"

"There are significantly less individual tasks, weapons... and no drones."

"Apart from Glass," Bee chimes in. "He's a drone if I've ever seen one."

Glass frowns at her, but she laughs it off.

Bear widens his eyes in surprise. "And you help us to..?"

"My primary function, asides keeping this vessel running smoothly, is to take control of it and pilot us through instances of [DATA REDACTED]."

Her voice changes so suddenly that it makes Bear jump, from a polite secretary to a harsh robot with no humanity.

Dusty winces. "She does that sometimes."

"Is she trying to talk about the phenomenon?"

"Aye," says Bee. "She can't, for some reason."

"We've tried to get her to mention it before," says Dusty. "Or to pick a name for it. But when she does, she goes quiet for almost the entire day and then comes back and tells us that she has performed an entire system reboot to her last known working configuration. We just let her do the robot thing now, it's easier."

"Excuse my little quirks," says May, and Bear has nothing to say. He's a child again, in awe at what he doesn't yet know. He watches the crew finalise their checks, and then braces himself as the engines are turned on.

"Well it's a pleasure to meet you, May."

"Likewise," she says. *"Now shall we get moving?"*

"Let's do it," says Dusty. "May: Ignition."

"Anything for you, dear."

"Viewport is opening, Bear," he turns to look at him. "You're safe, don't worry."

The entire vessel shudders and trembles, and the viewports open again as the protective armour slides back, revealing the snowbound, high-walled town of Forgehead beyond, with all of its looming steel structures and hangars and its clustered wooden shacks.

The Crawler turns, and Bear watches as Forgehead slides out of sight. The white wilderness, evergreen on snow, looms before them as they leave through the open gates of Forgehead. They burst out onto the open snow, the entire command deck swaying with the motion. Bear can feel the gyroscopes keeping them upright, counteracting the wild movement of the Crawler.

"Captain," comes May over the speakers. *"Forgehead have closed their gates behind us."*

"Understood."

Bear suddenly wishes that he could look back and see it one last time. He wishes he could see Calum and wave to him, wish him luck. But there is no looking back now. As the gargantuan Crawler, the Icebreaker, bursts out onto the snowfields and turns north, Bear wonders if he will ever see Forgehead again. He feels that familiar panic rising, and makes a decision to let it go. His father used to tell him that fear is a choice, and whilst he has found that to be provably false, he knows that he can choose his mindset. Bear exhales for a long time, and lets the awe take him instead, revelling in this dream come true.

"We are all green-lights here, Captain," says Bee, looking at her workstation readouts.

"Ok," he says. "May?"

"Yes, dear?"

"You have full control. Take us the programmed route."

"Of course."

Dusty leans back, taking his hands off the controls, which start moving by themselves. He unclasps his harness and stands up, stretching.

"Right, that's the hard part done. Glass, get the kettle on."

Glass undoes his harness, stands up, and leaves the cockpit, walking back into the body of the Crawler.

"Bear," shouts Bee. "Tell Glass what you take in your tea, quick, before he starts making it."

Bear's jaw drops. "You guys have got *tea?*"

Chapter 8

The common area is a small hold near the cargo bay, close to the bottom of the vessel. A folding wooden table comes down from the wall into a booth, with space for three each side at a push. Storage units and cupboards are stacked against one side of the room, with boxes of dried food, a kettle and a working tap crammed amongst them. It has one of the few working fridges Bear has seen – a rarity in Forgehead, given how effectively mother nature keeps things cold there.

Glass arranges little metal camping cups around a large teapot as Dusty unfolds their seating area for them. Bear has to duck every time he moves, lest the light fittings hit his head. Already the steady thump and hum of the Icebreaker has become little more than background noise.

"You want food, you can make some here," says Dusty. "We get a bit of everything we transport. So once we leave White Anchor, we'll have fish for a couple of days. Usually it's just long enough between stops to get thoroughly bored of something before you get a change. It's more variety than most people in the Coastal Union get, day to day."

Bear nods as he sits down, and Glass silently pours him a cup of tea.

"Had this before?" asks Bee, and takes a sip through the uninjured side of her mouth. Everything she does and says is slightly lopsided. Her jaw mesh seems to be holding her face together, though.

"Couple of times," says Bear.

She arches her eyebrows. "So you're either rich or you've got rich mates?"

"Well my dad built the prototype for the phenomenological sensors, so..."

Bee nods, as though she already knew this. "The *phenomenon,*" she says, as though testing out the word. "Interesting word for it. Not a Christian *or* a Gaian, eh?"

"Uh, no."

"Interesting," she says, implying by her tone that she thinks quite the opposite. "So you don't think we're living in a post-judgement, fallen world that missed out on the return of the savoir? No?"

Bear clears his throat and sips his tea. "Uh, I can't say I do, no."

"Fair enough," she shrugs after a pause. "But everybody prays to something, whether they know it or not."

Bear declines to voice his blatant disagreement, but his face tells Bee his opinion on the matter. She leans back in her chair, as though enjoying watching him squirm. She plays with the circlet around her hair, one hand still on her abdomen.

She remains silent, whilst Dusty and Glass fix the food for the team. He feels alone with her, unsure of what to say or where to look. He looks into the tea for a while. The heat coming from the cup warms his hands, but it reminds him of the heat from the glove. The screaming. The *smell* -

"You've really never prayed?" she prompts him, and he forces a smile.

"Nope. Never prayed. Been in some rough patches, sure, but no. Never."

"Rough patches? Like, as rough as what the Crawler drives through?"

"If you're asking if I'm familiar with the phenomenon and what it does to people, then yes. I'm well acquainted with it."

Her voice is an accusing whisper now. "You sure? Because I have, and I'll know if you haven't. It's not something that can be faked. Is it, Dusty?"

"Leave the boy alone, Beatrice," he shakes his head.

"I want him to answer me. I don't think anybody who has been through the *phenomenon* could come out the other side without faith of some kind. I don't care if he's Gaian or Christian, I wanna know why he's *neither.*"

Bear lowers his voice for her. "I've seen what it does up close. I've spent my life researching it."

"Yeah? And you *don't* think that it fits the biblical descriptions of Hell?" she starts quoting Last Testament scripture off the top of her head. "*They shall see in the fire all that they fear, and none shall escape unscathed from any past deed.* I mean, that sounds pretty -"

"I don't think it matters," sighs Bear, already impatient with her scripture. "And I don't think any of us actually have an answer to that question. I don't think it's the eyes of a conscious super-ego that lives within our planet and *hates* us, either, so you know my problem isn't personal to your faith. I just don't agree with your perspective."

No matter how cold he is with her, she keeps trying to press his buttons.

"So when do you think it'll end?" she asks, quieter now, less pressing. He has matched her, at least a little, and she's backing down.

"End?" he asks.

"Hell, Gaia, your phenomenon... y'know, the world changing and switching around all the time. It didn't used to be like this. Both Christian and Gaian alike agree that this whole charade is going to end soon, so what do you say? When do you think it'll stop?"

"When *we* stop it," he says. "I imagine you think it'll stop when the Son of God returns, right?"

"Behold, those who have suffered beneath great evil," she clearly relishes the chance to recite scripture at him. "I promise you this; that God judges all in the end, that all will be judged, and all will be with Him again. It is not for us to know *when*. It is just for us to know."

"You know your scripture," he smiles.

"I do. That's from the Book of Endings."

"Here's one," he says. "*Don't trust people who follow*

charlatans and con-men. That's from the Gospel of Bear, whatever verse you like."

She laughs, brushing off his bad manners. "Not Christian then, not Gaian either," she muses. "So what *are* you?"

"I'm figuring it out," he says, and takes another long drink of his tea. "Trying to answer the big question: what *is* it? And how do we stop it?"

"There's something to be said for the simplest answers," she offers.

"I'm not interested in simple," says Bear, smiling. "I'm interested in true."

"So you *do* have faith."

"Do I?" he asks, genuinely interested.

"You believe that you can answer those questions. Otherwise you wouldn't even try. You have faith in yourself."

"Maybe I do," he shrugs in mock-defeat. It is best to stay humble, he has found – and it does not endear him to people when he talks about himself in such a way. Of course he has faith in himself, he thinks. What else *can* be believe in?

"Maybe you're right Bear," she sighs. "Maybe you know better than the ancient stories that formed the most powerful cultures on earth. Maybe you've got us all covered and the church can relax. It's not like the Last Testament predicted everything that we've endured."

She's positively awash with sarcasm now. Bear knows about their beliefs, and the prophetic, doomsday foretelling of what has befallen the world.

"They're pretty vague stories, to be fair," he shrugs. "Easy to retroactively shape them into prophecy after the fact. But ok. What makes you so certain that *you're* right, then?"

She smiles, the kind of glowing smile that comes from inside, but with a shadow around her eyes. Bear is suddenly reminded that this woman was nearly torn to shreds by something they don't even have a name for – she's clearly far from fragile. Her smile is the kind held by somebody who has seen combat, and found that they enjoy it.

"I'm only alive because I prayed; and God had my back."

Bear searches her face for any hint of doubt, but finds none. She's telling the truth – or she thinks that she is.

"What happened to you?" he asks.

She laughs to herself. "You'd only try to explain it, Bear." Bee drinks the rest of her tea, hands the empty cup to Dusty, who has patiently watched the entire exchange, and stands up to leave. "I'm going to the bridge. Glass, join me."

Glass nods, and follows her out. Glass does not seem particularly pleased with what Bee was saying, but then he looks angry most of the time. Both Bear and Dusty notice her trying to hide the weakness in her abdomen as she walks, her hand always hovering close to where her wounds are, hidden by her vest and shirt.

Dusty sits down with Bear.

"You'll get used to her," he says. "She's been through the kind of thing that makes or breaks a believer. She'll lay off eventually."

"I don't mind a challenge," he says, and laughs nervously. "She doesn't need to like me."

"Good. And how are you doing, Bear?"

Bear shrugs. "Fine, I guess?"

Dusty looks at him sideways. "You sure?"

"Yeah."

"Because in my professional opinion, I'd say that you're exhausted; that you're bottling up some bad shit, and that you've just had to leave a friend in a horrible place. Lot of space for guilt, there, lot of space for bad feelings to bubble up."

Bingo. Bear visibly winces at the fresh reliving of all of his recent memories. He can smell the burning again, and wonders if he is enduring permanent brain damage or something.

"Yeah," he manages.

"You're going to be with us for at least a few days," says Dusty. "It's easy to feel trapped in here, to start going a little crazy. Whatever one of us feels, tends to affect everybody else. You keep an eye on yourself and tell me if you start getting stupid thoughts, ok?"

Bear nods. It's hard to remain composed when faced with the overpowering paternal concern that Dusty exudes.

"Good," smiles Dusty. "May?"

"Go ahead, love," comes the voice from the speaker in the corner of the room.

"When Bear has had some food, direct him to the passenger bunk please."

"Of course."

"I'm really not hungry," says Bear, who feels as though his stomach hasn't stopped churning since he left Forgehead.

"You were spiked up on adrenaline – enough to be shaking, don't think I didn't notice – you're going to crash soon, if you haven't already. Best that you eat something before you do. You don't need to impress us here, son," he chuckles to himself. "We've seen each other in all kinds of messes."

Dusty heads for the counter, and starts arranging something in a bowl with some water from the kettle.

As he works, Bear starts to feel himself buckle under the unbearable weight of the last two days. There's no reprieve coming – he won't be able to relax until he knows if Calum is alright; if Forgehead even makes it through the incursion. The thought of having to live in this constant state of near-terror, as though he's constantly falling, seems like an unscaleable cliff face set before him.

Sometimes this feeling, this sense of dangling over the void ,has come for him before. When it has, Bear has thrown himself into work, into distractions; but there's no real work to be done here. Not yet. The panic keeps trying to claw its way back in, and Bear knows that he cannot fight it off forever. Eventually he is going to let it overwhelm him, no matter how little he wants it to. Just thinking about it is making his heart pound.

Dusty turns around and sits a bowl of what looks like oats and frozen fruit in front of him, steam pouring off of them. The thought of eating anything makes Bear want to be sick.

"I'm ok, Dusty, thanks – really, I'm ok -"

Dusty sees the look on his face. He's gone pale white. It has come out of nowhere, faster than he can handle.

"Bear, are you -"

Bear vomits over the table, thin water sicky that burns his

throat and nostrils. He stumbles away from the table, trying for some reason to apologise, and Dusty catches him, muttering calming things as though he is a wild animal.

"Easy, easy," he says, "there we are, it's ok, it's ok -"

Bear's eyes water with the stinging feeling, and he gasps and retches as he clutches the table.

It all catches up with him as Dusty helps him to a clean seat, sits him down, and passes him a towel to start cleaning himself. Bear is shivering again.

"Dusty, those guys tried to *kill me -*"

"They sure did," he says, slow and steady.

"I set him on *fire,* he was screaming, -"

"Bear," he stops him. "Listen. There are bad, *evil,* people in the world who would do you harm. Who'd hurt those that you care about. Right? When they come calling, you can roll over and die, or fight back. There's no shame in what you did. You did *good.* Y'know, the way I see it? That guy killed *himself* when he crossed you, right? He fucked with you, and ended up committing suicide by proxy," he smiles, and Bear can't help but join him. It's a hell of a dark joke, but maybe that's what life on a Crawler does to a person. "Yeah?"

Bear nods, as Dusty's drawling, ancient wisdom sets in. As soon as it does, he feels himself strengthen. The certainty returns, and his free fall into the abyss ends, grounding him back in the earthly embrace of common sense. Dusty throws an anchor around him, so to speak. Brings him back.

Bear takes a breath.

He was attacked. He defended himself and his friend, and if he hadn't, they'd be dead. The natural order has been satisfied – they shouldn't have attacked him if they weren't prepared for a potentially violent death. Bear feels the weight of trauma lift, replaced with the steadying crutch of a task, a responsibility.

Forgehead will fall unless he gets the message to Union City to reinforce them; and he can help the Crawler crew as thanks in the meantime.

There is work to be done.

Dusty sees the transformation in his face and hands him

another towel. "Feeling better?"

"Aye," he says, and stands up straight from a slouch he hadn't realised he'd been holding, wiping his face clean. "Aye, I'm ok, I'm just – tired, and hungry. It's been a long couple of days."

"Good thing you weren't sick in your porridge then," laughs Dusty, and takes the cloth from him. "Take it to your room with you. I'll clean this up – May?"

"Feeling ok there, dear?"

"All good now. May, direct Bear to his quarters."

"With pleasure. If you'll take the door you entered through and keep left, look for a ladder..."

Bear quietly thanks Dusty as the old man starts pulling cleaning products out of a cupboard. He hefts his satchel as he follows May's scholarly tones.

His bunk turns out to be a sturdy single bed against a cold wall. May gives him a brief tour of the room: no windows, barely tall enough to stand in, with a harsh white light that hums, and a set of drawers for storage, with a small desk and a lamp, all part of the wall and incapable of movement.

Home sweet home, thinks Bear, and tries to lay down and close his eyes.

Immediately, the uneven thumping of the tracks becomes a distraction. Bear focuses his mind elsewhere, but the noise of the engine remains there. He lifts his bowl from the ground and devours the now luke-warm porridge. It's hard to swallow without water.

As he sits it back down, he realises that the thud of the engines is still there, still distracting. He feels like it is forcing his heart to beat in time with it. It puts him on edge – as though his heart will beat faster as they accelerate. He wonders if he might have a heart attack, and the worry makes his hear beat even faster.

The anxiety starts to build.

"Shit," he whispers. "Not again, come on."

He jumps as the walls speak to him, in a homely English

accent.

"Everything ok, Bear?" asks May.

"I'm fine," says Bear, then pauses and sighs. "Actually, I'm not. May?"

"Yes, dear?"

"Is there anything you can do about the ambient noise?"

"Of course. I can provide white noise to assist with sleep, or distract you otherwise. Do you have any preference?"

Bear thinks back to his troubled sleep as a youth, when his father would sit by his bed and try to bore him with scientific knowledge, the really dry stuff. How to calculate whether or not a rocket has enough fuel to hit the atmosphere. The different kinds of infinity that mathematics talks about. The links between mathematics, music and language; frequencies of words, the frequencies of each note. It was counter-intuitive; Bear loved the talks. It did, however, always succeed in putting him to sleep.

"May, do you have any recordings or anything? Or can you speak about something for a while, like science or history?"

"Would that help you sleep?"

"I think it might, aye."

"I do have access to an informational archive to help inform my decision-making. It draws from pre-cataclysm sources, plus my own post-cataclysm learning. I could select from a broad range of topics, but if science is your thing then perhaps I could recommend something from the pre-cataclysm archive?"

Bear is already intrigued. "You said a *pre-cataclysm* archive of information?"

"Of course – I am, after all, pre-cataclysm technology."

"Well you're damn right that's my thing," laughs Bear. "What kind of stuff can you talk about? Like, give me something at random."

"Ok, random selection. Give me a number."

"Uh, seventeen."

"Ok. What about early gene editing, viral bio-technologies and their subsequent usage as gene-specific viral weapons?"

Bear leans back in his hammock. "Yeah," he sighs. "That sounds good. Let's go with that."

"Get comfy then, dear," she says, and her voice takes on a newsreader's timbre, pretending to clear her throat. *"The early twenty-first century saw mankind finish the mapping of the human genome, and within the first two decades of the new century, this allowed mankind to use the mechanisms of certain bacteria to edit and replace specific genes within DNA. Whilst initially used for such global projects as the eradication of malaria and other diseases detectable in-vitro, its use quickly turned to genetic adaptations for soldiers and , worse, the creation of untreatable, hyper-adaptive viruses, which would later run rampant through vulnerable groups during the darkest years of social collapse due to the cataclysm. It is said that -"*

Bear doesn't hear the rest, for he is fast asleep.

Chapter 9

When Bear wakes, it is to May's uncharacteristically sharp tones.

"Bear! Bear, move your arse love, come on, time to get up."

Bear thrashes about in his bunk until he is clear and sitting on the edge of it. The thrumming of the engine has stopped.

"What? May? What's up, what is it -"

"Dusty is requesting your presence on the navigation deck."

Bear rubs his eyes, though he at least feels rested. "You mean the cockpit?"

"Six and half a dozen, love," she says. *"It's urgent. Come on, move!"*

"What time is it?" he yawns as he stumbles to his feet.

"It's currently six thirty two in the morning, but that's neither here nor there, we're an all-hours team after all."

"Bloody hell," he groans, grabs his satchel, and makes his way to the cockpit, up stairs that are practically ladders, through tunnels that threaten his forehead with their hanging pipes and cables.

When he enters the navigation deck through the sealed door, the other three are already in heavy winter gear, as though ready to venture outside the Crawler. They are dressed in thick white waterproof jackets, padded underneath with thick fleeced layers, reflective goggles atop their foreheads and scarves pulled around their mouths, leaving just their eyes visible. Thick headphones and secondary scarves that double as blindfolds hang around their necks – sensory blockers in an emergency, Bear realises.

Glass and Bee both cradle long wooden-stock pre-cataclysm hunting rifles, with elaborate scopes and white wrapping for camouflage. They probably cost more than Bear's house in Forgehead.

The Crawler viewports are completely open, and the sky in the distance is ablaze with the early winter sunrise, like molten gold pouring over the cloudless horizon. It is the first sunrise that Bear has seen from somewhere else – and though he has heard people talk about it, it takes him a moment to come to terms with the stark beauty of the world beyond.

"Glad to see you're up," says Dusty, and tosses him a thick winter coat. "You're taking a walk."

"I – what? What's going on?" he manages.

"Point of interest," says Bee, and points out the viewport. "Take a look. "

"Is it safe to – I mean, is there -"

"Hell ain't here today, lad," says Bee, patting him on the back as he approaches the viewport. "You can look outside. May wouldn't let us open the viewport otherwise."

Bear looks out, and it takes him a moment to pick out the details: there are bodies in the distance, near a line of evergreens, half buried by the snow.

"They look -" he stops himself. "Are they dead? Who would even be out here? Scouts? Cartographers?"

"We're going to find out, and log it when we get radio coverage," says Dusty. "You're a smart guy, and you know medicine. You're going to lend a hand."

Bear shrugs. The idea of leaving the Crawler doesn't appeal to him, but curiosity has always been his downfall. He'll join them gladly, if only to ask more questions.

"Ok," he says. "I'll help if I can."

"That's the spirit," says Dusty.

"This is what pitching in means on the Icebreaker," says Bee.

"You got a gun?"

"I've got a glove that shoots fire about six feet?" he offers, shrugging. "And shouldn't you be resting? Your wounds haven't -"

"No time to be injured," she shrugs. "I'll be fine. No sudden moves and my stitches will hold."

"That's not -" he stops, sighing in frustration. "Look, it was me that done them, they *won't* hold if you start doing athletics in the snow."

"Well, *you're* here just in case, right? Gimme some new ones." Bee sighs. "Now again. You ever used a gun?"

"Not really, no."

Dusty laughs. "Then you ain't getting one."

"See?" says Bee, turning to Dusty. "He has no field training, Dusty." From her tone Bear realises that they've probably been in here debating about whether or not to bring him along. He can see what side Bee falls on with little effort. "He'll be as good as a man short."

"Well it just so happens we *are* a man short," says Dusty, and something in his tone shuts Bee up. "So nothing will change. Consider it practice for when you have your own Crawler."

Her protests continue. "Me and Glass can't cover three-sixty degrees if the new guy doesn't know what he's doing. We're leaving a sector uncovered."

"I'll do as I'm told?" Bear offers.

"I'll be watching from here," says Dusty. "May and I have your backs covered, you and Glass focus on the front."

Bee looks uneasy. She turns and gazes over her shoulder out the viewport. Bear thinks for a moment that he sees fear in her eyes. She adjusts her circlet to sit above her goggles, needing something to fidget with. "Sir, I've already got a bad feeling about this; and that's without taking any additional risks."

"I'm not *that* bad -" begins Bear but she holds her hands up.

"Nothing personal Bear; but you aren't a field operative and you've got no experience. If this is another ambush, you'll just get us all killed."

Bear hears it, even though she didn't mean it: *another* ambush. Like the one that left her with half her face torn off and her abdomen torn open.

"It's not an ambush," says Dusty. "I know that last one rattled you - it rattled us all; but this is part of our job – our *duty*. One bad day can't ruin you, Bee."

She looks around at Bear and Glass, and then her shoulders sag.

"Fine. Fine, I'll lead the team out. With me, boys."

She stomps towards the door, and Glass follows. Bear trots after her.

"I'll be watching from up high," shouts Dusty. "I've got you all covered."

They depart from the cargo bay. A horn sound, and then the ramp drops, blowing snow into the sky as it hits the ground. A gust of frozen air hits them.

Bear follows Bee and Glass as they disembark and trudge out into the snow in their thick boots, scoped rifles at the ready. Immediately, the knee-high snow gets into his shoes and starts to soak his feet. He curses, stumbling after them as they forge onwards, tugging his satchel with him.

"Glass," says Bee, "watch the treeline."

He nods.

They are high above the lowlands, with the long white earth rolling away to their right until it becomes the mash of ice and water that is the sea. Bear takes it in for a moment as the sun starts to creep over the hills. To their left is the edge of a huge evergreen forest that looms like a crowd of thin men watching over them.

They seem so small, Bear realises. He'd prefer to be behind a wall right now; he feels exposed, like something might drop from the sky and spirit him away at any moment. He can't help but stare at the distant fields of ice. This is the furthest he's ever seen.

"Bear, move your arse," shouts Bee from up ahead, and he jogs with his knees high, plunging through the snow to catch them up.

Once he is at their back once more, he follows Bee's gaze and looks back at the Crawler.

Sitting atop the huge steel behemoth is the wiry figure of Dusty, his legs hanging down a manhole into the Crawler. He has a long metal weapon of some sort across his lap. Bee raises a hand, and he mirrors her motion.

"We're clear, let's go," she says.

Minutes later, they find the first body.

Glass keeps watch whilst Bee squats in the snow and brushes ice from a dead woman's face – dead *girl,* Bear corrects himself. She's young. Bee lifts her goggles, and sighs. There are splotches of red along Bee's jaw mesh, where her wound reopens every time she speaks.

"Poor thing."

She continues searching about the frozen corpse, scraping away the snow around her, searching the ground. Bee keeps clutching at her stomach, kneeling to hide it.

"What are we looking for?" asks Bear, watching, feeling relatively useless. He wants to ask her if she's ok, but he can already tell that she won't admit a thing.

"Insignia, tags, anything that would let us know who they were. Glass, search the other bodies," she orders him, standing up and taking his place. "I'll cover you."

Glass leans down and grabs a corpse by the lapels, hefting it out of the snow and shaking it.

"Jesus," whispers Bear. Glass handles the corpse like a puppet, ignoring the sunken eyes and hollow face. The frozen body sheds its snow, and reveals a jacket riddled with crimson wounds. Bear looks away, grimacing.

"Murdered," says Bee, and motions to another one nearby. "See this, Bear?"

"Yeah, I'm quite aware," he says, and steps closer despite his disgust. "Looks like knife wounds."

"Correct. The uniforms and badges tell me that these people were Scouts."

"Cartographer's Guild?"

"The very one," she nods. "Tough people – hard to ambush. Hard to kill. Especially with *knives* of all things. Scouts are always well armed."

"We're next to the treeline – easier to get into close quarters with cover, right?"

"Yeah, but not against Scouts. They'd know to be careful."

"Maybe they were surrounded, or clearly outmatched?"

"Execution, you think?" asks Bee. "Perhaps. Though you'd hope an execution would be cleaner. A slit throat, knife to the heart, that kind of thing. This is just a random pattern of stabbings. No direction, no skill. And that one -" she points to the body that Glass is searching, shot at least eight times. "Why waste ammunition on an execution? Eight or nine shots when one would do?" She looks around at the treeline, and frowns. "No. Not an execution."

"What are you thinking?" asks Bear.

"Maybe they were surprised because they thought they'd met a friend?" she asks. They look at one another, and she raises her eyebrows. "Right?"

"It's possible."

"Other troubling detail," she adds. "Where are their guns?"

Bear plunges his hands into the snow and rakes around for a bit, trying to help out.

"Glass?" shouts Bee. "You find any firearms?"

"Negative."

"Aye. Me neither."

"Bee," Bear approaches her and kneels in the snow next to her. "How many people are usually in a Scout patrol?"

"At least two," she shrugs. "Sometimes three. On a sled, normally."

"I see no sled," says Bear.

"Yeah, I was just thinking that. Very unusual."

Bear looks around, and sees only snow and sky. "And our missing sled should have dogs pulling it, right?"

She nods. "And I see no dead dogs. Or tracks."

"Exactly. Either the dogs ran off when the trouble started -"

Bee interjects. "They wouldn't. Scout dogs won't abandon their master. They usually stay by a corpse. Loyal creatures."

"*Or* their killers took the sled and used it to travel onwards," says Bear. "Act like friends, or act wounded and in need of help, then shank them when they get close. Take their guns. Maybe they disarmed one, took his gun, and shot the other at close range."

"Automatic gunfire," says Bee, looking again at the shot woman. "Close range, burst of fire. It's an explanation we can work with, at least."

Bear nods along, only to stop as a thought hits him. "What kind of guns do Scouts usually carry? Rifles like yours?"

"Oh, nothing like what we have. They only really need protection from wildlife, or to hunt in the event they find themselves without supplies, or cut off by the Devil's work."

"So, low quality weapons, cheap ammunition..."

"Yeah."

"Suppressors?"

Bee raises an eyebrow. "Yeah. Good for hunting. They're a holdover from the Scav war. Why?"

"I think that whoever killed these Scouts may have been the same men who made an attempt on my life – and Calum's."

"That's a leap – it's quite a distance from here to Forgehead -" she has the same realisation as him. "Though not with -"

"Not with a sled and dogs," he finishes her sentence.

Bee looks around, nodding as she talks. "Shit, Bear, that's not bad deduction."

He shrugs, laughing. "It's not deduction at all, actually, it's *inductive* reasoning -"

"Ok, you were doing well and you've ruined it," she says,

shaking her head. "Still, the time frames seem off. We'd need some way to confirm their actual time of death – and I don't know of any reliable way to do so. The cold won't let them decay at any appreciable rate. So it's a theory, but we've nothing solid."

Glass drops the body, shrugging, and returns to keeping watch. Bee pats him on the arm and opens her jacket, pulling out a notebook. Her mittens have a flap that allows her fingers to come out, useful for using a firearm or a pencil. She begins taking notes on the incident.

Bear has been deep in thought, prompted by Bee's wish to know how long these people have been dead.

"There might be a way," says Bear, and opens his satchel.

Glass clears his throat, and Bee looks up at him. He has his hand raised.

"Speak, Glass," she says.

"Ma'am, this place is making the hairs on my neck stand up."

Bee looks around, and then puts her notepad away and kneels down with her rifle unslung. They all stay perfectly still, listening to the wind. A cursory glance back at Dusty sees him sitting atop the Crawler, watching them like a father watches his children play.

"Can't say I share that feeling," she says. "No birdsong this close to the trees is strange, I'll grant you. Could be us causing that, though. I mean, the Crawler did just rock up. We ain't quiet."

"I mean," begins Glass, and struggles to find the words. He motions at his head, makes a kind of exploding gesture. "I mean in *that* way."

Bee opens her eyes, and plunges her hand into her jacket to pull her crucifix out, holding it in one gloved hand. "Oh, ok; sorry Glass. In that case we'd probably best get out of here."

"What's up?" asks Bear.

"Glass thinks that the Devil done his wicked work here; might still be nearby. Means that it's time to go."

"I – what?" splutters Bear. "He can just *feel* that? Like, where the phenomenon has passed? Well maybe that's what drove their dogs and sled off, maybe -"

"No point worrying about it now, Bear. You'll learn to trust Glass's instincts. Come on, back to the Crawler."

Bear looks from the corpses to his satchel. "Wait; just two minutes, I can test our theory."

"Bear, it's time to *go,*" she says. "Come on."

"Two minutes," he says, and kneels to get his sensor out.

Bee sighs, and looks at Glass. Despite his size and confidence, Glass appears on edge, glancing every which way. Bear knows that Bee is consumed by the same curiosity as him, she *has* to be. He heard her reasoning, her investigative brain. She wants to know the answer too.

"Glass?" she asks. "Do we *have* two minutes?" He considers it, and shrugs, nodding. "Fine," she whips around to Bear. "Two minutes, no more. Glass, count to one hundred and twenty."

Glass nods.

Bear talks as he works, like he usually does, pulling out wires and batteries and connecting sensors together. "Scouts would have phenomenological sensors, right? To anticipate it suddenly popping up in front of them?"

"Yeah, they usually carry one per team."

He pulls a few wires out of his own sensor, takes a knee, and begins patting down the dead body, trying to avoid the bloodied areas. He feels out their small, more modern sensor and claws at various pockets till he gets it out.

"I was raised helping to design these bloody things. The modern sensors store data up to about a week," he explains, as he connects his own sensor's playback circuitry to the Scout sensor. "Which means..."

He presses the recall button, and the LED screen lights up with a graph. The data from the Scout sensor is playing out on his, allowing him to scroll through their recordings and look for anomalies.

"Nailed it," he says, before his smile drops. "Oh. Oh shit."

"What is it?" asks Bee, coming closer and peering over his shoulder.

"That's normal background readings, see?" he points to the LED screen, where a readout that looks like a sound wave is modulating. "If I set it to display over a twenty-four hour period, then... See that massive spike there?" Bee nods. "That's phenomenal activity. Nothing else causes readings like that."

"How long ago?"

"Three days ago; about seventy hours, more accurately."

She looks up at Glass. "Two days ago we were attacked by Dreamers. Ambushed en route to Forgehead."

"And yesterday," says Bear, "Calum and I were nearly killed by two Dreamers using poor quality Scout weaponry - who neither of us recognised."

"This seems like way too much of a coincidence," she says. "But how did they..?" She shakes her head and turns around. "Glass, Dreamers can anticipate where the Devil will walk, right? You have permission to answer."

"It is said that a Gaian shaman is able to do so. These are rumours."

Bear makes a mental note to ask how Glass knows this, and makes a mental note of something else that Dreamers can apparently do.

"Then I think we know who tried to kill you, Bear."

"Dreamers, definitely," he says. "Probably the same ones who killed these Scouts."

"Ok," she says. "Good work team! Back to the Crawler."

She tugs on Glass to join her as she starts walking, but Glass is as still as a statue. He's staring into the rows of evergreens, and he won't move his eyes.

"Glass? Big guy, you ok?"

When he fails to respond, she shoulders her rifle and hisses for Bear to get behind them.

"What do you see?" she asks.

"We are not alone," he whispers, and puts his palm flat out to indicate that they should not move.

Bee kisses her crucifix, and keeps her eyes on the ground as her training kicks in. "Dreamers?"

"No," he says. "We'd have been shot by now."

Bear follows his eyes, but cannot see what he sees. He stays low, his heart racing, and puts his hand over his eyes.

Bee turns to the Crawler in the distance and raises her hand. Dusty mirrors her across the snow, mimicking her hand signal. She makes a few shapes that Bear doesn't understand, and Dusty raises his long, heavy-looking rifle to his eye and scans it across the tree line.

Dusty gives them a hand signal. A single finger, then a thumbs up.

"There's someone in there," says Bee. "Alive."

"Could be a third scout," says Bear. "Might be able to tell us what happened here?"

Bear sees the problem cast across Bee's face. Potential answers about something that seems to run deeper than she'd expected, at the potential risk of a fight - or worse, the phenomenon coming down upon them. Bear finds himself trembling.

"Glass," she says after a while, both of them holding their gaze on the tree line. "How strong are you feeling it right now? Scale of one to ten. Permission to speak."

"About a four, ma'am."

"Unlikely that we're about to walk into the devil's front garden then?"

"Odds are favourable to neutral."

"Ok. Bear, back to the Crawler. Glass, cover me while I check it out."

Bear immediately kicks off. "What? No way – if there's more to this, I want to know too -"

She turns, and the authority of her position seems to well up within her. She seems twice her usual size.

"Bear, if you're out here then you do as I say. This isn't civilian time now, this is fieldwork time, and you don't *do* fieldwork."

"I've walked into shit like this before," says Bear, surprised at how unwilling he is to back down. "I know what I'm doing. And I'm not *part* of your team, remember? I'm just a civilian volunteer. I'm coming."

Bee looks him up and down, but finds him unyielding.

"Fine," she shrugs. "But you look after yourself."

"It's what I'm used to," he says.

Bee turns and sets off towards the treeline. "Dusty has us covered. Glass, I want you weapons-ready in case this kicks off, ok?"

He nods, and flicks the safety on his hunting rifle off.

They stay low as they approach, weapons up, and Bear does his best to mimic their movements despite his frozen feet and chattering teeth. He keeps the sensor box in his hand, glancing down at it while he walks to readjust it for proximity readings.

It remains silent as they approach.

The treeline is only steps away, and the wall of firs and evergreens begins to resolve into a mass of trunks and green needles, snow coating their branches. The border to the forest is marked by the sudden coating of green on the snowy ground.

The needle flickers on Bear's sensor. It beeps.

"Guys," he whispers, feeling for some reason that if he speaks, the snow will fall from every branch. "There's something here, my sensor's going."

They stop and crouch in the snow, sheltered beneath the trees. Bee raises her rifle and scans around the trees, eyes like an owl.

As one, they all freeze, hearing a pained mumbling in the distance, then the sound of metal on wood. In Bear's mind it is man burning, screaming. He crouches behind a tree and stops breathing.

Bee turns her head and motions something at Glass, some military hand signal, and Glass nods and shoulders his rifle as Bee moves forward on her haunches.

Bear watches as she moves, and the mumbling grows louder. There's a frustrated shout, and they all freeze again. More mumbling, seeming to come from all around them.

Bear's needle spikes again, and he slowly begins to reach into his satchel for his sensory gear, anticipating the skull-crushing feeling of the phenomena coming for him.

Bee stands up and walks forward, then lowers her rifle.

"All clear," she says. "Fuck."

They follow her into a small clearing, bereft of light and snow. On every tree are the post-exposure sigils that Bear has dealt with before, spirals and cubes and layered tesseracts drawn in two dimensions. Branches are lain between various trees, forming links between them in a pattern that seems, to Bear, to have some kind of significance.

It is a blue print, he realises. Or perhaps a proof, a formulae of some sort. It has the structure of something scientific, with all the flair of the drug induced life-work of a great artist.

In the centre of the masterpiece is a man in the foetal position, naked and covered in brown crusted blood. Black blotches stain his body, frostbite eating into his extremities. His eyes are bloody and dilated, rimmed with blood. He is scrawling with a blunt knife on the ground beside his face, like a defeated prisoner scratching their will on the floor.

Bear has heard these groans before. He knows this man.

It is Old Simon.

Bear is unable to move, to register the hollow creature before him as the same man. Even as he watches on, his analytical brain finishes Simon's story. Addie was gone – dead. Whether Simon found the strength to end his suffering or not, Bear cannot know. Either way, he wonders if Simon came out here looking for answers.

Perhaps he wanted to see what Addie saw – to stare into Gaia's eyes and know the truth. He seems to have found her, Bear thinks.

Old Simon finishes etching a sigil on the ground with a blunt knife, and Bear's sensor spikes again.

"Don't look at the sigils," says Bear, his head already aching from being so close to them. He tries to keep his gaze down – but these runes are weak, unfocused. They aren't as bad as some he's been close to – not a massive danger.

"Yeah we know," says Bee. "Glass?" He turns to her. "Show on three," she says, and Bear watches them briefly play rock-paper-scissors. Glass goes rock, Bee goes paper.

Glass seems suddenly crestfallen, and then takes a breath and nods.

Bee steps forward and squats beside the man.

"Can you hear me?" she whispers. "Hey?"

"Bee?" Bear asks, and she stops to look at him.

"What?"

"I know this man."

Her face drops. He sees sympathy there, for the first time. She steps back, bowing her head, and allows Bear to kneel next to the deranged creature that was once Old Simon.

Bear gets close enough to see the his face, twisted in constant anguish. He's drooling and shivering, chattering to himself constantly. All of them are wincing with the aching migraine of being near the sigils.

But the wild eyes lock on Bear. Old Simon is in there somewhere, and he recognises something in Bear.

"Simon, it's me. It's Bear. Do you remember me?"

He nods his head violently and mumbles, then smashes his own head off the ground. Bee reaches past Bear and leans in, taking his head, stopping his self abuse, whispering calming things to him.

Bear searches in his satchel. "Bee, if I may?"

She looks at him as though he is interrupting surgery, until she sees the notepad in his hand.

"What's that?" she whispers.

"I think I know why he's out here. I don't know if he was anything to do with the ambush. I doubt it."

"He's looked into the abyss," she sighs, "that's for sure. How did he get out here?"

"He probably walked," says Bear. "Simon? Can you understand me?"

Simon sniffs and grinds his teeth, several of which have already cracked. They move like broken plates in his bloody gums.

"I'm sorry, Bear," says Bee. "He's gone."

"Maybe not," says Bear. "I can maybe get some information out of him."

"You think he's going to tell us anything useful?"

"Let me try, at least," he says. "I've done this before. A lot."

After considering it, she leans back and lets Bear in. He reaches out in sympathy and puts a gloved hand on the Old Simon's back. Old Simon is barely there. This is a wounded animal, fighting the end for as long as it can.

"He's been out here at least a day naked," says Bee. "He shouldn't have survived three hours, let alone the night. Incredible."

"Exposure fever," says Bear, looking over Simon's frostbite. "Long lasting spike in body temperature following exposure. It's why he's so skinny too, he's burned through all of his body's fat reserves. Well documented symptom. Was a time I thought that might cause the madness, but it's just another threat to anybody who's been exposed. Brain fever might kill them before the insomnia and organ failure does."

"So how do you do this, usually?" asks Bee.

"Watch," says Bear. "Ok Simon, how are you? We've done this before, haven't we? I've got some stuff I need to ask you, ok?"

The man is staring into the ground, hunched over like an animal. His muscles are all completely tense, his teeth chattering.

"I'm just gonna say some words," says Bear. "I just want you to listen, that's all, ok?"

He's still just staring, but his head cocks somewhat. It's as if he is hugely preoccupied with something.

"Crawler. Icebreaker. Bear. Bee. Glass. Dusty." He rhymes off some standard words that he's learned recently. He sets a baseline – there is no reaction. He's watching Simon's pupils, watching for them to dart to the left or the right.

"Scout," he says, and there is a faint dart left. "There we go, Bee. See that? The eyes often do that when recalling something from memory. Scout, the word, sparked something. Let's try another. Listening, friend?"

He trembles, trying to claw at the ground again.

"White Anchor," says Bear, and looks at his eyes.

Nothing.

"Red Lake."

Nothing.

"Union City."

Nothing.

"Forgehead."

Movement. "Ok, so you're from Forgehead." He looks at Bee, who is watching with great interest. "Let's try some more then. Crawler?"

Nothing.

"Scouts."

Nothing.

"Dreamers."

Nothing.

"He doesn't know the Dreamers by name, at least," says Bear. "Let's try this then: Addie."

Movement.

"He came here for his son, one way or another," says Bear.

"His son was missing?" asks Bee.

"No, no," says Bear, realising that she doesn't know what he does. "His son was exposed. By Dreamers, we now think. I believe that this man came out here in desperation, trying to find who or what had done this to his son."

"Well, he found it," says Bee.

"I know," sighs Bear.

Bee kneels beside him. "Can I try?"

"Sure," says Bear. "Be gentle."

"Hell," she shouts at Old Simon. Bear winces. "Devil," she tries.

Nothing.

"Gaia."

Movement.

"Ok, Gaia was here. Hell. Whatever."

Old Simon reels back on his haunches suddenly, like a dog about to attack. He bares his teeth, bringing his hands up to cover his terrified face. Bee pulls her rifle up, but Bear keeps the barrel down with his hand.

Bear shushes Simon and tells him to breathe. He struggles as he starts hyperventilating, and then a sudden moment of complete clarity, and he jerks forwards and grips Bear's forearms.

His bloodied eyes stare into Bear's as though he can see something in them. Simon starts violently shaking and sobbing, and clings to Bear like a terrified child. Bear puts his arms around him, holds the poor man, and looks up at Bee, who is watching with a mixture of terror and anger. Glass just stares.

Bear's head is pounding from proximity to the runes. They seem to be getting worse; he feels his vision starting to blur out of focus at the edges like a migraine starting. Bee is squinting through the worst of it too, and leans in to touch Bear's arm.

"We'll take him," she says, loud enough that the poor man can hear. "We'll take him to the Crawler now."

She helps him stand up, and he clings to her. Bear reluctantly lets go, and as she starts walking him to the edge of the forest, she gives Glass a pointed look, and he nods.

Bear follows at a distance, watching, close enough to hear. He remembers their game of rock-paper-scissors, which Glass lost.

Bee stands with him at the edge of the tree line, and moves as far as she can from him, all whilst keeping one hand on his shoulder for comfort.

"The Crawler will be in sight soon," she whispers, squeezing his shoulder. There's a look on her face of pained, forced happiness. "We're going to take you to safety."

Glass lifts his rifle to his shoulder and takes aim.

It dawns on Bear what is about to happen. He remembers Old Simon lamenting that he was not strong enough to end his boy's suffering. Bear remember how he was not strong enough to end his own father's suffering. He wonders if Simon knows.

Bee holds him at arm's length, hand on his shoulder. Simon is trembling, silhouetted against the sun.

"I want you..." starts Bee, catching herself. "I want you to think of something happy, ok? Keep the exposure at bay for now. We'll get you back to health, ok? No worries. You'll be warm aboard the Crawler. You know we've got *showers* and everything on there, roasting hot, and..."

Glass exhales and goes still. Bear wants to look away, but he cannot.

"And we'll get you better," she whispers. "You're going to be ok."

Bear sees her wipe her eyes, just briefly. Simon has his hands held close to his body, his feet curled and black, most of his toes and extremities gone with the frostbite. He keeps leaning his head to the side, as if listening for something.

Glass fires, and a cloud of red mist explodes from Simon's scalp. The life leaves his body. Bee immediately jerks her hand away and wipes her face. She shakes her gloves dry in disgust, and lets out a tense breath. Simon crumples on the ground.

Bear hears the engines of the Crawler surge to life in the distance, and he watches Glass work the bolt on his rifle and chamber another round, before flicking the safety back on and slinging it over his shoulder. He reaches down and picks up the brass casing, wisps of smoke coming from it.

"Christ," whispers Bee, and takes her sideways crucifix out to press to her lips. They shuffle out of the forest together. Dusty is bringing the Crawler to them at a slow trundle, and so they wait next to the body. "How long do you think he was there? A full day alone after an exposure? In this cold? Tough bastard, exposure fever or not."

Bear looks down at Old Simon, almost unrecognisable now, and the urge to be sick seems less so.

"I think I'm getting desensitized," he murmurs.

"It's better this way," says Bee, ignoring him. "Exposure cases get worse the longer we let it fester. Best not to get attached."

"What do you think he saw?" asks Bear, shuddering. It is the same question that always plagues him.

"Don't think about it," says Bee, putting her goggles and gloves back on. "He saw Hell and it saw him right back. Of course that breaks a man. Breaks them or puts the fear of God in them. Rightly so. Lots to be scared of. Hell just breaks people. Chews them up and spits them out. Except the really bad ones. Like Dreamers."

Bear looks away from the body, and Bee gives him a weak, somewhat condescending smile.

"Or maybe," she says, "there's a logical, scientific explanation for it, if we just do enough algebra."

"Maybe," says Bear, without a hint of doubt.

The Icebreaker reaches them, and they trudge towards the ramp once more.

Chapter 10

With their weapons stowed and field gear hung to dry in the cargo bay, they gather on the navigation deck and watch the snowscape trundle under the viewport as they crest the hills and turn towards the mountains.

Aware of the uneasy silence, Bee chooses to break it.

"Least we got to put the poor bastard out of his misery," she says. "As for the Scouts, we got their Guild patches, we can call it in when we get a signal. They had orders on them – a patrol from White Anchor."

"Good job," says Dusty, passing tin cups of tea around the group. "Did Bear do ok?"

Bear is watching, and Bee hesitates. "He was ok," she shrugs. "Lucky we didn't get shot at."

Dusty turns to Glass. "Glass? How did Bear perform? Permission to speak."

"Valuable input. credit to the team. Filled in well for Red."

Bee seizes up and glares at Glass. "That's *not* why we took him –"

"Now, Bee," Dusty begins, trying to defuse it before it explodes. "Nobody said that."

"Glass just did!"

Bear looks out the viewport, awkwardly trying not to get in the way of an argument about him. He hasn't asked since he came aboard

– doesn't want to put his foot in it. He knows that there were four, and there was an ambush, and now there's three. He didn't know the man's name, though.

Now he does.

"Well," says Dusty, "Glass calls it like it is; Bear *does* fill in well for Red's role."

"He's *not* Red, we don't *need* another Red."

Dusty shrugs. "Bear's a bit of a medic, a bit of an engineer, and he knows a lot of useful stuff."

Bee looks at Bear for a while, but Bear avoids her gaze. He stares out at the bodies in the snow instead. She follows his eyes, looks out the viewport to see what he's staring at, and then lets out a breath. Just more dead people in the snow. Same as last time.

"He *was* useful out there," she admits. Bear finally looks at her, and finds a grudging respect in her eyes. "New guy knows his shit."

"Thanks, Bee," he manages.

"While we're here, *why* are you so used to dealing with exposure cases? You said you'd done a lot of it. Who *are* you?"

"He's John Woods' son," says Dusty, as though this is not new information.

Bear feels his heart start pounding. "Dusty? You knew my father?"

"Knew *of* him, like I said. A scientist," he explains to Bee. "The man who invented the sensors we use. His son happens to be a bit of a scientist."

Bear leans back, his excitement gone. "There you go," he says. "That's who I am. My father's son. And to answer your question, I have to deal with exposure cases all the time; for my research."

"Christ," she whispers. "Sounds really fun."

"It's not."

"We're getting sidetracked," says Dusty. "Did you find anything else useful?"

Bee shrugs, and points to Bear. "New guy thinks that the people who tried to kill him in Forgehead killed those Scouts too.

Took their sled and guns, that kinda thing."

"The time frame checks out," says Bear, holding up his sensor in explanation.

"Question is: why?" says Dusty. "Why try to kill Bear at all?"

"They were probably gunning for Calum, to be honest," says Bear. "He's a bit more important than me. He knew that they had tried something at the radio tower, and he was organising Forgehead's defence."

"Yeah," says Dusty. "Get the Chief Woodsman out the way, leave Forgehead vulnerable for an exposure. That hard drive would have no doubt played the all clear before it was due. They could have exposed the whole town in one go, if not for the Chief Woodsman's intervention. That sound about right, Glass?"

Glass nods. "Fits with their goals."

"Sorry," says Bear, raising a hand. "So... do we mean their goal of exposing people that they think will survive it?"

Dusty shrugs and answers. "Why expose two or three at a time if you can nail an entire settlement and then just find survivors? Much more efficient. That seems to be what motivates them – they follow Gaia across the land like pilgrims. Survivors get recruited."

"You *say* they follow Gaia," says Glass, uncharacteristically speaking out of turn. "Others say that their shamans can call Gaia down upon their foes."

"Yeah well neither has ever been proven to be the case," says Dusty.

Bear tries to take it all in. A cult, killing Scouts, attacking Crawlers, attacking his friend and even him; all because they want to deliberately expose people. Who would *deliberately* do that to another person? He has so many questions, but he tries to pace himself. There's much to ask, and much to learn already.

"Can I ask," begins Bear, and all eyes fall upon him. "How does Glass know so much about the Dreamers?"

"Glass, if you wish to talk you can," says Dusty. Glass pointedly says nothing, and Dusty laughs. "Well, there you are."

Bear sighs; these people are all mysteries on some level – and then there's him, with a sensor and a glove that shoots fire and a vain hope that maybe he can contribute to what is happening. He feels, again, a little out of his depth – and annoyed that he can't just sit down for a few days with them and learn everything they have to teach him.

"Well, that'll be all, crew," says Dusty. "I've got the helm while May takes us up into the peaks. Once we're there, we should have clear signal to reach Union. Get some rest until then."

Glass nods and shuffles away. Bee taps Bear on the arm before he can turn and head for his bunk, and points to her jaw-mesh.

"This is getting itchy," she rolls her eyes, trying to downplay her suffering. "Ain't been changed. Mind taking a look?"

Bear nearly defaults to his statement that he isn't a doctor, that he assumes they would get her better treatment somewhere else – but he doesn't.

He said he would pitch in.

"Sure. You guys got a medical bay or something?"

She nods. "Follow me."

They are on the bottom floor of the Crawler.

"May," shouts Bee, as she grimaces and tries to turn the valve of the med-bay door. Bear can see her struggling from the effort, and remembers that most of her abdomen is torn to hell. He would offer to help, but in his head she just slaps him every time he offers. "May," she shouts again, finally managing to turn the wheel. "May, is the med-bay sterilised?"

"You've all been a bit busy, love," says May, apologetic.

"Is that a no, then?"

"That's a no, I'm afraid."

"Ah hell," she mutters, and she pauses and takes a breath before she opens the door as the lights flicker on. She gives Bear a pointed look that has something of an apology to it.

He sees why.

There's a single table covered in dried blood and soaked

bandages. The gore has dripped onto the floor and congealed into a dark brown stain.

There's a hand on the table. A man's, Bear guesses, with wisps of black hair at the base. An extremely clean cut, Bear notes. Phenomenological, he thinks, like how bits of Forestry recruits turn up after an incursion, thinly sliced like meat.

"I'll uh – I'll clean this," says Bee, the quietest – or most distracted - that Bear has heard her. "Give me a second."

"What the hell happened?" asks Bear, still in disbelief.

"Dusty and Glass tried to put me back together. That's about the gist of it," she says, and moves to the other side of the room where there's a large steel sink and a stainless steel cabinet. She starts running the tap, soaks a rag, and then turns to the hand.

Bear watches her stare at it for a moment. He's felt the same thing that he sees in her. He remembers being in the same room as his father's corpse, not long after he died. It took him almost an hour to work up the courage to touch it, let alone to try and move him. Bee is wrestling with that too.

Eventually she looks up and speaks. "Sorry. I don't know what we're meant to do with body parts, this hasn't, uh – we've never had to -"

"Medical waste," says Bear. "Separate it from normal waste."

"Don't have anything like that. Do we just give it to the crows, then?"

"Maybe, yeah."

She looks at the ground before moving to the cupboard and pulling out a black plastic bag and, with some effort, and more fear than Bear has ever seen her express, delicately drops the hand into the bag. She performs the movement without any skin on skin contact occurring.

She bunches it up and places it near the sink, then breathes out as though she's just locked a door shut on a barking dog. "Ok," she says. "Help me clean this?"

Bear shrugs. "Sure," and intends to talk as he helps her; but there is nothing he can think to say. He keeps coming back to the hand.

As they wash down the steel bed with bleached water, Bear decides to go for it anyway.

"Bee?"

She stops scrubbing for a minute, looking pointedly at the spot of blood she was cleaning, and answers as she finally continues.

"That's Red's hand," she says. "Assuming that's what you were going to ask?"

"Jesus," whispers Bear. "Can I uh -"

"Can you ask what happened?" she finishes his sentence without stopping her cleaning. "Of course you can. You're all about questions, right?"

Bear swallows, the bleach catching in his throat. "So... what happened?"

She looks up, but not at Bear, and begins. "We had been given a tip that there was a pre-judgement -"

"Pre-cataclysm?" Bear tries to clarify, and she gives him a pointed look before continuing.

"There was a *pre-judgement* ruin, an old army facility with some serious weaponry and stuff. Worth a lot of money. Maybe dangerous. Either way, we were en route to a delivery and it was nearby so we stopped and checked it out. I was on lead, as always. I had Glass come with us, and take an overwatch position while Red and I approached."

Bear watches her eyes go distant as she recounts it.

"It was a little concrete building, didn't look like much – but you know those old structures, most of them are underground anyway. So it was just me and Red that went in. I could've taken Glass, but Red knows – *knew* – tech and stuff pretty well. He was the best choice."

"What did you find?"

"Nothing. Empty building, no basement level. Maybe used for storage once. Dead rumour, bad intel, whatever." She stops scrubbing, now that the bed is mostly clean, and starts on the floor where Bear joins her. "Then Glass started shouting – which you've probably realised is not something he does often."

"Yeah,, about that; why doesn't he talk?"

"He has his reasons, not mine to tell. He broke his usual silence to warn us that we had people incoming – and worse yet, that, in his words, Gaia's fury was about to fall upon us."

"The phenomenon? You got hit by it?"

She nods. "I got my sensory gear on, and so did Red, just as it dropped. Then the gunfire started. We couldn't hear it well, couldn't see anything... but I could feel debris hitting us, concrete chips, feel everything shaking. To be blind and deaf and *then* get shot at? I knew I was going to die. Came to terms with it. Then the real shit started – we got that horrible feeling that you get when it's nearby, you know? The feeling like your tongue is being pulled out your skull?"

Bear nods, he knows it well.

"Well," she continues, having entirely stopped scrubbing now. "Hell had come for us. I didn't know what to do, so I got my crucifix out and I prayed as hard as I ever have. And I asked God to guide me, even as I felt the claws of demons cut into my stomach." She looks at him as though from a thousand miles away, her hand going to her stomach again. "There was a light, Bear," she says. "Like a beacon. And I took Red's hand, and I ran towards it. I could feel things tearing into me, trying to climb in through my mouth."

Bear looks at the black bag by the sink, with Red's hand still in it.

"When I fell into Glass's arms, this had happened," she points to her sliced-up cheek. "And my stomach, and my shoulder. And I was still holding Red's hand, but... the rest of him was gone. I hadn't even noticed," she remarks, as though bewildered by the whole experience.

Most of the blood is gone now. Bear begins to gather some medical equipment in silence. He walks to the closet and starts pulling bandages, gauze, antiseptic. Bee is still kneeling on the floor with the bloodied rag in her hands. Bear stops what he's doing and kneels beside her. She's staring at the rag.

"You ok?" he asks.

"It was a fucking setup," she says, and stands up and sits on the bed. "I should've known better." She snaps out of her momentary lapse of strength, and sits upright, her facial expression changing. Bear sees her put her mask back on, right before his eyes. "Right new guy, fix my face then."

Bear grimaces as he looks closer as the mesh. Her cheek has began healing, he notes, but he should really have been checking on her and keeping it clean. There are patches of inflamed skin starting to appear – possibly infection. Splotches of green and yellow, too.

"Ok, I might have to cut away some infected skin and really clean this out," he says. "It'll likely hurt like a bastard."

"There's vodka in the cabinet, too," she says. Bear finds it, and she gratefully accepts the bottle when he offers it to her. It has a label on it marked *Dusty's Reserve*.

"The miracle you mentioned earlier," says Bear, as she takes a swig and he sets about peeling the mesh off, a little at a time. She winces every time, but never makes a sound. "Was it that you made it out of the phenomenon alive? Or was it the light that you saw?"

"I was in Hell, Bear – and I asked God for guidance, and he guided me out of there. People don't just walk out Hell in one piece."

Bear removes the mesh and sees pus forming around the edges of her wound.

"Glass was there too, right?" he asks, trying to keep her distracted whilst she takes swigs from the bottle. "He talks like he's Gaian. He made it out ok?"

"Glass has faith – whether in Gaia or God, I don't think it matters. He believes in *something,* enough to put his life on it. As do I. Red? Well, he was like you. Didn't believe in much he couldn't provide an explanation for."

Bear lifts the scalpel from a sterile basin and starts cutting away at the green flesh of Bee's jaw. At least he can't see her teeth or muscle through it any more, but even when fully healed it's going to leave a rigid, bumpy scar down her cheek.

"You think that Red didn't make it because he lacked faith?"

She nods, wincing every couple of words as Bear continues working. "I had a light to run towards, despite having my sensory gear on. God gave me that light. I tried to lead Red as best as I could, but... maybe fleeing Hell isn't about running in a literal direction, you know? Maybe you can't get out without a guide."

"Maybe," says Bear.

She waits for him to continue, but he doesn't. Bear doesn't hear much that he can engage with – so she prompts him with something else.

"So you've studied this stuff, right?"

"I have, yes."

Most of the infected flesh is gone, and Bear lifts an alcohol swab and sets to work disinfecting the rest of the wound.

"Have you ever heard of anybody surviving physical exposure, you know, without an armoured suit or anything? I don't mean audio-visual exposure, I mean full on physical exposure. Not just seeing or hearing it. Being *in* it."

Bear thinks it over as he works. "Not that I'm aware of. Forestry don't even wear armour beyond their sensory blockers, and I imagine they would if they thought it would help. Accounts of actually being in the physical area of exposure are rare for that very reason, I expect. Audio or visual exposure is much more common to find – and easier to study. On top of that, it's hard to study physical encounters, what with the, eh... destruction that tends to accompany it."

"So," says Bee, her eyes watering from the pain whilst her voice is steady. "If you don't think that the planet earth is a huge conscious being that actively hates us for what we did to her; and you don't believe that we've been subjected to the judgement of God and live within the end times... what do *you* think did this to me? What cut my face open, Bear? What tore Red to pieces, if it wasn't Hell's footsoldiers?"

Bear steps back and looks at her wounds while he thinks. "Bee, the kind of answer you're looking for is the kind that faith gives. All I can do is guess at *what,* and *how.* Then try to prove myself wrong. If you want to know *why,* don't ask a scientist."

"I did ask *what,* though. As in, *what* did this to me?"

"Something sharp, edged, like a knife. Beyond that, I don't really know."

"Can't you look at the skin under a microscope and tell me that it was a six-foot tall guy with brown hair or something like that?"

Bear laughs. "Not exactly, no. Though if you have access to a microscope here it would be interesting to see what kind of damage was done to the cells, if I can see them at all."

"What could you tell about the wounds under a microscope?"

"Well, if the cells are directly damaged then whatever did it has to be on the nanometre scale, and thus not something inherently natural; barring maybe diamond or obsidian, I guess, but even then..."

Bee looks at him as best she can as he works on her wound. "You know all that, but you can't tell me what you think actually *did* it?"

"That's not the point of science," says Bear, shrugging. "I can guess, and try to prove myself wrong. That's all."

"Well, then, *guess*. Go for it. What cut me up, Bear?"

He blows a breath out between his lips, and waves his hands around.

"Beats me. Maybe, wisps of monofilament from whatever the phenomenon is? An area of physical instability that shifted your skin apart, on a molecular level? If it distorts space, it could have strands of hyper-thin material similar to matter in a black hole. It certainly causes reality to break down around itself?"

She laughs. "You're just as clueless as the rest of us, aren't you?"

"Of course I am," he smiles. "But at least I *know* I'm clueless."

She misses the jab, and he picks up his needle and begin stitching her cheek back together.

"Does it bother you, having a scar here?" he asks, and she shrugs.

"I used to be a Scout, Bear. I've never been one to bother much about looks."

Bear leans back and frowns, considering for the first time that she's a remarkably attractive women when she isn't being openly hostile towards him – despite the gaping scar. It doesn't diminish her brightness at all. Already she seems to have made it a part of her – or perhaps he has just never seen her without it.

"Not one for looks," he observes, "but you always wear your circlet, right? Isn't that for looks?"

She adjusts it absent-mindedly, and gives him a stern look.

"That's to keep my hair out my face when I'm shooting people. Plus, it was given to me by someone important."

"*And* because it looks nice?"

She laughs. "A *tiny* bit because it looks nice. But no; don't worry about my scar. I'll wear a scarf if I start to scare the children, y'know, when we do drop-offs. I prefer being away from people anyway."

"Long enough in this job, you have to get scars at some point, I imagine, right?"

She nods, but says nothing. Bear finishes his stitching just as May comes over the radio.

"Bee, we're almost at radio broadcast altitude. Finished?"

She looks at Bear for an answer, and he nods.

"Yeah, we're finished May."

"Dusty says he'll see you both on the roof."

Bear feels a surge of energy as they leave. His entire purpose here is finally on the cusp of completion. He can finally repay Calum for getting him out of Forgehead, and ensure that they survive the incursion.

Chapter 11

The rungs of the ladder stick to his bare hands as he follows Bee up onto the roof of the Icebreaker. He inhales the sharp, chill air and savours his current freedom from the fumes and smoke of Forgehead's industry. Mid day sunlight warms him a little, but his face is already going numb.

Dusty sits atop the Icebreaker, his legs dangling over the side. From up here, atop a ridge of several smaller hills, they can see almost the entire length of the Coastal Union. On the ocean horizon are the masts of a few large ships, and on the other side of the mountains lies the vast white wastelands of the inner country, where almost nobody goes any more.

"Afternoon," says Dusty, drinking from a flask of steaming tea.

They join him at the edge of the Icebreaker, dangling their legs off the side. Bear gets slight vertigo as he looks down at his feet and sees the forty foot drop onto the tracks or the rocks below.

These wide open spaces still terrify him. He can see further than he ever has in his life. The phenomenon, he thinks, could be on the other side of the world, and he might still see it from here. He can't understand how the others are so relaxed about it.

Dusty is holding a deflated, foil balloon attached to a wire. He nudges Bear.

"Ok son, we're going to contact Union City. For that, we need altitude. May?"

"Boss?" comes her voice, strange-sounding and tinny in the open air. She sounds less human up here, and more machine.

"We're going to do a radio message now, so fire up the necessary software."

"Already done, dearest."

Bee is keeping watch across the white capped hills and snowy slopes that lead down into evergreen forests; once a Scout, always a Scout. Dusty produces a lighter and holds the flame under the deflated balloon. Bear is confused at first, but then the heat triggers some chemical reaction, and the balloon begins to inflate and lifts out of Dusty's hands, lighter than air.

It's airborne, and drags the wire with it as it goes.

"Is that a transmitter?" asks Bear as he follows it up with his gaze.

"Aye – and a receiver. Beats having a tower on us all the time, eh? It'll keep expanding as it rises."

"Smart," says Bear, and laughs out of wonder. He keeps finding things to be impressed by.

Dusty pulls out an orange crate with a bunch of wires and microphones in it. He picks a microphone, connects it to the box, and plugs the box into an open port on the Crawler's roof.

"Ok," says Dusty. "Just let me do the usual stuff, and then I'll hand it over to you."

Bear clears his throat in surprise. "What? Me? Why?"

"So you can tell Union City that Forgehead is in danger."

"But I mean – why don't you just do it?"

"It wasn't me who promised to pass the message on, was it?" asks Dusty.

Bear sighs. "I guess so."

"So you'll be the one to do it. Then you've met your promise, right?"

He shrugs. "Yeah, good call."

Bee gives Dusty a bemused look from across the roof, like a daughter raising an eyebrow at her embarrassing father. Dusty switches on the radio, and screeching static is the first thing that they hear. It resolves as May does her thing, and her voice comes through the speaker first.

"We're all set up Dusty."

"How's the signal?"

"Weak, but there. Union City must be having a storm or something, lightning maybe. There's a lot of static. Scrubbing and compensating. Getting a clear signal now."

"Thanks," he says. "Usual checks, no unusual or high energy transmissions?"

"None."

"Then patch us through."

The radio signal erupts with crackles and pops, and then hisses as it resolves into a human voice, female, somewhat elderly, like Bear's old school teacher.

"Union City Comms, this is Margaret. State your name and -"

Dusty launches in with a speech that must have been said hundreds of times. "Captain Dustin Mckay, Interloper Initiative, Crawler Four. Call-sign: Icebreaker. Requesting open channel for referral."

"Oh hello Dusty," comes the reply, immediately more casual. "How's life out there?"

"Oh it's not so bad Marge. Couple of stiffs to call in, Cartographers probably," he says, and then lifts the patches that Bee recovered from his pocket and reads out a series of numbers.

"Heard and noted Dusty, I'll see that it's passed on. Anything else?"

"Yeah, I've got a young man here from Forgehead who has to pass you some information. I'm putting him on, his name's Bear."

"Ok, go ahead."

Bear takes the microphone from an eager Dusty, who is watching with interest.

"Uh, hello," says Bear. "Uh, this is Bear. Uh, Benjamin Woods. Forgehead, uh, science...team? I guess. Requesting, uh..."

Dusty leans over. "You want Forestry."

Bee is laughing, hand over her eyes. "Forgehead science team, he says. *Benjamin,* he says."

Bear scowls at her. Nobody has called him his birth name since his father last did. "Yeah, uh, sorry, can I speak to the Forestry please."

"Of course son," comes Margaret's motherly tones. "What's your message?"

Dusty leans over again, whispering. "She'll pass it on, just tell her what you need said."

"So," Bear clears his throat into the mic. "Uh, Forgehead is experiencing a phenomenological incident -"

"A what?" comes the reply.

"A phenom -" he sighs. "Gaia is falling upon Forgehead."

"Oh bloody hell," she whispers. "That's awful news."

"Yeah," he says, and the nerves kick in. "And two people made an attempt on the Chief Woodsman's life, but he survived, but their radio gear is shot up and damaged, so they're isolated and vulnerable, so they're requesting immediate reinforcements from Union City, and, uh, we think that Dreamer cultists are trying to isolate Forgehead to conduct a mass exposure, so help is needed urgently, since they'll be defenceless."

"Take a breath son," she says.

"Sorry."

"Ok. Union City will dispatch what we can spare to help Forgehead out. I'll pass on your theory about the Dreamer cult to Vigilant Ophelia and our Forestry commanders immediately. Cavalry will be on the way."

"Uh, thank you," says Bear with a breath of relief, unable to believe how simple and straightforward it seems after how much thought he had put into it. "Thank you so much."

"Don't mention it," she says.

Bee is shaking her head. "That was like watching someone crash a sled in slow motion."

Dusty gently takes the mic from him. "That's me back on now, Marge."

"Oh hello Dusty. Anything else I can get for you?"

"Just a check in. How's the high road to White Anchor?

Anything awful coming in on the weather scans? Is the route still... y'know, is it still the same route? No Cartographers out there recently?"

The reply comes after a pause, for a change. "We're actually experiencing serious interference between here and White Anchor at the moment Dusty. Maybe a storm or something? So be careful if that's where you're heading next."

Bee hears this, and looks to the horizon. "No storm clouds," she says. "Clear blue all the way."

"Thanks Marge," says Dusty. "Take care. Say hi to your brother for me."

"I will," she says. "Are you holding up ok? You sounded a bit shook when you called in that ambush a few days -"

"Yeah we're all good," says Dusty. "Stay safe, Marge. May, disconnect."

And the line goes dead as May disconnects them. He turns to Bear.

"Neat, huh?"

"Yeah. That was easier than I thought."

Bee laughs again. "You didn't make it *look* easy."

"It was my first time," Bear defends himself. "I'm just glad they're sending help."

"Well, any settlement under attack is bad for Union City's reputation – they want people dependent on them, but that also means actually protecting them. One of the few good things about the Council. Well done son, you've saved Forgehead."

Bear smiles and shrugs, dangling his legs over the Crawler's edge. "Oh, I mean, I really just made a radio call, didn't I? No big heroics there."

"But you promised that you would, and you did, miles from home and hearth too. That's the important thing. Now on to other important matters; May?"

"Yes, my dear?"

"White Anchor sounds like it might be having some weather issues messing with comms. Try to hail them, please. We can take the balloon to max altitude if needed."

"I'm telling you Dusty," says Bee. "It's all clear weather, no storm."

"Let's see what the radio says, Beatrice."

Silence for at least twenty seconds, at which point even Dusty starts to look concerned.

"Uh, May?"

Then her voice comes as usual.

"Darling, there's an issue."

Bear sees Dusty's face change, and he listens intently. The look on both Dusty and Bee's face makes his stomach turn.

"What's the issue?" he asks quietly.

"Well, when I try to hail White Anchor, I'm having to filter out a lot of [DATA REDACTED]"

Bear jumps at the sudden drop in emotion and robotic tone of her voice. Dusty turns to him and puts a hand on his shoulder to calm him.

"Bee, wind the radio balloon down and lock up behind you."

"Aye, sir," she says, and begins reeling it back in with a winch as Dusty urges Bear towards the hatch, but Bear stops them.

"Is it the phenomenon?" asks Bear.

"Either White Anchor is *being* hit by it," says Dusty, "or it's *about* to be. Either way, those people are in deep shit."

"What are we going to do?" asks Bear.

"We have a delivery of steel from Forgehead to exchange for fish," he says. "It's not high priority. We can miss White Harbour."

"What?" asks Bear, and Dusty stops and turns at the tone in his voice. "We're just going to abandon them?"

"The Forestry deals with this shit, son, not us. We aren't soldiers, we aren't scouts – we do logistics."

Bear wants to argue the point, but he remembers that the only reason he's here is precisely because the Crawlers don't hang around when the phenomenon hits.

But something catches in his thought process, and Dusty sees it in his face. Bear knows that phenomenological incursions aren't *this* common. First they went for the Icebreaker, then they went for Forgehead, now White Anchor is about to get hit? This is no coincidence, and Bear can feel that itching again, as though he at the precipice of something.

"What is it, son?" asks Dusty, seeing him deep in thought.

"Dusty, what if it's deliberate?"

"Go on."

"What if the Dreamers are hitting settlement after settlement with the same tactics? Union can't help them all at once, can it?"

Dusty scratches his chin, folds his arms, and considers what Bear is saying. Meanwhile, Bee finishes winding in the radio wires and turns to them.

"He might be right," she says. "Maybe this is another mass exposure attempt. Dreamers are getting bold, we know that."

"And if it is," says Dusty. "Then they need Union City's help too. We could put another call in?"

Bee shakes her head. "Union City is going to be stretched to breaking point with one or two settlements down, if the Dreamers hit all of them, then they won't be able to respond. Not with sufficient force. Not against armed assailants, let alone the armies of Hell."

"Shit," whispers Dusty.

Bear raises his hand. "Does White Anchor have a radio tower?"

"It does," says Dusty. "Why?"

"Well, we think that their plan in Forgehead was to use the radio tower to broadcast a false all-clear. Otherwise, they'll need to go in once the sensory gear is on and take it off people. I mean, it'll be easy – but that takes a lot of manpower and time, right?"

Bee nods with him. "Yeah – that was probably why those two in Forgehead went back to the town, right? So on the plus side, Forgehead's probably safe, Bear."

"Yeah, but White Anchor didn't get a warning like we did. They'll be sitting waiting for the all-clear and they'll have their sensory gear pulled right off. Union won't get there in time."

Dusty is nodding now. "These people need help," he says. "We need to get on the radio."

"To Union?" asks Bee. "Captain, Union is *days* away – we're *hours* out. We're probably the only people in the vicinity. They need *us.*"

"You know I can't risk a Crawler like that, lass. If the Dreamers are there, we're walking into a firefight, and we're walking in blind and wounded."

"They won't be expecting us," she says. "We never go into hot zones, we're the *last* thing they'll be expecting. Let May take us there! If Hell has come to White Anchor, we can use May to do this without even looking out the windows. We've trained for combat in an incursion. Hell, *I'll* lead this mission if you want -"

"You aren't Captain yet, lass," he says. "But I take your point." Dusty looks away for a moment, deep in thought, and then nods. "Ok. Bee, get the balloon back up. May?"

"Yes, love?"

"Patch her through to Union City when she's ready. Bee: tell them that White Anchor is under Gaia's gaze, attacked by Hell, whatever – and tell them that Crawler Four is responding. Tell them that the Icebreaker is en route."

"Of course," says Bee.

"And May?"

"Hm?"

"Switch us to War Configuration."

"Yessir," she replies, curt and proper, to-the-point.

Her voice and tone change even as she replies, and the lights in the Crawler's hatch dim slightly as the power is re-routed. From the outside, they see the Crawler start to change. There's the sound of sliding metal all around them and rattling machinery as things *move* all over the Crawler.

"To the nav deck with me, Bear. Bee, get that balloon up and do your thing."

She nods and starts messing with the radio balloon, whilst

Bear follows Dusty down the ladders and into the Icebreaker once more. Dusty rushes them to the nav deck, and Bear notes that his slow gait and elderly kindness have all but vanished as he barrels down the narrow hallway. He stops halfway, when they are alone, and turns to Bear so suddenly that Bear jumps in surprise.

"Listen to me," he says, stern and low. "You're coming with us because there's no choice. If you want to go to your room and lock the door? If you want to put your sensory gear on until this is over? I will not judge you. I won't even tell anybody. You have that choice. Ok?"

Bear takes a breath. It'd be easy. But he can't bring himself to take the easy way out this time. Is it adrenaline or excitement, he wonders, that are driving him now? Most likely, he feels, it is curiosity.

"I'm sticking it out. Just tell me what you need me to do."

Dusty smiles, and Bear sees another side to him in that cheeky old grin; for the first time, he sees underneath the grandfatherly kindness, and sees a man who relishes danger.

"That's the spirit," he laughs, and whacks Bear on the arm. "Just follow orders and you'll probably survive. Let's tell Glass the good news."

They burst through the nav deck door and Glass is on his feet, his rifle in his hands, having realised that they are on a war footing. Behind him, the glass viewport shows a new overlay of targeting matrices and armour integrity, as well as power reserves and ammunition counts for various weaponry across the Crawler. Nothing is reading at 100%, Bear notices. Damage from their previous run in with the Dreamers, probably.

His stomach flips again at the thought, but the fear doesn't paralyse him this time. He's unsettled, but it feels far less intense than the fear that he felt in Forgehead.

Glass asks no questions, but his face is essentially one massive question mark, so Dusty answers him:

"We're hitting White Anchor, Glass. We think that the Dreamers are trying to pull a mass exposure there."

Glass smiles, something else that Bear has just seen for the first time, and raises his hand.

"Permission granted," says Dusty.

"Are we going to catch *them* by surprise for a change?" he booms.

"We are," says Dusty. "May?"

"Sir?"

"You have the helm. As soon as Bee is back inside, you take us to White Anchor. Full speed."

"Aye-aye, Captain."

Chapter 12

Bear straps into the fourth seat in the nav deck, and watches the other three out of curious observation.

Glass has one hand on his rifle, one on the controls, and is swaying silently on the gyroscopic chair as the Crawler roars through the snow drifts, following the mountainside down towards the coast. He says nothing, and his face betrays no anticipation nor fear; but Bear can see how he handles stress: with silence and stoicism. Glass has battened down his hatches, waiting until the storm is over.

Bee is the opposite. She is actively checking her rifle, using her legs like stabilisers to keep her balance, and her face is a mixture of stern readiness and wide eyed awareness. Her jaw mesh is bloodied but holding, her circlet off-centre and tilted. She seems to deal with stress, Bear notes, by preparing and planning over and over again. He can almost see her lips move as she goes over plans in her head.

Dusty seems the most relaxed, if not excited, during the mountainside descent. He handles the ride like a rodeo, leaning into the bucks and turns of the Crawler, eyes on the horizon the whole time, singing softly to himself under his breath. There's a long-barrelled revolver hanging beneath his long overcoat in a shoulder holster of brown leather, and a bottle of Dusty's Reserve hanging in a little wicker basket under his control console.

Bear wonders how he looks to the others. Probably like a child, trying their best to seem brave but obviously terrified. His satchel hangs around his shoulders, and he holds his fire-gauntlet ready in one hand, currently inert in case they crash. He keeps checking inside his satchel, ensuring that his sensory blocking gear is there; just in case. It is, resting beside his father's notes. He shudders, wondering when he'll get a chance to read them, and what they might say. Perhaps, he thinks, he will just never read them.

May's voice comes over the speakers, clipped and professional now.

"White Anchor is about to come into view, estimation: twenty seconds."

Everybody looks up at the viewport out of instinct.

"May, you've done the usual scans?" asks Dusty.

"Affirmative. We are all clear."

"Any signs of life?"

"The town has no radio chatter. Preparing thermals. Stand by."

They turn the corner, and the nav deck falls silent at what they see.

"May," whispers Dusty. "Stop the Crawler."

The Crawler whines to a halt, still rumbling. They stand and walk to the cockpit together, all of them, in shocked silence.

The snow field before them, wide and flat, is dotted with bodies. At least twenty, maybe thirty. Bear watches in horror as the heads-up display on the viewport starts tagging and counting them, marking them as points of interest.

The town itself sits in the distance, a sprawl of low buildings huddled against the coastline, the horizon hidden by great concrete walls. Tall though the walls are, the gates are open and unmanned.

"This was an attack," says Bee. "Whose bodies are those? Dreamers or Forestry?"

May answers. *"From here, I can identify Forestry patches."*

"There was a fight, then," says Bee, noting the blood spray on the snow. "This was recent."

"May," says Dusty. "How many?"

"Twenty eight bodies, by my count."

"Out in the open, too," says Bear, confused. "Wouldn't they try to find cover? Why would they be out here?"

As if in answer, the viewport zooms in on the bodies. Their heads are covered in full-face helmets. Sensory blockers. Some of them still carry flame guns and fuel tanks on their backs, half buried in the snow now.

"Because," says Dusty. "They thought they were coming out here to burn it away. They walked out here, blind and deaf by their own accord, to do their job as usual. They didn't know they'd be fighting other people."

"Then the Dreamers would have just gunned them down," says Bee, shaking her head. "That's probably most of the White Anchor Forestry out there. Dead. A massacre."

Bear finds his voice, his chest tight with fear. "Leaving it defenceless. Do you think the Dreamers are still in there?"

"If there's anybody left to expose, maybe," says Dusty. "But May isn't picking up any of the typical signals – she'd be shouting about redacted information if she was. There's nothing to expose anybody to."

"We're too late," says Bee.

Glass raises a hand, and Dusty nods for him to speak.

"Perhaps we are just in time. Many possibilities. Maybe there's something we're missing. Maybe it's still ongoing. We have to check."

Dusty nods. "Glass is right. We've come this far – we need to see what the situation is. May?"

"Sir?"

"Take us up to the gates and drop the ramp. We're going in."

"Aye, Captain."

"Glass, go and prep the field gear. May, how's the radio situation now?"

"Still down as far as I can tell. The radio tower here must have been taken out, or otherwise disabled. Radio is totally silent."

"Ok," says Dusty. "Then we're on our own. Bee, you let Union know that we were coming here earlier, right?"

"Yes, sir."

"Then we go in. Glass will take point in case of exposure, have sensory gear ready. Bee, you're leading."

She hesitates, then nods. "What's our objective?"

"Search for survivors. Quick sweep. White Anchor's radio tower is close to their port, so we're gonna go and see what's happened. If it's been shot up like Forgehead's was, then we know who's responsible. Be quick, be quiet, and don't waste time helping exposure cases. If everybody is gone, Union can purge the place."

She bites her lip. "Yes, sir. Just me and Glass?"

Dusty looks across at Bear, and raises an eyebrow. Bear takes a deep breath, and shrugs.

"Me too," he says. "I'll come along. I want to see this."

"Ok," says Bee, returning his shrug. "Come and get your coat."

"Bee?" shouts Dusty as she leaves the nav deck with Bear following. She turns back, and something unsaid passes between them. "Be careful."

"Aye-aye, Captain," she forces a grim smile, and leads Bear to the ramp.

Bear looks at the heavy white jacket in his hands, wondering how he'll fit it over his overcoat, and feels the frigid air settle over him as the ramp grinds down towards the ground. Glass stands beside him in his white coat and goggles, rifle in hand, silent.

Bee spends a moment at a rack of weaponry and returns with a stubby black pistol that she hands to Bear. He takes it, unsure of quite what to do, and she points out the three main features:

"This is the safety, keep it on unless I shout otherwise. This is the trigger, don't touch it unless you're ready to end something's life. And this is the barrel. Don't point it at something unless you are prepared to see that thing destroyed. Point it at one of us and we'll take it off you. Got it?"

"Uh -"

"Good. Your mittens have a flap to let your fingers out, you won't be able to use the gun otherwise. This is a Glock 17. Pre-Cataclysm, reliable. 9mm. There's seventeen shots in the magazine, hence the name. Probably. If something needs more than seventeen shots, you're not going to kill it with 9mm anyway. Once you run out, that's you. Aim centre mass – and if something is worth shooting, it's worth shooting at *least* twice. If you're fighting for your life, dump half the magazine into them, ok? Bullets are cheap. Life is expensive."

"Thanks for the crash course," says Bear, sighing. "Fingers crossed I don't need it."

She puts the pistol in a shoulder holster and helps him wrap the holster under his arm, and put his jacket on over it. This close to her, Bear can feel the heat from her body. It's a welcome escape from the cold. Then his jacket is wrapped around him, and he's ready.

Bee looks around at her squad, and then nods to Glass, and motions with her hand for them to disembark. They step down the ramp, into the thick snow, into the silent town.

The sky is clear blue, no clouds. The only sound is their feet crunching on fresh snow as Bee leads them inside.

"This snow should have been cleared. Dates the attack to at least the last snowfall. Glass, take note."

He nods, and Bee motions for them to continue.

They leave the destroyed gate behind them and make their way, spread out across the main road, into the town of White Anchor. The gate seems to have been blown down by something, but there's no evidence of explosives or anything else. Bear makes sure to remember it.

Along the street are the Gaian banners and dream-catcher decorations that Bear recognises from the walls of Forgehead. He notes that they do not seem to have stopped anything.

There are cups, glasses, plates strewn around on the dirt path, and the smell of cigarettes, marijuana, sweat... All around are crudely drawn runes, nothing like the real ones that would be giving Bear a migraine right now. Writing is splashed across the walls:

Mother Gaia Calls Us Home

To Dirt We Return

Apocalyptic revelry. They must have been in the midst of another street festival when the alarm sounded. Bear chuckles at the irony: dance and sing and beg for Mother Gaia to take you back into herself, but when the alarm goes off you'd best run for your sensory blockers. Hypocrites, probably just there for the party.

Glass pays it no mind as they pass, but Bee seems disgusted.

"Imagine worshipping your own end," she sneers. "Throwing parties for the end of the world. Bloody Gaians. No offence Glass."

He shrugs: none taken.

Bear keeps pace with them as they round the corner to the first real dwellings, stone and brick buildings pressed together as though for warmth, their doors situated a man's height below ground, with rickety stairs leading down into the earth, wood on dirt. Bee motions towards them, and Glass keeps watch as she descends the stairs. Bear follows, and she reaches the door and gently pushes it open.

"Let's see if there's anybody inside."

Bear is painfully aware that they are out of sight of the Crawler now. It feels like he's connected to it by a lifeline; like every step he takes away from it is a step further into danger.

She makes a motion to stay silent, one finger on her lips, and Bear follows her through the door, into the dark. She shines a torch mounted on her jacket around the single room dwelling, and gasps.

There are four bodies, with old fashioned sensory gear on, lying on the bed together. There's a man and a woman, and between them lie two young children with smaller sensory gear.

They are breathing. There are rations and water beside them as well as chamber pots. Bee gives Bear a look of relief, and whispers,

"We're going to have to wake them – they can tell us what's happened."

"There was no all clear," says Bear. "Even though the phenomenon is gone. No Forestry to give the signal."

Bee nods, and moves towards them.

Bear finds himself disturbed by what he sees. In all the times he's had to lie down with his sensory blockers on and wait for the all clear, he never realised how vulnerable he was; indeed, how vulnerable they all are when the phenomenon comes. He checks his satchel and finds that his sensor hasn't picked anything up, and breathes easy for now.

"Oh no," he says; a thought strikes him. The hard drive, the radio tower. "Bee?"

"What?" she hisses.

"Are they linked up to a radio?"

She looks in the doorway, peers for a moment. "No," she says. "No radio. Poorer family, I think."

"We should check those *with* radio access. I think that's what they planned with Forgehead."

"To broadcast an all clear, right? But the phenomenon is gone -."

"What if they were going to broadcast something worse? Like an audio recording of the phenomenon – they could expose everybody that way?"

"Shit," she whispers. "Ok. Let me wake them alone and get a report, then we'll check closer to the sea for the wealthier homes, those with radio antennae."

Bear nods, and ascends the steps to the main road. Glass is staring both ways down the road, rifle at the ready, and barely acknowledges Bear as he joins him.

Feeling like there is a taboo in breaking the silence, Bear takes a brief walk around the street as he hears scuffling and whispering from the house that Bee is in. The windows are all covered up, and there is no crackling of fire.

The street itself is a main road that travels the length of the town until it hits the sea, where there is a squat lighthouse with a series of radio masts above it; Bear realises that they must just use the lighthouse as a radio tower, probably for its height. There doesn't seem to be anything amiss, but Glass raises his rifle to his eyes takes a better look at it.

"See anything?" asks Bear, but Glass looks at him, says nothing. No indication either way. "Great. Good teamwork. Thanks Glass."

Bee finishes up inside, whispering a farewell to the family, motioning for them to put their blockers back on as she reemerges.

"Don't take them off until the all clear comes from the Union Foresty, remember? Ok, bye, thank you," she mutters as she closes the door behind herself. Glass and Bear turn to her, waiting.

"So, everybody had similar dreams last night, and they've been like this ever since. They didn't hear any gunfire or explosions, nothing else strange, they've just been waiting patiently as usual. Poor things are terrified, as expected."

"Ok," says Bear. "Now the richer families."

"Follow me," says Bee, and sets off down the road towards the sea wall.

Bee pulls them to a stop by a house with a small porch, indicating a wealthier family's abode, and they stack on the door.

"Same again, you both keep watch, while -"

She stops, listening. They all freeze, silent.

Scratching. Scraping. Bee curses under her breath, nods to Glass to join her, and together they push the door open and step inside. Bear follows, shielding his eyes, but still curious.

Bee reels back the second they step inside, wincing, eye's closed. She's cursing, and batting invisible flies away from her face. Glass, seemingly unaffected, stands and watches.

Inside, in perfect unison, a woman in a nightgown and two young children are kneeling before a wooden wall. They are still wearing their expensive sensory helms, full face covering masks, giving them a strange faceless quality. The children are holding their mothers hand, one each, and the children are scratching symbols into the wall with their nails. Behind them, the father lies in a puddle of spreading blood, his helm a few feet away from him. Exposed. He appears to have torn the radial artery from his wrist with his teeth, leaving blood everywhere.

Glass stands in front of Bee and Bear to protect them. Bear swears he can hear chanting from under their sensory blockers.

The mother and two children, unable to see or hear, turn in unison to look at the squad. There is absolute silence, and the mother stands up, looking *right* at them, right through her blockers.

Glass, brave though he is, closes the door, turns to the two nursing their headaches from the runes, and motions for them to leave. Bee pats him on the arm.

"We're too late," she says.

"The radio tower," says Bear. "They must have got to it. The hard drive must have phenomenological audio on it or something. I didn't even know such a thing was possible. Recordings of it are just as bad?"

"At least the Dreamers will be long gone then," says Bee. "Mission over. Anybody with a radio in White Anchor is probably gone."

"Poor bastards," says Bear.

"Fuck," hisses Bee. She steps off the porch and starts storming back towards the Crawler, far on the other side of White Anchor. *"Fuck!"*

Bear goes to follow her, feeling a sickening lurch from the realisation that this could have been him.

Beep.

There comes from his satchel a sound that he hates; the sound of his sensor picking up phenomenological activity. Bear's heart drops into his stomach. Glass glares at him in realisation, as Bear lifts his sensor out of his satchel.

Beep.

Phenomenon near. It's set to long range, low sensitivity – this isn't the runes setting it off.

It must still be here.

"Bee," he shouts. "My sensor is going off!"

She turns, eyes wide, and motions for them to hide. Glass grabs Bear, and together they run to the side of the street, into the stairwell of one of the poorer households, using it like a trench. Bear starts scrambling for his sensors, feeling the panic rising in his gut once more.

Beep Beep.

Bee catches them up and gets down into the stairwell with them. The sensor is picking up more now, and Bear is rummaging in his satchel for his own sensory gear.

"We can make it back to the Crawler," says Bear. "It's faint, but I'm picking up phenomena, getting stronger. It's coming. There's time. Not much, but there *is* time."

"How long?" she asks.

"Minutes?" he suggests, and realises that she is considering *not* immediately retreating. "Bee? Bee, you can't be serious -"

"I'm not thinking of staying, Bear. It's not that. I think that we've just walked into an ambush, and I am assessing our options.*"*

His heart almost stops. Every corner suddenly has death around it. "What? What ambush?"

"The attack happened last night, right? The Dreamers have been and gone – but Bear, they ambushed the Crawler before. What if they waited? In case we turned up. They knew we'd be nearby. Maybe they want revenge; I mean, we did kill quite a few of them. They must have known we'd come here. It was next on our schedule, and they might know our schedule if they ambushed us outside Forgehead. Think about it."

"Shit," he breathes. "You think this is a trap?"

"Any strategist would consider it. They were gonna do this anyway, why not leave some people behind to hit us again? If they did, then now is when they'd strike. When we're far from the Crawler, all alone, and their best friend is closing in. This is how they operate. Call down Hell on us, and strike while we're blind. Shit, maybe they *can* control it?"

Glass raises a hand, and Bee gives him permission to talk. "Ma'am, we should make for the Crawler immediately."

"You're right. Glass, check up top. Be careful, be quick."

Glass checks, and stops. He stares.

"Oh no," he whispers.

Bee and Bear stand up and see what he does.

Down the road, standing in broad daylight, are a group of men and women with guns in their arms, staring right at them. Four that they can see, with more joining them and staring, emerging from similar underground dwellings, from around street corners, more than a dozen now. They are dressed like Gaians, with thick wolf furs and metal hung around them like armour.

"God above, this is *perfect* for an ambush," she hisses to herself. "They must have hidden in the houses. God damnit, Beatrice what the hell were you thinking?"

"They planned this," whispers Bear. "What do we do?"

A man steps out into the sun from the same building, and raises his hands in mock surrender. He is clad in a long brown greatcoat and little else – Bear can see bare skin beneath it, covered in lines like tattoos. He is otherwise bald, with a long beard and ice blue eyes, and built like a fighter. Bear notices that he's in his bare feet, even in the snow. He carries no weapon that he can see, though a satchel similar to Bear's hangs at his side. He looks like a shaman.

"Identify yourself!" shouts Bee, and raises her own rifle. His own men raise their machineguns, and Bear instinctively raises his own hands in surrender, before Glass makes him lower them.

The man begins pacing towards them, hands raised, speaking to his soldiers.

"Easy, easy," he says as though calming a dog, lowering their barrels. "No need for gunfire. Safeties on, children."

His voice is soothing, jovial, as though he's known everybody here for years. He walks at an angle, always slightly leaning over, leaning back.

"I said identify yourself," says Bee, centring her aim on his torso.

He stops walking twenty paces from them, and regards them across the snow.

"Well it's my old friends," he smiles. "The crew of the Icebreaker. Minus Dusty," he murmurs as he looks across them, "and plus one replacement. I am very sorry about Red, by the way. Total accident. I understand if you're upset, but we really did not intend for him to be hurt."

Bee catches her breath, unable to respond.

"Who *are* you?" asks Bear, but already the cogs are turning in his head.

"My name is Messenger," he says, and clasps his hands behind his back in a show of comfort. "Now you're *new,* who are *you?*" He peers at Bear like he might at a puzzle, smiling. "Have we met?"

"Don't answer," says Bee, and Bear shuts up.

"Answer or not, I'll find out," Messenger laughs, shrugging.

Bee glances over her shoulder. Bear can hear her breathing heavily. She's afraid. Glass is yet to move. He's like a statue, rifle ready. They have a decent position, full body cover in the stairwell, like a foxhole to fire out of – but there's nowhere for them to run. No way to manoeuvre. They'll easily be flanked, overrun, or some bright spark will throw a grenade into their trench.

"Beatrice, relax, girl," says Messenger. "This was the only way to talk to you; since your radios aren't working."

Bee taps the radio on her chest, and only static and bursts of noise come out the other end.

"Phenomenon," whispers Bear. "Shit. Radio is out for everyone."

Messenger turns to his soldiers, and they catch his eye. "I've got it from here, lads. Make yourself scarce before Dusty blows a bunch of you apart again. Except *you* three."

They nod, and scatter into the streets, save for three of them, who take up positions in cover, though their weapons stay down.

Bee doesn't fire, nor does Glass, as the others retreat.

"See now, this is a bit nicer than our last meeting," says Messenger. "You should start by lowering your gun, Beatrice, we're not going to get any talking done over a scope. I'm not armed, am I? My soldiers aren't even pointing their weapons."

"You killed Red," says Bee, and puts Messenger's head in her sights. Bear watches her, ready to move as soon as she fires. But the shot never comes.

"You know fine well what killed Red," he lowers his voice in a serious tone. "And it wasn't *me*."

Beep-beep, goes Bear's sensor. He twitches, and Messenger looks straight at him.

"Ah, an old sensor. I miss the old models. Mother Gaia is getting closer. I invited her along, I have to admit, and I hope you don't mind. Too dangerous to confront you lot without her balancing the scales." He smiles as it all starts to fall into place. "Dusty doesn't know that this is going on, does he? He won't come in, guns blazing, to rescue you like last time. Will he, Beatrice? No. He won't. It's just us here. So let's talk."

"Dusty will come before the phenomenon does," says Bear. "He won't risk us getting exposed."

"Before the what?"

"The phenomenon," he repeats.

"That's not what it's called," laughs Messenger. "Her name is Gaia, and she speaks through me – and to me."

Messenger shows Bear his palms, as if to prove a point.

Bear looks at Messenger's palms, covered like the rest of him in spiralling runes and tattoos. He feels a sudden sharp pain in his head, like a migraine. He blinks a few times to get it away, but it feels like he's stared into the sun.

Runes. He has runes on his damn hands.

How?

"Don't look at his palms," mumbles Bear, and feels hands on his shoulders.

When his vision returns, he finds Glass looking into his eyes in fear, making sure he's ok. He blinks the worst of it away, but his head is pounding now, his vision blurred.

"I think we should all walk away from this," says Messenger, hiding his palms inside his clasped. "No need for any blood shed. Or you could hang around and try to fight us with your sensory gear on. That went really well for the White Anchor Forestry, I'm sure you saw."

"You tried to kill us," says Bee. "Now you're letting us walk away?"

"Kill you? Bee, you're smarter than that." He shakes his head. "I want you to face the truth, look into Gaia's eyes and embrace what you see. But I'd like it to be on your own terms."

"Why?" asks Bear, rubbing his eyes.

"Because you're Crawler crew; the best of the best, the Coastal Union's finest. If anybody could survive exposure and come out the other side in one piece, it's you lot. You all belong among our ranks, talented people worthy of the world that Gaia is bringing upon us, and I think you all know it. If there's one thing I unequivocally want, it's people like you lot. The world is going to need thinkers and doers, when Gaia is done here."

"I'll decline that offer," says Bee, and Bear hears fear in her voice. They're outgunned, on the verge of risking exposure, and help isn't coming.

"Oh, everybody declines at first; they're so afraid. Afraid of what? They're own potential, maybe? No, no, I think that everybody is afraid that Gaia will look at their soul, will take the measure of them, and find them *wanting*. Aren't we all a little scared that we fall short? That we aren't all that we can be?"

"You've survived exposure," shouts Bear, still fighting a migraine, piecing it together. "Those runes; they're post-exposure runes."

He nods. "Very well done. Someone here knows what they're talking about. You're a smart one. What's your name, boy?"

Bee looks at him and shakes her head, chopping her hand across her neck, but Bear is thinking. He's been in his fair share of fist fights growing up; most guys in Forgehead have been part of the town's legendary bar brawls. He's no stranger to it. But talking around a problem will at least give them time to think, to manoeuvre. He's no soldier, but he can give the soldiers time to formulate a plan of their own. Talking is one thing he is good at – shooting, less so.

"Bear," he shouts. "Benjamin Woods."

Silence.

"Interesting. You must be from Forgehead," comes Messenger's reply. "I think I've read some of your work."

"Then you know there's more to be gained from me by talking, than by killing me."

"I'm not killing anybody," says Messenger. "I just want to talk. I reckon you're curious to know what it is that people see, Bear. Aren't you?"

"Bear, don't listen to him," says Bee, trying to drown out Messenger. "Dusty will be here any minute. He'll figure out what's going on when the Devil rolls into town. May will detect it from a distance, he'll come."

"Dusty doesn't even know this is happening," says Messenger, cutting her off. He makes his pitch like a guru, like a salesman. "We could make this easy. I'll help you through the exposure. We can talk it through, first. I know how scary the idea is, but I'll take your hand and guide you. All those you see around me are survivors, too; I chose them, just like I'm choosing you."

Bear recalls the words of Pig and Rat in Simon's cellar, talking about how Addie, Aiden, had been chosen but had failed.

"Did you choose Aiden, too?" he shouts. "Young lad. Engineer from Forgehead."

Messenger closes his eyes, rubbing his nose, frustrated. "Yes, I chose Aiden. He had all the hallmarks of a survivor."

"What *are* the hallmarks of a survivor?" shouts Bear. "What makes you think he would have survived?"

"He was pragmatic, curious, and accepted the world as it was, not as he'd have liked it to be. Just like all of you – just like *you*, Bear. Whether now or later, you're going to have to face reality. I'd recommend embracing it before it's forced upon you. It's far, far easier that way. Ask Bee, ask Glass. Better to choose to descend into Hell than to be thrown in, right Bee?"

Bee takes a breath, but remains silent. Her scope is focused on Messenger's head.

Bear winces at the pain in his head, and tries to look at Messenger again, just at his eyes – but even his bald head is covered in strange runes.

"How many people have you killed trying to find the few that might survive, Messenger? That's just murder, in my eyes."

Messenger answers him, with a sadness on his face and honest eyes. The two meet eyes across the snowy street for the first time.

"Every failure weighs on me, Bear, but I have to keep trying. The South was consumed by Gaia, and so *few* survived. When she comes for the north – and she will, make no doubt, and soon – I want the Coastal Union to be *ready*. I want the suffering to already be over, and for us to welcome her when she arrives."

"So you're exposing *everyone?*"

"As many as I can."

"You're murdering people!"

"They'd die in agony when Gaia comes for them, Bear. I'm skipping the middle man. Better – kinder – by my hand, than by hers. Gaia has no mercy for the weak. This is a cull to save the species, not some insane slaughter. Those who do not survive, I put out of their misery."

Bear wants to ask how he knows this, to determine if Messenger is a mad prophet high off his own supply, or if he has evidence, but he feels Bee changing stances beside him and knows what is about to happen. He's interested Messenger enough to distract him, letting her act. He tenses, ready, realising that Bee has heard enough.

She nods to Glass. She knows something, and Glass nods back, out of sight. Bear wants to tell them to wait. There's so much he wants to ask this man, so many questions.

But it's too late.

Bee raises her rifle and fires. One of his guard's head snaps back in a spray of blood.

The guards take a second to get their weapons up, taken by surprise, unable to get their aim; but Messenger hasn't moved. He seems to be watching, unflinching. He looks disappointed; annoyed.

Gunfire erupts, blowing chunks out of the stones above their heads, showering them with snow and debris. Bee steps up to take aim and Bear joins her, trying to see what they're dealing with.

They see Messenger, still in the middle of the road. He does not even blink. Instead, he drags one hand across his torso and removes his great coat, leaving himself standing there topless in the snow. He's slim, built like a gymnast, covered in those tattoos, the runes.

Bear briefly sees his entire body, and feels a sense of horrifying vertigo before he clamps his eyes shut. What little of the runes that made it onto his retina stay there, pulsing, sending spikes of pain through his temples.

Beep-beep-beep-beep, goes his sensor.

beepbeepbeepbeepbeepbeepbeepbeepbeep-

His sensor is screaming. The phenomenon is here. The image

of Messenger's body is engraved on his eyes. He has a strange depth to him that seems to bend space around him, like looking down a tunnel, and there was so much *light* but; nothing like the sun, nothing like real, natural light, just a kind of glow, just shapes within shapes -

He realises there's shooting going on, and forces himself to breathe. Only now does he realise that he's been curled like a child, whispering to himself. He wonders if Messenger has just exposed him without Bear realising it.

"We have range on them," shouts Bees as they scramble to their feet in the stairwell. "They have submachine guns and pistols, we have rifles. Keep them at arms length until Dusty reaches us."

"He'll have heard the shooting right?" shouts Bear. "He's coming?"

Bee says nothing. She keeps firing, racking the bolt on her rifle like a well drilled machine, alternating with Glass to keep up a steady fire. Messenger is *doing* something, Bear can feel it. Space is changing, compressing, everything seems far away and closer simultaneously.

"Come on Dusty where the hell are you?" shouts Bee.

Bear keeps his head down as Bee rises to her knees, shoulders her rifle, and deafens him with another shot before racking the bolt on her rifle.

"What the hell *is he?*" she shouts as more snow and masonry explode above them. "I can't even look at him, it's like he's all light. He's coming closer, I think, I can't tell. Ah fuck, space is all weird again, I can't focus!"

"Allow me," booms Glass, and stands up, firing again. He seems barely affected.

"Wait," says Bee, "do you feel that?"

Glass turns to her, nodding. "Cavalry is here."

In the distance, they hear the roaring of the Crawler's engines. The sensor in Bear's satchel is emitting a constant whining now.

"It's getting closer," Bear shouts again. "It's him! It's not the phenomenon, it's Messenger that it's detecting."

"Just hold on," shouts Glass. "If he gets close, put your gear on. I'll hold him."

They hear shouting coming from down the street, and more gunfire. It's Messenger's voice:

"Time's up, take them alive before Dusty gets here!" He addresses the crew: "You can still surrender. There's still time to talk! All can be forgiven!"

"They're trying to flank us," shouts Bee, and both her and Glass rise and get another shot off before intense submachinegun fire forces them back into cover. "Shit, missed, my fucking eyes -" she rubs her eyes, gnashing her teeth. "He's a demon or something, I can't even look at him. Bear, shoot something!"

"He's just a man," grumbles Glass, and pulls a machete out of his jacket. "He comes any closer, I've got him."

Bear reaches into his jacket and fumbles for his pistol – and just in time.

A man appears at the top of the stairs from their left, submachinegun raised to his shoulder, and Bear raises his pistol and stares blankly at him.

The man shouts: "Drop your weapons!"

Bear pulls the trigger.

Click.

The safety is still on. They stare at one another, the Dreamer unwilling to break an order and open fire. Bee spins during his hesitation and fires from the hip, lying on her back, and blows the man's heart out through his spine. He crumples to the ground.

A sickly white glow appears above them, around them, and the air seems to take on the texture of creaking metal – there's singing voices, from all around, perfectly out of tune - Glass grabs Bear's satchel and jams Bear's sensory gear onto his head as Bee does the same, their voices disjointed as everything seems to fall away. Words separate as though they are without meaning, nothing has any *context -*

Messenger is here, and it seems that he has brought Old Mother Gaia with him. Hell. The phenomenon.

Then the world snaps out of its daydream, as the Crawler finally arrives. Bear doesn't see it, but he can sense the carnage it brings, can feel the impact through the earth.

Crawler Four explodes onto the street, a mechanical leviathan, every weapon onboard pointed downrange at their enemies. Heavy machine guns open fire, punctuated by the whine-boom sounds of railguns rhythmically targeting and eliminating any exposed hostiles.

Bear can feel it through his bones as the Crawler advances, clearing a path.

The sensor is going wild, but he can't hear it any more. There's only the shaking of the earth in his bones. All else is darkness, and Beethoven's music in his sensory earphones.

Glass hefts both of them to their feet, shouting,

"Go!"

But they do not hear, of course. They feel Glass's hands on their backs, and they run. Blind, they sprint for the ramp. As soon as their feet are onboard, it begins to close.

Glass holds both of their hands as they stumble and lie there, breathless, blind and deaf. The air changes, it is warm and smells of oil.

The Crawler.

Bear can't see anything in the dark behind his blindfold, but he can imagine the blood covered snow and sprawled, mangled bodies of the Dreamers down the street, holes the size of his fist punched through their torsos, and more than one red shadow plastered against the wall where a railgun round has hit somebody.

And Messenger – whatever he is, whatever *it* is, that endless glowing man-shaped creature, coming for them, all shapes and light, space cracking apart where he walked.

Then the ramp closes shut. The gunfire stops as suddenly as it started, and they feel movement.

Bear is filled with a primal fear that he didn't know he was capable of, and he remains curled in a ball until Glass pats him twice and gives him the signal for all-clear.

Safety.

Glass and Bee are rubbing their eyes and wincing, but nobody is hit; there's no blood.

The Crawler is moving; they can all feel the crashing and

bucking of the machine going over buildings, and then a loud thud as it collides with the wall.

"The fuck is May doing? May?" shouts Bee, looking up at the roof as they stand. "*May?*"

"MAY IS OFFLINE," comes the robotic, emotionless response.

"What the hell -" begins Bear, but he is cut short.

Gunfire thuds into the side of the Crawler, like a demon pounding on the walls, and they all stand and run for the ladders, making for the nav deck. The Crawler has stopped completely, but now choruses of gunfire join the orchestra playing on their outer hull. The Dreamers are still trying to break the Crawler.

"May," shouts Bee as they sprint through the corridors in single file. "May, perform a hard reset of all systems."

"NEGATIVE. ALL RUNTIMES ARE CURRENTLY BUSY."

"Shit, shit, shit," whispers Bee, and then they're at the nav deck door. "Glass, go in and check that the viewport is closed. If it isn't, bloody well *close it.*"

Glass opens the door, and Bee and Bear avert their eyes as that same sickly white glow blows through the door. They clamp their hands over their ears as the walls begins to twist inwards on them, everything becomes *deeper and rotates, inwards, from outwith, from inside -*

Glass slams the button that closes the viewport, and metallic sliders block the light out. He comes back and pats them both, signalling all clear.

The vertigo passes. The nausea stays.

When Bear opens his eyes, they are rushing into the dimly lit cockpit. Gunfire is still rattling the craft, shaking it, drowning out their voices. Dusty is slouched over the foremost control panel, one hand on his abdomen where blood is pooling. He's breathing heavily, his ears and eyes covered by heavy-duty earphones and a thick blindfold: his sensory blockers.

Bee is shouting, "Dusty, oh Christ alive, Dusty -"

There's a pop followed by a thundering blow to the Crawler, and the heads-up display on the viewport flashes red as the entire cockpit trembles, throwing Bee to the ground as she scrambles for

Dusty's chair.

"Bastard tried to drive blind," says Bear. "Why is May offline? We need her to drive, right?"

Bee shakes Dusty, and he barely breathes a response. She instantly changes, goes cold and still, calm as the mountains:

"Glass, take the wheel and get us out, we're driving manual, navigate using the sensors. Full power, blow through the fucking wall if you have to. Bear?"

"Uh, yeah, sorry -"

"Save Dusty."

The words hit him like cold water, and he sputters twice before nodding.

"Ok," he says. "Ok," and kneels beside Dusty as Glass takes up the controls. "Uh, Bee, I need the medical bay, or -"

"Don't move him. I'll bring you stuff, stay up here," she says, and dashes for the door.

Bear gently pats Dusty on the chest, and gives him the all-clear signal, before removing his sensory gear.

Dusty looks up into Bear's eyes, and smiles through the pain.

"Good thing we brought you, eh lad?"

Bear forces a smile. "Try not to move, or talk."

"I'm shot, son," he winces. "May tried to target that glowing bastard and it overloaded her. She shut herself down. Had to go blind, drive manual. Got shot trying to find the fucking buttons. Dunno how many of them I hit, tried my best though. Should know my own Crawler better -"

"Shh, shh, it's ok. Relax, try to breathe."

Bear lifts Dusty's shirt and can't see anything for blood. It's everywhere. Dusty lies back on the nav deck floor, bleeding freely onto it, clutching his abdomen as blood seeps through his hands.

Glass engages the engines again, as the display on the heads-up slowly ticks down. They're losing armour integrity in several key areas, and -

BOOM

Another explosion smashes against the Crawler. There's a red flashing light in the nav deck now, and one of the segments reads zero percent armour integrity.

Glass shouts something, a vague command to hold on to something. Bee appears at the door and tosses a first aid kid to Bear, who stows it beside him and holds on as Glass surges the Crawler forwards.

There's more gunfire, and then bumps and thuds as though they've crushed people under their treads. Glass grits his teeth and slams the Crawler into reverse, and Bear braces himself as they're all flung across the nav deck. The entire vessel rocks as they burst through something -

- and then it's smooth driving, albeit in reverse. Glass is watching the sensor readouts: radar, thermal, and laser range finder, working with his head down like a pianist. The gunfire trails off, and it feels like they're on open snow again.

Glass turns the Crawler one-eighty, picks a direction, and guns it blind, wrestling the controls as the Crawler rattles and churns across the snow.

Bear looks down at Dusty, and realises Bee is staring at him, white-faced.

Dusty has stopped talking, stopped smiling.

"Dusty?" she whispers.

Bear feels for a pulse.

Still there. He gets to work.

Bear pulls a bottle of water out of the first aid kit and splashes it across the wound, cleaning the blood off until he sees the tiny entry hole.

Small calibre, low velocity, that's what Calum had said they use, right? And it had already went through thick glass and lost most of its energy.

He can do this, he tells himself.

Anatomy comes to him easy enough, that was an early subject he enjoyed. Gunshot wounds aren't something he excels in, but he understands the physics. It's all about energy transfer.

He lifts Dusty's abdomen up, and checks about underneath his back for -

An exit wound.

He breathes a sigh of relief. A bullet that had stayed inside him would have transferred all of it's kinetic energy, maybe even fractured like a grenade inside Dusty's abdomen – far too much damage for his amateur hands to repair.

But entry-exit? Straight through? Possibly. Sub-sonic? Even better. No supersonic shockwave to kill the cells in his organs. Bear can't see any of the signs of internal bleeding or organ failure; that's the next phase. He searches the first-aid kit, and finds the ballistics gel. Only the best medical kit for the Crawlers, obviously; this stuff is like gold dust in Forgehead.

"I think we're going to be ok," says Bear. He squeezes the gel into the wounds, and it expands like shaving foam and then solidifies like insulation, sealing one wound shut, before Bear turns Dusty over and does the other one just the same.

"Bear, is he -" starts Bee, and Bear turns him over. The colour has drained from his kind old face, his lips curled back and mouth open.

"He needs fluids," says Bear, and checks for a pulse. It's there, but weak. "Do you have anything for blood transfusion? Plasma?"

She nods, and stands.

"Glass," she shouts. "Dusty is incapacitated, making me Acting-Captain. New orders. Carry Dusty to the med-bay with Bear. I'll take the helm."

"Negative, ma'am."

Bee stops, staring at him, and Bear doesn't know if he's ever seen such anger on somebody's face.

"Glass, look at me," she snarls, but he does not.

He's driving, eyes ahead. "Ma'am, if I may. Messenger said that Gaia was falling upon White Anchor. We escaped. For now. We cannot drive blind for more than a few minutes. We risk the entire Crawler dropping into an ice field. If we have to endure Gaia's presence any longer, then we need somebody who can have the viewport open without risking exposure. That's me. With you two in the med-bay, there is no exposure risk here. Ma'am. I think that I should drive."

It's the most Bear has ever heard him speak in one go, and already he has a hundred more questions. Bee curls her lips, and then sighs.

"I take your advice, Glass. Carry on."

"Thank you, ma'am."

Bee bends down and, with surprising strength, scoops Dusty into her arms like a wounded child. Bear follows her to the med-bay, still shaking.

As he leaves, he looks back to see that Glass is ok; but he can't see his face. Only the pool of blood at his feet from Dusty's wound.

As they leave and close the door, Glass opens the viewport, and Bear makes a mental note to ask Glass why exposure doesn't frighten him; because Bear doesn't know if he's ever been as frightened as he is right now.

It couldn't be that Glass has already survived exposure, he wonders? All of the little hints and clues that Glass has mentioned suddenly come back to him now, and he adds it to his pile of questions, wondering if he'll ever get to ask them.

Chapter 13

Dusty opens his eyes shortly after his first plasma infusion, lying flat on the same med-bay bed that Bear had sat Bee on earlier. Bee is holding the plasma bag high above him, while Bear monitors the flow into his veins.

"He's stirring," says Bear. "Dusty? Hey old fella, how are you feeling?"

Dusty groans. "Like I've been fucking *shot*, son."

"He's fine then," says Bee, and laughs out of pure relief.

"How bad is it?" asks Dusty, wincing.

"Abdomen shot, clean through. Nicked a blood vessel or six, judging by the bleeding, but your internal organs seem ok. We'll know soon if something important has burst, I guess. "

"That's reassuring," sighs Dusty. "What the hell happened? Is everybody ok? Where's Glass?"

"Driving," says Bee.

"Ah, smart – in case of exposure."

"It was his idea," she shrugs.

"Speaking of exposure," whispers Dusty as they lean in. "That glowing bastard; May tried to target him, and it frazzled her. She shut down – meant I had to manually drive in with my sensory gear on. He's got something of Gaia about him, I think. Never seen that before."

"He's covered in post-exposure runes," says Bear. "That could explain it. Looking at his palms hurt my eyes in the same way that the runes do."

Dusty gives a sad laugh of defeat. "Well, shit. I guess that's a thing now, then. The computer can't target him, you can't look at him –"

Bee smiles and pats Dusty's chest. "I guess we'll just have to settle for Glass hitting him with a machete, eh?"

Bear folds his arms and finds the courage to break a taboo. "Ok, I've got to ask," he says. "Why doesn't exposure bother Glass? What's his deal?"

"Why would exposure bother him?" asks Bee. "He's already survived it."

Bear closes his eyes in realisation, nodding. "I knew it. That makes sense. Right. *Right.*"

"He used to be Forestry," says Dusty. "That's all I'll tell you. The rest is Glass's story to tell, not mine."

"Yeah, like he'll talk to me," he shrugs.

"He might, given time."

The trio stay in silence for a minute as Bear works on his stitching, sewing Dusty together again. Bee breaks the silence in good humour.

"I guess I'm not Acting-Captain any more then?" she sighs melodramatically.

"Not any more, lass," he says. "So what's the situation in White Anchor? Some bastard debrief me."

Bee drops into her more professional tones. "Ok, so: White Anchor got the dreams last night, realised that the Devil was taking a stroll nearby. Whole town got into their sensory gear to tough it out, the Forestry got ready for a fight... and instead, the Dreamers showed up outside, gunned them down, got to the radio tower and, we suspect, played some of Hell's song down the microphone. Everybody who was hooked up to the radio waiting for an all-clear is gone, we reckon. Then Messenger – that's the bald bastard with the tattoos – said that he had called his demons down, and we had to fight for our lives. I think he wanted us alive, boss. Like, he *really* wanted us alive."

Bear interjects, at what he considers the most alarming point of the story. "Dusty, he said he could *call it*. Calling the phenomenon. How is that possible?"

Dusty frowns, both in pain and in confusion. "It's not. Old Gaia does as she damn well pleases."

"He also admitted that it was him that ambushed us," says Bee. "Y'know, when Red died. He knows us by name. He called me Beatrice."

"I'd have guessed as much," says Dusty. "And most folk know us by name, lass."

"But he doesn't wanna kill us, right Bear?"

"That's what he said," agrees Bear. "He wants to expose us. Wants us on his side, he says. He thinks that what happened in the South, y'know, when the phenomenon rolled in and the southerners had to flee north? He thinks that's going to happen to the Coastal Union, too. Clearly he subscribes to the Gaian apocalypse as his mode of thinking."

Dusty grunts, takes a breath, and tries to sit up. Bear almost tells him to lie down, but thinks better of it, and helps him sit up.

"Then we're still in danger," says Dusty. "First the ambush, then Forgehead, now White Anchor. If he *can* call Gaia down wherever he wants, then there's no limit to how many people he could expose."

"What are our orders, Captain?" asks Bee.

"We need to get up high, hail Union City, tell them everything. I can do it myself, but there's risks. It'd be a damn sight easier if we could get May back. I might open a channel with audio exposure risk – May can check for that herself."

"I could try fixing May?" asks Bear. "I'm decent with pre-Cataclysm stuff, just show me where to go." Dusty and Bee look at one another, raised eyebrows, and then a pointed look passes between them and Bear interjects.

"Ok," he stops them. "I've seen you two do that look a bunch of times – just tell me what you're thinking. If you think I can't do it or that I'll mess it up and break it then just tell me and -"

"It was Red that always maintained May," says Bee, and that

stops him.

Bear feels like he's just dropped a precious vase, and winces at himself. "Ok," he says. "Sorry, I didn't -"

"No, you're right. It's worth a shot," says Dusty, and pats Bear on the arm. "Bee will show you where May's console is."

Bee nods, and motions for Bear to follow her. As they leave, Dusty shouts after them.

"Bear? Bee?"

Bee turns around. "Captain?"

"What do you think will happen to White Anchor? Does it seem like they have a chance?"

Bee looks at her feet, bites her lip. Shrugs.

Dusty nods. He understands.

They both understand. This was no victory. This was barely an escape. Bear realises it too as the Crawler carries them over the snow fields. The phenomenon will still come to White Anchor – and that family in the basement, and all the other families, will be exposed to Messenger's great awakening, and for almost all of them it will be a death sentence.

Bear feels the weight of it all piling on his shoulders again, and is only saved from despair by the knowledge that he currently has a job right in front of him:

Fix May.

Bee sits on a metal chair behind Bear, in the lowest room of the Crawler. Beneath their very feet lies the treads and the snow, and the rumbling here is fierce and constant. The engines lie behind a door with a keypad, whilst Bear rests in front of a thin, A5 sized tablet. Wires lead from its dock into the walls. It is as though May's chamber is an antechamber to the engines. Bear wonders the extent to which May can protect anything – but given that she used to be a battleship, he has no doubts as to her capabilities.

"Pre-cataclysm tech," he says to himself, surprised by how quiet the engines are. "This is a tablet."

"That's May," says Bee. "She's in there."

"Always impresses me how much data our ancestors could fit into such a small space. So – how do we turn her back on?"

"She's already *on,*" says Bee.

"Of course," says Bear. "The problem is likely that all of her processing power is being used. She's trying to process what she saw when she targeted Messenger. That's how I think the phenomenon damages our minds – a total overload of sensory information. It gives *us* a migraine – it gives her, well, computer problems." He leans back and strokes his chin. When he touches the screen, it lights up and tells him in plain text:

Security Lockout In Progress.

"I've used pre-cataclysm laptops and stuff before – can't we just end her current process and let her drop it?"

"She isn't an old junker that you can just mess about with Bear," sighs Bee. "She's advanced military technology, remember?"

"Ah yeah – she was a battleship first, right?"

"Yeah. So it's probably a little different than just pulling up a task management window and restarting her."

Bear thinks again, trying to put himself in the minds of May's designers.

"Ok. Imagine that you're the captain of the most high-tech vessel ever made, and the bloody computer initiates a security lock. There must be some fail-safe to force May to wake up... She can hear everything we say when she's on, right?"

"Yeah, the Icebreaker is her body; we just have to say her name and she tunes in."

"So vocal commands are a thing. It makes sense that you'd keep your input channels open then, right? Even during a lockout, you want to record what people might be saying or what could be going on. Which means we can say things *to* her. She just can't currently speak back. I think."

"I mean, yeah – if you give any vocal commands though, you just get angry-May-voice telling you that it's pointless. If there were a way of telling her to wake up, she would know surely?" says Bee. "We've asked her how to avoid this, and she said she didn't have enough data to answer us."

Bear sidles his chair next to the tablet, as close as he can, and clears his throat.

"May: current status?"

The voice that comes out is May at her most robotic, with no emotion.

"ALL RUNTIMES ARE CURRENTLY BUSY. MAY IS OFFLINE."

Bear flinches. It seems to come from all around them, rattling the walls. "May," he tries, throwing things at the wall to see what sticks at this point. "Describe your currently running programs."

"ALL RUNTIMES ARE CURRENTLY BUSY. MAY IS OFFLINE."

Bear rolls his eyes, whilst Bee watches, absent mindedly rubbing her torn jawline. "I can see a pattern here," she whispers.

"May," he says, exasperated already. "State your serial number."

"ALL RUNTIMES ARE CURRENTLY BUSY. MAY IS OFFLINE."

"May, perform a factory reset."

"ALL RUNTIMES ARE CURRENTLY BUSY. MAY IS OFFLINE."

Bee puts her hand on his arm. "It's ok, even Red couldn't get her out of this lock-up. We'll wait it out as always."

Bear ignores her. "May, can you start up in safe mode?"

"ALL RUNTIMES ARE CURRENTLY BUSY. MAY IS OFFLINE."

Bee pats his arm again. "Bear, come on -"

He pulls his arm away from her. This is what his father left him: the stubbornness that will not allow him to ever leave a problem unsolved.

"May," he begins again. "What is your name?"

"ALL RUNTIMES ARE CURRENTLY BUSY. MAY IS OFFLINE."

"May, what is your purpose?"

"ALL RUNTIMES ARE CURRENTLY BUSY. MAY IS OFFLINE."

He can hear himself getting frustrated, and feels Bee's eyes on him. She seems worried.

"Bear, it's ok -"

"No," he turns to her. "It's not. May is broken, we need her online. I can do this alone, so if you've got other things that require attention, then go."

She purses her lips, and Bear can see that she is about to share a number of thoughts on the matter with him, most likely in a loud voice. To her credit, she stops herself, and lowers her voice instead.

"This isn't a test. You don't need to prove anything to us."

Bear takes a breath, and turns back to the tablet. "May," he tries. "Enter administrator mode."

"PLEASE STATE THE ADMINISTRATOR PASSWORD."

Bee sighs. "Bear for – wait-"

Bear is staring at the tablet as though it will disappear should he take his eyes off it. "Bee," he whispers without looking at her. "Go get Dusty."

"Aye-aye," she mutters, and dashes out of the room.

Dusty appears with a walking stick, wearing only his blood-soaked trousers. Bee holds a blood bag above his head, his drip still in his forearm, and his abdomen is a mess of red bandages. The colour is returning to him.

"Dusty you're -" Bear begins, and is taken aback at how vibrant Dusty already looks. "Bloody hell, you've gotten better pretty quick."

"I heal fast," he shrugs.

"Not bad for a..." Bear squints, guessing, "sixty year old guy?"

Dusty laughs. "Way off. Bee said you needed me?"

Bee stands behind him like a daughter, her strong arms hanging over him with the blood bag. He eases himself into a seat and she kneels on the floor beside him.

"Aye," says Bear. "Listen to this. May? Enter administrator mode."

"PLEASE STATE THE ADMINISTRATOR PASSWORD."

Dusty raises his eyebrows. "Now that's one we've never tried. And the admin password... Usually that's for when you want to change May's settings and preferences. Haven't heard that in a *long* time."

"Do you know the admin password?" asks Bear, on the edge of his seat.

He looks around at Bee. "I'll be honest, it's long gone from my memory. Can only think of one other person who might have kept a record of it."

"Oh for Christ's sake," whispers Bee. "Red? Right?"

"Red, yeah."

"So it's gone forever," she throws her hands up.

"Maybe not," says Dusty. "Red kept a journal, mostly for maintenance stuff I think; issues that he noticed, ideas to improve the Crawler. It'll be with the rest of his personal effects in his room."

Bee is staring at the floor, saying nothing.

"Could somebody bring me it?" asks Bear. "He might have written the admin password inside."

Dusty and Bee look at one another, and Bee bows her head.

"I think I should go and get it," she says, but there's a deep fear in her eyes that tears at Bear's heart.

"How about I do it?" he suggests, realising the weight of the situation. Though they have not answered him yet, Bear is already on his feet, making it easy for them. "Look, I'll do it, if you'll allow me. Don't worry."

"I guess," says Bee, reluctant but glad to be spared the pain. "Thanks, Bear. It's the third one on the habitat deck. Next to yours, actually."

Bear nods, and leaves.

Red's room is unlocked, and Bear steps into a small but colourful gallery of oil paintings and blueprints, paper and pencils, calculators and wiring, circuitry and tools. The paintings themselves immediately strike him, propped up against furniture on the floor as if Red was in the middle of moving house. There are four. Each one is a distinctive colour, and yet the tones of the faces painted seem to perfectly match those that they portray. The artist was talented.

The paintings are of the crew. Bee is painted in yellow and gold to match her hair, and behind her stands the sideways crucifix in black, like a shadow. She looks stern but quietly content in the portrait, as though aware of a joke that nobody else can know. There's no scar on her face here, and it strikes Bear as odd to see her without it.

Glass is in green, with the Gaian symbology of the world-tree stretching up behind him. He has his usual stern expression on, but something in the painting has given him an aura of protectiveness, his head tilted back to look down upon the viewer. Bear feels as if any room that this painting hung over would always be safe.

Dusty is in blue, with lighter metallic tones that match his grey beard and hair perfectly. He's the only one who is outright, genuinely smiling in his painting, and though the colours are cold, the expression is warm and paternal, as Bear has come to expect from Dusty.

Then there's the fourth one, painted in red of course. It's a man who Bear has never met before – but he recognises him as a kindred spirit. He has the air of curiosity to his eyes that Bear sees in the mirror. His hair is as orange as the sunset, thick and curled, and he wears spectacles and grows his beard out long like the fishermen do. He looks content. The background has little on it beyond the base layer of colour, and the beginnings of some equations. A rationalist, thinks Bear, just like him. Bear wonders if Red ever left any equations on the barbed wire at Forgehead's Forestry HQ. He wonders if Bee and Red clashed over their beliefs.

The painting, he realises, has been left unfinished.

And so it shall remain.

A pang of sadness hits him, for in these paintings he can see, can almost feel, the camaraderie that this crew must have all shared. He sees himself awkwardly stepping into Red's shoes, and suddenly feels an appreciation for Bee's unwillingness to just accept him – and the pain that the crew must have been in since.

Bear does the mental maths – it can't have been more than a week since the ambush where Red died. Barely any time to grieve at all, he thinks, judging by his own experiences. Bear joined them little more than a day after Red's death.

There's a black notebook on the desk, and Bear takes it and briefly flips through it. He feels like he could be reading his own notes back. He skips past the journal, the bits that look like diary entries, out of politeness. Those aren't his to read. He never knew the man.

In the back pages, however, are the kind of things that he can absolutely understand. There are theories expressed within that he recognises as though they were his own, simply written in a different hand. Ideas about the phenomenon, about the legitimacy of Gaian beliefs, all on the same pages as his thoughts on fuel efficiency, armour plating and weather prediction.

And there, on the back pages, circled with *IMPORTANT DO NOT FORGET* written next to it, is a jumble of letters and numbers.

"Well that looks about right," whispers Bear, and leaves with the book in hand. He closes the door quietly, out of respect, as though Red still lived there.

He stands again in the room with Dusty and Bee, holding the book open as they watch, the tablet still inert.

"May, enter administrator mode."

"PLEASE STATE THE ADMINISTRATOR PASSWORD."

Bear clears his throat. "1, A, 1, R, 2, W, 3, C, 5, W."

The same robotic voice comes back.

"PASSWORD ACCEPTED. ENTERING DEBUG MODE."

The screen on the tablet goes dark, and then lights up. Bear looks at Dusty and Bee, beaming, and finds them smiling to themselves.

He's done it; or, at least, opened the way towards doing it.

"Ok," says Bear. "Let's see what we've done."

He sits down at the tablet as the others scrape their chairs over towards him to watch. Bear flicks through menus and submenus, reading, taking in what he sees, talking as he does so.

"There's a *lot* going on here, but I think it stems from her targeting optics. She has software for spotting patterns, right? That's how she can pick out patterns from the visual or audio information, and decide things. For example, *this one is human, that's a gun, there are four dead bodies,* and so on. Very advanced stuff, even by pre-cataclysm standards." The other two are looking on, but say nothing. Bear has the floor, it seems. "Her exposure during phenomenal events has triggered this before, right?"

"Yeah," says Dusty.

"And it happened when she tried to target Messenger, who was *at the least* covered in post-exposure runes. It hurt us to look at him – it would have hurt her too. Her entire computational power, which is *considerable,* you can see here," and Bear points to a set of menus and processor reports. "This shows us that within a couple of seconds of trying to target him, she starts to think she's under attack by a cyberweapon or something. She shuts down to do an entire system purge, but she needs to know what's attacking her – she needs to log it. That's what hangs her up, she has to write an error report."

"...That's it? She's trying to write a debrief?"

"Well the error report is taking days to write because how the hell do you write a report on the phenomenon? What would it even say? How does she use numbers and letters to describe what her sensors pick up? This is something that *breaks* the human brain when we try to perceive it through even *one* of our senses. Maybe there aren't any words for it – certainly not for a computer. But she thinks she's *under attack,* Dusty, when she looks at it.*"

"You keep saying that, like it's important," says Dusty. "What are you thinking?"

"It might mean that there's something universal about the phenomenon, or even just the runes. If a computer has a similar breakdown to a person – but we can repair May afterwards... This might lead to treatments, perhaps an induced coma to stop the psychological disintegrations post-exposure, I need – can somebody get me some paper, hold on -"

Bear reaches around for his satchel and starts taking notes. Midway into his first page, Dusty leans over.

"Bear?"

"Hm?" he continues scribbling.

"Bear, can you turn her back on?"

"What? Oh, of course, sorry."

He flicks around a few menus on the tablet, and then hits the central button. It goes black, then lights up, then dulls.

"Just deleted the ongoing error report, that should be her. May?" he asks the walls of the Icebreaker. "You there?"

There's the sound of a well spoken woman yawning and stretching; a cute addition for an AI without a body, thinks Bear, and she even sounds like she's just woken up. Bear idly wonders if making herself an endearing character is part of May's programming.

"Well, good morning my lovelies -"

"May!" shouts Bee. "You're back!"

Dusty seems to glow, already forgetting his injury.

"I am darling, I am. Sorry to leave you all in the lurch there. Last I was aware, we were in some serious – oh, goodness, the Icebreaker has suffered serious, serious damage. We need immediate repairs, I'm surprised we're still going."

"Bee," says Dusty. "Work with May to pinpoint priority repairs and get them done, have Glass help you."

"Aye-aye Cap. What about Bear?"

They both look at Bear, in another world, scribbling his notes down. Bear knows that they are talking about him – he just cannot bring himself to stop putting his thoughts down. These are too important, he thinks; connections are forming in his head, ideas and theories are coming together.

"I think he's busy," says Dusty. "Drag him away if you really must."

She laughs. "I think I can manage on my own for now."

"Good," says Dusty. "May?"

"Oh Captain, my Captain?" she sings.

"Take the helm, tell Glass that you're back, and get us to the nearest suitable peak for radio."

"Of course, love."

"May?" asks Bear, emerging from his studious scrawling. "With Dusty's permission I'd like to change some of your operating parameters." He looks up at Dusty, who thinks for a second, then nods.

"Go ahead, my dear."

"If your sensors pick up a pattern that you interpret as a cyber attack, instead of trying to file an error report, just shut down for your safety's sake, ok? Then we can reactivate you when it's clear?"

"I can certainly do that, not a problem."

"There," says Bear. "Now she'll still shut off during phenomenal incursions to protect herself from damage – but she won't *stay* shut off for ages. We can reset her manually down here."

"Good work, lad," says Dusty, and pats him on the back. "You get stuck into those notes, and let me know if you come up with any other improvements."

"Of course," smiles Bear, just glad to be of use.

It is nightfall by the time the Crawler crests the peaks overlooking White Anchor. The Icebreaker rumbles to a juddering halt, the entire craft shaking as it stops. The top hatch flies open and the crew emerge, one at a time, in their white coats.

Dusty pushes the orange box of radio kit up first and starts wiring it in as the other three sit around him. Glass carries his rifle, and keeps watch as they set up, though Bear wonders how much watch one can keep in the crushing darkness. Despite the stars overhead, he can barely see his own hands in front of him.

"Can you guys even see in this light?" asks Bear.

He can practically hear the smile in Dusty's voice. "I can do this by feel if needed son, don't worry."

Bee turns to Bear. "No lights, that's the rule. At this time of night, we'd be giving away our location to anybody who's looking."

"Like Messenger and his cult?" he suggests.

"Exactly."

"Speaking of... might be worth checking in on White Anchor? While we're here?" suggests Bear, but both Bee and Dusty give him looks of pity in the darkness.

"Even if they survived, Bear," says Bee. "Their radio tower is compromised, remember? We'd get nothing back anyway. Nobody there to receive it."

He accepts defeat, and Dusty preps the balloon. His fingers are deft and sure despite the rest of them chattering in the frozen night. Bear has to remind himself that this old man took a bullet to the abdomen only six hours ago.

"May?" asks Dusty.

"Yes, dearest?" her voice is strange and tinny in the open air.

"I'm taking the balloon to full height. Keep me posted as we go, ok? As many details as you can get."

"Certainly."

Dusty produces a lighter, and their faces are briefly cast in orange as he lights it, cupping his hands around it to conceal their location. He holds his lighter under the balloon and it inflates rapidly, soaring, rattling the spool of wire as it drags it upwards, expanding all the while.

"Anything so far, May?"

"Nothing, Captain. Airwaves are pretty much dead apart from the usual interference. East of our position there's a significant disruption."

"Phenomenon," whispers Bear. "Right at White Anchor. It matches up. He *can* call it to him -"

"Birds," says Bee, loud enough to make them all jump. "Coming our way."

She points to the horizon and they see what she does. Flocks of blackbirds, silhouetted against the moon.

"I don't get it," says Bear. "They're just birds."

"That's because you're not a Scout, Bear. This is the kind of stuff that Scouts have to know. Those birds aren't nocturnal. Birds at night means they're spooked. They're coming from White Anchor, right Glass?"

"It would seem so," he nods.

"Confirming our fears," she says, and they all hear the resignation in her voice. "They're fleeing. White Anchor has gone under. Poor bastards."

Glass pats her shoulder. "Perhaps we drove off the Dreamers. Do not surrender to despair just yet, Beatrice."

Bear raises an eyebrow. It's the most sincere, and kindest, thing that he has heard Glass say. Maybe the huge golem is human on the inside after all, he thinks.

"Balloon has hit maximum altitude," May announces. *Deploying."*

There's a sound like leathery wings above them and Bear flinches out of instinct – then the birds pass overhead, and Dusty slaps his back. HE can hear Bee smirking in the dark.

"Relax, son," says Dusty. "May can see more in the dark than we can, and she's keeping watch. Aren't you, May?"

"I am always paying attention to our surroundings in case danger emerges."

"See?" he smiles. "Now, May: Get me Union City on the line."

"Of course." There's a silence, and they wait as May works at her task. *"Serious distortion still, Dusty."*

"Still? That's been there since earlier today. No storm stays put for that long, does it?"

"There's precedence, certainly. Could be that the storm is moving towards us."

"Ah well, wouldn't that be great? Are there any weather reports circulating the air waves?"

"None – Forgehead and White Anchor haven't reported their local weather for days, obviously. Union City depends on them to get meteorological readings of the region – we're functionally blind."

"A storm would be the last thing we need right now," says Dusty. "Scrub the interference and get me Union, girl."

"I'm trying, Cap. Scrubbing the signal, compensating."

They wait, Glass and Bee watching now. There's a tension that Bear can't place – he feels it himself. He's on edge, waiting for something to go wrong. Perhaps the birds have unsettled him, he tells himself.

"We're through, Cap. Automated response, transmitting…"

They all freeze. Everybody knows what an automated response means, from any town. They hear Marge's voice, unmistakable from before, speaking through the radio.

"Automated message," she says, her voice firm but unable to hide the fear underneath. "Union City has experienced shared dreaming, and is currently in lockdown. The Forestry are hard at work, preparing our defences and keeping us safe. Please stay away until the all-clear is sounded. Union City is currently unsafe to approach. God and Gaia bless us." There's a pause. "Pray for us. This message will repeat."

The message repeats, but May drops the volume so that there's just Marge whispering through the speakers, repeating the same phrases that have just turned their blood to ice and dropped their hearts into their stomachs.

Bear doesn't know if he's ever felt so suddenly alone, so isolated from safety and warmth, as he does right now. He looks at Dusty, a hunched figure in the dark, and cannot find any reassurance there. Nobody says anything. There is only static, interspersed with Marge's voice. When Dusty finally breaks the silence, his voice is hoarse.

"May," he says. "Emergency channel, broadcast a code red. Hail all Crawlers, order them to stop and set up radio beacons. Then tell them that Union City is under direct attack. We are needed. Gather thirty kilometres east of Union, we'll ride to their defence with all four Crawlers once we're together."

"Hailing. Standby."

Bear's mind is racing. "Dusty, if we have an emergency channel to use, could we warn -"

"It's comms that only the Crawlers use," says Bee, cutting him off. "Pre-cataclysm stuff. Reserved for emergencies only. Nobody else would hear us, anyway."

Dusty holds a hand up to silence them, as though he's concentrating. They all listen to the static as May tries to hail the other Crawlers.

"Captain," says May, and they can practically hear the worry in her voice too. *"Captain, there's no response. We're past the expected response time, they should have given us at least a ping-back."*

"Wait another minute," says Dusty, nodding.

"Why wouldn't they respond?" asks Bee. "The hell is wrong with them? It's a *code red.*"

"Maybe we weren't the only Crawler that got ambushed," says Dusty, as it all falls into place for him. He sounds as though he's reading out a eulogy. "Shit. Messenger has been ahead of us the entire time – what's to say the others weren't ambushed too?"

"Surely not," says Bee. "It's the Crawlers for Christ's sake, you can't just shoot them up, they've got more armour and weapons than pre-cataclysm battle tanks. Besides, we'd have *at least* received emergency distress signals if they were in real danger -"

"Unless it all happened under Gaia's presence," says Dusty. "No radio out of that. Just like White Anchor – Crawler's would be totally contained while the crew used sensors and radar to pilot through it. They don't have May like we do. If somebody could sneak up on them, cut a hole in the side, trap them, expose them... Isn't that what Messenger wants?"

Bear feels himself growing nauseous. He no longer feels safe out here, under the open sky. He thinks he can hear wings, but he isn't sure.

"Doesn't every crew have someone like Glass?" he asks. "Someone who can stay aware during exposure risks..?"

"People like me are very, very rare," says Glass, breaking his usual mute rule to answer Bear. "So no. Most crews do not have an exposure survivor."

"Dusty..? It's been three minutes. No response."

Dusty doesn't move. The group fall silent – even May shuts off the static from the radio. Dusty raises his clenched fist to his mouth and bites down on his knuckle as if to stop himself from screaming, and faces away from the group for a moment.

"Dusty?" whispers Bee, stepping forward. "Captain?"

He holds his hand up to stop her, and they all stand in the darkness, completely alone under the freezing night sky.

The wind starts to pick up around them.

"Ok," says Dusty, turning around, wiping his eyes clear. "We go to Union. It's where he's going to head next, right? So we beat Messenger there and we warn them, we get their defences ready and we help them ride this out. When Messenger turns up, he'll have hundreds of flamethrowers pointing back at him – and us, too. May, will the Crawler hold together until then?"

"It should do, provided we don't -" May suddenly goes quiet, and the wind howls in the silence. Snow starts to fall.

"May?" asks Dusty.

"Captain," her voice has dropped the charm. She's a soldier now. *"I am sensing* [DATA REDACTED], *north of our position and coming our way, estimated time of impact: two minutes. It wasn't a storm, Captain."*

Dusty throws the hatch open without another word.

"Everybody into the Crawler, sensory gear at the ready, *now!"*

The crew scurry down into the warm light as the snow starts to whip around them, and the birds caw and circle overhead. Bear swears that he can hear something like crunching glass in the distance, and whispering on the wind.

He questions if the birds are whispering, if he can really hear them calling his name, before dismissing such nonsense. No, he thinks. He is sure he heard them. Something is calling his name, the birds, calling to him -

Then Bee slaps him on the shoulder and pushes him onto the ladders, as Dusty begins barking orders as he takes his last place on the ladder.

"May, what are our chances? We're low on armour, how exposed are we going to be -"

"There are four open breaches that constitute a major exposure risk. I can seal the doors leading to the habitation deck, I advise that you all take cover in a single bunk room, from where I can focus our defences."

"I will keep watch," says Glass. "If we are in one room, I can cover the door."

Bear is confused as he is bundled along the corridors, and Dusty slams the hatch above them.

"Cover the door?" shouts Bear. "Cover it from what?"

Bee turns around as she drags him down the corridor. "From whatever slashed my face open. We're going through the eye of the storm lad, come on!"

"But I thought we were safe in here?"

"Don't know if you noticed," she shouts as they run. "Messenger's boys blew a couple of holes in us. We're compromised. We could be boarded."

Boarded. The word fills him with dread. Bear has studied the phenomena his entire life, trying to understand it. Now, out here, without the protection of the Forestry and no help coming, no cavalry on its way, he feels a fresh appreciation for just how helpless he is against it.

Bear is terrified – but that doesn't stop him from thinking.

"Wait," shouts Bear. "What if this is Messenger – he registers on my sensor as a phenomenon! What if he's planning an ambush."

"Already considered it," says Dusty as they bundle into Bear's bunkroom. "I'm not taking any risks. May?"

"Captain?"

Dusty slams the door shut and turns the handle, locking them in, and begins handing out the sensory blockers.

"May, I am lifting all restrictions on weaponry. Fire everything we've got the second we hit the danger zone, and keep us at full speed. We'll blow right through it. Don't even let it get close."

"Sir, I will be unable to target anything effectively; with my sensors down for protection from exposure -"

"I don't care what you're shooting *at,* love, just keep fucking firing. Spin up the napalm canisters and set us to full speed. We aren't taking a single risk here."

"Aye sir. Sensors tell me we're closing."

"Everybody hold hands," says Dusty, and sits down with his blindfold already on, his hands out. The room is not compromised – not yet, but they can't take that chance. As Bear puts his hand in the cold palm of Dusty and the warm, thin fingers of Bee, he sees Glass unsling his rifle, and a length of rope.

"Bear," shouts Dusty. "You been through one of these before?"

"I mean," he stutters, "I've went into runed areas, and I've had to endure days of -"

"No but have you ever actually been inside this thing?"

Bear's stomach drops. "No."

"Whatever you do," screams Dusty as the noise gets louder. Something is scraping the outside of the Crawler, like a thousand tree branches. It sounds like the flock of birds are trying to get in. "Under no circumstances take your gear off until you get the all-clear, or Glass removes it, ok? Under *no* circumstances. No matter who asks you to do it. No matter what you hear. Do you understand?"

Bear nods, and Glass starts moving behind him. Bear holds off on his blindfold out of curiosity.

He watches Glass tie himself by his belt to the bunk, and brace his legs as though they're about to hit a hurricane. His rifle is trained on the locked metal door, and his face is pale white as though he's going to be sick. He unhitches his machete from it's sheath on his belt, and lays it on the bed beside him.

"I'm ready," he says, and Bear realises that he's speaking to something that Bear cannot see. He is addressing the storm.

They all put their earphones in and Bear slides his blindfold down over his eyes. He fights the urge to be sick; he can feel himself shaking, feel the panic and the nausea gripping him.

Bee is whispering something – a prayer, he realises. They hold one another's hands all the tighter. Whatever Bee thinks of him, in that moment he knows that they are both grateful for a hand to hold.

"It's here, hold on everybodddyyyyy -" May's voice wraps into a long, distorted screeching, and Bear feels the pressure inside his

skull. He hits play, and Beethoven's Symphony Number Five in C Minor blasts into his ears, drowning out the noise.

He knows fine well that he's gritting his teeth and screaming at nothing, but he can't help it. Every sway and jolt that the Crawler makes as it speeds over the snow throws his balance off. He cannot tell which way is up, he cannot remember which hand is Dusty and which hand is Bee.

He loses his frame of reference. Space changes so suddenly that he cannot tell where he is. He is weightless.

They hit the phenomenon.

Chapter 14

Bear's music drowns out the worst of it, sparing his sanity. He feels his body sway backwards and forwards, and then

he's falling

vertigo -

screaming

"Glass? Bee? Dusty?"

nothing

wind, there's wind and

rain, black rain, soaking him. Trumpets. There are trumpets sounding, too loud, his ears are in agony, just

got to

need to take the pressure off my ears, just take them out

no

no, under no circumstances Dusty said

he sees black tendrils in his vision, he can see through his own eyelids, through the blindfold

There is no way to stop seeing

drifting through all of them, he can see the room perfectly why can he see, shouldn't he have his blindfold on? Wait a minute

the tendrils go through their hearts, black tendrils,

black rain, through all of them

TAKE IT OFF

one of the walls has cut Bee in half, she doesn't mind but it looks so

look at me

they've hung Dusty upside down, he's burning, they're taking out his

now my bones are cold

look at me boy   black tendrils inside of them

Can a soul die?

shapes

within shapes, over and forever

dead insects cover the floor, crunches as he steps on them

going to be sick, he says, and eyes

his eyes are sealing up

wax

never open his eyes again

he is being stood on, he is crunching under the pressure, popping like a tiny bug

who's singing?

singing? Who is

LOOK AT ME

no directions, no context

metal wires inside his bones, everything is pulling him apart

eyes sewn shut,   can't breathe,   pressure on his heart, vomit in his mouth, blood

EYES ARE ITCHING, TAKE THE BLINDFOLD OFF AND LOOK AT ME

hands on him,

hands everywhere, pulling him

DOWN INTO THE EARTH TO JOIN YOUR FATHER

forest, trees, every tree is the same, far as he can see

how can he see

blindfold,

earplugs

TAKE THEM OFF

LOOK AT ME

hands

one set of hands too many, who else is holding his hand, how many hands does he have?

Red's hand, he's holding Red's hand now and

There is an oak tree atop a hill, framed by the setting sun.

A man lives beneath it. No – not a man.

But it looks like a man.

A hand bursts from the ground amidst the roots, clawing for freedom – and Bear recognises it. He wants to reach down and pull the hand, pull the creature out of its prison.

Something does not feel right.

Bear breathes, and

And

and

He breathes.

Vertigo is gone. Darkness is coming in, safe and warm. Familiar. Like sleep. Blindfold still on. Fabric on his head, music in his ears.

Two hands in his. Bee squeezes his hand.

All Clear, comes the hand signal on his chest, and someone pulls his ear plugs and blindfold away. Glass is kneeling in front of him, and briefly checks him over. Their eyes meet.

"You ok?" asks Glass.

Bear wants to nod, but instead he throws up, and Glass takes it as a yes. Bear watches him wake the other two, who are sitting cross legged and shaking, trembling. As Bear looks around the room, two things take him and drive that cold fear back into him.

First, is that Glass is wounded. There's a thin laceration from his collarbone down his t-shirt, where the fabric has split and been stained with blood. His machete is in his hand, and his rifle's bolt is locked back.

He's fired every round in the magazine.

The door itself is another story.

It's lying on the floor, covered in thin lacerations as though razor wire had threshed through it. It's bent inwards in the centre from whatever force blew it off its hinges. Almost a foot thick metal, and it's been cut like butter and crumpled like foil.

As Glass gently wakes the others and checks on them, Bear turns to him.

"Glass? Glass, what happened -"

Glass turns and shakes his head as he helps Dusty and Bee out of their gear.

"You are safe. Count your blessings. Thank whatever you pray to."

Bee pulls her knees up and hugs them, her other hand bringing her crucifix up to her lips as she kisses it and crosses herself.

"I knew God would see us through," she says, getting her breath back. "I knew. I knew."

Dusty shakes his head. "I'd be trusting Glass if I were you, lass. You ok, big guy?"

Glass starts reloading his rifle. "It's a superficial wound," he says. "Gaia does not reclaim us today."

Bear notes that there is a strange residue on the blade of his machete.

"Glass, did you actually hit something with that?" He nods, and Bear has to force himself not to overreact. He is lost for words. "Seriously? Nobody has ever thought to put that stuff under a microscope?"

Dusty shrugs. "Nobody wants to risk exposure, son. It's from something anomalous – might have the same effects. You want to press your eyes up against it and take a look, you be my guest."

"Well what if Glass were to look at it and just *tell* me what he sees under the scope?"

Bee leans in, as though telling a secret she is tired of telling. "Bear, maybe we don't *want* to know, yeah?"

Bear stands up in surprise. "Ok, ok – but I do? Glass, come on – even a vague description? What attacked us? What was it? Humanoid? Is there something predatory in there?"

Glass keeps loading his rifle as the rest of them get to their feet. The Crawler is still moving beneath them.

"Glass? Glass?" asks Bear, and when he gets no response he stands up. Glass looks at him, sensing the fire that's building in him. Everybody in the room looks at him now. "Glass, this shit is the greatest threat that anything on this planet has ever faced, and you're just sitting there with information that could turn it all around and you're not going to say a fucking thing? What's wrong with you?"

Glass doesn't move, doesn't say anything. He looks at Dusty, who gives him permission with a nod of his head.

"You wouldn't understand," he mutters. "You don't want to know."

If a pin were to drop, everybody would hear it.

"Are you dense?" asks Bear, taking his jacket off, feeling himself about to overheat as his anger grows. He must be bright red in the face, he realises, as he throws the jacket at the corner of the room. "Have you got fucking brain problems? I've studied this thing my entire life, you don't know if I'll understand! You've got no idea! Try me!"

Glass looks at Dusty, but this time it is Dusty asking permission – and Glass who nods.

Dusty looks between the two, then whispers something to Bee. Both of them leave the room without a word. Bear watches them go without a word, half-expecting Glass to hit him with the rifle. Once their footsteps fade into the distance, Glass lays the rifle down on the bed beside him, safety on.

"Are you sure you want to know, Bear?"

"Yes."

"Are you absolutely sure? Because I cannot un-tell you. And once you know, going through a patch like that will never be the same. Because you'll know what you're going through."

Bear feels himself shaking. "I know lots of messed up stuff, I can handle it. What is it that's inside the phenomenon?"

Glass nods, and wrings his hands together, takes a deep breath. "When we are near Gaia, she forces us to face ourselves. It is you that you see. You, that tries to kill you."

Bear feels every hair on his body stand up. "Me?"

"We all see ourselves. I have asked others. I have seen *my* self. If Bee or Dusty were to look, they would see *them* selves. I do not know what May sees. I don't know the science. There are many of me, and Bear; I recognise them. I know them, and they know me. They want to take us away, replace us. They want to take us to wherever they are. I have the distinct impression that they... feed upon us, perhaps. I have seen them infest a person. They climb in through the eyes, through the ears. They do not exist in the way that you and I do, I think. They are not really here. But they want to be."

"Like other versions of us?"

"The worst versions, it seems. Wherever Gaia moves, she lets them through. They come with her. And they reach through into this place, reaching for me – for us. When they come through, they look like long black cracks in the air. If you have been exposed, you can see what is really there. Thin dark tendrils that feel for warmth and light. They cut through almost everything. They only look like us from certain angles. There are flashes, moments where you can see them clearly. They are very hard to shoot, but a bullet will kill them. From most other angles, they are too thin to hit. Very few things can stop them. They'll cut through steel like it's nothing."

Bear is trying to remember this, all of it, unable to believe that he is actually getting an answer to the question. He needs a notebook. Glass continues.

"Worse: everything inside Gaia's aura has too many angles, and distance ceases to have meaning. Everything keeps moving. Space doesn't matter. Like in a dream. You just shoot what you can, and *some* rare metals will stop the tendrils," he hefts his machete, with thick parts of it cut away by the threat he is describing, eating into the blade. "This is made of a pre-Cataclysm metal. Same metal as the Crawler's armour. It does better than most metals. Asides that, it doesn't seem to like fire. Metal and fire, and explosives. We don't have anything else."

Glass is shaking, Bear realises, and that's what he takes away from this more than anything else. He's just as human as the rest of them. He's terrified, just like they are.

"Sometimes they get in, sometimes they don't. I believe that is what causes exposure. An overwhelming of the human mind. I do not know what protects somebody – only that seeing them is enough. Once you see them, they see you, and they will not leave you alone."

"Was that what happened when you were exposed?"

"We are not going to discuss what happened when I was exposed," says Glass, and there can be no arguing with his tone. "Suffice to say; I saw them. They saw me. I experienced a lifetime of *something,* a connection to something larger, but the experience did not destroy me. I do not know why it destroys most people. They do not seem to care that I survived. They still try to climb down my throat."

"And the others don't know this?"

"They know some details. They don't *want* to know. The nightmarish visions are bad enough. Things screaming into your head. I think it is these apparitions that tell us to take off our masks. They try to climb inside of us, and when they do, they turn us into another breach from which their siblings can crawl. It makes more of them. Then they fight one another, usually."

Bear does not know how to respond properly to the news that

he is hearing. Glass can see the damage beginning to take a toll on Bear, and pats him on the shoulder.

"Ignorance is bliss, yes? The others know that whatever it is, it shakes me up, and that's enough for them. If they knew that something from another place wanted to turn them inside out, maybe they wouldn't have the bottle to endure this."

Bear sees Glass's hands trembling. He's lost a fair bit of blood. "Are you ok, man?" he asks the giant.

"It certainly raises questions about existence, does it not?" asks Glass, staring past Bear. "What are they, exactly? When victims are exposed to the singing, is it those strange doppelgangers that are calling to us? Why are they so hateful? What happens to those they kill?"

Bear can see that Glass does not like to ponder these questions – even to a man of science like himself, these are questions that he is nervous to answer. He is not sure that he will like what he will find.

"Glass?" asks Bear, pointing at the blood dripping on to the floor. "Are you *ok?*"

Glass shakes his head. "I'm a bit shook up, I'll be fine."

"Let me look at your wound -"

"I'll be fine."

"Glass. Infection kills people – let me treat it. We need you up and working."

Glass raises an eyebrow. "It's 'we' now, is it?"

Bear feels the sting, but accepts it. He shrugs. "Yeah, it's 'we'. Forgehead might be gone, same with White Anchor, now maybe Union; and the other three Crawlers are gone too? I don't see that we've got anybody else we can rely on. It's just us out here."

Glass nods begrudgingly. "Point taken," he says. "Ok, doc. Patch me up."

Bear nods, and together they head to the medical bay. His head is spinning from this revelation, but he is more upset by the new questions it has spawned. He had not expected such a human-centered answer. Perhaps the phenomenon defies explanation, and Glass's experience is simply the feeble human mind trying to come to terms with the infinite. A connection to something greater, Glass had said; but to what? What does this tell him about reality? Doppelgängers from where? What do they want? Are they predators? Extra-dimensional entities, perhaps? What does this say about the universe? Is this a confirmation of a multiversal theory, of higher dimensions layered above this one?

Bear is overwhelmed. Lost. In his desperation, he decides to focus on the task at hand: keeping the crew alive. When in doubt, his father always told him, find some work to do. A busy mind is a quiet mind. Which may explain why Bear has worked relentlessly since the day his father left him.

Bee and Dusty are already in there, as Bee changes the bandages around Dusty's abdomen. Bear gets a good look at his wound as they enter and greet one another, the whole crew together again. Dusty, it seems, is mid-conversation with May.

"Do we have enough armour plating in storage from Forgehead?"

"We do love, yes."

"How much ammo did we use up?"

"Almost all of it. We have railguns and the ballistic weaponry online, but I will be trying to conserve ammunition, in anticipation of further danger."

"So we're out of napalm," sighs Dusty.

"I'm afraid so, love. Enough for a little bit of a fire but not much else. As you asked, I burned it up getting us through [DATA REDACTED]."

"Ok crew – we can spare maybe an hour tops – we'll all pitch in to get as many repairs done as we can. May, can you prioritise the repair work for us and we'll hit the most important stuff first?"

"Of course love, just let me know when. I'll keep us on towards Union City in the meantime, till we find a safe spot to stop."

Bear leans in for a peak at Bee's handiwork. Dusty's wound has almost entirely closed over already.

"That's healing pretty damn fast," says Bear.

"I'm young at heart," says Dusty, and covers the wound as though self conscious. "I heal fast. Glass tell you what you asked about?"

"He did -"

Dusty holds up a hand. "Keep it to yourself."

"I understand," says Bear, and turns to Glass. "Just patching the big guy up."

Glass nods his approval to Dusty, having seemingly returned to his usual mute status for now. Bear makes a mental note to ask him about that too, at some point.

"You doing ok, Bear?" asks Bee as she starts bandaging Dusty up.

"I mean – all things considered, yeah I'm doing ok. Feels like we're up shit creek with no napalm, but I'm alive I guess."

"Chin up soldier," she gives a grim smile. "You've just walked through Hell and made it out in one piece."

"Eh, I've got Beethoven to thank for that. And Glass. And May."

She shakes her head, and taps the crucifix sitting outside her shirt. "And Him."

"Yeah, thank him for me too will you?" he relents, letting her have this.

"Oh he knows," she winks, and Bear rolls his eyes. She pats Dusty's bandages. "Finished, Dusty. Table's all yours, Bear."

Bear asks Glass to sit on the table, and hopes that focusing on the medical work will distract his mind from the five hundred questions that it are spawning every second. He finds no such luck. As the team chatter amongst themselves, throwing out suggestions and tactics for when they hit Union City, Bear is focused only on what he has just learned:

That there are life forms of some kind within the phenomenon. Versions of themselves? That Glass has survived exposure, knows what it looks like, feels like. He has to know more.

Bear has to update his notes, apply this new knowledge to his prior assumptions and see what changes. He has to interview Glass properly.

Bear is thinking about spaces beyond the third dimension. He exists in three dimensional space, but is moving through time, the fourth dimension, in a straight line, in one direction. What could come above that? The space in which all possible things reside, perhaps. He remembers speculating over whiskey and a log fire with his father, talking about such nonsense.

But, he thinks: maybe this is a breakthrough. Gaia distorts space, they *know* that, he can prove it; it's how the sensors work. Space and time are linked, so what else might Gaia affect?

Gaia, he sighs, laughing at himself. The *phenomenon,* he corrects his own thinking.

He has so much to do. So much to learn. He hasn't even touched on Glass's experience with exposure yet; he adds that to the list. He only hopes that the world will hold itself together for long enough that he can answer those questions – and that is what really scares him: the thought of getting so close, and never knowing.

"Dusty," May interrupts his thoughts. *"Darling, I've prioritised the repairs. I'll park us somewhere with good visual cover, shall I?"*

"That would be great, love," he tells her. "We'll go team handed, get it done as quick as possible – Bear, you nearly done?"

Bear swabs the last of Glass's wound and winds a bunch of bandages around it, sighing.

"It'll do, I suppose," he says.

"Thank you," whispers Glass.

But Bear is already back in his own head, a thousand questions spinning over and over again.

"Then come on," says Dusty. "Repair time. Glass, grab the tools."

"Aye, sir," they both echo Dusty's words, and follow him outside as Glass pulls his bloodstained, torn t-shirt back on with little mind to its condition. Bear finds his head in the clouds – he's struggling to concentrate on anything except the questions that he has.

He needs some answers before they ride into another battle.

Crawler Four, the Icebreaker, lurks amongst the trees like a hidden giant. Here, atop the peaks that border off Union City from the rest of the Coastal Union, the trees are ancient, gargantuan things, spaced well apart and almost perfectly uniform.

As they step out onto the crunching snow in the fresh light of morning, Dusty tells them that the uniformity of the trees is because the forest is man-made, and hundreds of years old. To Bear, the trees seem far too big to be any younger than a thousand years, but he shrugs; trees are one area he has little knowledge in. Perhaps the phenomenon touched them – perhaps time has been different for them. He feels as though there is no frame of reference for anything anymore.

Glass and Bee carry sheets of metal, welding masks, and backpacks filled with kit that will power the cutting and welding tools for repair work.

From the outside, Bear finds a new appreciation for the quality of the Crawler's armour. The old girl is hanging in pieces. Gunshot dents number in the thousands, and there are thick black scorch marks and crumpled metal where the grenade launchers met their target. Further up, above the treads, there are long thin lacerations just like the ones on the door to Bear's bedroom.

Bear can't help but visualise the crew huddled as black tendrils pour through cracks in space towards them. He looks over at Glass, whose face is hidden behind the welding mask, and wonders what else the man has seen.

So many questions, Bear thinks; so many things that he had always wondered, always wanted to know, to ask – and here is a man who has seen it all and yet is reluctant to speak of it. Aside Glass, the only person who can speak with any authority on the matter is Messenger, who claims to have survived exposure.

There is, of course, one other person he's aware of who could talk of their experiences with exposure – but that's his late father, with his long sheaf of rambling from post-exposure psychosis before his death. Bear remembers those notes, stuffed in his satchel, and shudders. They might discuss what one sees looking into the phenomenon – but Bear still does not know if he can ever bring himself to read those pages. They contain the complete annihilation, neuron by precious neuron, of his father.

He heard his voice, he is sure – in the phenomenon, demanding his attention. Again and again, his dreams are filled with his exposure-sick father, screaming for Bear's mother – herself dead for as many years as Bear has been alive. That begging for the end, that desperate attempt to hang on to his sanity and to make sense, still resonates years later.

He still isn't sure if his father chose to leave the world by exposure, and leave him alone or not – and he has buried that wound deep enough that it might be too late to reopen it. He has learned to live with it. Nobody, he thinks, should have to see their father as though he were a child.

He realises that he is staring at Glass, and the rest of the crew are staring at him. Someone is talking, and he isn't responding.

"Uh, sorry," he snaps himself out of it. "What?"

"I said," says Dusty, folding his arms, "are you going to help us or what?"

"Uh sure, sure," he mumbles, "just tell me what you need."

"Help Glass with that sheet metal, we'll weld it over the breaches."

"Isn't that a little slapdash?" asks Bear, as the Crawler's skin takes on the appearance of a patchwork quilt of various metals.

"It'll have to be, we don't have time," says Dusty. "We'll make proper repairs once we're back home in Union. Till then, I want us able to endure another run through Gaia's worst if we have to."

There it is again – one mention of Gaia, of what they experienced, and Bear's mind is off wandering. He absent-mindedly picks up the sheet of metal and hefts it over to Glass.

Glass turns around and lifts it, welding mask still down, sitting sideways on the tread itself. He feels a faint hostility from Glass as he approaches, as though Glass can already tell what's going through his head.

The friendly giant who had looked him in the eye and answered all of his questions earlier is gone again, replaced with the golem who does not speak without permission. Bear considers dropping it, giving up his questions – but he knows he'd never forgive himself if he doesn't take his chance to ask everything on his mind.

"Glass," begins Bear, and Glass fires up the welder. Sparks fly across the snow. He shouts over the din. "I need to ask you some more questions." Glass says nothing; keeps welding – but Bear can see his head move as he talks, and knows he's hearing him despite the racket. The other crew members are out of sight now, attending to their own repairs on the other side of the Crawler.

"Glass? I know you can hear me. It's ok to talk – I've got a list of questions that are bugging me, things I need to know before I can put them aside."

The welding noises stop, and Glass lifts his mask. Bear sees his stern and unforgiving gaze beneath the mask, and Glass shakes his head, putting his mask back down.

"Oh come on," pleads Bear. "You've already helped so much – but I didn't get to ask anything about exposure. I've studied it my entire life, Glass, please. If we're riding into something life-threatening then I might never get a chance to ask you again."

Glass continues welding, and after a while he stops, lifts his mask, looks at his handiwork, and sighs. He turns to Bear, and just as Bear expects him to speak, he gestures to a sheet of metal. Bear rolls his eyes and hands it to him, huffing and puffing as he heaves it over. Glass takes it in one hand and angles it against the armour, pulling his welding mask down.

Bear climbs up onto the tread beside Glass. He knows that Glass is acting differently for a reason. He's a straightforward person, black and white. He was fine with telling Bear about the experience of being inside the phenomenon; yet the second that actual exposure comes up, he clams up again.

Perhaps, thinks Bear, his exposure was traumatic. It usually is, he understands. With some apprehension, Bear realises that he's going to have to put Glass in an emotional state to get anything out of him. Bear doesn't like to do this, but he'll gladly take a few punches if it means that Glass gives him *something* he can work with. He has to play the long game.

Bear watches him. Glass lifts the welding torch to return to work, but as he kneels to start welding, Bear jumps up and – without stopping to think – slaps it out of his hand. It clatters to the ground.

Silence.

Glass removes the mask and looks up at him, still kneeling, but he doesn't react further. He seems to be waiting for Bear to do something. He remains silent.

"You don't want to answer my questions?" asks Bear. "Fine. As long as you can *tell* me why you won't. Because the people of the Coastal Union are entitled to some answers too. If you know something that might help me form a protective measure, or a cure, then you have a duty to those people. *Why* won't you help me?"

Glass shakes his head, gritting his teeth. He picks up the welding torch, and Bear slaps it out of his hand again. Glass twitches, almost reacts, and Bear steps closer.

"Why won't you help me?" repeats Bear, and Glass places his welding mask on the ground and stands up. He's a head taller than Bear and twice as wide, but Bear is too deep now to back down. "Why do you need permission to talk? Is that it? Is that something to do with it? Can I give you permission to talk? Does it have to be Dusty? You've spoken without permission before -"

Glass picks up his mask as if about to strike Bear, and Bear shies back. Glass roars in anger and throws it down into the snow. He grabs Bear by the shoulders.

"Stop this. Stop it. Now."

Bear meets his eyes, hard though it is. "No," he manages, shaking. "You want to hit me, go for it, but I won't stop asking until I get a good answer."

Glass snarls and tightens his grip, but he lets go without warning and Bear nearly collapses. Glass begins climbing down from the Crawler treads, and Bear sees his intention. He's going to get Dusty; he'll try to avoid Bear, to swap work partners, whatever is required.

Bear is going to have to really push him if he wants to know.

"Was your exposure painful?" he shouts after Glass, and Glass keeps walking, deaf to him. He dials it up a bit. "Who died, Glass?" Still nothing. Glass is getting away. Bear takes a deep breath. "It was your fault, right?"

Glass stops.

There we are, thinks Bear. That did it.

He turns and stares across the snow at Bear, who still stands on the Crawler's track. Glass is daring him to continue; he has violence in his eyes. Bear has to press the moment while he has his attention. Bear climbs down to face him.

"Because you know, if you feel guilty about that? Then you're killing even *more* people by refusing to help me. You're letting people die from exposure when, maybe, I could prevent it."

"You could prevent it?" asks Glass, breathing heavily now. He starts pacing back towards Bear, and Bear suddenly fears for himself. "You?"

He suddenly feels his confidence disappear as Glass approaches, furious.

"Yeah," he manages.

"You, who have no faith, have no understanding, who hasn't seen *any* of the things I've seen, *you* could save people from exposure?"

"I can try, Glass," he says, and has to stop walking backwards – he's at the edge of the Crawler tread. Glass puts his hand above Bear's head, slamming it into the metal tread-guard, bearing down on him.

"You'll stop Gaia? All by yourself?"

"Yes," says Bear, and Glass is in his face now. Glass grabs him by the collar, and Bear holds on to his wrists.

"With some microscopes and some sensors and a calculator, right? You'll just work out how to stop Old Mother Gaia, the being that encompasses all things. Right? You want to know the truth, Bear?"

"Y-Yes."

"She can't be stopped," he whispers, and Bear realises that the welding has stopped elsewhere. The others have heard them. "Do you even know what you're talking about? You're talking about the centre of creation, the bonds between all things past, present and future. You're talking about infinity, Bear, about a concept! Maybe you ask me some questions, and maybe I answer them as best I can, but what then? You won't have a clue what I'm talking about. Even if you do, what then? Your science does not apply to these things. You are a man of the material, trying to understand the immaterial. What will you do with my answers?"

"I'll work out how to protect people – or how to stop her."

"You can't. There's no way to stop her. You can't stop time, you can't protect people from something they're a part of, Bear. She's everything, and everything is her. She is awake and she is testing us and we are failing."

"That's Gaian dogma, Glass, you're spouting someone else's beliefs. Tell me what *you* saw, what *you* believe, and we'll figure it out together."

"You won't understand, Bear," he says, shaking his head. He seems full of sorrow. "You can't understand. Not till you see for yourself."

"Try me," says Bear, trying to soothe the mood. "How about you *tell* me and we let the data sort itself out? Look at us! We've had people march out blind and deaf with flamethrowers to fight this thing! For decades! And most people don't even know what they're fighting! You could change that, you're one in a million, you're a miracle -"

"There's nothing to tell! That's what I'm trying to say! You're coming at this like a scientist, but this thing doesn't obey rules like you want it to, it won't fit in a box."

"It has to, everything does – or else I'll create a new box," shrugs Bear. "It's either matter, energy, or both. Even knowing *that* would be a -"

"Didn't you hear me? It *doesn't fit* into your view of the world. Gaia shows us that everything is part of everything else. I *know* that Bear, it doesn't have to be proven. I've looked Mother Gaia in the eyes, and let me tell you Bear, she *hates* us. She sees us, and she hates us. Everything I've said? That is what you see when she stares into your soul, and forces you to look at yourself and your place in everything."

"A spiritual experience, then? Something that alters perception?"

Glass turns away, frustrated, running his hands through his hair. When he turns back, he is clenching his fists, his jaw, he looks on the verge of losing it.

"It's not like it comes with an explanation Bear, it's just... I can't describe it. It's... you experience, you *see,* with eyes that you don't have. You see everything. It doesn't stay long, but you experience, I think, a... *connection* to everything else that exists. Briefly – and it changes how you see things after. She's all of creation made manifest, contained within herself, and you see that you're a part of it. I think."

"You *think?*"

"Yes, that's what I think. Now, I've answered your question. Are we done?"

"You *think* that? How can you just think it? Don't you know what you experienced? Can you describe it to me -"

"No, I can't," says Glass, getting closer again. "I did as you asked, even though I didn't want to. I've broken promises to myself even discussing this, all because you think you might be able to do some good with my experience. Well, you can't, and you won't. Take one thing away from this, Bear, please: there is no way to undo what Gaia does, or has done."

Bear is still stuck on Glass and his inability to explain what he experienced.

"I mean," begins Bear, "was it visual? Did you *see* something?"

"Yes," Glass throws his hands up. "But from outside, as though I was separate."

"Sounds like an out of body experience." Bear feels his heart pounding. "That doesn't make any sense, though - why can't most people handle that? What's different about you?"

"*I don't know!*" shouts Glass, breaking. "I've watched men far better than me go in, and lose their shit just being close to it. I don't *know* what breaks them, or why people better equipped than me didn't survive what I did. I just... did."

Bear sees a thread and pulls on it. "Perhaps they weren't your betters?"

Glass simmers down, though he's still bubbling under the surface. "You didn't know my team, and you don't know me. I've answered your question as best I can. That is the end of it."

Bear catches it; *my team*. He isn't done. He can keep pushing. Glass has barely answered anything.

"Your team? You were Forestry, right?" He can see that he's right by the indignation on Glass's face. Bear knows that he should stop, but he can't: he's finally getting answers. "Could you tell me about your team? Comparing what was different between them and you, and we can cross reference -"

Glass goes quiet, and Bear knows that he may have stepped over the line. Too late now, he thinks.

"I've helped you, Bear," he lowers his voice into a growl. "No more questions."

"But this might be it!" shouts Bear. "We're right at the cusp here."

"I said no more questions."

"And I'm asking you anyway, this is too important Glass," he steps up, chest to his chest, and jabs him in the chest as he shouts it. "This is bigger than you and whatever shit you're carrying, ok? This is life or death for everybody in the Coastal Union."

"Bear," he pushes him back. "You need to learn when to stop picking at scabs – lest there be blood."

"Are you threatening me?" he laughs.

Too far. He shouldn't have done that.

In response, Glass grabs his collar and throws him aside with a roar. Bear hits the snow hard on his back, knocking the wind out of his lungs. He groans and tries to breathe, tries to get up, but Glass leaps down and is moving towards him already, snarling.

"Yes I'm threatening you – or do you need me to put that under a microscope too, so you can *analyse* it? I said *no more*."

He leans down and picks Bear up by the collar of his jacket. Bear may not be a fighter, but he's proud, and he's no stranger to a scuffle after ten pints. As Glass is lifting him, Bear throws himself upwards with the momentum and rams his forehead into Glass's nose.

It cracks, and Glass is briefly blinded by the tears in his eyes. He reels backwards and Bear scrambles to his feet, facing Glass across the snow as they both recover.

He hears birds overhead, cawing.

Only now do Bee and Dusty appear around the corner of the Icebreaker, having heard the sounds of a fight breaking out. They see blood on the snow, and Dusty whips his coat back and puts a hand on his pistol.

"That's enough," he shouts.

But neither Glass nor Bear are listening.

"He could have just *answered* my questions," shouts Bear, as Glass leans over and breathes blood down his chin. "I'm trying to save people, and he's too busy feeling sorry for himself."

"I answered your questions!"

"But none of the important ones -*"*

"Bear, shut up," shouts Bee. "Glass, are you done?"

Glass holds a hand up, and stands up straight. He smiles, blood glistening between his teeth, the bottom half of his face red. It's a cruel smile, and it unnerves Bear.

"Bear wants to speak to someone who's been through exposure," says Glass. "So he asked me; because he's too much of a coward to just read his dead father's notes."

Maybe it's because of his smug smile, or maybe it's because there's a heavy truth to it, but Bear loses it. He charges across the snow and tackles Glass to the ground, but Glass was clearly expecting it. By the time they hit the snow, Glass is on top of him. Bear takes one good, solid punch on his cheek bone before he gets his hands up to defend himself, and -

There's a single gunshot.

Everything stops. Just as well; Bear doesn't know if he'd have come out of this with all of his teeth. Glass looks around at Dusty like a dog caught misbehaving. Bear winces, keeps his arms up, his face already red and aching.

"That is e-*fucking*-nough!" shouts Dusty. "Glass, get off of him. Bear, shut the *fuck* up or *I'll* hit you as well."

Glass gets off of him, and together they sheepishly get to their feet. Dusty is holding his long barrelled revolver in the air, and Bee stands behind him, red faced like she's about to join the fight.

"We had one hour," shouts Dusty. "*One* hour of grace to fix our girl up before we ride into hell again so that *maybe* we stand a chance of surviving, so that *maybe* Union *fucking* City doesn't get exposed in its entirety, and you two – *you two* – think that this is a good time for a little scrap." He holsters his revolver and buttons his jacket shut in one fluid movement. "Pair of you ought to be ashamed of yourselves. *Unfuck this. Now.*"

Glass looks at the ground along with Bear, neither of them able to meet Dusty's eyes out of shame. Bear knows fine well that he pushed too far – and that some of what Glass said was true. The answers to almost all his questions likely lie in his father's notes; if he could only bear to read them.

"I am going to assume," says Dusty, "that this is the end of this. I won't hear of this happening again. Will I?"

They both mumble 'no'.

"Now shake hands and apologise," says Dusty, and stares at them until they work up the shamed courage to extend a hand to one another.

"Sorry," mumbles Bear. "Got carried away."

"As did I," says Glass.

"I kind of deserved it," whispers Bear.

"Yeah," says Glass. "We done?"

"We're done."

They both stare at the ground, and though they can't see, Dusty gives a nod to Bee.

It's over.

"Bear," he says, "come and work with me, I'll show you how you can help us make up the time we just lost. Bee, you help Glass."

She nods, and the two new pairs split up.

Chapter 15

Bear and Dusty work in the kind of silence that can only follow a disciplinary telling-off. Bear works in a kind of quiet shame, focusing on doing a job that will redeem his reputation a little. Dusty works in a different silence, tense and focused, as though his mind is in three places at once, and held there precariously.

Bear holds the sheets on as best he can while Dusty welds them to the side of the Crawler. After ten minutes of quiet work, the atmosphere eases somewhat, and Dusty begins to narrate what he's doing like Bear often does when trying to teach.

"The plating is actually a composite," says Dusty. "That means _"

"More than one kind of metal," says Bear – can't help but complete Dusty's sentence. "Yeah, I know what composite means. Steel?"

"Mostly," says Dusty. "The original Crawler armour is something we're not sure about. The plans said depleted uranium inside a stainless steel shell. The replacement panels we order from Forgehead are just layers of steel tempered to different levels of hardness."

Bear nods. "Like pre-Cataclysm tanks. They're bloody heavy, these plates."

Dusty gives a grim agreement. "Yeah, and every time we have to patch the Crawlers up with new stuff, they lose a little of that pre-Cataclysm technological edge."

"Weird," says Bear, as he hefts another one from the pile and works with Dusty to raise it onto the tread. "I always assumed the Interloper Initiative built the Crawlers themselves. I thought Union City commissioned them or something."

"Nah, nah," says Dusty, getting his breath back. Bear notes how quickly he has healed from his gunshot, and is intrigued again. "The four Crawlers were a relic I found down south, in those strange years following the worst of the Cataclysm. When there was still something to loot from the ruins." He laughs, darkly. "When you could still *get* that far south."

"You've been south?" asks Bear, impressed. To his knowledge, the south was a no-man's-land. Of course, back then, it was just like anywhere else. Then the phenomenon rolled over permanently, and the southerners came north in such a massive wave that the Coastal Union ended up fighting with them; The Scavenger War. That was a fair while ago – giving him another reason to wonder how old Dusty is.

"Well – this was a long time ago, like I said. But yeah, I've been south."

"What's it like?"

Dusty puts his hands on his hips and takes a deep breath. "Quiet. Cold. Felt like we were being hunted the whole time."

"By the phenomenon?"

"Aye. It was everywhere down there, even back then. Getting that way up here too," he sighs, and pops his welding mask back down as Bear manoeuvres the plating over the gap.

Bear feels the same old urge rising. To sit Dusty down and interview him. To ask him how old he is, to ask about the south – the frozen, uncharted south. Now everybody thinks that the Coastal Union is going to end the same way – except now there's nowhere for anybody to run. Nowadays, they can at least anticipate and fight back against the encroaching phenomenon as it spreads over their land like prying fingers.

Dusty sees it – reads Bear like he usually does, and says,

"You have about fifty questions, right?"

Bear shrugs. "I like to know things. It stresses me out when I don't – especially when you consider how rare and fragile some of this information is."

"Can I ask you some, for a change?"

"Sure," says Bear. "Shoot."

"What *is* your end goal is with all this?" asks Dusty, and Bear realises that he probably heard his entire argument with Glass.

He sighs, shrugs. "I mean... I've wondered myself what I'll do once I actually have a model or something for the phenomenon. It was my father's work, you know, his entire life."

"Is that why you pursue it?"

Bear thinks, looking off into the trees, somewhere else for a moment, before turning back to Dusty. "No. No, it's not out of duty or anything. I think it's..." he sighs. "I think it's anger. Revenge, maybe."

"Because it killed your father?"

"It didn't just *kill* him," he frowns. "It annihilated him. Tore his brain apart. It killed his thoughts, his intelligence, his speech, his words, any capacity for clear thought. It killed him as a father, it killed him as a man. Memories, personality, sense of humour, everything. All stripped away, one at a time, until even the thoughts in his own head were useless to him." He stops and takes a breath. "Smartest guy in the world. Then he got exposed. On the tenth day he started screaming. Few exposure cases last a week, let alone ten days. He screamed until he died - three days later. What can do that to a person?"

Bear fades off, and Dusty gives him a sympathetic, sad smile. "It's hellish to watch somebody go through it, isn't it?"

Bear hears the shared experience implied. "You've done it too?"

"You don't get to my age without watching a few friends go that way," says Dusty. "Especially in this line of work. First one was my wife. A long, long time ago."

"I'm sorry," says Bear, almost out of instinct.

"As am I."

"So don't you want to know?" asks Bear. "Don't you want to understand it? Don't you want to try and stop it happening to anybody else?"

"Of course," says Dusty, shrugging with a tiredness that

betrays that his age. "But Bear... if my wife had been struck by lightning, understanding how lightning works would bring me no closure. I still couldn't beat the lightning. It's a force of nature. People used to attribute lightning to the gods – much like we do now with the phenomenon. Understanding it might help, sure, but it doesn't stop it."

"But we could manage the danger. I mean, we build lightning rods on our towers now, right? Imagine that I could build walls that would guarantee to keep it out -"

"And it will still be a part of nature that we have to live with," says Dusty. "We understand cancer. We used to be able to cure it, in some cases. But we can't stop it from being part of nature, just like we are."

Bear stops, and considers it – and then shakes his head.

"I have to disagree, Dusty," he says. "And maybe that's where I disagree with most on the subject of the phenomenon. I don't think it's part of nature – and I don't think we have to just accept it. I think it's malevolent, and understanding it is the first step."

"What's the second step?"

Bear comes to realise it as he says it, the answer to a question that has bothered him for a decade – what *will* he do once he understands it?

"The same thing it does to us," says Bear, and a dark cloud crosses over his face. "I'll annihilate it."

"That's like saying you'll kill the sun," laughs Dusty. When Bear looks over at him, there's no humour in his eyes, and Dusty realises he is serious.

"It sounds impossible, right? Well, splitting the atom once sounded impossible. Reading the human genome, walking on the moon, colonising Mars, the sound barrier, light field storage, *fusion*. They all sounded impossible once."

"That was pre-cataclysm, though," says Dusty. "We've fallen a long way."

"We were just as human pre-cataclysm," says Bear. "We're no different now. Just as capable, if not moreso. We're the smartest thing that we know of in the universe. This thing is a challenge, sure; it's a threat, a serious one. But nothing is as dangerous as humanity when our back is to the wall. Back then? If we had really wanted to kill the sun, we probably could have," he states, and looks Dusty dead in the eye. "Or at least conquered it. The phenomenon has made a dangerous enemy in us."

Dusty sees a kind of determined insanity there that unsettles him. Bear, he thinks: nice boy, very smart, knows medicine and science – but maybe don't let him near the weapon controls when he has that look in his eye. Dusty puts down the welding mask and torch, and folds his arms.

"I get why you asked Glass about himself. I do, really. But you've got to understand," says Dusty. "All of us here have been through *something* we'd rather not relive. Glass has probably endured more than most. He doesn't want to relive it, and you can't force him to."

Bear feels self conscious, aware that he keeps pushing the issue, but he cannot drop it.

"But Dusty, if I can find out what was different about his squad and him, it might show me what makes someone immune, what lets someone survive. That's a *huge* breakthrough, right?"

"Yes - and that's a noble goal," he sighs, "but not if it disrupts the crew. We rely too much on each other, and if Glass is distracted, you're putting our lives at risk. I can't allow that. Ok?"

"But -"

"The answer is 'yes', Bear," he says. "Tell you what, lad. Once we hit Union and get them safe and sorted? Once Messenger is in a shallow grave, and I know the location of my other three Crawlers? I'll sit down with you for a pint, me, you, Bee and Glass. And you can ask us any damn thing you like. Least I can do for all of your help. Deal?"

Bear breaks out of his brooding, his dark meandering, and smiles with genuine excitement. "Sure, I mean – that'd be great!"

"Incentive to get us all through this alive, too," he winks.

As if on cue, there comes the chirping of birds in the early morning glare, that same strange gargling caw again, and the crows fly overhead.

"Every time I hear that bird sound," says Bear, almost to himself, as he watches them fly overhead, "I get unsettled."

"As you should," says Dusty, and begins packing his things away. "It usually means that Gaia's gaze is shifting. The birds never used to make calls like that when I was a boy. They had to make a new one for what they were experiencing. Gives me shivers still. Sounds like they know it shouldn't exist, that it's wrong."

Bear shudders as the crows pass, and hears the crunching of feet on snow. Bee appears from behind the Crawler treads.

"Dusty," she shouts. "You hear the birds?"

"Aye lass. Let's pack up. Our hour is almost up – onwards to Union."

"We get the repairs all done?"

"The important ones. No more breaches; that's the important thing."

Bear can't help but shudder at the thought of another trip through the phenomena without an intact hull. The visions and nausea are all bad enough without the constant fear of being cut into pieces by *something* leaking out of a crack in space.

Glass joins them to pack away the last of their stuff, and Dusty leads them to the rear ramp. Glass and Bear avoid one another's gaze at first, but eventually Glass gives him a brief pat on the back, and Bear has to assume that he is telling him that all is forgiven. He gives him a reassuring nod, and no more is said.

As the ramp lowers, May's voice cuts through the still winter air, tinny on the outer speakers.

"Dusty, I've got something. Distress call."

Dusty stops, and they all feel him suddenly charge with a kind of static anxiety.

"From who?"

"Crawler Three, the Polaris. Automated distress beacon, which means -"

"Their Captain activated the dead man's switch."

Bee sees the curiosity in Bear's eyes and indulges him. "If a Crawler Captain knows they're going into a situation where it's unlikely they'll come out, they can flick the dead man's switch. If they don't de-activate it within one hour, it sends out the distress call."

"It might have been active for some time," says May as the ramp comes down and they board. *"Even the distress signal won't get through to us if the* [DATA REDACTED] *is bad enough to block radio. We may have just gotten a clear shot at it."*

"Where is it?" asks Dusty as they hang up their coats. The ramp begins closing behind them, and they watch Dusty carefully, waiting for orders.

"Twenty one miles north-west, approximately. About an hour, at cautious speed. Twenty minutes if we throw caution to the wind."

"That's on our way to Union," says Dusty. "This is..."

"Too good to be true," says Bee, voicing the crew's suspicions. "I'm sorry Captain, but it's far too convenient. Right in our path, just as we've fixed up the Crawler? If Messenger says he can call down the wrath of Hell where he so pleases, he could bait us into this and expose us all, just like he wants. I'm not afraid of a gunfight, but we're in no shape to fight him again."

Bear wants to agree, but feels like he may have pushed his welcome a bit too far as of late, and so he stays silent until Dusty looks straight at him.

"Well?" he asks Bear. "What do you think, lad?"

Damn it.

"Well, if the other Crawlers are unaccounted for – and if Messenger thinks Crawler crews are the best candidates for his little cult, then... Yeah. I'm sorry Dusty, but this seems like an ambush."

Dusty bites his knuckle, clearly struggling with something. "Whether it's an ambush or not, both situations assume that we've got an Interloper Initiative crew stranded, hurt, held hostage, maybe dying, and we cannot ignore that."

Glass raises his hand, and Dusty nods for him to talk. "Sir, it doesn't matter. It's on our way. We swing by, stay far off, May can tell us if anything is unusual. At the first sign of danger, we break contact and flee. We stay aboard the Icebreaker."

Bee folds her arms, unhappy. "How many ambushes are we going to walk into? I don't know if we'll make it out of another one. We've all been wounded asides Bear, the Icebreaker is low on armour and ammunition, and -"

"Ok," says Dusty. "I've made my decision: we do a fast drive by. If Messenger has set a trap for us, we blow him and his friends to pieces with what weaponry we've got left. May?"

"Sir?"

"How are our armaments looking?"

"As before – a very small amount of napalm left, some heavy machinegun rounds, a dozen of railgun slugs. Not much ammunition for anything really, but if I'm able to use my targeting matrices then I can be as efficient with ammunition as possible."

"One shot, one kill, right?"

"Provided I can actually target them, Captain."

"Ok," says Dusty. "If it was us in the shit, then I'd expect any other Crawler crew to respond to a distress call with full force. We never leave any of our own behind – that said, I understand your apprehension. We give it our best. Watch each other's backs."

Everybody nods, but it's a non-committal, reluctant agreement. Dusty nods, acknowledges the atmosphere.

"Fair enough. Everybody to the nav-deck. Weapons ready, coats on. We don't know what we'll find."

"Aye aye, sir," comes the chorus, and even Bear joins it.

The nav deck is a mess, but Dusty gives it little heed as he takes his seat at the central console, and wraps his overcoat around himself. He uncorks the bottle of Dusty's Reserve hanging in a pouch below the controls, and takes a swig, grimacing. The Crawler's engines roar and it begins rumbling forwards. He passes the bottle around the crew, and even Bear has a quick swig of it. It hits like paint thinner, all fumes and spirits, and makes his eyes water.

The rituals begin. Dusty is singing softly to himself. It's a far cry from the eager atmosphere as they approached White Anchor. The deck is sombre now. Bear can hear only the deep, focused breathing from Glass and Bee as they check weapons and load magazines. Bee's face is twisted, a dark red blotch covering her cheek. Glass's wounds are hidden beneath his white coat, but the careful way that he moves tells Bear how much pain he's in. The big guy isn't at one-hundred percent, not even close.

Bear puts his satchel around his torso and checks the pistol holster hanging by his ribcage. It gives him a strange comfort that he isn't used to.

The first time they went into a situation together like this, Bear could not stop himself from shaking. Even in the warmth of the nav deck, his body was trembling in its entirety. Now, Bear feels a low calm settle in his bones.

Things, he reasons, could not get much worse. This might be his last hour of life, unknown to him, before he meets his end. And what could lie beyond that? All of the evidence points to there being *nothing*. How many methods did he already attempt, trying to contact his father beyond the grave? What was he looking for exactly?

He knows what he was *hoping* for, with those nights spent poring over ouija boards and EMF detectors: he had been trying to put his mind at ease over his father's passing, trying to answer questions that had no answers.

It all comes back to his father's suffering. Many nights, Bear lay awake, asking himself: the suffering had to have stopped in *this* world, right? He was at peace now, surely?

But what if that was wrong? What if there was an afterlife – and his father was in the same state there? What if the insanity of exposure had tainted him and followed him to his final rest?

It was these kind of thoughts that would occasionally cause Bear to rise from bed and wander naked out into his garden with a shovel, and stand over his father's grave, listening, waiting for the slightest hint of movement down there. Even months afterwards, when there would be nothing but worms and bones to dig up, Bear couldn't shake the idea that his father was still in danger, still in need of his help.

It left him in tears every time, staying out there until his bare skin would start to lose feeling.

No experiment that he could conceive of, no sane theory, would alleviate that hellish curiosity, and it chipped away at his mind until his resolve shifted: if his father was beyond his help, then he should turn his attention to those that he *could* help. Those yet to be exposed – those recently exposed, whose experiences might shed light on the process.

And so his lifelong study of the phenomenon had begun.

Now, he muses, he is riding on an Interloper vessel, heading straight into what is most likely an ambush. He briefly wonders how he got here. Things have gotten so much bigger than Forgehead in only a day or two.

May interrupts his thoughts, and he realises that everybody else in the room has been in a similar state of reflection. They all snap to attention.

"Two minutes out, sir," she says, clipped and proper in her military tones.

"Everybody," says Dusty, "eyes front. May, close up the viewport. If it's an ambush, they can waste their bullets on our steel plates instead of my abdomen this time."

"Yessir."

Bear looks out the viewport one last time before it closes over. The landscape ahead of them is a rolling sea of low hills and forested valleys – like an old riverbed. The trees are thicker ahead, wild and uneven evergreens under the midday sun. Poor visibility, bad terrain. Perfect for an ambush, again.

"Keep an eye out, May," says Dusty. "Any heat signatures, let us know – but verify and ID before opening fire. Don't want to hit our own people, if this distress call is genuine."

"Yessir."

There's a clattering from above them as the weapons emerge from their nests on the roof and sides, and May's sensors begins sweeping the landscape. The beeps and whirrs on Dusty's screen tell them nothing of interest. The forest is devoid of human life.

"One minute until we reach the Polaris," says May.

"I hear you lass, just keep us steady and reduce speed. Run us parallel to the treeline, give us a clear escape route."

"Yessir."

A soft beeping on Dusty's console begins to increase in frequency until it's a low whine.

"We're here," he says as the Crawler slows and finally eases to a stop like a train pulling into station.

The engines remain on.

"May," says Dusty. "I assume we are safe to open the viewport?"

"Yessir. The signal is dead ahead, one hundred metres. Should be visible."

"Open the port up, let us see."

The viewport unfolds like petals and shifts backwards with a heavy clang, shaking the entire vessel. All eyes are fixed on the snow beyond.

Trees. Evergreens, boughs, and snowy furrows.

"No Crawler could fit between these trees," says Dusty. "If they did, they'd have left a visible trail where they flattened the forest. If the distress beacon is inside, it must with a person. Maybe they lost their Crawler?"

"This is a *textbook* ambush, Captain," says Bee. "They want to force us out of the Crawler where we're vulnerable."

Dusty nods. "May? Definitely no heat signatures?"

"None, sir."

Dusty shakes his head. "I know how it looks. Chances are we're going to find a body."

"It's a setup," says Bee.

"It's a possible lead – a body might tell us what happened to the other Crawlers."

Bear nods. "Good point. Might be our only chance to get a lead on the location of the others."

"Ok," says Dusty. "Bee -"

"Sir, listen to me," she begs, and Bear hears the apprehension in her voice.

"Bee," he continues over the top of her. "Watch the Crawler. If anything happens to me, you are acting-captain."

She's caught off guard by the reversal, keeping her safe instead of piling the danger on her shoulders.

"Sir?"

"You heard me. You are acting-captain. Your orders, if we do not return, are to get to Union City and warn them of what's coming, after which... Well, I leave the Crawler and what remains of the Interloper Initiative in your hands. If it turns out that we're the only Crawler left, then your job is to rebuild the Initiative. Ok?"

"Sir, you're taking a huge risk."

"I can't ask you to do this, Bee. It's my call, it's my risk. Glass, you're coming with me." Glass nods. "Ok, let's go -"

"Wait, what about me?" asks Bear.

Dusty looks at him for a moment. "You want to come too?"

Bear isn't sure what is driving him. He knows it could be dangerous, and he still has yet to even fire a gun at someone. He threw up the last time he hurt somebody.

But they really are all alone out here. He feels a strange loyalty to this crew, these people, despite the rough time he has had with them. If they are willing to risk their life for their other crews, it seems only right that he helps out.

"I want to pitch in," says Bear. "That's all."

Dusty mulls it over, then concedes. "If you want to come, suit up."

"Aye-aye," says Bear.

"Sir," says Bee. "I should come too then -"

"Someone has to survive this, Bee. Come the worst case, that's you."

"Aye-aye, sir." Bee looks at the floor, then gives a weak salute – she knows there's no arguing.

Dusty stands up and unhoslters his long-barrelled revolver. "Glass. Bear. With me, we're going out."

Bear takes a deep breath and follows Glass and Dusty out the nav deck door, towards the ramp. He knows – they all know – that it could be an ambush. But the other Crawlers would do this for them – that's what it means to be part of the crew.

The ramp kicks up the snow as it lands just outside the tree line, and the three of them trudge into the knee deep drifts, weapons out.

Bear pats his satchel, at ease feeling the shapes within. He nestles his hand inside and worms it into his gauntlet, checking that his sensor is switched on as he does so. He brushes against his father's notes and shudders. There will come a time soon for reading them. He makes himself a promise to do it soon – he has faced worse things by now, there is no excuse.

Pistol in one hand, gauntlet on the other, he follows Dusty into the tree line. Dusty pushes through the branches between boughs with his revolver pointing ever ahead. Glass taps Dusty's shoulder, his rifle ready, signalling that it's clear.

Dusty pushes into the trees, and they follow.

The sunlight fades immediately as they step into the forest, and the snow here is only ankle deep. Evergreen needles litter the ground. Bear can hear himself breathing, can hear his heartbeat and little else besides their footsteps. There is total silence – even the rumbling of the Crawler's engine seems far and distant, muffled somehow.

There's a light ahead, soft red, casting a bloody glow on the snow around it. None of them can see where the light is coming from. Its source is blocked by the trees. Glass points to it, and Dusty nods.

They move forwards, and spread wider as they move, fanning out to flank the light, approaching it like a threat.

In a clearing a few feet across, they come upon the distress beacon. It's a small box, roughly the size of a radio, with a red flashing light on it.

There is no body.

No footprints.

No message.

Dusty kneels down next to it and switches it off. The red light dims. He turns it over and checks the wires, studies it briefly, then tosses it onto the ground, looking around.

"This isn't one of ours. This is jury-rigged," says Dusty.

Bear looks around, expecting the ambush to hit them at any

minute – but there is only silence.

"I thought only Crawlers used this kind of comms?"

Dusty nods. "Somebody has learned our ways. This was placed here for a reason."

Bear hears something like bird calls. Like the crows gargling high above them. His sensor beeps in his satchel.

"Run," whispers Dusty, patting them on the shoulders as they turn. "Now."

The silence is shattered by a sudden groaning noise, loud moaning on the wind, as though the air is tearing itself apart. The trees crack and bend around them, and their shadows are flung across the ground as the sunlight intensifies.

Space begins to change.

The light is all around them, bending.

"Follow me," shouts Glass. "Put your sensory gear on, they're here!"

Bear rummages in his bag as he runs, trying to grab his blindfold and earphones. The air is fracturing like thin ice as he moves through it, struggling against it like a web. There's singing, discordant, distant. The cracks form lines that coalesce into *runes* that ache to look at.

The air opens like a door, twenty steps in front of them, and Bear briefly gets the impression of the deep earth, of the ancient darkness below the ground that has never seen sunlight, and is tangled with roots older than the mountains. Something moves from those roots, reaching out with a single hand, pulling itself out of the earth, forming a human shape.

Messenger is birthed out of the cracks in the air, softly glowing, followed by his soldiers holding onto him, a human chain.

Dusty shouts something, but the sounds seems to hang in the air around his mouth, and Bear cannot hear him. Nothing makes sense. His sensor is giving off a constant whine.

Bear takes the safety off of his pistol, aims at Messenger, and fires. There's a soft explosion of light around Messenger where the bullet should have hit, and then several more as Glass and Dusty open fire. Every bullet bends around the aura of light, and nothing hits

Messenger. He has some kind of protection.

Bear's eyes and head are aching already, like the world is forcing itself in through his ears. He cannot bear much more of this. Bear's teeth feel like they're going to explode, like his eye balls are going to pop.

He is moving in slow motion – like running in a dream. He tries to grab Glass, then Dusty, but he can barely move.

Reality is breaking around him.

Messenger gives a signal and one of his men raises a grenade launcher. He fires, and Bear sees the spirals of air trailing towards them.

It detonates nearby, a concussive grenade. Snow and tree bark fill Bear's mouth. He is lifted and thrown through the air, briefly blinded by intense light, till he rolls to a stop on the ground.

Strong hands grab him and pull him to his feet. He is nauseous, disorientated, betrayed by his own senses. He can barely tell which way is down. More bullets fly. Branches and pine needles burst upon impact.

Glass shouts something, but he sounds far off. Bear realises that Glass is not holding him. He turns and looks up to find the shirtless, tattooed figure of Messenger, holding him by the back of the neck like freshly caught prey.

His gun is lying on the ground next to him, just within reach.

"Take the others," Messenger shouts to his men, and Bear scrambles for his gun. Blood is running down Bear's forehead from a scalp wound, his vision is blurred; he lunges for his pistol, grabs it, and twists on the ground. Messenger watches him as one might watch a pet learning a new skill. Amused, and interested.

If something is worth shooting once, he remembers Bee telling him, then it's worth shooting *at least* twice. Bear empties the magazine, one shot after another, till it clicks empty.

Messenger doesn't so much as move, nor flinch.

Each shot provokes a burst of light from some kind of shield around him, and the bullets never hit their target. Bear looks over his pistol in awe, and then glances around for help as Messenger lunges for him and pins him to the ground, trying to restrain him.

He's *strong,* shockingly so. Bear can hardly stop him as he is bundled over onto his front, held down with his arms pinned. He can't move.

There are gunshots in the distance. He hears his name being called. It's Glass, breaking his silence to shout on him. Then the roar of the Crawler, and the whine of railguns powering up. There's a loud crack of air splitting, and a *splash* nearby as the Icebreaker's guns vaporise a Dreamer.

He hears his name being called again. It's Dusty, screaming his name now. More gunshots, more shouting. He can't tell who is winning.

Messenger clamps his hand over Bear's mouth, and Bear can't scream to them, can't tell them where he is. Messenger is strong and fast, and holds him against the snow like a ton-weight.

White-cold fear begins to take him, as he realises what is happening. The overwhelming sound of gunfire is coming from submachine guns, not the single-shot rifles of the crew. They're losing, being pushed back, away from him.

The crew will have to retreat without him.

Something else is coming too. His sensor is still going insane in his satchel. If he could reach his satchel, he could grab the glove -

The glove.

The glove is on his hand already. The glove that incinerates people at close range.

Bear chooses a moment when Messenger is giving orders to his men, and twists like a snake, rolling to the side. Messenger loses his grip on Bear, who kicks himself free and rolls away, rising to his knees.

Bear points the glove at Messenger. The Dreamers look on, weapons raised, with Messenger shouting for them to hold fire.

He sees the fear in Messenger's eyes, and he knows that this bulletproof man can be killed. The pilot light flickers to life. Messenger is about to say something, to make a plea to Bear. He is *afraid.*

Bear hears footsteps nearby, and Messenger raises his hands in fear, in defence.

Bear hesitates.

He can hear the screaming of the Dreamer in Forgehead, smell his burning skin, and he hesitates.

A machete falls across Bear's wrist, and cleaves his hand from his arm. It hits the ground with a dull thud. Bear gasps and gulps as his blood sprays onto the snow. He falls back, open mouthed, staring at his wound, trying to twitch fingers that aren't there.

As he collapses to his knees he sees Messenger's horrified face. He clutches at his forearm, trying to stop the bleeding, panicking.

"You *idiot,*" shouts Messenger, "get a tourniquet on that before he bleeds out, *where are the other two?*"

The Dreamer is stammering in a panic. "H-he was going to -"

"Where are the other two?" screams Messenger.

"Uh, the Crawler started coming through the forest sir, we had to fall back, we lost Carlson -"

"Damn it," he says, as Bear's vision begins to fade. Someone has lifted his wrist and is wrapping a belt around it. "Well, we've got one. With me, to the other side of the forest."

"Sir, they'll follow us, surely -"

Messenger shakes his head. Bear's sensor is still going crazy. He can feel himself starting to slip away.

Bear sees Messenger begin tracing shapes in the air with his hands, mirroring the strange runes on his chest.

"Not if Mother Gaia stands between us and them. Their Crawler is far too beaten up to endure a trip through it," he says. "And then we can get Bear's exposure out of the way, without forcing it upon him. Two birds, one stone. If they come for him, we'll grab them too. They're weak. Losses?"

"Three of our men sir. Delaney got hit by their rail gun, he's... He's -"

"Leave the bodies, nothing we can do for them now," he sighs. "As for you, little Bear. You'd better have been worth all of this."

Messenger crouches down beside Bear, who is pale and fading, unable to talk, shaking violently. He can hardly muster the breath to scream. Two of the Dreamers are crouched beside him now, trying to administer bandages and anti-septic, injecting ballistic foam into his wound. It's a perfect, clean cut, a cross section of his bone visible under the blood.

"Try to keep him conscious," shouts Messenger. They can hear shouting in the distance, a woman's voice. It is Bee, he realises. She's screaming his name. "Ok, let's move, they're coming for him."

"Will we make it in time, sir?"

"Of course. Gaia is almost here, can't you feel her? Someone bring his satchel, too."

They all begin to chant something, and Bear closes his eyes, reaching for his satchel. He needs to read the notes. If this is the end, then he wants to know what they say. He wants to know what his father wrote – if his exposure was deliberate, or forced upon him.

But a Dreamer bats his weak arm away, lifts the satchel, and slings it over their shoulder. They leave his severed, gauntleted hand on the ground.

It's the last thing that Bear sees before he finally falls unconscious.

Chapter 16

Back at the Crawler, Bee throws open the roof hatch despite Dusty and Glass chasing after her, rifle slung over her shoulder, red in the face.

"Bee, *stop!*" shouts Dusty, his voice strained by grief. "That's a fucking *order!*"

She ignores him and leaps down the side of the Crawler onto the ladders. She gets halfway down before impatience takes her and she leaps into the snow, tumbling and righting herself.

"Bear!" she shouts into the forest, and then takes a breath and raises her rifle to her shoulder. She bursts into the treeline at a jog, rifle up, swinging it to clear her corners as she moves through the snow.

"Bear, answer me!" she shouts. She can hear Dusty behind her, shouting her name. She pushes forward, finding the first Dreamer – or what is left of him. The Dreamer took a railgun slug to the chest. There are some bits of bone embedded in the tree, and the ground has the look of a snow angel, made in blood, where he was vaporised.

A quick death, she thinks, as she moves forward. But that is not Bear.

There lies another Dreamer, clearly shot in the throat, then at least once more in the abdomen. He' is gasping and shaking as Bee moves past him. She gives him just enough attention to kick his grenade launcher out of his hands.

"Shit," she whispers. "Shit-shit-shit -"

She stops when she sees the tracks converge – and the bare footprints that must belong to Messenger.

Bee finds Bear's gauntlet in a puddle of blood, lying on the ground. Inside it, she finds Bear's hand.

She covers her mouth before she can scream, and forces it to stay down. Bee drops to her knees, the wind punched out of her. It had to be the hand.

It had to be Red, all over again.

"Not again," she whispers. "God, no, not again -"

Dusty catches her up, gasping for air, and drops to his knees beside her. He places his hand on her back, and holds her. He gently tries to pull her away.

Glass approaches, head bowed. He lifts the gauntlet, and Bear's hand falls out of it. He holds the gauntlet, staring at it for a long time as Dusty and Bee wrestle in their grief.

"Come on lass, no sense seeing this, they could still be near, and Gaia is coming -"

Bee shakes him off with surprising strength and unzips her jacket. She pulls a hand-axe from inside and staggers to her feet, surging forward after the trail of footprints.

"Bee -" shouts Dusty as he chases her.

She storms after them as though she is possessed, and in that moment she may as well be. It takes Dusty tackling her to the ground and pinning her there, wrenching the axe from her hands, before her anger turns to grief and she screams aloud, in frustration and sorrow.

Glass is behind them. "Gaia is watching," he shouts. "She's coming. Time to move."

"Hell's coming girl," says Dusty. "Hell is coming, we have to go *now*. You understand?"

Bee understands – she just doesn't care.

She's already in Hell.

When they are back aboard the Icebreaker, they sit on the

nav-deck. Bee nurses a cup of strong, sweet tea, still shaking. They are all pale-faced, staring blankly. May has the helm, steering them away from the forest, as Gaia's gaze; as the phenomenon; as Hell itself descends upon the woods.

Finally the Crawler comes to a stop. Dusty takes another swig from his bottle, and passes it to Glass, who does the same. The Captain's chair and the co-pilot chair are swivelled next to one another, leaving Glass sitting across the controls from them, alone.

"Captain," comes May's voice, heavy with sorrow. *"It's behind us. Out of visible range; behind the hills."*

"Keep the viewport shielded anyway," he mumbles.

"The minute that thing passes -" Bee begins, her voice still trembling.

"I'll go after him," says Dusty.

Glass looks at him, eyebrows raised, but remains silent.

"You?" asks Bee. "Yourself? Why not me, I should go. God has guided me through Hell before, maybe I can survive it with sensory gear on."

"It was my call," he says. "I'm Captain, Bee. That means that I'm in charge. That means that when things go to hell like they just did, I have to take responsibility."

"Then we should all go -"

"It was *my call,"* he stands up, slamming his hand on the controls. "It'll be me that goes after him. I am not risking my crew again. Our enemy is far more capable than we ever imagined. We aren't taking any more risks. Once Gaia looks the other way, I'll go after him. You'll be acting-captain."

"Sir," whispers Bee. "That's suicide."

"That's what it means to be in charge. It's not a privilege, it's a duty - and I'd do it for any of you." He walks to the console and takes a drink of his vodka, pinching the bridge of his nose. "God damn it, Messenger can – he can genuinely just appear out of *thin air."*

Glass raises his hand, and Dusty gives a weary nod. He says, "This is not something that I was aware could be done. Nor did I expect bullets to fail so consistently."

"He's bulletproof, he can appear out of thin air..." Dusty rubs his eyes as though he's about to pass out. "May can't even target him."

"Could this be pre-Cataclysm technology?" asks Bee.

"No," says Dusty. "It's like nothing I've ever seen. It shouldn't be possible, in all honesty, but these are strange times."

"It's the runes," says Glass. "He has mastered them. I've never seen ones like his before. And I've seen plenty. Gaian shamans dream of such mastery. Messenger's runes are exquisite. Subtle, but powerful, filled with meaning. There is depth to them."

"I wonder if he's got a rune that stops me putting an axe through his skull," says Dusty.

Bee gives a grim nod. "I volunteer to deliver it."

"You?" asks Dusty. "You'll be in Union by then."

"Sir?"

"Once I leave, I'll order May to begin a forty minute countdown. If I don't return to reset it, she'll consider me KIA and promote you to Captain, Bee. Understand?" Bee gives a weak nod. "And my final orders are for you to head to Union and *save it*. Ok?"

"Yes sir," she whispers.

"I'm going up top," says Glass. "I'll be able to see which direction Gaia is moving. I'll let you know when she's gone."

"Good man," says Dusty.

Glass leaves, and Dusty stares across the room at Bee. It's her that breaks the silence.

"I should have been out there," she says.

"Maybe. But that wasn't your call. That's why it's me going after him."

"You'll die."

"Beatrice," he sighs, and sits in the Captain's chair. In moments like this, Bee remembers how old he really is, and how much of this he has had to endure, and how tired he must be. "If you're going to be Captain, I need you to understand this; to *really* understand this. Everything that happens to us, good or bad, is ultimately *my* responsibility."

"What about Red?" she asks, and there's a tense silence. "That wasn't on you... You think that was my fault. I know you do."

"Red..." he sighs, stops, rubs the bridge of his nose again. "Red died because of my decisions, one way or another. I took the job, I led us there, but -"

"But?"

He sadly nods. "But I think you hold some responsibility, yes. You led the team. And I worry about leaving you in charge if you can't accept some of the blame. You've never once acknowledged that it might have been your fault." Bee nods, says nothing for a while. Dusty picks up and continues. "I worry, Bee, that you aren't your own ultimate authority. You understand? When everything goes wrong, I have myself to blame. I'm responsible, in every analysis. For you, there's always going to be another authority, whether God or Satan, to blame for everything. And a Captain can't *have* an authority higher than themselves. Not out here. It's all on you."

"Then who does the Captain draw his strength from?"

"Whoever they need to. I'm not talking about strength, I'm talking about making hard decisions. I'm asking you to put yourself as the arbiter of your own choices. I know that when Gaia hit you and Red, you prayed. What you should have done, was to start giving orders. Understand?"

"Do you think Red would have lived? If I had?"

"Maybe?" he shrugs. "Maybe not. We'll never know. But I need this from you, Beatrice; I need to know that if it happens again, you are capable of bearing that burden yourself. Because I probably won't be there."

"Don't talk like that -"

"I won't live forever. I'm older than I've any right to be, especially in this job, and young folks keep dying, when you and I both know that it should be me. Are you capable of bearing the weight? Do you *want* to?"

Bee looks into a dark corner of the nav deck for a long time, and takes a breath to steady herself.

"Yes."

"Good. And you understand how important the Crawlers are? The Initiative?"

"Yes."

"Without us, the Coastal Union falls to pieces in a couple of weeks. It's back to the Scav Wars again, it is right back to subsistence living and tribal law, and all of our progress disintegrates. The Icebreaker is probably the last Crawler left – that means you'll be the last Captain. You'll have to build it all again from the ground up. Are you up to that?"

"I think so. Yes. Yes, I am."

"Then you understand why I have to go after Bear on my own? You can't help me with this one. You have a job to do."

She nods, and then rushes forward without warning and throws her arms around Dusty. He holds her like a grandfather would hold his youngest grandchild, rank and orders forgotten for the moment. When she pulls away, stubbornly wiping her eyes, he reaches out and fixes her circlet, and lightly touches the wound across her cheek.

"Now you're ready to be a Captain," he says.

They stop as they hear the hatch going – Glass returning. He pops into the nav deck and straightens up as though nervous, or embarrassed. It's a strange look for him.

Dusty takes a shuddering breath. "Is it gone? Is it time?"

"No sir," says Glass. "It's uh- It's not moving."

"What? May?"

"Readings don't show the usual [DATA REDACTED]. *No gradient in the readings. Nothing I can predict. It seems like it's there to stay, at least for now."*

"Bastard," whispers Dusty. "Ok, we do this the old fashioned way. May? Unlock the Captain's armoury and detach whichever of our flame guns has a little napalm left in it. I'd hoped it wouldn't come to this."

"Yes sir."

"You have a Captain's armoury?" asks Bee, incredulous. "Why

didn't we know about this?"

"Because it's never been this bad before," he shrugs, and paces towards his room. "And I hoped I'd never have to use it. Come with me. I'll need help putting it on."

Bee and Glass give each other confused looks, and follow him.

A panel has slid back beside Dusty's bunk in his otherwise messy room. Empty bottles of his reserve, boxes of revolver rounds, and dust-coated stacks of maps and pencils fill the space – but to the left of his bed is a small room the size of a walk in wardrobe.

Inside is an old fashioned diving suit, in steel grey instead of brass. The front of the helm has had it's mesh replaced with a steel block, and it appears airtight. The arms and legs are joined like old plate armour, protecting most of the body from harm. There are valves all over it, pipes and metres. Electrical wires too, Bee notes – though for what, she doesn't know.

"This is literally a diving suit," says Bee.

"It's made from the same material that the Crawler's pre-Cataclysm armour is, and equipped with sensory blockers," says Dusty. "It's ridiculously heavy, needs a power source to be of any use. Back in the day, it was one of our first prototypes for dealing with Gaia when she made an appearance. It's my best chance at going through it."

"Hold on, hold on," she shakes her head. "You're going to walk *through* Hell. Yourself? Dusty when you spoke about going back I thought you meant once Gaia had passed."

Glass raises a hand, but doesn't wait for permission. "I have to accompany you. You don't know what you're walking into."

"I know exactly what I'm going into son – I've been doing this most of my life. I'm not hanging around in there for long. This should get me through in one piece. Might give me some protection from gunfire as well when I reach Bear."

"Dusty," says Glass, folding his arms. "If anything happens to the helmet, if there's a slight leak -"

"Then I get exposed," he shrugs. "It's been a long time coming.

Should still leave me with enough time to save Bear, provided he's alive. We only found his hand, after all. At least Messenger doesn't want to kill him, so there's a chance he's alive. Worst case scenario, I'll settle for just killing Messenger."

"Dusty this is *insane*," says Bee. "The Crawler itself barely gets through unscathed. You'll be blind and deaf and surrounded by demons. Take the Crawler! We'll *all* go."

"We've been through this," he shakes his head. "Besides; she's falling apart. We can't risk it." He places one hand on the old suit of armour. "This is our only choice. Glass, you stay with Bee. I do this alone. May?"

"Dusty?"

"Set a timer. Once I leave the Crawler, start counting. If I do not report back within forty minutes of leaving, I want you to list me as killed-in-action. Bee is to be promoted, and given the Captain's tour. Tell her all the stuff she doesn't know, bring her up to speed. Get her to Union safely, ok?"

"Yes, Captain."

There's a sadness in May's voice that cannot be programmed – but she accepts the order.

"Now you two. Help me into this thing."

The ramp comes down, and Dusty stands at the top of it in the heavy, suffocating suit of armour. He clanks when he walks; and walking is a serious effort. His pistol hangs at his side in a holster, and Glass steps outside and heads around for the ladders. Dusty tries moving his fingers, and finds them too heavy to really use. He'll be useless until the power comes on.

When Glass returns, he is holding one of the Crawler's flame guns in two hands. It's heavy even for Glass. It resembles a syringe duct taped to a lighter, with a barrel full of unlit napalm for the pilot light to ignite, and pressurised pumps that will send it in a long arc wherever it's pointed. It's supposed to be mounted on the massive Crawler; it is not designed for comfort, or for hand held use.

Bee hands him her rifle as Glass straps the flame-gun across his back, on a harness that allows it to swing down at his hip so that he can fire it one-handed, using the armoured exoskeleton like a frame.

He's a walking tank, but the armour is the only thing that is holding him up.

"Dusty you can't walk like this," says Bee.

"Not when it's switched off maybe," he says. "Do me a favour and connect the power module on the back, lass."

"What?"

"There's a black box in an armoured hatch, it's a pre-Cataclysm battery. Should have some charge left."

Bee finds and opens a small hatch and sure enough, a small black box with a positive and negative sign on it. She pushes it properly into place, and the joints and hinges of the diving suit begin to hiss with pneumatic pressure.

Dusty suddenly stands up straight in the armour. Through the open port, Glass sees his face flush with relief as the weight is taken off of him.

"Powered exoskeleton underneath it all," says Dusty. "I know my limits."

Glass pats the armour. "If you see the Dreamer with the other grenade launcher, take him out first. There were two, and I got one in the forest. I don't know where they got grenade launchers, but they're your only real threat. You aren't invincible in this, but their submachine guns aren't getting through it."

"I know, I know," he says. "Now, Glass, I'll be blind so I'll need you to point me towards the tree line. Bee, you get back inside. There might be some of it in the sky, don't want you seeing it and getting exposed."

She nods, but watches from the top of the ramp as Dusty clanks down it with Glass in tow. At the bottom, Glass shuts the helmet and, faintly, Bee can hear loud music coming from the armour.

He's sealed in, she thinks. May as well have closed his coffin lid on him.

Glass slaps the back of the armour, and the helmet shakes as

Dusty visibly nods.

He begins walking, rifle and pistol clanking off his armour, flame gun at his side, and a long handled fire-axe in his other hand. Glass watches him go, and when he finally returns to the top of the ramp, he has fallen silent once more.

They stay there, listening, until they can no longer hear the thump-hiss of Dusty's footsteps. Then they return to the sealed nav deck as the ramp closes, and Bee lifts Dusty's Reserve out of its hammock and sits in his Captain's chair, sullen-faced.

"Drink?" she offers Glass.

He nods, and she pours two glasses and passes him one.

"To Dusty," she says, and Glass clinks his drink against hers.

"To Dusty."

Glass reaches into his coat and puts the gauntlet on the dashboard. He and Bee look at one another questioningly.

"I'm not toasting Bear yet," she says.

"You think he could be alive?"

"He damn well better be," she says, and finishes her drink. "It's just a hand. The Dreamers likely know how to tourniquet an amputation."

"Thirty-nine minutes and counting," says May.

"Thanks May," says Bee. "But I don't need one every minute."

"Understood."

Bee begins to recite her scripture, praying to herself.

"Behold, those who have suffered beneath great evil," she closes her eyes, reciting scripture from memory again. "I promise you this; that God judges all in the end, that all will be judged, and all will be whole again. It is not for us to know when. It is just for us to know."

"Why that verse?" asks Glass.

"The last book of the Last Testament, the Book of Endings.

Reminds me that this is all going to be over one day," she smiles at him. "We just need to survive. That's all He really asks of us. To keep going, and trust that this is all *for* something." She dips her head and closes her eyes. "If you'll excuse me, I'm going to pray."

"You're praying for Dusty and Bear?"

"For all of us. Every single one. Same as I always do."

Dusty is in the dark, with deafening music blaring in his ears. Classical violins scream, as he puts one foot in front of the other, waiting with every cell in his body for the vertigo to kick in and the phenomenon to hit him. His finger rests on the flame gun's trigger. His body feels weightless, due to the incredibly complex mechanical systems at work. This was cutting edge before the Cataclysm – now there is likely nothing like it left in the world.

All is dark, but Dusty is at home in the dark. His own breath is hot on his face as it bounces off the inside of the helm. He feels powerful, young again, as the pneumatics kick in and spur him onwards.

Already his mind is playing through the worst possible scenarios: Bear exposed, shuddering and mumbling, his mind already breaking under the strain. Maybe he has already bled out, if the Dreamers don't have enough medical experience to handle a violent amputation. Messenger could have stepped into thin air and vanished with him – they could be long gone. He can't help but picture Bear clutching a bleeding stump, lost and afraid, wondering where Dusty is.

Maybe he won't even make it through the other side, he thinks. Maybe the armour fails and it tears him apart, or he loses his mind anyway and opens his helm and jams his revolver against his temple.

Dusty puts one foot in front of the other.

One foot in front of the other.

Maybe it's time, he thinks. Countless years of avoiding it, of jamming his ears shut when it's near, of letting May drive them through it. Maybe it's time that he sees what Gaia seems intent on trying to show him. Maybe it's time to see what his wife saw, before her mind quietly stepped out of her body, leaving Dusty to watch her die.

Or maybe Messenger is right, Dusty thinks. Maybe he's tough enough, maybe he's one of the rare few who will not go insane.

The cataclysm, despite its best efforts, could not kill him. Nor could the horrors of the South. The diseases that followed the early settlers could not end him, nor could the madness of the Scav War. How many times has he rode head-first into the Hell that infests his home? And how many times could he really expect to come out the other side in one piece?

This is a long overdue debt, Dusty thinks to himself. A price paid for all the good luck that has kept his crew together until the last few days. It has all gone so wrong, so very quickly.

He is weary, tired of surviving whilst the young and the brave, the beautiful and the intelligent people all around him, die violently under his care. His wife, his first crew, his friends – either the South, the Scav War, or the plagues took them all from him.

Then it took Red.

Now it has taken Bear.

It is about time it took him.

But not before he saves the new lad.

One foot falls in front of the other. Dusty puts his head down and picks up the pace.

One foot, then the other. Then the vertigo begins.

He feels like he is falling forwards, blind and disorientated, and stumbles as he pushes onwards.

He grits his teeth, bracing for the feelings before they hit him. There are flashes of light, like stars zipping past him in the dark. He screws his eyes shut, afraid of what he might see, and flicks the pilot light on the flame gun.

Something whispers nearby, directly into his head, over the volume of the music. Dusty, terrified, shaking in his armour, roars and pulls the trigger, firing the flame gun in a wide arc and burning back the voices.

There are things moving in front of him, he can *feel* them.

Then he crosses the threshold and reality

shatters like a

w i n d o w

Take off the Helmet, Dusty.

She's a robot, old man, she's not your wife, your wife is de

Something is climbing up the inside of his leg

Fire. Fire in front of him, flame gun trigger depressed, he's screaming, something is cutting into the armour, it's tangling him like a

net,

a

spider

web

There's screeching from the armour, something is cutting into it.

Black acid, black tar, black water flooding into the helmet

blacktarblacktarblacktarblacktarblacktarblacktarblacktarblack

More flame

armour is being torn to pieces

black water, filling his lungs

can't breathe got to take the helmet off, got to -

No water. He's imagining it. Dusty keeps firing, and as he does, reality returns to normal for a moment, a pause, just a breath to let him

covered in insects

long thin legs, thin enough to pierce his armour and

He can hear May, but she keeps telling him that he is dead

hot, too hot, got to take the armour off

Something wraps around the shoulder of his armour and tears at it, and he feels the unmistakable blast of cold air as his bare shoulder is exposed under the armour.

It's going to get in.

It's going to climb in here beside him.

More flames. He dumps the last of the napalm into an arc of fire and runs through it.

The armour is overheating, he's sweating into his own shut eyes. Dusty roars in terror and swings the axe in front of him as though chopping his way through jungle, eyes screwed shut, locked in his own tomb.

The axe connects with something, and it reels back. He feels the armour being torn apart. He's wading through black water that eats at the metal, corrodes it, his feet are burning, it's inside his skin now, inside his body.

He's aware that he is changing shape, conforming to some pattern that he cannot see. Something is trying to grab at him.

A presence in front of him.

He cannot see it, but he feels the world bending around it, space sloping down towards it, shifting into impossible shapes layered upon one another.

There's something huge in front of him.

Dusty realises that he cannot make it through.

He stops.

Everything in him says to turn and run; that it is foolish to even try and fight. Dusty spits.

Foolish to even try; Dusty has been called a fool for many things – he isn't about to stop now He did not come here to give up – nor has he any intention of dying peacefully.

Dusty throws the empty flamegun back behind him, aware of the leviathan emerging from the ground in front of him because he can *feel it in his soul.* His pistol and rifle swing on harnesses by his side.

He wields the axe two-handed and staggers forward, roaring a challenge into his own darkness. Dozens of cold hands are scraping and pawing at the armour now. He cannot help but find them familiar. Like he knows them.

Something cuts cleanly into his shoulder.

"You can't have him," he roars. "He's my crew, he's *mine!*"

Dusty senses something moving towards him and ducks low, swinging the axe upwards like a knight, and it connects with something. Space contorts and whatever was in front of him dissolves back into the ground, and Dusty screams in fury and breaks free of whatever crowd is holding him down, throwing his assailants to the wind.

And what a wind.

He's being pushed back by some intense kind of force, like an electrical storm, and everything in his body feels charged, but he can't push hard enough, can't make it -

Something doesn't want him to leave this place. A hundred pairs of hands claw at him, dragging him to his knees.

Dusty raises his pistol and fires. Like a peel of thunder, it blocks out all else for that moment. He feels the shock of the shot in his arm, and it reminds him what he is capable of. He is reminded of his strength.

Whatever is holding him staggers backwards when he shoots it, and Dusty takes a step forward.

Another shot.

Another step.

It begins to relent. Another shot. Another step.

The force abates, weakening like strained, wet wood as he pushes through it. Whatever dwells within this dark place, it pushes and tests its strength against Dusty, desperate not to lose.

He feels like there are cables pulling on every limb, and one by one he roars as they begin to snap, one at a time, losing their grip on him.

They break.

It clears.

It stops.

Everything suddenly feels cold, fresh, new. Space has rotated back to normality, everything lines up now, everything exists as it should. The music in his ears is untainted, pure and clean on its own. Dusty can hear only his own breathing above it.

He drops to his knees, gingerly opens the hatch on the helmet, leaving the music on, and sees -

Snow.

Snow and, to his sides, pine forest.

He checks the sensor built into his suit's forearm. Phenomenal audio is low enough to give him a headache but otherwise looks ok. He presses a button on the lapel of his helmet and the music stops.

Silence.

Dusty vomits into the snow, and realises now how much pain he is in. His entire body aches, like every muscle is torn.

The axe is coated in some strange black fluid and the head has been severed cleanly in two. He reaches back and finds his revolver and Bee's rifle still hanging there, in one piece. The armour on his sleeves is cut and scratched, with blotches of it eaten away as though by acid. Something corrosive had him in its grasp, of that much he is sure.

His shoulder is aching from where something has sliced neatly through the bare skin, but has missed the muscle. Dusty takes a breath, spits the vomit from his mouth, and stands up.

Bear is not here.

He presses onwards, one heavy metal foot in front of the other, and soon finds tracks in the snow. He has emerged from the forest at a kind of horse shoe clearing, near the bottom of a small valley. Atop the valley are clear fields of snow and rock, looking down into where he is.

The tracks are easy to follow. Six of them, he counts, in shoes. The smudged lines of someone being dragged. More tracks; someone in their bare feet. Messenger.

He hears the crackling of the air like glass behind him, like something slowly pushing its way through a bedroom window. Something is singing underneath the ocean, it sounds like. It's moving towards him, chasing him; but Dusty is focused on the barefoot tracks in the snow.

"I've got you now, you bastard," he whispers, and heads onwards, away from the protection of the tree canopies, armour hissing and screeching with every heavy step.

Behind, the phenomenon rumbles after him, reality distorted in a slow tidal wave of light and sound. Ahead, over the lip of the valley, Dusty can see smoke from a camp fire.

Chapter 17

Bear opens his eyes.

Day time still, late afternoon perhaps. The day is still bright and cold. His vision is bleary, everything is in agony. There's a dull throbbing pain, constant, in his wrist. He looks down, sees the bloody bandaged stump, and the adrenaline wakes him up like an electric shock.

His heart starts pounding. Panic constricts his chest and his throat. It all comes back to him, and he looks around wild-eyed, hyperventilating. Someone has their hands on his shoulders to hold him still. There's a well-stoked campfire in front of him. His legs are burning from the heat and he scuttles backwards, but his back is against a cut tree stump.

"Sir, he's awake," says the deep voice above him.

Over the fire, he sees Messenger. He seems to occupy several places at once, as though there are several of him vying for existence. Bear cannot tell if this is another spatial trick, or just a combination of the fire-haze and his blurred vision. Messenger has Bear's satchel at his side, lying open. The sensor has been lain aside, batteries removed, and the two pale folders sit on Messenger's crossed legs.

The first folder is his research from Forgehead, largely pointless now that he has learned so much more about the phenomenon. Those research notes are currently in Messenger's hand. Sitting on his other lap, dangerously close to the fire, is the envelope containing his father's notes.

Messenger is chewing on a half-burned hunk of meat,

probably rabbit, as he reads. He looks up at Bear, and smiles. He is wearing his great coat, buttoned up to the neck, sparing Bear the headache of seeing his rune-tattoos, though he still in bare feet despite the cold. The runes on his bald head are still visible, but they do not seem to cause Bear any discomfort.

"How's your pain?" is the first thing he asks. "We have some more painkillers if you'd like – though I do want to keep you conscious and we've already given you a fair amount."

Bear is bewildered. He darts his eyes around, and gets his bearing.

They have built a small camp atop a hill overlooking the forest, but shielded from view. Bear can sense Gaia nearby, just over the lip of the hill. He averts his eyes and stares at the ground. The Dreamers have thrown some shawls on the ground to sit on, keeping him off the snow for now. He counts six Dreamers, in warm clothing, scarves covering their mouths, and the same bright and aware look on their faces. They are all armed – one of them with a single barrelled grenade launcher. Only Messenger carries no weapon.

A few hundred paces away, down a gentle slope that is out of sight, is the treeline of evergreens where Bear was separated from his crew. The air crackles in the air like a hallway of mirrors, and he averts his eyes again, heart pounding.

The phenomenon is very close.

He wonders who else is hurt, if they got away ok. He hears no engine, no movement – he remembers Bee calling his name, but cannot hear her now.

Messenger reads his mind.

"Your friends are ok," he shrugs, and keeps reading Bear's research. "They evaded us yet again. Hopefully they come for you, and we get them all safe and sound."

Bear goes to speak, and realises that his throat is painfully dry. He rasps a response, and at Messenger's behest a Dreamer passes him a wooden camping-mug of cold water, probably melted snow. It stings Bear's throat and he winces, almost grabbing it with his non-existent hand.

Despair lingers at the edge of his thoughts. Nobody is coming for him. He's on his own. He fights the fear down by reminding himself that this is ok. Bear is used to being alone.

"Calm yourself," says Messenger, seeing the whites of his eyes bulge. "We aren't going to hurt you. I just want to talk properly, while we have time. I do apologise for your hand, but Robert here tells me that you were about to immolate me, and he acted to protect me."

Bear hears the words, and realises that he cannot turn off the part of himself that picks up little details. Bullets seemed useless against Messenger – but immolation was something worth removing Bear's hand over. A weakness, maybe? There is a campfire between them. Bear remembers how strong Messenger was – in his current state, there is no way to overpower him. He files it away in case it becomes an option.

Bear nods, instead of replying. He must conserve what strength he has.

"You can speak," says Messenger, and tosses a rabbit leg onto Bear's lap. Bear flinches out of reflex, staring at it suspiciously. Messenger rolls his eyes. "It's not poisoned Bear. I thought you were the smart one. You've endured serious trauma, you need food."

Bear takes a bite, the first proper food he's had in recent memory, and the warmth and burst of energy it brings starts to settle his body and put him at ease. He leans back on the tree stump.

He feels a little of himself coming back, and takes a moment to eat his rabbit leg before saying anything. He lets Messenger stew a while. The longer this takes, the longer the Icebreaker crew have to do something. He goes over his options, and rapidly arrives at a conclusion:

He is in all likelihood, going to die very soon.

Bear takes his time and enjoys what little pleasures remain. A strange peace falls over him. He has no clear path out of here, no way to save himself. Physically, he is almost useless right now. No weapon, nothing else to use. If he's going to survive this, it may well require a miracle.

"Feeling a little better?" asks Messenger. Bear nods without looking at him. He's busy looking off at the horizon, at the sunshine. Trying to preserve that feeling somewhere that it cannot die. He thinks about his father, wonders if maybe he felt this way near the end. Accepting of it, maybe.

"Bear?" says Messenger. "I'd like to talk, if you don't mind."

Bear smiles. He remembers his father telling him to find the good in every bad situation – and perhaps this is the worst situation that he can imagine or remember. If there is any good to be found, it is that he has been given an interview with a man who holds many answers to questions that he has. Maybe he doesn't have to die with out any answers after all.

Messenger may not realise that he is about to be interrogated, but that suits Bear just fine.

"So talk," says Bear. "Why don't you tell me why you haven't exposed me yet? I half expected to wake up face first in the phenomenon."

Messenger clears his throat. "Because I would rather that your exposure was voluntary, Bear."

"Like it was voluntary for everybody in White Anchor?"

"That's me playing the numbers game. You're a special case, Bear. I have high hopes for you – so taking some time and care with your exposure is just fine."

"And you're going to try and convince me that it's a good idea?"

"Yes," says Messenger, laughing to himself. "Yes, I am."

"Then clearly you don't know me, or anything about my history."

Messenger smiles, and there is no warmth in it. It's a coy, smug smile. "Oh, I think I know more than enough about you Bear. Everything worth knowing."

"Bold claim," shrugs Bear.

"Let me see," says Messenger, leaning over the fire. "Rationalist, scientist, doctor – though that last one is sketchy. As I understand it, you spent two to three weeks learning everything that you could about medicine as you... *tried* to treat your father's post-exposure madness." Bear looks away; that one was right on the money. Messenger continues, pressing the opening. "You've been flitting around ever since looking for answers and coming up against brick walls again and again. Nowhere that you belong, no place to really call home any more... Even your research, brilliantly presented though it is, is years behind what all Dreamers intuitively know, and even what Union has managed to figure out. Not to mention, you've made yourself a criminal by even investigating it."

"Ok," sighs Bear. "That's fair."

"You're only just putting together that there's something unusual about the dreams that occur before – you call it the phenomenon, right? Before the phenomenon hits a town. You're *just* putting that together. We've understood the meaning and purpose of the shared dreaming for years. Not even to touch on the things people see in Gaia's reflection, or what we can do with runes and their proper usage. You're in the stone age, Bear, for all your effort. I can help you to leave it, and reach a new level of understanding."

"So tell me," says Bear. "Explain it to me, then. I don't believe you."

Messenger leans back and smiles. "How can I describe colour to a blind man? You lack the structures in your head to comprehend what I would tell you."

"I'm sick of being told that I won't understand this shit," says Bear. "Try me."

"But it's true. It would be like trying to fit a cube into a circular hole; there is simply nowhere for the information to *fit*. Why do you think so many go mad upon exposure, Bear? A sudden influx of knowledge that does not fit anywhere in their brain, information that they cannot or will not accept. That information has no way of getting out except through the desperately scribbled runes that they draw on the walls. A feeble attempt by them to rationalise what they have experienced."

"We know about the link between exposure time lines and rune-drawing, it's well documented."

"Yes but you don't *understand why,*" says Messenger. "You don't know what it's like, Bear. Imagine..." Messenger closes his eyes and searches his head for examples. "Imagine reading a sentence in a book. It doesn't make any sense. Now it's in your head, and it's in another language, so you can't understand the context but there's meaning there, and it leaps out at you. You've experienced something incredible. You briefly, vaguely, grasp the meaning of the text, despite not knowing the language; and what little you grasp hints at the ultimate knowledge, the keys to every secret, the grand unravelling of all mystery... and maybe also something incredibly dangerous. But it makes no sense to you. It stays in your head, just beyond your mental reach. And if only you could *understand*. If only you could *show somebody!* But it stays in your head, and it itches away at you, and you have to get it out somehow because it's taking over every thought, every neuron in your brain, and you find that you are spending all day just thinking, that you cannot *stop* thinking! You're forgetting to eat, and you *know* the symbols, you *know* the lines, but you can't connect them to anything *solid* that would let you finally rest..." Messenger trails off, looking expectantly at Bear. "All in an instant – and you've peered at all of creation, at Mother Gaia, and what you saw has broken your mind. Overloaded you. You can't get it out now. It's locked in there with you, and it grows, until there is no space left for you in your own head."

"And that's exposure madness," says Bear. "Right. There's nothing there that I don't understand."

"But you've never experienced it," says Messenger. "Imagine enduring that, Bear... but surviving and coming out the other end. When you do so, you find that you have earned knowledge that you could not possibly otherwise understand. You see anew. Every snowflake is suddenly a universe, staring back at you. "

Bear frowns. "Yeah, with a one-in-one-thousand chance of survival. I think I'll stick to the scientific method, thanks. It's slow but it's effective; and there's less risk of me dying."

"Or maybe you're just remiss to let go of the methods of your father, Bear. Only child, right? Mother died when you were too young to remember?" Messenger leans forward as his words hit home, and Bear feels his stomach turn. "Father dead, all alone in the world. Still seeking his approval a decade after his passing. But really, you're afraid to walk down the same road that he did."

"Because I know where it leads," says Bear, feeling his face flush red. "I've seen where it leads."

"For him, yes," shrugs Messenger. "You know what I think? I think that you are afraid that you will succeed, where he failed – because that means that you've surpassed him, and then you really are on your own Bear. As long as you keep this -" Messenger holds up Bear's father's final notes - "like some kind of holy text? You have something ahead of you. Some final untouched memory of him. I think you're a coward, Bear, unable to face the world alone."

"I haven't read it," says Bear. "And I am quite ok with being alone."

"You haven't read it?" Messenger raises his hands in mock surrender. "My apologies, I misread you. Why exactly have you not read it?"

"Because it's unscientific. And he had lost his damn mind at this point. I don't want to remember him like that – and I'm afraid that -"

Bear cuts himself off. He can't say it. There's a block there. Say what, that he's afraid his father's notes will confirm that he left Bear willingly? That whatever is wrong with Bear, he wasn't good enough to be worth staying around for; staying alive for.

"Afraid of what?" asks Messenger, with sincere concern.

"Afraid it confirms what I already know."

"That he left you alone? Knowingly? Deliberately?"

Bear nods, and Messenger nods with him.

"Fathers can do terrible damage to a child with such simple decisions, can't they? Your father left you alone, so you're taking out your anger on the world, is that it? You want to destroy the thing that killed him?"

"I do."

"Or is it that you're jealous of it? He chose the phenomenon over you?"

Bear says nothing. He looks into the fire.

"Maybe I can help you," says Messenger.

Bear finally looks up. "Help me with what?"

"I know more about Gaia than anybody else alive – and my real interest lies in securing a future among the new world for those who are worthy. I believe you to be worthy, Bear. I'd like you on my side. Help me build this new world – thrive in it – and I will help you figure out how to make the world safe for us all."

Bear is almost tempted, but there's something snake-like about Messenger. He sees Messenger's angle of attack here – how obviously vulnerable Bear must seem, to anybody who poses like a father to him, standing in for what he has lost.

"Or maybe you want to see how easily I can be manipulated?" says Bear, pressing his attack."Do you think I don't know what cold reading is? Don't you think I've pored over every record of psychics, mediums and diviners that I could find? And they were all *frauds,* Messenger. Just like you. You're no great prophet – I don't think you even understand the phenomenon."

Messenger is briefly taken aback, and Bear gets a glimmer of anger from him. He's wounded him, and that gives Bear some pleasure.

"A fraud? Bear, I *stepped out of thin air* and blinded you all with light from my hands. I'm *bulletproof.* How am I a fraud?"

Bear shakes his head. "So you understand the runes. That's good, that gives me hope – because if you can summon the phenomenon to you, then that means that it can be controlled and manipulated. Which means that I can control it too, in theory. But I don't think you *understand* what you're doing. I think you're just drawing shapes that you've learned. I don't think half of those runes on your body *do anything.*"

Messenger leans forward. "You don't know what you're talking about."

Bingo, thinks Bear. He's baited him in. Now for the big one:

"Then enlighten me. What *is* the phenomenon?"

Messenger throws his hands up. "How do I describe -"

"Oh stop with the metaphors and just *try*. What is it? Is it a field? What does it behave like? How long does it take from calling it till it arrives, does it have a consistent speed? Give me details!"

Messenger winces, and screws his eyes up as though he has a headache. Bear can see that he is getting to him, and realises that his life might be ended all the faster if he pushes too hard.

"Bear," says Messenger, his tones soothing and calming now. "Bear. Listen to me. You're a man of truth. You seek the truth, that's who you are. Am I right?"

Shit, thinks Bear. He had the chance, and Messenger has swerved it. He isn't going to get as many answers out of this shaman as he had hoped.

"I guess," he agrees. "I'm a man of science."

"But you can't tell me at what specific point a person becomes a corpse. You can't tell me if two people consider *red* to be the same colour. You can't tell me the weight of the soul. Gaia is one of those questions. She is not something that science can *conquer.*"

"But you can control it, right? So she follows rules."

"I can ask her to strike. I can *see* the runes, the writing of them, the casting of them. But it's, it's, it's -" he waves his hands in frustration. "It's not like writing computer code: symbols in the correct order, in the correct context, for a given effect? No, no. It's just not like that. And Bear, I know that you think everything can be understood, but no matter what cryptography or code breaking you try, you will *never* understand how this works without being exposed to the truth." He motions to the runes on his body. "This is not like a written language, it cannot simply be replicated and studied."

"But why not?"

"Because you exist in three dimensions, Bear! And you struggle to even perceive *them* properly. There is no way that you could understand runes that are written two spheres above your plane of existence, in hyper-shapes and perfect symmetries that echo above and below in all directions, through all time, forever. Do you begin to understand how small you are?"

Bear understands the words, certainly – but the specifics he is losing. He feels like he's hearing a lot of jargon. "Different dimensions I can understand. You're talking about dimensions above ours?"

"Like all dimensions, in all combinations, across all times, forever – and try to draw a shape on *that*, Bear. It has to echo, in harmony and symmetry, through the hyperstructures that permeate all things, at all levels... just to have any effect."

Bear considers what he has heard, and takes a deep breath. "Messenger, I don't think *you* understand those words."

Messenger scrunches up his face in frustration. "I can see these things because I have been *awoken!* You are smart, Bear, you are frighteningly intelligent; but you are a child in this world. These are things you will never understand unless you open your third eye. You must learn to see without eyes, to hear without ears, to speak without tongue. Let yourself die and be reborn, in the only crucible that matters."

"Die?"

"Yes, Bear, die – and *be reborn anew*. That's how one survives an exposure; by accepting the complete destruction and reconstruction of the self. And I *know* you will survive it, because I am preparing you for it right now. We die and are reborn every time we learn something new, and you may be the most learned man in the Union. You can see in ways that I cannot. And I hope that you will help me Bear, I dearly, dearly hope that you will help me."

Bear hears a genuine plea in Messenger's speech. If nothing else, Messenger at least believes his own dogma. That said, Bear is aware that nothing Messenger has said is a solid answer.

"Why would I help you?"

"Because I am trying to secure a future for mankind in a world with Gaia, and Bear, heaven help me, I need a scientist."

Bear sees no con here; no lies, no trick. Messenger is begging. Genuinely begging.

"Secure a future?" he asks, always looking at the details before the broader picture.

"From Gaia, from Hell, from the phenomenon, whatever you choose to call it," says Messenger. "Just like you are, Bear. The rest of the world is gone, and we act like the Coastal Union isn't going to follow it. The South showed us what happens when Gaia - your phenomenon - comes for us in force. Nothing that we do can stop it, no amount of fire will be enough. When she arrives, and she stays, what do we do? When the fuel for the flamethowers runs out, what do we do?" Messenger tosses the last of the rabbit bones into the fire, shaking his head. "You thought the cataclysm was bad? Humanity will disintegrate, there'll be barely any survivors at all. We need to be prepared for that, so that we can fight through it and rebuild."

"Messenger, you're *bringing it down* on people! How are you helping?"

"There's only one path for humanity's future, and it lies in accepting a future with Gaia. Only those who can survive exposure are going to continue the species. We are a new breed, Bear. Adapted, evolved, to live in this new world. But that doesn't mean that we're safe inside it. Gaia is still a threat, and we need smart and capable people to figure out how we live alongside her."

Bear understands a little better now. "You're just as afraid of it as we are. You can call it, but you can't *stop* it."

"Of course I'm afraid of it – it kills people, us included. We're just able to *see,* and that makes it much more survivable. I need to restructure society as quickly as I can, so that we can prepare for her coming. For that, I need to expose as many as I can, with as few casualties as possible. We do not have much time, so yes, sometimes corners must be cut."

"And what about those who *aren't* adapted? Do they get to chew their fingers to stumps while the rest of us live on?"

"What did the dinosaurs do when the world cooled? They died off, and mammals thrived," says Messenger. "You're arguing against the natural order. As a scientist."

Bear takes a moment to process that Messenger may be correct. "So that's it? That's your grand plan – put everybody in the Coastal Union through an ordeal with a one-in-a-thousand survival rate, and hope that the people you have left want to build a society with you?"

Messenger looks into the fire, then shrugs.

"Yes."

Bear rubs his eyes with his one hand, and knows that Messenger is approaching his do-or-die pitch, the part where he'll either win Bear over, or kill him. Bear has to attack, has to keep him off balance, to buy more time.

He raises his voice, and challenges him.

"Messenger, there are only about a hundred thousand people *left,"* he shouts, and the other Dreamers turn to listen, as though they haven't been listening already. "You'll end up with a hundred people, statistically. A *hundred* people – you can't even get a sustainable population out of that without everyone having webbed toes, you *idiot."*

Messenger waves his hands, trying to discard the objection. "No, no, Bear, I believe that there are other communities of Dreamers out there, in the forgotten parts of the world. Take the South for example."

"There's nobody in the South," he says, but it's more of a question. "It's deserted."

"Is it?" asks Messenger, and the all-knowing look returns. "Have you been there?"

Bear has to stick to his principles. He takes a breath. "No, I don't *know* that for sure I guess."

"Exactly. I have. A Dreamer can walk freely in the South – and there is life down there. The world survives, Bear – this was never an apocalypse. It was an evolution. The cataclysm let humanity crawl out of another ocean, grow legs and walk on a new, unexplored land... A spiritual awakening, to let the gifted minority rise to the top, and leave the dross behind."

"Dross like my father," says Bear, and Messenger winces as he realises he has spoken out of turn.

"I didn't mean that quite so harshly," he holds his hands up in apology, and runs them over his sweating, bald head, down through his beard, braiding it idly as he goes. "I am trying to tell you that you are part of this minority. You must have felt it before, that you could leave these people behind?"

"Of course I've felt that," says Bear, leaning back. "But I don't think I'd survive an exposure, and I don't want to die. That puts me firmly against you."

"We're on the *same* side," urges Messenger.

"You want to kill me," he whispers.

"You'll *survive!*"

Bear feels himself going red in the face as his anger returns. "You've read my research paper there, right? The last entry on it, the boy in the basement? I bet your lackeys told him the same damn thing. Before he was exposed, and he went insane. How many people do you tell this to? How many people actually believe you?"

"I do not relish these results, Bear, but I am perfecting a process. The people you see around you were the ones I got right. This isn't random chance, the numbers are better than could be expected. I'm doing what *has* to be done! It's this or extinction."

"Tell me one thing," says Bear, shooting for, at the least, an answer to his big question. "How did you expose Addie?"

"Addie," whispers Messenger. "Forgehead boy?"

"He was exposed in Forgehead. Within the walls. No alarms, tripped no sensors, nothing. How?"

Messenger looks curiously at Bear, then at his father's notes.

"You really haven't read these?"

That one question sickens Bear to his stomach. The implication is obvious – that Addie and his father were, in fact, similar cases.

"No, I haven't."

Messenger puts them to the side, patting them. "Bear, sometimes people seek me out. Gaians, usually, who want to experience enlightenment, who prepare extensively and then test themselves. I visit them personally, spend time with them, assess if I think they'll survive – and then, yes, there are ways that I can bring exposure to somebody, wherever they are. I can act as a channel for Mother Gaia, and allow people to see what she is. I did that for Addie."

"And he died."

"He did."

Bear fights the fire in his chest, and summons the courage to ask his question, even though he's shaking.

"And a man called Alan Woods. My father. Did he once seek you out that way too?"

"I was wondering when you might ask me that, Bear," says Messenger, with a sad smile. "I knew your father, yes."

Now the foundation drops out of Bear's world; that whatever he thought of his father, he voluntarily sought out exposure. Whatever his reasoning, his father had decided that the answers to his question were more important than raising his son. He feels the hero that he has chased after for his whole life crumble inside of him. Everything feels a little off centre now, a little hollow.

He feels the rage towards Gaia, Hell, the phenomenon, fade. It burns down to embers, to mere curiosity. It didn't take his father from him – his father removed himself from the equation.

Left him alone.

"You didn't know," says Messenger. "I'm sorry to be the one to tell you, Bear."

"You knew him?" he asks.

"He was a great scientist. As a young man, we were both part of an ill-fated expedition to the South, to investigate what had happened there."

"He never told me."

"Maybe he wanted to protect you from all that we learned."

"What did you learn?"

"That Gaia is coming, Bear. The Coastal Union is not going to last forever. This is what I've been telling you, that humanity is running out of time. Maybe that's what drove him to try and understand it; trying to protect you."

"Don't make excuses for him," says Bear. "He left me alone to satisfy his own curiosity. How did he get exposed, then? Did you – did you help him?"

"I did. He sought me out."

"Did he ever say why he wanted to be exposed?"

"He didn't, no. But if I were to guess, I would say that he wanted to finally answer the questions that had plagued him for his entire life."

Bear takes it in, and feels a small part of himself die, and wither.

"I hope it was worth it," sighs Bear.

"I can't answer that, Bear," says Messenger. "But you can do things differently; you get to decide, Bear: are you going to help me save humanity, or not?"

Messenger falls silent briefly, and Bear jumps on his chance. Bear feels adrift, unsure of himself, but he knows that exposing people en masse still is not the way forward. There are so many avenues that they can still explore.

"With all you know," pleads Bear, "with all the secrets you have answers to... you could help me build a wall that protects people, you could help me design a weapon to neutralise it forever, or predict it better than the dreams can. But instead you're going to force me to go through the worst thing that I can imagine."

"If those things might work, I'd consider them, but they will not."

"Listen to yourself, you don't believe that! You don't know

what the phenomenon is, you've just found out how some of the controls work. You think cavemen understood fire, understood exothermic processes and combustion, or molecular bonds and their energy? Of course not, but they knew how to *use* it. You have the answers that I need to figure out what the hell that thing actually is. Look, maybe we *are* on the same side..." Bear pauses, breathless. "But you're going about it wrong."

Messenger's face clouds with doubt, and Bear begins to feel hope, for the first time, that maybe he might not die here today.

"Then you *are* willing to work with me?" Messenger grins. "Bear, I knew you'd see sense."

"I'm willing to try and save the Coastal Union," says Bear. "Of course."

"And could you convince your friends aboard the Crawler of that?"

"Wait," says Bear, suddenly remembering the Crawler. "The other three Crawlers, you hit them too! Where are they? Were they necessary casualties too?"

Messenger says nothing, but Bear instantly realises that something is amiss. Messenger is shocked – taken aback.

"What?" asks Messenger, flat and confused.

"The other Crawlers," says Bear, but he sees no recognition in Messenger's eyes. "They all went... you don't know? You don't know."

"We haven't targeted any other Crawlers, Bear, I barely have enough manpower to target one. We made our own distress signal to dupe you, yes, but..." mumbles Messenger. "Have they – are they -"

"Out of contact. We thought that you got to them."

"We weren't able to pinpoint their locations. I mean, we tried, but -"

"Then where are they?"

At that moment, Messenger and all the Dreamers move in sync, looking up at the evergreens behind Bear. Bear almost looks, but something stops him – the sound of glass crackling, or faint singing in the distance.

"She's here," says Messenger, confused. "It's early. Why is she here, she's not supposed to move until I call her -"

"Sir, what do we do?" asks one of the Dreamers.

Bear sees fear in Messenger's eyes; he's just as afraid of it as Bear is, no doubt about it.

Above them, the birds let out their gargling caws as they flee towards the sunlight. Bear feels a cold and absolute fear seize him. It is behind him. His satchel and his sensory blockers are one good lunge away, but Messenger might still have other ideas, and Bear is in no shape to fight.

It'll have to be words.

"Messenger," he pleads. "We can continue this conversation, but you have to get me out of here. Think about what I said, ok? You need to pass me out my sensory blockers, I've got -"

Messenger has not looked away from the trees yet. "You'll survive," he shrugs. "Trust me."

Bear wants to know so badly what he is looking at, but he knows it would be the last thing he sees. Messenger opens his mouth to speak, visibly perplexed and struggling with what he can see.

"Impossible," whispers Messenger. "It can't be. Is that -"

A single shot rings out, and the Dreamer holding Bear's shoulders slumps over.

The one with the grenade launcher shouts something, and the rest of them dive to the ground. He aims his grenade launcher and, before he can fire, his spine explodes out of his back. He crumples like a paper box.

Messenger rises to his feet, shouting commands.

"To me, get close to me for protection! Return fire! Return -"

A volley of shots hit Messenger's invisible shield, like electrical sparks, causing him to pause and flinch.

Bear takes his chance and lunges for the bag. Over the sound of gunshots, something is beginning to worm its way into his ears, like cold fingers.

Is that his voice, he hears?

His own voice, *yes*, singing to him, promising to *drag him to hell, with a throat clogged full of blood,* whistling through the cracks in the world. *Just let me in through your ears here, Bear, and I'll show you how*

      bad

          things

              could

                  be

He jams the earphones in and hits play, sweating, certain that he has just skirted audio-exposure. He still has the blindfold in his hands. He almost puts it on, but he stops himself. He knows which direction it is coming from; if he keeps facing away from it, he should be fine, and he can look for a chance to escape. If he is blind, he stands no chance here.

What he does not know, what he does not see, is Dusty. Alone, he emerges from the treeline in a hissing, thumping suit of powered armour, a rifle in one hand and his long-barrelled pistol in the other, walking forward under a hail of submachinegun bullets that bounce off of the suit like water. He has his head down, eyes focused through the open window in the helm. He fires as he moves, charging up the hill towards Messenger.

Chapter 18

Bee stares out the viewport of the Crawler, perfectly still. Glass cleans his rifle behind her, and occasionally looks up at her; she can see him doing so in his reflection in the viewport. She wonders if Glass knows what she's doing; if he knows that she's *waiting*.

But Glass says nothing, as always.

"May?" asks Bee after staring into the treeline for an age.

"Yes dear?"

"How long left on Dusty's timer?"

"Two minutes and ten seconds, love."

"Ok," she whispers, and rests her elbows on her knees, her jaw in her hands.

Her cheek is still a gaping wound, but Bear's handiwork has held together for now. It hurts more than she'll admit, a constant aching that sharpens when she talks or chews. She can feel things moving in her jaw when she tries to press her teeth together. Not to mention her abdomen – every mission, every step, every shot she fires, it feels like her gut is tearing itself apart.

She brings one hand to the horizontal cross dangling from her neck, and whispers a prayer as the countdown approaches, explaining her requests to God as she does so. She prays first for strength rather than safety, for Dusty had always told her that you can't make the world safe; rather, you must make yourself strong. She prays second for wisdom rather than guidance, for Dusty only recently told her that her decisions must be hers, not God's. What she is about to do can come only from her, as Captain; the highest authority aboard the Crawler. She prays, finally, for forgiveness rather than permission. For she is about to break a promise to her oldest, dearest friend, her Captain, a man to whom she pledged her gun and her service.

The nav deck turns red, and there's a soft ringing like alarm bells.

"Countdown finished. I regret to inform the crew that Captain Dustin McKay has been listed as Killed In Action." Bee doesn't react, but she sees Glass look up from his rifle. He watches her stare out the viewport, waiting. *"As per his instructions, Acting-Captain Beatrice Thomas is henceforth promoted to Captain, if you have -"*

Bee doesn't wait for May to finish.

"May, this is your Captain speaking."

"Yes?"

She spins around in the pilot's chair, hands on the controls. "May, take us to a war footing. Belay any previous orders. Keep the viewport open."

"As you wish, ma'am."

Bee grabs the emergency pistol from under the controls and turns around, fire in her eyes, and finds Glass staring at her in confusion.

"Glass, take the wheel; you're driving, big guy." He raises his hand to speak, and Bee stares at him. No permission given. "Your objection is noted," she says, "now get on the wheel. That's an order."

The Crawler is shifting around them, taking on its war-form. The engines burn hot and loud, and Glass slides into Dusty's old seat and takes the controls.

Bee checks the load in the backup pistol, then roots around in her pocket and brings her sensory blockers out.

"Glass, we're turning May off and driving full speed through those woods, front armour is still decent and we can crush our way through. The Devil might have his legions on the other side, so I'll have my senses blocked up until you give me the all clear. Don't stop until you see either Dusty, or Bear, ok?" Glass raises his hand again before Bee can put her blockers in. "Go on," she sighs.

"Ma'am, Dusty specifically requested that we *not* do this. I understand your affection for him. I share it. But he is most likely dead or exposed. As is Bear. The Interloper Initiative itself is more important than any one of our lives."

"Objection noted," says Bee.

"My apologies, ma'am. I would be remiss if I didn't speak my mind."

"Dusty *is* the Interloper Initiative, Glass. He's saved all of our lives more times than I can count."

"Then I merely wish to inform you that with the viewports open and May turned off, we may be vulnerable to attack. Quite badly so."

"You have your machete and your rifle there right?"

"Yes ma'am."

"Good. Here," she comes over and rests her pistol on his shoulder, pointing forward out of the viewport, already cracked and splintered from the Dreamer ambushes. "I'll keep this pointing forward. If I feel you tap on my arm, I'll fire once for every tap, ok? An extra gun. I'll hold on to the back of your seat with my blockers in."

"Yes, ma'am," he nods, and positions himself so that her pistol points dead ahead. "I'll do my best."

"Attaboy," says Bee. "May?"

"Ma'am?"

"Switch yourself off until further notice, we're going somewhere dangerous and I don't have time to come reset you."

"Yes ma'am. Farewell, and good luck."

"Glass? Take us through. Flatten the trees, follow the burned vegetation, and stop for nothing except our crew mates."

"Aye-aye, Captain," he says, and guns the engines.

Bee puts her headphones in and pulls her blindfold over her eyes. She presses play on a thirty hour long playlist of death metal, and grips the back of the chair. The Icebreaker, Crawler Four, held together with amateur welding and second hand steel, bursts across the snowy wastes towards the evergreens.

Glass sees the speedometer max out seconds before they hit the tree line, and adjusts his aim to smash the trees apart where they are blackened and still half aflame. Dusty has left a trail of brimstone and ash behind him, and the trees explode into ash as the Icebreaker hits them at top speed.

He feels the Crawler slow as the dead trees drag on her body, but its engines are more than up to the challenge. Tree after tree thuds against the sloped front hull and crashes aside as they plough onwards. It was built for this.

Still, Glass realises, Gaia is not here. She must have moved.

Nowhere to be seen; until suddenly, she is before him in all of her violent glory.

Glass wants to close his eyes – the familiar sight of his goddess, staring into his soul in judgement, still has the power to put him into a helpless terror. She resembles a terrible black orchid, a trillion petals of every possible size, filling the world before him. Her gravity pulls him forward into the void. Direction ceases to have meaning; there is only Gaia, and the Crawler.

Black tendrils surround the Crawler, prying her open. They snake out of the impossible spirals that surround them. Reality cracks and bends under Gaia's presence.

Something flutters in front of him, a cloud of moving objects, and then every piece of glass on the viewport shatters at once and the navdeck is filled with those awful black tendrils. Glass throws his arms up, swinging backwards with his machete. He cuts into them like ropes, hacking them apart, and hears Bee cry out in pain.

Glass catches glimpses of himself, sickly and pale, eyeless and screaming, pulling himself through the gaps torn in the air. These demons reach for him, folding through the air, forming impossible shapes.

Outside the cockpit, reality is gone, replaced with an unending tunnel of darkness that goes on forever, down towards Gaia. They are falling. Tendrils are stretching in through the broken viewport now, lashing around from corner to corner. Glass ducks as they scrape across the controls, severing the electronics within. Everything forms in spirals that he cannot anticipate – and if one of those tendrils catches either him or Bee, he knows that it will sever their limbs without effort.

Something appears on the view port's edge, out of focus, as Glass tries to use his peripheral vision. It's him, elongated, forcing himself through the gap in reality, pasty and pale. Every time Glass sees himself like this, he feels a sickening mixture of sympathy and hatred. It is undeniably him – and it is desperate, starved and fighting to survive, just like him.

As it reaches for Bee the tendrils come straight from his mouth. Bee is cowering behind him, pistol ready. Whatever it is, it wants to turn them both inside out. Glass remembers what it felt like, the first time he had to watch one of these things crawl in through his eyes and live inside his head. He will not let the same horror befall his friend.

He taps Bee on the arm, and a shot rings out, blowing his imitator off the remains of the viewport. Light begins to form in the endless dark. There is snow. Trees. The forest and snow beyond them is upside down, inside out, and Glass has to close his eyes and navigate by memory alone.

Switch on May, he thinks. *Get some help, you can't do this alone -*

A dozen tendrils drift near his head, slicing at his skin.

Wait for it, he thinks to himself. *Don't activate anything -*

They're going for his eyes now, and he puts one arm across his face, swinging his machete in front of him, trying to clear a path.

Just a few more seconds.

Black tendrils brush up his arm, severing tendons and opening his forearm to the bone as he screams and drops his machete. Bee is screaming his name as she fires again. She pumps the trigger until the pistol clicks empty.

The navdeck is full of the tendrils, arterial spray covering the controls from his arm now, and -

White snow.

Blue sky.

They are clear.

The Icebreaker bursts out of the snowy trees. The birds vanish with the tendrils. He yanks the earplugs from Bee's head and rips her blindfold off. She gasps in fear and retches as she tries to stand. #

"MAY!" he roars, diving for the controls.

"May," shouts Bee. "Come back online!"

Her voice lifts their spirits. *"I'm here, I'm here."*

"Good, get me the -" Bee sees the view outside. "Oh holy mother of Christ."

The field of snow before them is an open gun battle – and before them, a metal suited man charging ahead at a dead sprint, firing a rifle in one hand and a revolver in the other, as he closes with his enemies.

There are four Dreamers that they can see – and one bald, bearded shaman, wearing a brown great coat in front of a roaring campfire. And beside him: Bear, his earplugs in, staying low amidst the gunfire, facing away from them.

"May, give me the loudspeakers," she shouts, and grabs the microphone from the control board.

Dusty is pushed back, dozens of bullets slamming into his armour as he sprints through the storm in his powered armour. Shot after shot fails to find the window to his skull, ricocheting off into the snow. He can't hear a damn thing over the grinding of his armour and the clang of gunfire.

Messenger stands dead ahead, taunting him, deflecting every shot that he lands.

"Bear!" he screams. "Bear, stay down!"

He twists and gets another shot off, and another Dreamer goes down.

But now Messenger is moving, and Dusty can't hit him at all. Messenger bends down to one of the fallen Dreamers and stands up with a single barrelled grenade launcher.

"Shit," whispers Dusty, and looks around.

No cover. Nowhere to hide.

Just an open field and the snow. Dusty closes his helmet and charges. Messenger fires, and hits Dusty's armour dead on. There is a moment of silence where Dusty is deaf and airborne. Then he smashes into the ground, the armour contorting and twisting as pieces of it fly off.

Dusty hears nothing but ringing in his ears; he can't tell which way he is lying.

He has the presence of mind to realise that the power to his armour is gone. He can hardly move it; it's broken. He's no longer in a protective suit, but a heavy metal prison with no power. He smacks the release button in the inside of the left wrist, and the back of the armour pops open as bullets smash into the remains of his suit.

Dusty is dumped into the snow, wheezing, his entire body in agony.

But there's no exposure. The phenomenon isn't here.

It's gone.

His wrist has dislocated, leaving his hand dangling like an accessory. He can't feel anything yet, but he is well aware that the pain is on its way once the shock and adrenaline wear off.

Dusty crouches behind the pile of armour in his duster jacket, behind the only cover in the field, and waits for Messenger's second round to hit. His revolver lies in the snow just feet away; otherwise, he is unarmed.

More shots hits the snow near him – they're flanking him, getting around his cover.

He has no weapon, no armour...

"You tried, you old bastard," he whispers to himself, and pulls a short knife out of his left boot, and tries to get his eyes on his attackers.

Finally, Dusty realises that the ground is shaking. He looks behind him as a familiar voice cuts across the wastes – a woman's voice.

"Cavalry's here, lads!" comes Bee's voice from the Icebreaker, amplified by the onboard speakers. "Keep your heads down!"

Aboard the Icebreaker, Bee throws down the microphone and gives her orders as she sprints for the roof.

"Glass, get us close and pickup Dusty. May?"

"Yes Ma'am?"

"Detach all roof weaponry for me. How many railgun rounds do we have left?"

She reaches the ladders.

"Four, ma'am."

"Anything else?"

"That's all."

"Damnit, it'll do -"

She leaps the ladders and throws herself out onto the roof. Shots hit the metal around her and she dives forward to the firing port, where the main railgun has risen from its position and now sits ready for her to use.

It's almost as large as she is, but Bee is strong and scared; right now, she could likely lift the entirety of the Crawler by herself, if she had to. She manoeuvres it around like the ton-weight it is, a sleek tube of magnetic coils attached to the Crawler with almost forty different power cables. Lying down like a proper markswoman, Bee eyeballs her first target and flicks the red switch to power up the rails.

There's a Dreamer in yellow, making his way over Dusty's left flank.

Bee judges the distance, the lead, the shake and sway of the Crawler itself as Glass drives them onwards, wind whipping her hair back – but her circlet keeps her eyes clear as always.

The coil whines with power; ready to fire.

She depresses the button on the side, and the whining stops . There is a sudden electrical discharge, and the magnetic slug is accelerated to seven times the speed of sound. The air detonates around the barrel. It makes a sound like lightning. When she looks up from the railgun, there is but a red stain on the snow where her target was.

"Three rounds left," she whispers, and scans the field. It is

Messenger who is holding the grenade launcher – the primary target. She turns the railgun on Messenger, and it starts charging with a whine. "Bulletproof, eh?" she grunts, taking aim. "I wonder if a twenty-millimetre solid slug counts as a bullet, you cheating bastard."

Bear ducks and watches, deafened by his own music, as he feels the ground tremble. To his left, a Dreamer suddenly evaporates into red mist and the air crackles with electric charge.

Railgun shot. His heart leaps: the Icebreaker is here.

Messenger is right next to him, rummaging through a dead Dreamer's pack for another grenade round. Bear is weak, woozy, and one-handed – but if he can stop Messenger from loading another grenade then surely, he thinks to himself, the Crawler will win the day. Nothing else the Dreamers have can even touch it.

And the runes; Bear has deduced that he can do something about them. Messenger said that they had to be perfect, after all. Bear wonders how hard it is to sabotage them. They're only ink on skin, after all. He can sabotage the rune itself, and end whatever protection it is granting Messenger.

Messenger finally finds a grenade, red faced and desperate as his men keep working towards him for protection. One of them is screaming to retreat, but Messenger will have none of it. Only now does Bear see that he is, truly, a fanatic. Willing not just to die for a cause, but to let other people die for it too. Messenger reloads the grenade launcher with a snap.

Before he can aim, there's a blinding flash of gold, and a whining crash loud enough for Bear to hear it over his music. There's a crater where Messenger used to be, and lingering bursts of golden energy dancing like glitter.

Messenger himself has been blown off his feet, landing behind Bear. He is scrambling to get up, totally unscathed. Clearly, railguns will not get past his bulletproof runes – but Messenger is stunned, and off balance.

Bear seizes his chance. He plunges his one hand into the fire, grabs a burning log, and charges head on at Messenger.

One of the Dreamers opens fire on him, but he is close enough to Messenger that the bullets burst into golden energy before they can hit him. The Dreamer is shouting to protect Messenger, but he explodes into red mist before he can finish his sentence.

Bear launches himself onto Messenger before he can rise, and hears Messenger curse and roll, trying to get away. Bear presses the burning log into Messenger's arm and they both scream together as Bear's palm, and Messenger's rune-covered arm, bubble and singe under the log.

Messenger strikes him hard across the face and throws Bear off, bloody-mouthed, tearing his ear phones out. There's no phenomenon – no audio risk. Messenger's punch hurts him, but it lacks the terrifying strength that he had before. Something changed – Bear has broken one of the runes. Messenger stands up, looking at his arm.

"Wrong rune, Bear," he grins through blooded teeth, and kicks Bear in the ribs, throwing halfway down the slope towards the fire; and away from the guns of the Crawler.

He begins pacing towards Bear, who is struggling to get up. On the ridge, the last Dreamer explodes, and Messenger does not even acknowledge it. He is focused on Bear. Messenger stands above him, and places a bare foot on his chest, crushing his ribs.

But so focused in Messenger that he misses the vital detail; from behind them, a wild man in a long duster jacket crests the ridge and sprints forward, revolver ready. Messenger hear the footsteps too late and turns, trying to raise his arms. Dusty's shots bounce off his golden shield, but Dusty closes the distance with unbelievable speed, faster than Bear has ever seen anybody move.

He drops the revolver, catches it by the barrel, and uses it like a hammer. He hits Messenger across the jaw with it, him to the ground. Messenger drops, and Dusty kicks him onto his back and points his revolver in his face. The long barrel presses into Messenger's forehead.

The Crawler is nearby, it must be, Bear can hear the engines – but there is no strange sounds or bird calls, no crackling of glass...

Bear turns around, risking a look.

No phenomenon at all.

Just the Crawler, with Bee standing atop of it holding a full-sized railgun like she owns it; and Glass, bloodied and clutching his forearm at the controls in the shattered, open viewport.

Dusty and Messenger are staring down the barrel at one another. Bear has never seen Messenger frightened, and he does not look afraid now either.

"Let's test a theory," says Dusty. He places one foot on Messenger's chest, presses the revolver right onto Messenger's palm and fires a round through it. Messenger cries out and tries to clutch his bleeding, hanging fingers.

"Guessing the shield only works at a distance, eh? Good to know. I suppose those runes don't work when you rip them up either, eh?" He turns to Bear. "Which one of these makes him bulletproof, Bear?"

"If I had to guess," he breathes, "I think the one on his chest?"

"Good enough," says Dusty, and takes a small knife from his sleeve. He kneels down, and slashes apart the rune on his chest. Messenger grits his teeth, but does not flinch. Dusty has to shield his eyes, their heads aching, as he pulls Messenger's jacket off of him, revealing his runes.

Messenger does not cry out as Dusty slashes a few of them apart – he does not make a sound. He tries to struggle, but Dusty now seems far stronger. Whenever he tries to raise a hand, Dusty stamps on something, or drops a knee into his soft flesh. Bear feels like he is watching a butcher doing his work.

"Dusty, that's enough," he says – but Dusty is no longer here. He completes his work without looking up, without talking.

Dusty eventually stands back, leaving Messenger covered in bloody cuts, and admires his own handiwork. He paces away as Messenger writhes on the ground, and takes aim from a slight distance at Messenger's injured hand. He fires again, blowing his hand apart, and Messenger screams, clutching his wrist. "Seems bullets work just fine on our boy now," Dusty beams. "Consider that a hand for a hand," he gestures at Bear. "Good work, Bear," he looks up at Bee behind him, atop the Crawler. "Bee, you got this bastard covered?"

"I do, sir," she shouts, shouldering a scoped rifle.

"And Bee?" he shouts. "Didn't I give you very specific orders, lass?"

"Yes, sir," she nods. "You also told me that a Captain is the highest authority there is – and I'm Captain now. I made a decision."

"Yes, ma'am," Dusty smiles, and looks over at Bear. "Bear, you ok?"

"I mean, uh, no," says Bear, as he laughs nervously. "I've lost my bloody hand. Otherwise I guess I'm alive?"

"Anything you want to ask this guy before I introduce send him to meet his goddess?"

"Well I – wait, what? You're going to shoot him?" Bear stands up and grabs his satchel and his father's notes, stumbling towards Dusty. "Hasn't he suffered enough? Look at him!"

Messenger lies in a pool of blood.

"Of course I am," says Dusty, and puts his boot on Messenger, who is curled in the foetal position. Dusty is awkwardly trying to reload his revolver with one hand, since his wrist is evidently shattered and his hand is limp. Everybody seems to be breaking or losing hands today, thinks Bear.

"But Dusty -" he begins.

"That is -" Dusty cuts in, and points his gun at Messenger's head. "Unless he tells us where the other Crawlers are. Then I might let him live."

Messenger is saying nothing, just lying beneath Dusty's boot, staring at them, a wounded animal.

"Dusty," begins Bear. "He doesn't know. Honestly."

Dusty looks down at Messenger in disgust. "He can tell me that himself."

"He doesn't *know*, Dusty."

"Is that true, Messenger? Answer me."

Messenger looks away. "You'll kill me either way. You'll kill a hundred thousand people with one shot, and you won't even realise it."

"You mean the whole Coastal Union?"

Bear interjects. "He thinks he's saving everybody."

"Well that's ill-informed, isn't it?" asks Dusty, and then turns his attention back to Messenger with a sigh. "Sounds like another fanatic to me. Nothing to gain from letting him live then -"

"Nonono," shouts Bear. "Wait. Don't shoot him."

Now everybody is looking at Bear. Dusty shrugs. "Why not?"

"Because, Dusty, this guy knows things that I couldn't discover in a hundred years. He represents a major leap forward in our understanding of the phenomenon. Let me take responsibility for him, we'll take him to Union, lock him up?"

"He's a huge danger, Bear, we can't risk him just stepping back into space and escaping to continue his work."

"He can't," says Bear, and he meets Messenger's eyes. He looks desperate; defeated. "Not without the runes, and you've broken them all."

Bear sees Messenger in the same way that he saw Old Simon; naked and bleeding, mad and desperate. Messenger never once asked them to stop, or begged for mercy. Dusty is right; the man is a serious threat with his runes intact.

But without them?

He's a specimen that Bear desperately needs – a book of answers waiting to be decrypted.

"This better be worth it, Bear," says Dusty, relenting. He puts his revolver away.Dusty signals to Glass to come and help him, and takes one more look at Messenger.

"You really, *really,* owe this guy," he tells Messenger, pointing at Bear. "You owe him your life. Remember that."

Messenger says nothing, but he watches Bear with a knowing look. Even as Glass binds him and carries him to the Icebreaker, Messenger holds his gaze.

Bear stashes his father's notes back in his satchel as they return to the Icebreaker. Messenger has finally passed out from the blood loss and is slumped, unconscious and caked in dried brown bandages, in the loading bay. Glass has tied his wrists to a pipe.

From here, he seems less intimidating, and more like a homeless madman. Bear feels genuine pity, an emotion he is not too used to. This man knew his father – and Bear has to add more to the list of questions he has. He wonders briefly if he wants to know more about his father now – there is a bitterness there that he has been nursing for a long time, and now it has been confirmed: his father left him for his own ends.

Then Bear looks away, because people are talking at him, and he needs to pay attention. People are hurt – Glass's forearm has been slashed open, Dusty's wrist has been shattered and his shoulder is covered in a weeping cut that needs treated immediately.

And Bee, though not hurt with the same physicality as the rest of him, is swaying with bags under her eyes as she pats them all on the shoulder and, with a smile, and tells May to hand control back over to Dusty.

Bear realises, again, that he is being spoken at.

"What?" he asks, emerging from his stupor.

Bee smiles and pats him on the shoulder. "I said, thank God you're alive."

It might be the nicest thing she's ever said to him.

Bear smiles. "Thank God if you want, Bee. I'll thank *you.*"

"May?" asks Dusty, staring at his limp, useless hand.

"Captain?"

"You have the helm. Take us to Union City. Full speed."

"Aye-aye sir. It's good to have you back."

"Good to be back," says Dusty.

"Apologies, sir, but I never doubted you'd return. I was talking to Bear."

She is obviously taking a moment to lighten the mood, but nonetheless, Bear blushes.

Bee slaps his arm. "Told you; she's sweet on you."

Chapter 19

"This has been used to transport horses before," says Dusty, slapping his hand on the sealed stable door in the cargo bay. "He won't get out."

Bear, Bee and Glass, bruised and bandaged, stare in through the stable window. Messenger is on the other side of it, making no sound. His eyes opened when they sealed him inside – after letting Bear pore over his naked skin and check that not a single rune remained unbroken. He has been cleaned, his wounds freshly bandaged – he no longer hurts to look at, but he must be in pain.

Messenger holds Bear's gaze through the window. Bear cannot tell if it is a warning, a vendetta, or something worse. Messenger will not break eye contact, until Bear eventually turns away. The rumbling of the Crawler is the only sound, with the wind howling through the broken nav deck above them.

"What a creep," says Bee. "But unless he has some trick we haven't anticipated, then I don't think he can hurt us anymore."

"The runes were the key," says Bear. "The minute I burned his arm rune off, he lost some of his strength." Bear laughs, and rubs his eyes with his good hand. "I don't know where I'm even going to start with logging and studying all of this stuff. I want to find a way to record the runes without them hurting my eyes, for one, and then look at categorising them into an iconographic database, perhaps with -"

Bee puts a hand on his shoulder, and he stops. "Not now, Bear. Now is the time to rest."

Bear smiles, but with a frown. "I don't *want* to rest. I want to solve this."

"Tough shit," says Dusty, and motions for them to follow him to the nav deck. They are all glad to leave Messenger his icy blue eyes. "Once we hit Union, we're all due a drink. And I promised Bear an interview with all of us. He has some questions, I believe."

"I don't know how necessary that is now," says Bear. "I mean, I got an interview with Messenger himself after all. Learned a lot."

"You might get another one," says Dusty, with a knowing smile. "I imagine Union will want to speak to him, and they'll probably want you there. May?"

"Captain?"

"How close are we to Union?"

"Two minutes until visual. Shall I stop for radio confirmation that it's safe?"

"It's safe," says Dusty. "No warning signals, flares, nothing?"

"Nothing on emergency frequencies, sir."

"Thanks girl. That'll be all, take us in."

Dusty leads them to the nav deck, and Bear feels his stomach flutter as he takes his seat. They crest the white hills around Union, and May has the self-awareness to pause atop the peak and give them a second to adjust.

Union sprawls before them, bustling with people, vehicles, horses and carts, with herds of animals led in for the market and the slaughter. Houses cluster like smokers in the cold, wisps trailing skyward – and what a sky. Above Union is the vivid baby blue of a summer sky over crisp white snow, fresh and new.

Bear can't help but laugh.

"We made it," says Bee, to herself. "They're out of their alert. Union is ok."

"May?" says Dusty. "Pop the radio balloon, love. Get me Marge. Tell her we need Forestry escort for a high-risk prisoner, plus medical and mechanical assistance – and get a message to the Council."

"Aye, Captain."

Dusty nurses his hand, which is bandaged to his wrist with a splint to hold it in place. His first-aid was always patchy at best, and with only one hand he now requires Bee to act as his other hand.

"Bear?" says Dusty, turning around in his chair. "Your entire purpose here was to deliver your research to the Council, tell them about Forgehead. You still want to do that?"

Bear sighs, and shakes his head. "Dusty, Forgehead was one of many that got hit. My research is..." he opens his satchel and pulls it out, leafing through it. "I mean, it's good stuff; but none of this is new, or groundbreaking. The things I've seen out here? The things Messenger said, that Glass has told me?" He nods over to Glass, who returns the motion. "Those are world-changing revelations. My research is going to have to step it up a gear. This?" He waves the folder of research in his hands as though it is rubbish. "This is already outdated. I've got so much more work to do before I can show the Council anything that would impress them."

"You promised, though," says Dusty.

"I promised to help Forgehead, to get them help – and I will. I just hope that they're still holding out."

Bee butts in. "White Anchor too – we need Marge to do a check in. We should swing by the comms tower first, Dusty."

"Agreed," he says. "I'll not be able to rest for the medics until I know how extensive Messenger's damage has been."

Bear listens, and hears the pop of the radio-balloon above them, as they trundle towards Union City. Its walls are tall and wide, and as they approach, Bear sees the familiar sight of charms and letters stuck to the wall, plus the hand-painted modern graffitti.

There are paintings of trees and birds, of animals long extinct. It's not just statements of protection or belief, he realises. Some of the paintings are of human faces in swarms of insects, of smiling wolves with human teeth; doors with long hands creeping around them, stairways with shadowed figures at their bottom.

People put their fears on the outside of the walls, Bear realises. Where they'll never have to look at them. From a distance, it is beautiful. Up close, it just saddens him.

It also hardens his resolve; that people should not have to live like this. Whatever Messenger wanted, he's been beaten. Now Bear has him as a resource, and can put him to good use. Messenger may save the Coastal Union yet, without quite meaning to.

The long walls meet at a metallic gate which opens with a cheer from the waiting crowds – the guards on the watch towers, the men patrolling the walls, raise their rifles and cheer in unison. They fall silent, as they see the damage the Crawler has sustained.

Some of them peer through the viewports, and see the bedraggled, half-dismembered crew of the Icebreaker, and fall silent. They hush their comrades, scolding those who are still whooping.

In silence, Crawler Four trundles to its rest. Outside, there marches a legion of heavily armed Forestry, some in sensory blockers. Behind them are medics with stretchers, mechanics with bags of tools, and a rumbling bulldozer with chains to pull the Crawler home, should it need it.

"Let's go see Marge," says Dusty. "May, you have the helm."

"Aye, Captain."

Bear pats away medics who try to grab at him, talking about his hand, about sepsis and infection, about a thousand things that he already knows about. They obsess over the crew like celebrities as they descend the ramp, but Bear holds the medics off long enough to turn and watch the Forestry leading Messenger down the ramp.

He walks in chains, his head bowed, his body a mess of dried blood and bandages. Bear feels like he has betrayed Messenger somehow, and he feels that same strange pity again. The man in chains before him had tried to expose him and break his mind – but in his heart, Bear can see his point.

They both want the same thing, he thinks, but Messenger sees no value in the masses of bodies that will line the foundations of his future. As he is led out in chains and cuffs, under guard from flamethrowers and machete wielding guards, Messenger lifts his head and looks straight at Bear.

He rasps when he speaks, and Bear barely makes out what he says.

"Don't read the notes," he hisses, and Bear sees real concern, real fear, in his face. "You aren't ready yet. Don't read your father's notes, Bear."

Without thinking, Bear nods. He's not sure what Messenger means; a threat, perhaps? A warning? Nevertheless, he feels as though he understands. The notes are in his satchel, the heaviest thing that he carries. Then Messenger is gone, led into a horse-drawn cart with his guards, and pulled away, a shawl over him for warmth.

"Guards," says Dusty. "Take me to the comms tower – then we'll accept medical attention."

The medics protest, of course – but who would deny Dusty?

Marge's office is wooden panelled and wide, with an open window that she sits beside, lined with snow and bird feeders. Robins and starlings peck at the nuts in their mesh as she smokes a rolled-up cigarette out the window. The tower has windows all around, with a small crew of radio techs. Sunlight beams in, along with dazzling rays from the snowy mountains, on all sides.

She looks nothing like what Bear had expected. He had envisioned the eternal grandmother, short and homely. Instead he sees a woman built like a yew tree, wiry and thin, with long white hair pulled back into a ponytail. She wears a fake fur coat, and large aviator sunglasses.

"Dusty," she grins, her twenty-a-day rasp giving her a voice like a match being struck. "Council were worried for a while there. Thought there was no help coming."

"There nearly wasn't," says Dusty, and paces across the room to gingerly embrace Marge. She gives his dislocated wrist a look of concern, and he waves her away. "Just a massive break, it'll heal."

She laughs. "Always does with you. You needing something special?"

"Forgehead, White Anchor, check ins, post-anomaly casualty lists, Scout reports, anything you can get me."

She waves him away like a pest, and chuckles inwardly. "You can drop the worry, if that's your aim. Forgehead reported all-clear yesterday. White Anchor this morning."

"What?" asks Bear, stepping out from the doorway that they are all huddled in.

"But the anomaly rolled through White Anchor uncontested," says Dusty. "We didn't know that there would be anybody left to report in?"

"Let me see," she turns and scrolls through lists on her ash-white computer terminal, that whirs and beeps as she does so. Seriously old school technology, thinks Bear. "Casualty lists... four in Forgehead, two listed as stress-induced heart attacks, and two from a flame-gun exploding apparently. White Anchor suffered high casualties, but it seems most of the working population made it through all right."

"Brief exposure window," says Bear, stroking his hair out of a mix of relief and uncertainty. "Forgehead had its Forestry and its leadership intact when she hit. At White Anchor – we must have interrupted Messenger's plan, driven him off. They got lucky."

"You tell me," shrugs Marge. "It's a positive outcome compared to the usual reports, so I ain't complaining son."

"Marge," says Dusty. "Can you get me Forgehead's Chief Woodsman? His name is Calum."

Bear's heart stops, and starts again when Marge shrugs an agreement and turns to punch a frequency in. Two minutes later and the medics finally negotiate a deal with Dusty – that the crew can be treated except for Bear; *he* gets as long as wants on the radio. He's earned it.

Marge confirms the connection, and hands Bear the receiver.

"Bear?" comes Calum's voice through the radio, and Bear bursts out laughing.

"Calum?"

"Mate! You're ok? You're at Union?"

"I'm – well, I mean I lost my hand, but I'm doing ok, I -"

"You *what*? What happened?"

Bear closes his eyes, savouring the moment, and Marge smiles at him from across the table, leaving to get herself a cup of something strong.

"Mate, I've got so much to tell you about," he says.

The medics fuss when Dusty insists that they treat the crew in the pub, wasting no time in demanding a clean and quiet table for his crew. No barman would turn away the Icebreaker crew, he knows – not when they are all clearly wounded, and have walked out of Hell itself, and are asking for a pint.

When Bear is brought in they fuss even more, but within seconds Bear is engrossed in a discussion about crush-injuries and the dangers of tourniquet removal, as the medics tend to his hand. It is a weeping stump, Bear sees as they remove his bandages, and raw, swollen. He slams back shot after shot of whisky along with the rest of the crew as they rebind his wound and try to drain the massive swelling.

It looks like a club of flesh on the end of his arm, but he cannot bring himself to look away. There are still strange sensations, as though his body thinks the hand is still there.

Eventually, though, they are left in peace, with the day-time tavern empty asides from them.

"The Icebreaker is going to take days to fix," says Dusty, when he has poured another whisky for everybody. Bee's cheek is healing nicely, but her drink keeps dribbling through the wound, prompting her to constantly clean her cheek with a napkin. Glass, though he thinks nobody notices, is having trouble keeping a firm grip on anything with his wounded forearm. The shot glasses keep sinking out of his fingertips.

Bear keeps trying to use his non-existent hand to lift things. Dusty keeps knocking his over. Every single one of them understands the quiet frustrations of the others, and says nothing.

"What do we do for those days, then?" asks Bee. "Help interrogate Messenger?"

"I want to find our missing Crawlers," says Dusty. "The Coast will be suffering without them. Dogs and sleds can't do what we can, no matter their number. We're running at twenty-five percent capacity with three Crawlers missing."

"Messenger didn't even know they were gone," says Bear. "I

believe him."

"Then we have no leads," whispers Bee. "Nowhere to start."

"We'll think of something," says Dusty. "What about you, Bear?"

Bear looks around at them, a little drink at this point. "What about me?"

"Your mission is complete. You made it to Union. What now?"

Bear feels his stomach sink. He curses himself for assuming that they'd want him to stay on – that he'd have earned a place automatically. But Bear has always been alone, really. It's nothing he can't handle, he tells himself.

So he answers:

"Well, I've got a lot of work to do. I don't know if I can just go back to Forgehead, you know? If I can live inside those walls again, knowing how much there is to see outside of them. I've got questions that need answers, research and experiments to carry out. Maybe I'll stay here, try to put together a team, maybe pay some ex-cartographers to take me out into the wilds, or -"

"Sounds like you'd be perfect," says Dusty, slamming back another shot. "Want a job?"

Bear chokes on his whisky trying to agree. "Of course?"

"There's an interview process," says Dusty.

"Oh Dusty," says Bee. "Are we *still* doing that?"

"Everybody else had to, I don't see why not."

She rolls her eyes, and looks at Bear. "It's an embarrassment," she says. "But it's easy."

Glass raises a hand, and Dusty nods his permission. "Speaking of interviews: Bear was promised an interview with us. This once, Bear: do you have any questions for me?"

Bear looks long and hard at Glass, thinking – but he is as surprised as Glass is by his own answer.

"No," he says. Glass barks a laugh of surprise. "No, I don't. Nothing that you haven't already answered. I'll try to answer those questions myself," he says. "After all, not everybody wants to know the answers. Hell. Maybe not every question has an answer."

"I'll toast to that," says Dusty. "And to a new member of the crew of the Icebreaker." He clinks his glass against Bear's, against Bee's, against Glass's. "Welcome to the Interloper Initiative, son. Interview pending, of course."

Bee puts her hand over her mouth in an exaggerated whisper: "You've already got the job, I reckon," she winks.

Bear loses a fight to keep himself from smiling. He sinks his whisky and slams the glass down. He keeps trying to use his missing hand, and cursing.

"Maybe I should get a round in," he says. "Though I might need a hand bringing the drinks over."

Bee spits her whisky out.

When Bear is next alone, it is on the porch of the now-bustling tavern. Dusty is inside, regaling drinkers with tales of the Crawlers, putting feelers out for leads on their current locations, while Glass and Bee both seem ready to fall asleep on the table as their adrenaline finally crashes.

Bear watches the snow fall, and tries to put his hand out to catch it. There's a phantom feeling there, he knows. That kind of thing is common knowledge - but why, then, he wonders, can he feel the snow landing on his phantom hand.

And why is the snow *slowing* where his hand would be?

The physical hand is gone, sure, but maybe there's more to this world than the physical. Bear focuses on his absent hand, and he has to conclude that there is something where it used to be.

He wishes now more than before that he could ask Messenger.

One of the snowflakes stops, resting on the space where his hand should be.

The tavern door flies open and Bear shakes his head clear.

"Whisky must be hitting me," he slurs to himself.

Bee sees him staring at his missing hand. "You ok?"

"Going to take some getting used to," he shrugs.

Bee comes and stands beside him, arms folded around herself. "I think we're going to turn in for the night," she yawns. "You coming?"

"Aye."

"Hey," he nudges him, "what did Messenger say to you earlier? I saw him whisper something but my hearing on my cut-up side is a bit dodgy."

"Told me not to read my father's notes," says Bear.

"You going to?"

"Well," he shrugs. "I'm not sure. Messenger knew him, he says. Told me that my dad chose to be exposed. Don't really know if I want to read them, after hearing that."

"Yeah," she nods, then frowns. "Listen, Bear, you were with him for quite a while. I heard you talking to him in White Anchor. It worries me how similar you guys can sound. He's a snake, man. He's a fanatic, and he'll use you for whatever he wants. Classic psychopath. Don't let him pull your strings."

"You think he was trying to manipulate me?"

"I think that he had access to your dad's notes, and to your research, and I think maybe he's trying to put ideas in your head."

Bear considers it and realises that he hadn't given it that much thought. Messenger could be trying to sway him, lying to him – ultimately, he might still want to expose everybody, including Bear.

"Shit, you're right. I'd missed that. Maybe I *should* read them then?"

"You're thinking in straight lines, that's your problem," she smiles, coming to stand beside him. "Embrace the wispy, wavy world of the spiritual. Get some metaphors in your life, man. It'll help, on the Crawler. Trust me."

Bear chuckles. "I'm too straightforward for all that."

She shuffles closer beside him now. "So why didn't you read them before?"

Bear shrugs. "Afraid it'd confirm what I kinda knew. That he put his research above me, left me behind to fend for myself."

Bee shares a sad nod with him. "Yeah. People do shit like that

– ask any of us. But hey, you're crew now, right? Anything you need to talk about, you come to us?"

"Right," he smiles. "Thanks, Bee."

She returns his smile, crooked with her wound, and pats him on the shoulder. "Hey, no problem, new guy. Good night."

"Night," he pats her shoulder as she walks away -

- with the hand that isn't there.

She doesn't notice. Her jacket ruffles and they both hear his pat. It happened, he thinks, it definitely happened.

Impossible.

Bee walks into the night in her white, fur-collared coat, leaving Bear standing in the snow staring at the hand that isn't there any more.

Absolutely impossible.

His mind is racing, filling with thoughts and ideas too quickly for him to process. He feels faint, about to collapse.

No rational explanation for this.

Bear sits down heavily at an outside table, pulls his satchel onto his lap out of the snowfall, and in the flickering light of a gas lamp, pulls out his notebook and a pencil.

He starts scribbling furiously, alone in the darkness, his handwriting a drunken scrawl.

"Impossible," he whispers.

And he knows a man who deals in the impossible. The first thing that he jots in his notes is a reminder for when he is sober:

Speak to Messenger.

End Of Book One

The Interloper Trilogy continues in

Book Two: The Hundredth Question

Printed in Great Britain
by Amazon